The Mexican Cowboy, Coyote, and The Thing in the Sky

The Mexican Cowboy, Coyote, and The Thing in the Sky

Bruce Saunders

Quartet Global Books

Acknowledgements

Kaiti Saunders made this book possible
Laura Saunders saw me through to the end
Dana Gaskin Wenig edited this work
Thom Laz illustrated the work
Jack Remick published the work

The Thing in the Sky

I t was November. The night was clear. Speckling trails of fire occasionally lit small threads stretching through the star-jammed sky.

"It's space debris that made a wrong-turn decision and is burning up," the Mexican cowboy thought, as he sat rocking on the raw wood boards of his porch in the high-back slatted rocker he'd been given by the mother of Celesto, the runaway child he'd found happily playing far up Salerno Canyon.

He listened to sounds in the night: the swish and inaudible *peeeeeeeeee* of a bat orbiting the dry land under it, the threatening/inquiring soft call of a saw-whet owl, the incoherent jumble of mumbles coming from wintering yellow-crowned night-herons, snow geese and cranes in the Bosque several miles away.

As he rocked back and forth and listened, the still air was becoming slightly turbulent. Little gusts of wind, both cold and warm, blew into the Mexican Cowboy's face. He felt an odd prickle of fear in his gut and chest. He looked down and saw his left fist had clenched by itself.

"What's this about?" he asked himself.

Looking at the dry mesa a step down from his porch, the Mexican Cowboy noticed little puffs of dirt coming into being, swirling, moving from side to side, disappearing.

He heard the soft *"shsshsshing"* of flower stems in his garden rubbing together, twisting and bending, moved by turbulent puffs of wind.

"Something's going on," the Mexican Cowboy said aloud.

He went inside and without turning on any lights, found a lukewarm bottle of beer, popped the cap off, and went back to the bare wooden, dusty rocker on his porch.

Sipping, waiting, watching, listening intently, he heard sounds animals make at night growing louder. Frogs were *"birriping"* unceasingly. He noticed interlaced tense-voiced chipmunk chatter—when chipmunks ought to be sleeping. The Mexican Cowboy thought he heard the snort of a puma from Chappal ridge behind him. He even heard what might have been the grunt of a black bear. And the coyotes. The coyotes were talking faster, more intensely, impolitely interrupting one another.

"Something's definitely going on," the Mexican Cowboy said.

He got off his rocker, went inside once more and into his bedroom. On his knees, his fat belly drooping over his belt, he felt around under his low, messed-up bed for the shotgun he kept there. Finding it, coughing with dust in his mouth, he went outside and sat in his rocker again, the gun lying beside him on the porch. He was more alert than before.

The sky overhead was becoming mottled with faintly colored clouds of different shapes. The masses were forming and dissolving, swirling, turning into a miles-high, miles-wide stage complete with cast, looming in the southwestern sky. As the clouds moved faster, some seemed to touch the distant peaks of the Ruidoso Mountains. Flashes of lightning acted like stage lights. Oranges and greens began to appear in the dangerous sky.

"A big storm is coming," the Mexican Cowboy said to himself.

The animal noises around him intensified. Howling sounds, mewing and barking were perfectly synchronized with the thunder. Overhead, flashes in the sky appeared that were as soft and rounded as a headlight reflecting off a deer's eye.

Suddenly, nervously, without his usual "Here I am again" howdy, Coyote crept up on the Mexican Cowboy's porch. Coyote was agitated, more reserved than the Mexican Cowboy had ever seen him.

"What's happening?" the Mexican Cowboy asked.

"Big stuff," Coyote said.

"You worried?" the Mexican Cowboy asked.

"Being scared is a way of life with me," Coyote said.

"You hungry?" the Mexican Cowboy asked.

"I'm a coyote. I'm always hungry," the Coyote said.

The Mexican Cowboy went back into his adobe house again and brought from the kitchen a bowl of food he'd fixed for a later dinner.

"Want some gordo gallo-chorizo con frijoles?" the Mexican Cowboy asked.

"You mixed this stuff all together?"

"Only had one bowl," the Mexican Cowboy said.

"Has it got chiles in it?"

"I'm a Mexican. Everything I eat has chiles in it," the Cowboy said.

The Mexican Cowboy pulled his rocker closer to the porch's edge so he could see more of the sky. He scooped out a large fistful of the sloppy greenish-brown goop from the pottery bowl and dumped it on an unpainted board in front of his friend, Coyote.

He held out his hand for Coyote to lick it clean.

He got back in his rocker and with the bowl on his lap he opened a sack of tortilla chips that he bought a month ago at Santo Pui grocery store in Cordoba. He ate slowly while Coyote gobbled.

"The fur's prickling on the back of your neck," he said to Coyote.

"And the anus gland is sweating under my tail," Coyote said.

"Your nose is twitching from side to side. You are sniffing a lot. What are you picking up?"

"Something big is happening. I can smell it," Coyote said.

"It's just rain coming," the Mexican Cowboy said. "We need rain here. You hate rain. But you know we need it. Is that what's bothering you?"

"Do you hear all the animals talking nervously?" Coyote asked. "Smell the air. Look up at the sky. This isn't about rain. This is bigger than rain. More scary than rain. I'm excited and I don't know why," Coyote said.

"What's it smell like?" the Mexican Cowboy asked.

"It smells like…" (and Coyote made a couple of sentences out of coyote whines, teeth snapping sounds, throat growls) "That's our name for it. You humans can't smell it so you don't have a name for it," Coyote said.

Just at that moment the sky lit up with streaks of eye-burning fire running in all directions. There was a horrible, dissonant, crashing sound, like a punk rocker running his gritty palm up the steel strings of his guitar with the amplifier turned all the way up.

There was a noisy din rising in the multi-lit sky, like an orchestra of second graders tuning up.

Dark shapes, masses of clouds perhaps, were forming, moving, engaging.

The Mexican Cowboy and the Coyote watched with blooming excitement, apprehension, tension, as constantly reshaping and re-coloring cloud masses appeared to jell and become moving figures.

The Mexican Cowboy and Coyote saw different things.

Coyote saw the coyote god El Latrano, Santo Coyote, seated on a mountain of steaming clouds, his head back, howling to coyotes everywhere. El Latrano was mottled orange and blue. He had a checkered band around his abdomen and was spotted like a jaguar. His eyes were black and his tongue was long and forked. He wore an Aztec headdress, feathered, multicolored. He was fearsome. Coyote knew El Latrano demanded instant respect. Coyote could smell the insistent, imperious divine being He is.

Coyote lay down, put his head between his front paws, and averted his eyes. With his nose sniffing unceasingly, he cowered respectfully, panting softly, his ears relaxed. He feared for his life. He hoped for a blessing.

What the Mexican Cowboy was seeing was completely different. The sky had turned into a newly revealed universe of divine human-like figures.

The Mexican Cowboy first saw his own version of a coyote god, El Timador, the Trickster, playful, vexing, witty, dressed like a clown, with the mind of a philosopher and the behavior of a bar fighter.

The Mexican Cowboy got up and sat on a step of the porch, his back against a post.

He watched. He was enthralled.

And he was frightened too.

He forgot all about his friend Coyote.

Unnoticed by either of them, dogs of all kinds, and cats too, were gathering in the yard in front of them. The animals were moving around anxiously, watching the sky intently, with fear and devotion. And excitement was building. More bats were flying overhead. The migrating birds in the Bosque were squawking louder and louder. Jackrabbits and hares were hopping excitedly in the yard. The dogs were whining, howling, panting, barking louder and louder. The screeches of the cats, so painful and riveting, became exactly the right dissonant music for what was happening in the sky.

The Cowboy saw Kweo, the Wolf god, in the sky. Wakas, the Cow god, and Mosairu, the Buffalo god, were there too, dancing, moving swiftly around each other in the moving drama in the heavens. The Bear god, Hon, and Chop/Sowi-ing, the antelope/deer god, were kicking and running like children in a school yard. Kyash, the Parrot god, was flying among them and Mongwu, the Great Horned Owl god, was flapping and gesturing furiously in front of what appeared to be a gate.

"It is war," the Mexican Cowboy said.

"It is the animal gods fighting," Coyote said.

In the yard in front of them, tails wagging furiously, animals were baying, screaming, intermixing, bobbling, jumping, spitting, and falling down. An un-orchestrated cacophony of animal, bird—and even reptile—voices.

The Mexican Cowboy now began seeing New Mexican Santos colliding and bumping together in the sky.

Saint Raymond the Unborn was holding up his skirts and holy lamp and was running about the sky kicking.

Young Jesus the Nazarene, his arms high, wearing a loincloth, was darting in and out of the masses of Santos, chasing what appeared to be a ball.

Saint James the Greater was galloping his horse around the field in the sky, guiding his mount with a rosary for reins.

On the edge of the sky, the Mexican Cowboy saw Our Lady of Guadalupe jumping up and down, her skirts flying, holding her crown on her head with one hand. The smell of roses came to the Mexican Cowboy.

Inigo Lopez de Loyola, his wounds raw and dripping, was making mystical gestures in the middle of the moving clouds. Even St Christopher seemed to be shouting as he was traveling through the sky.

It was a terrible moment. It was a heretical moment. It was an interfaith moment. It was a moment of thrill and opening, of warming spiritual feeling, a moment of desperate awareness that lasted for hours. Then...

Suddenly, with a finish that began with a giant, ear-bursting crash of thunder, the sky's vivid colors began fading. The rumbling sounds diminished. The heavenly cast grew more indistinguishable from the clouds and finally disappeared.

Stars began to come out again.

And the animals gathered in the front yard, some of them very happy, others seeming very disappointed, grew aware of the enemies around them and trotted, padded, hopped, flew and crawled away into the emptying night.

Silence. Coyote came over cautiously and sat on the porch step next to the Mexican Cowboy.

The Mexican Cowboy reached out to stroke his friend's back. Coyote whined with pleasure.

"It is over. Shall we go to sleep?" the Cowboy asked.

"You sleep. I'll stand watch," Coyote said.

The Mexican Cowboy went inside and brought out his bedroll. He spread it out on the porch. He took off his hat and his boots and crawled under the covers.

As he lay looking at the bright, calm sky, he asked Coyote, "What do you think that was all about?"

"Perhaps they were playing soccer," Coyote said.

"Good night," the Mexican Cowboy said.

"Sleep tight," Coyote answered.

Coyote and the Porta-Confessional

It was a Thursday in late fall and the Mexican Cowboy's hands were getting arthritic. While making his breakfast he'd dropped one of the last hand-painted, chipped pottery bowls he used for cooking and eating. He picked up the pieces and took them out to the pile of broken pottery near the old, red, rusty, long-levered pump he used to get water. Now, it was about ten-thirty a.m. and he was rocking on his porch, staring out at the native grasses and shrubs and the medium-sized peachleaf willow tree in front of his house, pondering where his life was going. A lot seemed to have gotten left out of his life so far.

He looked up when he heard the unusual sound of a car approaching. He recognized it as the old, nicely maintained Cadillac of his friend (and foe), Howie Waters, the perpetual mayor of Cordoba—the mostly one-street town not too far from the ranch—driving toward him. Mayor Waters parked in front of the little, adobe-plastered, wooden ranch house and climbed onto the porch.

"Howdy, how's it going?" Howie said. Howie, short and round, was wearing the grey suit and imitation Stetson hat he always wore.

"Hello," the Mexican Cowboy said warily back to the Mayor.

"I need some help," the Mayor said. "Can you do something for me?"

"More than likely," the Mexican Cowboy said. "What's the problem?"

"It's a church fuss. You know Mrs. Whitenose, that prissy parishioner who puts up Father Gallapo when he comes twice a month to lead masses at Chichimaya?" the Mayor said—referring to the old beaten down church at the edge of Cordoba.

"Yeah, so what?" the Mexican Cowboy said.

"Mrs. Whitenose can't stand him anymore. Father Gallapo needs to be hosed off because he stinks, she says. He pays her nothing. He won't do favors for her. She's pretty sore. She won't let him back in her house. Can you put him up?"

"I can keep him for you," the Mexican Cowboy said. "But I'm going to need food to feed him. And some bowls too. I only got one bowl left in the kitchen."

"I can get you some food. And some bowls," the Mayor said. "How many bowls you need?"

"About five," the Mexican Cowboy said. "This is a big deal for me."

"Five bowls are all you want for keeping Father Gallapo when he comes here?"

"What else do I need?" the Mexican Cowboy said.

"That's for you to say," the Mayor said. "Okay. I'll get the bowls for you. Thanks for taking care of him. I won't forget it."

"You always forget things I do for you," the Mexican Cowboy said.

"I don't forget that you help me out when I need it," the Mayor said. He touched his hat brim, raised a hand in farewell, got back in his polished old black Cadillac, and drove away.

The Porta-Confessional

Thursday afternoon, round four, Father Gallapo drove up in his serviceable 1970s Ford 150, colored khaki—like New Mexico sand. The truck was pulling an outhouse on a trailer. The outhouse had two doors. The Mexican Cowboy had heard about Father Gallapo before and recognized him from descriptions. The old Priest was tall and thin, his body bent slightly at the waist, and he was smelly. He had a do-it-himself goatee and he looked somewhat like Don Quixote.

"Damn," the Mexican Cowboy said under his breath. "With him I'll look like Sancho Panza. And he's probably going to try to make me tilt at windmills too."

With the Mexican Cowboy watching, the Priest expertly backed his truck and parked it near the water pump. The trailer with the outhouse on it was neatly positioned under the north side of the ranch's sole tree—the coolest place to put it.

The Priest got out of the truck and, standing on the running board, started rummaging through a pile of hay in the truck bed. He pulled out a big, flowery, hand-painted pottery bowl. With the bowl in hand, keeping his eyes friendly, innocent and needy, he walked toward the house like a beggar.

"What you got there?" the Mexican Cowboy said by way of introduction.

"A bowl for you. The mayor sent it. There are more in the back of the truck. Want to help me get them?" Father Gallapo replied. The Priest put the bowl he was carrying down on the porch, turned his back on the Cowboy, and started walking to the truck.

The Cowboy didn't have much choice but to follow him. "He's already gotten control of me," the Cowboy said with a sigh.

Father Gallapo climbed into the truck bed, his old joints creaking, got on his knees like he was about to pray, and began hunting through the pile of hay. One by one he fished out four more bowls, handing each to the Mexican Cowboy. With pain showing on his face, he climbed out, went around to the passenger door, and took out four heavy sacks of groceries. "I'll carry the bowls," he said grabbing them, and started back toward the house.

"I'm going to be his slave," the Mexican Cowboy said, picking up two of the bags and trudging after him.

Back in the kitchen the Mexican Cowboy set the bowls on a bare shelf and then put away the groceries. "Tortillas, rice, beans, flour, oil, meat, ice cream, beer, and wine. The Priest knows what I like to eat. We'll get along."

Out on the porch the Priest was sitting in the Mexican Cowboy's rocker. "You hungry? Can I fix you something to eat?" the Mexican Cowboy said.

"I'll eat, but I'm hungry for something else," Father Gallapo replied.

"What's that?" the Mexican Cowboy asked.

"I'm hungry to fight sin. I'm hungry to fight sin wherever I meet it," the Priest said.

"What kind of sin do you want to fight?" the Mexican Cowboy asked.

"Any kind of sin at all."

"You hate sin?"

"I love sin. If God hadn't made sinners I couldn't have been a Priest," Father Gallapo said.

"There are a lot of sinners out there," the Mexican Cowboy said.

"Not so many as you think," Father Gallapo replied. "The problem for Priests is there's a lot of goodness around." He paused a moment to see if there was an objection. Hearing none, he continued. "The church has done a pretty good job of beating sin out of people. If they do nothing sinful, they don't need to go to church. If they sin, we confess them, they do their penance, God forgives them, and they don't need a Priest until they screw up again."

"Why can't they screw up and just live with it?" the Mexican Cowboy asked.

"Sinning messes up their heads. They don't feel good. It's like they are sick and know what's doing it to them. If they are big sinners they are hurting big. And only a Priest can fix them," the Priest said.

"Fixed a lot of folks, have you?" the Mexican Cowboy asked.

"Some. I had one guy who took a lot of confessing last month."

"He screwed up big?" the Mexican Cowboy asked.

"Bigger than anyone on the planet."

"You can't tell me who it was?"

"Nope."

"You can't tell me what he did?"

"No," Father Gallapo said. "But things he did messed you up too."

"Where was he when you confessed him?" the Mexican Cowboy asked.

"Down in Crawford, Texas. I'm an itinerant Priest, you know. I do a Mass down in Texas once a month. This guy heard about me and asked me to see him. I knew he was going to need a lot of confessing. I took my porta-confessional with me," the Priest said.

"Porta-confessional?"

"The thing that looks like a two–hole outhouse on the trailer back of the truck."

"You pull that around everywhere you go?"

"I need it. And not just for confessing. There's a composter under the penitent's bench," the Priest said.

"So this guy in Texas sat on top of your poop while you confessed him?"

"He didn't notice. He couldn't think clearly. And he mumbled too. It was hard to get sense out of him," Father Gallapo said.

"A boozer?"

"He got into about every form of evil there is."

"He's going to Hell?"

"Not if his wife can help it. If he hadn't married her he'd have surely sinned himself to Hell fifty times over."

"He listens to her?"

"Almost never. But she was his first lady. She stood behind him and shoved. She's done good."

"What church did you take him too?" the Mexican Cowboy asked.

"He wouldn't leave his ranch. After all the bad things he'd done he was scared of what's out there. So I took him into the porta-confessional," the Priest said pointing to the outhouse on the trailer parked under the tree.

"Isn't it a sin for you to make them confess on top of your poop?"

"God didn't say so," the Priest said.

"Well he ought to know," the Mexican Cowboy replied.

After a pause in the conversation, the Mexican Cowboy asked: "Why aren't they letting you stay in town?"

"Because I'm poor, I'm scruffy, and my mind works different than theirs. There's too much philosophy in me. And way too much demanding love. I'm fit only to be an itinerant Priest," Father Gallapo said.

"An outcast?" the Mexican Cowboy asked.

"Not according to God," the Priest replied.

"Do you fight back?" the Mexican Cowboy asked.

"I don't fight back. I lead forward," the Priest said.

"Well come on in, Amigo, and I'll fix us something to eat," the Mexican Cowboy said. "I'm poor, scruffy, and different-minded too. It might be good to have someone staying here who can lead me forward. Things have been the same for me as long as I can remember."

Coyote's Yearning Arrival

It was after seven and the sky was darkening. Dimming rays of the sun setting over the ridge to the west behind the adobe ranch house were turning the Manzano Mountains a deep watermelony purple.

Father Gallapo, well fed, happy and sipping a beer, was sitting on the wooden porch in the rickety green slat-backed rocker that Celesto's mother gave the Mexican Cowboy for finding her lost child.

The Mexican Cowboy was heading across the dry yard toward a large pile of sand. He was carrying the bowls he had used to make their dinner with. Using a cloth torn from a ruined shirt, he put fistfuls of sand in the bowls and started scrubbing them clean. When the pottery bowls were tolerably clean he stacked them and walked further away from the house, to the pump near the small arroyo, to rinse the bowls out.

It was almost dark now. While he was pumping and rinsing, he heard a familiar voice from the low arroyo beyond the pump.

"It's me again. Howdy," Coyote said softly. "Who's the smelly guy on the porch?"

"A Priest," the Mexican Cowboy said. "Mayor Waters wanted me to keep him for a few days. Howie gave me some cooking bowls as a bribe."

"What's the little house on top of the trailer?" Coyote asked.

"It's a portable confessional," the Mexican Cowboy said.

"I sniffed around the trailer. It smells like an outhouse up there," Coyote said.

"It's that too."

"Well we don't want your visitor to know you are talking with a coyote," said Coyote.

"Probably not," The Mexican Cowboy replied. "That could turn out bad for both of us. I'll leave some food out for you by the kitchen door. He brought a lot of food for us."

"Thanks," Coyote said. "I'll keep out of sight."

The Mexican Cowboy stacked his bowls again. Smoothly waving the stack in the cooling air to dry the bowls, he walked back to the porch.

Father Gallapo had been watching the Mexican Cowboy cleaning the cooking dishes from his rocker. When the Mexican Cowboy got back again, the Priest said earnestly: "Why didn't you bring your dog up on the porch?"

"Long story there," The Mexican Cowboy said.

"Put the bowls away and come tell me the story," the Priest said. "I'm a good listener."

The Mexican Cowboy took his time putting the bowls back on their shelf in his kitchen. He hadn't felt so undecided in years.

"If I tell him I talk with a coyote he'll think I'm nuts. If I tell him I love this coyote more than anybody, he'll pass that along to someone in church on Sunday. People in Cordoba don't like me already. If he tells them about Coyote they'll hate me, call me a fool, and try to kill Coyote," he was thinking. "What am I going to tell him?"

The Mexican Cowboy popped caps off a pair of beers and went back to the porch. He handed a beer over to Father Gallapo and sat down on a cement block beside him, his back against the adobe wall. He was quiet—stewing and getting angrier—because the Priest was messing with his head.

"Okay," Father Gallapo said, "Why can't your dog come up on the porch with us?"

"He isn't a dog. He's a coyote," the Mexican Cowboy blurted without thinking.

"I got it," the Priest said after a moment. "Why can't your coyote come on the porch?"

"You want a coyote to come here on the porch?" the Mexican Cowboy said, surprised.

"Why not?" Father Gallapo said. "You've got rattlesnakes and frogs under your porch, haven't you? You've got bats over the porch at night, falcons during the day. You've got rats sneaking up at night to eat food you dropped on the porch. You've got hummingbirds sucking nectar from the morning glory flowers in front of your porch. You got spiders and lizards and ants on the porch. You even got me on the porch. Why not invite the coyote up here too?"

"People around here think coyotes are vermin. They shoot 'em," the Mexican Cowboy said.

"Coyotes are not vermin in God's eyes," the Priest said, with remarkable force. "Get him up here."

"He's afraid of you," the Mexican Cowboy said.

"I like coyotes," Father Gallapo said. "They get kicked around a lot. And what do they do to deserve it?"

"How can he trust you?" the Mexican Cowboy asked.

"Bring him up," Father Gallapo ordered. "Tell him every one of God's creations is a friend of mine."

"First I want to know how you are going to treat him," the Mexican Cowboy said. "He's a friend of mine."

"I'm going to treat him the way God treats him," the Priest said sternly. "The same way I treat every creature God loves."

"Does God love coyotes?" the Mexican Cowboy asked.

"You betcha," the Priest said. "Now go get him. Here, give him this to sniff," the Priest said, handing over a not very clean handkerchief.

The Mexican Cowboy reluctantly obeyed and trudged back to the arroyo, where Coyote was likely to be hiding. Hopping over the bank, he sat down on the dry arroyo's bottom and waited for Coyote to come to him.

When he did, Coyote seemed unusually timid.

"He wants to meet you," the Mexican Cowboy said.

"Does he have a gun?" Coyote asked.

"Not that I saw. Come on."

"I'm not going up there," Coyote said.

"He's okay. He's real and he's serious. He's odd, he's strict, and he talks like a philosopher. He says he loves all creatures too much to be allowed to be a full-time Priest at one church. He says people in this parish think he's a nut or a heretic"

"Why?" Coyote asked.

"Because he doesn't do his laundry often, and he doesn't say what they expect him to."

"Why don't they go to a different church?"

"The nearest one is thirty-five miles away."

"He's messed up," Coyote said.

"He makes God out to be bigger and more tolerant than they want God to be."

"We're talking about your god or mine?" Coyote said.

"Ours maybe," the Mexican Cowboy said.

Coyote stopped and thought about this.

The Mexican Cowboy waited a minute and then held out Father Gallapo's handkerchief. "He wants you to sniff this."

Coyote put his nose near the handkerchief. He sniffed. And sniffed. And sniffed.

The more Coyote sniffed the handkerchief, the less wary he seemed to get. Then Coyote finally stopped sniffing and said: "Tell him I'll meet him halfway."

"He's good at going halfway," the Mexican Cowboy said. "I'll get him."

Meeting of Conflicted, Advanced Souls

Back at the porch now, the Mexican Cowboy said to the Priest, who was sitting comfortably in the rocker: "Coyote's willing to see you. But you got to go out to him."

Father Gallapo groaned, stood up—the Mexican Cowboy heard his joints cracking—and came down the steps to the Cowboy. Slowly they walked over to where Coyote waited, near the arroyo. Every step of the way the Priest held his hands out, palms up, so Coyote could see he wasn't carrying any weapons.

About twenty feet from Coyote, the Mexican Cowboy said: "Stop here. He doesn't want you to get too close."

"I understand," the Priest said. "Tell him I'll stay put and he can come to me."

Raising his voice, the Mexican Cowboy introduced the Priest: "This is Father Gallapo. He won't come closer without your permission. He wants to meet you."

"Howdy," Coyote said softly.

"Howdy back. Sorry I don't speak coyote," the Priest said.

"You know coyotes talk to each other?" Coyote asked.

"Suspected it," the Priest replied.

"Why do you want to meet me?" Coyote asked.

"I want to meet everyone in God's creation," Father Gallapo said.

"I thought coyotes were excluded from your god's creation," Coyote said.

"That must seem so to coyotes," the Priest said.

"If your god cares for coyotes why doesn't he come see us?" Coyote said.

'Why don't you ask Him that?" the Priest said.

"You are a Priest. You talk to him all the time. Why should I do the asking?"

"Because you've got a soul," Father Gallapo said.

"How do you know that?" Coyote asked.

"Any creature that talks and reveals what's inside himself must have a soul," the Priest said.

"Have I revealed anything?" Coyote asked.

"More than you think," Father Gallapo said.

"What did I reveal?" Coyote asked.

"That you—and possibly all coyotes—are angry with God because you have awakened and realize that you are spiritually bereft."

"You are assuming a lot," Coyote said.

"That's a Priest's job," Father Gallapo said.

~*~*~

This was one of the hardest moments in Coyote's life.

He was scared to death of going closer. But he also wanted to be near the Priest.

Keeping his distance—his mind racing—Coyote thought about the night not so long ago when he had seen El Latrano—his god—in the sky.

He thought about the longing he'd been feeling to move nearer to his god, to know El Latrano better, see Him more often.

He thought about the loneliness of coyote life.

He thought about how much he owed the Mexican Cowboy for being an incredible loyal and good friend.

He thought about whether humans might actually be able to help coyotes, make their lives better, give them space and the freedom they needed to become more than they were being allowed to be.

Why, he asked himself, should humans be the only species allowed to advance? And what did god have to do with a species' advancement?

But: the Mexican Cowboy said this god stuff was a crock. Was he right?

Should he risk himself and find out?

Hard as it was for him to do this, he decided to put inherited coyote wisdom aside and move closer to Father Gallapo.

"I'm coming your way," Coyote said.

"You won't regret it," the Priest replied.

The Priest stood still, arms out, palms up as Coyote warily approached him. Ready to bolt into the arroyo, Coyote circled the Priest, sniffing him all over.

At last he moved closer and put his nose against Father Gallapo's outstretched hand. "You smell all right," he said.

"If you guys can stand each other for a while, let's go up on the porch," the Mexican Cowboy said, and walked away.

"You first," Coyote said to the Priest.

"Much obliged," Father Gallapo said, and started after the Mexican Cowboy.

Last in the train, some distance behind the others, Coyote followed them back to the ranch house. His good ears heard the Priest's knees complaining as he got back in the rocker. But Coyote wouldn't go up on the porch.

"You want some supper?" the Mexican Cowboy asked Coyote.

Coyote nodded and the Mexican Cowboy went inside.

The Priest was silent, rocking, perhaps meditating. Coyote sat at the bottom of the steps and waited. He was surprised at what the Priest said when he finally started to talk to him.

"Do you have religious feelings?" the Priest asked Coyote boldly, without preliminaries.

Should I tell him or not? Coyote asked himself. All right. Let's see what he has to say.

"Things have happened I can't explain," Coyote said, thinking about the night he'd seen the coyote god in the sky.

"How do you feel about those things?" Father Gallapo asked.

"I want more things like that to happen. And I want them to be explained too," Coyote said.

"We've got things to talk about then," the Priest said.

"Maybe," Coyote said.

Dinner

Twenty minutes later the Mexican Cowboy brought out a bowl of water, and another bowl heaped with leftover Anglo/Mex food: tacos, tamales, frijoles, enchiladas, and a piece of raw meat.

He stepped off the porch and put the bowls down carefully in front of Coyote. "Eat up chum," the Mexican Cowboy said.

"Thanks," Coyote whispered.

While Coyote ate his food, the Mexican Cowboy and Priest sipped beers and talked.

"What do you think of my friend?" the Mexican Cowboy asked the Priest.

"He's special, maybe more special than either you or I know," Father Gallapo said.

"Besides the fact he can talk to us, what's special about him?"

"If a coyote can talk, if a coyote can think and feel, if a coyote knows what he's done, if he can feel guilty, if a coyote looks up at the sky on a clear night and sees something mightier than him, if a coyote feels that he's not alone and this life is not all he has, if he feels he has a friend who'll always love him, who can forgive him if he asks the right way, if a coyote knows what sin is and knows he can be forgiven, well then that coyote is very special and a Priest's just got to be willing to confess him," Father Gallapo said.

"Take him out to the trailer and confess him then," the Mexican Cowboy said.

"He's got to be baptized first," Father Gallapo said. "In a church."

"You are going to turn him into a Christian?"

"I'll leave what he gets turned into in God's hands," Father Gallapo said.

"You going to baptize him with your church's holy water?"

"I don't think that's the right water to use on him. You got any special water around here?"

"Just what comes out of that pump down by the arroyo. It's never let me down."

"That's holy enough for me," the Priest said. "Take a bowl and go get some of that water. We won't need much."

"I'll do it tomorrow, if it looks like Coyote's going to agree to get baptized."

Listening while they were talking about him, Coyote finished his dinner. Too much, he said to himself, and backed softly into the dark night. Crouching, he slunk away. He needed time by himself.

The Priest looked up and saw Coyote was gone. "Where'd he go?" Father Gallapo asked.

"Don't know," the Mexican Cowboy answered. "Coyote 'Howdies' politely, but he never says 'Goodbye.'"

"Will he come back?" the Priest asked.

"God knows," the Mexican Cowboy said, only partly in exasperation.

Bedtime Prayers

It was after midnight now, on Friday morning. The Mexican Cowboy was in bed, trying to sleep. He was in a whirlpool of swirling emotions, battling a momentum of propelling forces that would not let him rest. To make matters worse, the house's old wooden floors and walls planked with dry and cracking rough-hewn cedar were acting like an amplifier. Wind gusts on the house's walls and windows made annoyingly loud creaks and rattles. It didn't help that the Mexican Cowboy could hear the Priest moving around and talking to himself just several feet away on the other side of the thin wall.

He wished Father Gallapo would shut up and go to sleep. But a cracking sound as the Priest was kneeling warned the Mexican cowboy that his guest was going to say his prayers first.

As the Priest began his praying all the outside noises the old house was amplifying so strongly waned. The Priest's words, perhaps unknowingly spoken too loudly, came to the Mexican Cowboy as clearly as if they were kneeling side by side.

Oddly, though, the house was amplifying more than just the Priest's voice. The Mexican Cowboy could make out too the other side of the conversation the Priest was initiating, just as he had been able to listen-in when another guest had talked on his cell phone where the Priest was now praying.

As clearly as though he were listening with earphones on, the Mexican Cowboy received the exchange that was taking place in the next room.

It startled him when he realized the Priest was praying in a way the Mexican Cowboy had never heard of before. Father Gallapo was engaging in 4-way prayer, going back and forth simultaneously with God, Jesus, and the Holy Spirit.

He was asking all of Them for guidance.

"Help me decide if what I'm about to do with Coyote is right?" the Priest asked his Advisers.

To God, the Priest said: "Your First Commandment is that we should have no other god before You. Does that mean that we are allowed to have other gods along-side, but slightly beneath you?"

The Mexican Cowboy heard God, speaking in a multidimensional voice that was at once absolutely authoritarian yet unguided, say: "**I meant what I commanded.**"

Simultaneously Jesus said, in a voice as laden with Holy Love as a human soul could bear: "*Love your Fellow Being as you would like to be loved by all Beings in my Father's creation.*"

Simultaneously the Holy Spirit said briskly and efficiently: "Priest, you are Our executive on earth. We delegated responsibility to you. It is up to you to figure out how to make things go right and well for all creation. We leave making day-to-day executive decisions to you."

To the Holy Trinity the Priest asked: "Do coyotes need a god they can believe in?"

God: "**If coyotes have souls they have a god.**"

Jesus: "*I want coyote to be loved by you as I am.*"

Holy Spirit: "That's for you to decide."

To Jesus: "I don't want to harm Coyote."

Jesus: "*Bless you Father. You are a Loving man. Where in my teachings do I say: 'Harm Coyotes!'*"

To Holy Spirit: "Did you catch that?"

Holy Spirit: "I was online with you."

Father Gallapo, his knees aching, said to the Holy Spirit: "Tell me what I'm being told here? What's right for me to do? You explain better than the others."

"What's right is always what a holy man decides and does," the Holy Spirit said.

Jesus chipped in: "*Remember: with Me, God headed off in a new direction.*"

Father Gallapo: "God seems to do that a lot."

God: "**Farmers need to keep doing new things to raise their crops rightly.**"

Father Gallapo: "Too many metaphors. Be plain with me, Guys. What is truth here and how does it apply to me?"

Jesus: "*Funny. Pontius Pilate asked me the same question during a moment of extraordinary doubt he was having.*"

Priest, feeling weary and frustrated: "Okay, Bosses. I give up. It's my problem, I know. Thanks. Good night."

Chorus: "*Sleep tight.*"

The Mexican Cowboy heard more knee-creaking as Father Gallapo got into bed and pulled the brightly patterned wool blanket over him. He was sighing.

Ten minutes later there was snoring on both sides of the thin wall.

Early Morning Atop the Rock of Ages

Around six on Friday morning Father Gallapo's body was aching so much he couldn't stay in bed any longer. He got up, put the same clothes on yet again, and went into the kitchen looking for something to eat. With a big chunk of bread in his hand, he slipped out the kitchen door quietly, not wanting to wake the Mexican Cowboy who certainly deserved his sleep.

The sky was pale blue and cloudless. The sun's rays were almost horizontal. Standing on the little patio made with irregular pieces of flagstone tapped into sand, looking at the hummingbirds diving into the morning glories, hearing the screech of a hawk overhead, the Priest thought about what he wanted to do. What he really wanted to do. His prayers last night had left him disconsolate, self-doubting. With a mix of chagrin and self-assertion, he said to himself: If They won't guide me I'm going to have to guide myself.

Father Gallapo walked away from the house, his truck, the arroyo. He crossed the small mesa and began slowly climbing onto Chappal Ridge, west of the ranch house, lit in stunning detail by the early morning sun. The ridge was peopled with giant boulders and he threaded his way carefully through those, watching for rattlers, but mainly looking for a place to sit.

About two-thirds of the way up the ridge and panting now, Father Gallapo found the perfect big rock to sit on. About twelve feet high on the downhill side, the giant boulder was nestled against a smaller rock. Its top was flat, and it had indentations on the uphill side that looked like perfect steps an old man could use. Up he went, his knees creaking and spiking with pain.

On top, he sat down, his aching knees stretched out before him; eating the last of his chunk of bread he looked out at the view.

He was captivated by the earthly beauty of this part of God's creation. A staircase of boulders fell away below him. He could clearly make out the old ranch house with its tattered porch, the gallant tree by the arroyo surviving where none of its fellows did, the trailer he'd parked under the tree and the truck by it.

With his gaze he followed the curving dry bed of the gently winding arroyo. His eyes moved across the rough mesa dotted with patchy native plants all the way to the sharp edge of the purplish Manzano Mountains in the distance. Looking up he saw the first trace of high cirrus clouds in the light blue eastern sky. The sky was threaded with the east-west remains of contrails, all that was visible of the invisible tunnels above him crowded with humans.

Crossing the mesa he'd seen grasshoppers and spiders among scattered plants that were gleaming with a faint sheen of dewdrops, several pygmy blue butterflies flying aimlessly above them. Looking down at the ground closer to him he saw a horned toad, round and pointed, fat and flattened, with its head bent up sitting near an anthill, waiting for food to come its way. In the dirt beside him a whiptail lizard, sinuous, alert, and four-legged, was looking skyward for its next meal—and for birds who intended to eat him. The lizard had reason to worry. Maybe looking for whiptails to eat between the boulders below the Priest, a cactus wren was jumping and scratching, jumping and scratching.

The morning light on his face was healing. The Priest felt less confused, more certain. Just at the moment he made up him mind what he should do about the profound and treacherously heretical problem he'd been given to wrestle with, he was startled when a soft voice near him said:

"Howdy. It's me again." Coyote was sitting on the small rock next to him, not in arm's reach but near enough to seem friendly.

"I've been thinking about you," Father Gallapo said.

"Same here," Coyote replied.

"I've decided that I want to move you forward, in the only way I know how."

"What way's that," Coyote asked.

"I want to baptize you so I can hear your confession."

"Why would I want to confess anything to you?" Coyote asked.

"So you can ask for and I can give you God's forgiveness," the Priest said.

"Why would I want to be forgiven by your god?" Coyote asked.

"I understand that point of view," the Priest said. "This is going to sound bad to you. What I am wrestling with is why my God would want to forgive you."

"Maybe he thinks I've sinned," Coyote said, with a grin.

"Maybe you have sinned," Father Gallapo said with a severe look back at Coyote. Coyote withered a little.

"What do you think I've done that I need to confess?" Coyote asked.

Thrilled, the Priest said to himself: We are there. Now, God help me, I've got to find out what in hell a coyote would need to confess.

Coyote waited patiently while the Priest thought about how to work the problem of finding out what was in Coyote's soul. He thought, How should a human Priest go about learning what counts as sin in the coyote world? What are the risks here for me? Well, he decided finally. I've got much to learn. Let's start by finding out what Coyote thinks of the Ten Commandments.

"Are there any laws in the coyote universe?" he began by asking.

"Keep moving, keep yourself fed, feed your pups, and stay out of sight," Coyote said.

"Do coyotes have any gods?"

"Not until recently," Coyote answered.

"Any drawings, carvings, statues?" Father Gallapo asked.

"None I've seen."

"Do you honor your mother?"

"I don't know much about her," Coyote said. "She had lots of pups. I didn't mean much to her. I walked away from her at the same time she walked away from me. Family life doesn't mean much to coyotes."

"How about your father?"

"Never met him. Don't know who he was. Coyotes don't have dads," Coyote answered.

"Ever commit adultery?"

"Never, or always—depending which way you are looking at it. Coyotes don't marry."

"How about your neighbor's wife?"

"Coyotes never settle down. We don't have neighborhoods and neighbors."

"Done much killing?"

"Lots. Except when I eat what the Mexican Cowboy gives me, I've got to kill to live. I like killing. I'm good at it too."

"Stolen anything?"

"There's a tangle here," Coyote said. "Coyotes don't have possessions, and if something isn't owned it can't be 'stolen.' Owning means a lot less to coyotes. I can't think of anything I ever 'owned.' And neither can any coyote. If I find something I want, I take it. If another coyote wants it and he can take it from me, he can have it. But he won't keep it either. We don't want or get to 'keep' anything. And if coyotes did, how could we carry around the things we were keeping?"

"Ever tell lies about other coyotes?"

"Coyotes can be deceitful with each other, but we aren't very good liars."

Father Gallapo sighed and leaned back on his rock. "We're not getting anywhere," he said.

"That's not true," Coyote said. "I'm getting somewhere."

"Where?"

"The questions you are asking make me realize how much wiser you are than I am. That wounds me."

"Why does that realization wound you?"

"Because I recognize how far coyotes need to go to understand themselves and their god."

"Perhaps you will lead them," Father Gallapo said.

"Humans are happy to be led," Coyote said. "Coyotes will always want to be independent and free."

Sounds like Texans, the Priest thought to himself.

"Humanity leans toward the material, the bountiful, the useful, but they aspire also to the infinite, the immaterial and the beautiful," the Priest said, over-reverently.

"Coyotes are less sophisticated. We concentrate mainly on killing rabbits."

"If you have no sin, and it looks like you don't, we don't need to go further," Father Gallapo said wearily.

"Hold on. Suppose I have no **human** sin," Coyote said with an expression on his face that mixed satisfaction with yearning. "Suppose I have **coyote** sin. Who does the listening, judging and forgiving then?"

Speaking sternly now, the Priest said: "Priests do the listening, God does the judging and forgiving, and there is no appeal. Are coyotes willing to accept God's strict laws?"

"Did humans have a choice?" Coyote asked the Priest softly.

"Do Coyotes want to learn my Faith's requirements, its beliefs, canons and practices?"

"Do humans want to learn coyotes' ways, beliefs and practices?"

"We are getting nowhere again," the Priest said.

"Not so," Coyote said. You are making me realize that I cannot have my god without a faith and a faith's laws."

"Will you obey?"

"I doubt that my god will put obedience at the top of his list of commandments."

"Will you believe?"

"What if I have a direct connection to my god and argue with him, as Adam, Abraham, Moses and Jesus did?"

"Then you will be a Prophet."

"I am eager to be a Prophet," Coyote said.

"Are you ready to move forward?"

"I'm still on the line," Coyote said.

"If you are the First," the Priest said, "that means you have been chosen to be a leader. Will you proselytize and spread the faith among coyotes?"

"Hard to believe that can happen. Coyotes only talk about themselves."

"Do you want to confess?"

"If my god asks me to."

"What would you want to confess then?"

"My lack of belief in my god before he showed himself to me in the sky."

The Priest put his arms around his knees and began rocking back and forth like an autistic child. His face was red. He was warm and exhausted. He wished he had never ignored Mrs. Whitenose's obvious needs for more of his attention. Coyote sat patiently watching him.

"All right," Father Gallapo said finally and grimly. "Let's go to Chichimaya church tonight and I will baptize you so you may confess to me."

"In whose name will you baptize me?" Coyote asked.

"I will baptize you in the name of your coyote god. I'll be acting as a surrogate for a presumptive 'coyote Priest.' When Judgment Day arrives my defense will be that this was my contribution to interspecies religious cooperation."

"What will you baptize me with?"

"Water from the Mexican Cowboy's pump."

"That will do," Coyote says.

His knees aching, Father Gallapo struggled to his feet. He started unsteadily down the boulder's backside, watching his step. Coyote was waiting below him at the bottom—as though to catch him if he fell. The Priest felt a surge of liking for Coyote. Clear of the boulder, and without realizing what he was doing, he patted Coyote on the neck and head, like a dog. Coyote didn't flinch.

They started back to the ranch house together.

Back at the Ranch

As he neared the Mexican Cowboy's little patio, Father Gallapo looked back at Coyote, who had been lagging behind. He wasn't there. Coyote had vanished.

"Just like him," the Priest thought with a wry smile. He went into the kitchen.

The Mexican Cowboy was there, making their breakfast. The little kitchen was filled with the sounds and smells of an Anglo/Mex breakfast being made—the clanking of a bowl as Cowboy tossed chopped vegetables and chiles into it for topping the omelettes, the faint dry smell of chorizo being heated, the bubbling of a coffee pot on the stove.

The Mexican Cowboy was humming a *Norteño correo*—something about Texas Rangers and migrant workers. He was obviously feeling happy.

On the other hand, Father Gallapo was feeling tired and pensive. He did not want to talk to the Mexican Cowboy about his conversation with Coyote, but he felt it would be wrong to keep it to himself.

"I was up on the ridge, sitting on a boulder, talking with Coyote," he said.

"Go well?" the Mexican Cowboy asked, his mind mostly on the meal he was cooking.

"We talked about baptizing him tonight."

"He agree?" the Mexican Cowboy asked.

"He had his doubts. When he asked why he should be baptized, I told him that when you are baptized you are enlightened by the Grace of the Holy Ghost."

"And?" the Mexican Cowboy said, concentrating on his cooking.

Coyote said: "My God's not a ghost."

"What's the sin he wants to be forgiven for?" the Mexican Cowboy asked.

Dodging the question to protect Coyote's privacy, the Priest answered with vagueness: "I wondered if it might not be fornication, since he and his partners were unmarried."

"Never heard him worry about that," the Mexican Cowboy said, starting to dish up.

"He sired lots of pups," Father Gallapo said, sitting down at the kitchen table.

"Pups are good," the Mexican Cowboy said. "I wonder if Jesus made a mistake by dying before he had children."

"Sounds like you need a girl friend," Father Gallapo said.

"Want some coffee?" the Mexican Cowboy countered with.

"Did you see the Coyote god in the sky that night?" the Priest asked the Cowboy, before beginning to eat the food put in front of him.

"I did. And he was weirdly dressed, like an Aztec with a feathered headdress."

"What did Coyote say after the storm?"

"He said religion was conflictual for coyotes. And when I went to bed, he said he was going to stand watch and pray for guidance."

"Who did he want to guide him," Father Gallapo asked, before taking a sip of his boiling coffee.

"You maybe?" the Mexican Cowboy answered, heaping sugar into his coffee cup.

"I'm going to take him to Chichimaya tonight and baptize him. You want to come?"

"That would be okay with me," the Mexican Cowboy answered.

"Fine. When you take the bowls down to the sand pile and pump, would you mind pumping a little water into a bowl and bringing it back with you?"

"Going to bathe his soul, are you?"

"You don't think I'm going to take a bath, do you?"

"No. Then you wouldn't smell the same. Keep that in mind when you are with Coyote."

"Funny," the Priest said. "I sniffed him and I couldn't smell a thing."

"And we believe we are superior," the Mexican Cowboy said, getting up to do the dishes.

Holy Night at Chichimaya

Late Friday night, with Coyote in the front seat beside him and the Mexican Cowboy sitting in the bed of the truck with his back against the cab and his feet in the straw, Father Gallapo drove to Chichimaya Church, at the edge of the small, mostly one-street town. "Usually I only go here on Sundays," the Priest said to Coyote.

Behind them and carefully holding the bowl of water he'd pumped from the well, the Mexican Cowboy was surprised it wasn't spilling much. "That old bent Priest's driving's pretty steady," he said to himself. The Mexican Cowboy watched the rough dirt road unfolding behind the jiggling porta-confessional on the trailer. Comfortable enough riding in the bed of the truck, he started feeling nervous when the Priest drove onto the big, uneven, dirt parking lot beside the church.

The Priest got out of the truck and Coyote jumped out after him. The Mexican Cowboy put down the bowl of water he'd been holding, climbed out, lifted it over the edge of the bed, and followed the Priest and Coyote who were already walking towards the unattractive church.

Chichimaya Church, called *El Santuario de Nada* by locals, was on the edge of Cordoba, the little town left shrinking by a distant by-passing freeway. The church was a faded yellowing, adobe-plastered cement-block building, with a small wooden tower that had no bell in it and was home to a large family of bats. The church was nobody's shrine.

The Cross blocking the way to the Church's small porch and doorway was made of 2x6s nailed together by a local carpenter. There was no fountain, no flowers, and no welcome sign near the walkway leading to the door. The only thing remarkable about the church's exterior was a chunk of rotten cottonwood screwed to the front wall. It had been unearthed when the cross was planted. Don Bernard Makko, a recently deceased church member, claimed the piece of rotten wood was a remnant of a Penitente cross, carried south by Hispanics fleeing the angry Pueblo tribes which friars had clumsily tried to convert. Father Gallapo thought the rotten chunk was a piece of firewood left over from a Christmas luminaria, but he kept his mouth shut about this.

Because it was untended, the church had no visiting hours. The little church's double doors were uninspiring, with no ornamental carvings, and they were marred by a yellowing notice of Mass times. Father Gallapo unlocked the door with a key he had picked off a nail on the backside of the cross in front of the door. He led his nervous followers inside, passing through the small vestibule with a birdbath used as a holy water vessel, which a deacon bought forty years ago at Sears in Albuquerque,

"Sometimes I remember to fill it," the Priest said.

"Where do you get the water?" the Mexican Cowboy asked, trying to see the dark church's insides.

"From the sink in the bathroom," Father Gallapo answered.

"Do you want me pour the rain water in there?" the Mexican Cowboy asked him.

"No. Take the bowl up and put it down by the altar," the Priest said.

Father Gallapo moved around the church lighting several heavy, badly-gilded candleholders holding thick white candles which had once been tall. Being better able to see now, the Mexican Cowboy noticed that the church's pews were just long benches with slatted backs. The altar was wooden and draped with a white cloth. There were some cheap, unidentifiable painted saints—made in Mexico he knew—in niches along the walls. There were two undecorated windows on the east wall and two wooden chandeliers overhead holding unlit naked light bulbs.

Father Gallapo pointed to the crucifix behind the altar. "It was bought in Juarez," he said. "It's badly painted and there are some odd, yellow-colored spots on Our Savior's loincloth. Mrs. Whitenose is the sole Altar Guild member and she can't stand ladders. That's why she doesn't take off our Lord's loincloth and wash it."

"'Fraid of what she'd see?" the Mexican Cowboy asked. "Why don't you do it?"

"It is unCatholic to say this, but I like Him that way. The old guys who still come to Masses call Him 'the Pissing Jesus.' I think the yellow spots are evidence of Christ's human side."

"Roman soldiers didn't take Jesus to the urinal before they nailed him to the cross."

"He couldn't hold it in?" The Mexican Cowboy replied.

"Do you think you could in His place?"

"Depends on how much beer I drank at my last supper."

While the Priest talked to the Mexican Cowboy, Coyote cautiously explored the church, hunched over with tension, sniffing and looking at every-thing inside the building.

Ignoring Coyote, the Mexican Cowboy turned around and saw the only unexpected sight inside this church. It was a wide, hand-made wooden ladder leading up to a small choir loft over the vestibule. The pipes of a long unused organ dominated the choir loft.

"That pipe organ was put up there by a benefactor who wanted to get rid of it," Father Gallapo said. "It was never hooked up."

Father Gallapo opened a closet door on the side of the altar and took out a white surplice and pulled it over his clothes. "Mrs. Whitenose cleans and presses it for me," the Priest said.

Coyote was standing near the back of the church, still sniffing and looking around.

"I'm ready for you," the Priest said.

Coyote came hesitantly towards him.

"Next to me," Father Gallapo said, moving in front of the altar.

Quivering slightly, Coyote moved next to him.

"Kneel," Father Gallapo said.

"I can't," said Coyote.

"Well, then tell me how do coyotes submit?" the Priest said.

"Roll over and show their throats," Coyote said.

"Do it for me," the Priest said.

Coyote looked at the Mexican Cowboy with something like desperation in his countenance.

"You wanted to do this," the Mexican Cowboy said. "So do it."

Realizing he'd done what no coyote ever wants to do—trapped himself—Coyote submitted. He lay down, stretched out, rolled over and closed his eyes, quivering like a sheep awaiting the slaughterer's knife.

Standing over Coyote, Father Gallapo began speaking in Latin. "*Quid petis ab Ecclesia Dei,*"

Coyote looked up at him blankly.

"Say '*Fidem,*'" the Priest said.

"What's it mean?" Coyote asked.

"This isn't going to work," said the Priest. "Okay I'm going to have to treat you like an infant."

"That's a mean thing to do to me when I'm being submissive," Coyote said.

"Hush," the Priest said.

Father Gallapo burst into Latin, pausing momentarily between each sentence. Neither Coyote nor the Mexican Cowboy could fathom what he was saying.

"Bring me the holy water please," Father Gallapo said to the Mexican Cowboy.

With fear and trembling Coyote watched, upside down, as Father Gallapo took a large spoon out of his pocket and dipped it into the bowl of arroyo pump water the Mexican Cowboy was holding. Coyote could hear the Priest's knees creak as he leaned over him and dabbed rainwater on Coyote three times: on his throat, on his forehead, and on his nose. With each spoonful of water the Priest said Latin words Coyote couldn't understand.

Coyote lay still and quivering.

Father Gallapo, after saying a final sentence in Latin, straightened up, and beaming said, "We're done."

"Can I get up now?" Coyote asked.

~*~*~

Father Gallapo makes a gesture like a dog trainer releasing a dog from a down-stay command. Without realizing he's acting like one of the hated dog slaves, Coyote rolls over and stands up.

He's wobbly and feeling woozy, and very unsure whether what he's done is the right thing. He needs to sit and he does, looking dazed.

The Mexican Cowboy, feeling worn out himself, steps back from the altar and flops down on the first row bench. He looks at Coyote—who is staring up at the small choir loft at the back of the little church. Coyote's nose is pointing right at the organ.

The Mexican Cowboy looks up at the organ loft, sees nothing and turns around. Looking at Coyote again he notices that Coyote's head is perfectly positioned to block the steady light coming from one of the candles behind him.

Coyote is still looking up, fixing intently, perhaps worshipfully, on something in the choir loft. Coyote cocks his head, and suddenly the Mexican Cowboy sees a halo of pure light surrounding Coyote's head and snout.

"My god," he says. "Coyote is a Saint."

Coyote, his eyes and nose still fixing on the choir loft, begins whimpering. His body tenses as if he is getting ready to jump up there. Currents of fear, excitement, and exaltation are vibrating inside Coyote. The smell coming from the loft is unmistakable. Coyote has only smelled it once before, the night when different gods were mixing it up in the sky.

Something is on top of the organ pipes. That's where the smell is coming from, Coyote realizes.

In the darkness above the pipes Coyote can just make out El Latrano, Senor Coyote, sitting on the mountain of organ pipes. He is mottled orange and blue, and he's wearing his feathered, multi-colored headdress.

In the coyote way of speaking—with gestures, emitted odors, whines and barks—El Latrano 'speaks' to Coyote. An enormous wave of pleasure sweeps through Coyote's body as he grasps his Lord's message.

"You have done well, my Son," Senor Coyote says.

"My son? He calls me MY son? He says I am HIS SON!" Coyote is ecstatic. No male coyote ever called him 'son' before. Always fatherless like every other coyote, Coyote feels a tsunami of love and need swelling in his heart.

"I have a father! I have a father! My Father knows me! My Father loves me! My Father will guide me and keep me safe."

"What's that odor?" the Mexican Cowboy asks Father Gallapo.

"Don't know. Something here smells weird to me. And what's Coyote saying?" Father Gallapo asks the Mexican Cowboy.

"I don't know. Some thing's crazy going on here," the Mexican Cowboy whispers to the Priest.

They both look at Coyote.

Coyote is transfixed. He is uplifted and exalted. Slumping on his belly, he rolls on his back, puts all four of his legs in the air, and allows himself to be bathed in the sacramental blessing his Lord is sending down to him with smell. Under Coyote's tail his glands begin radiating wellbeing and happiness.

If the humans in the church had coyote noses, they would smell the divine things that are happening. But they are not completely oblivious.

For long moments there is no movement whatsoever in the church.

Father Gallapo is feeling someone speaking to him in a language he could never learn.

The Mexican Cowboy is feeling himself embraced, praised, respected, and loved, emotions he associates with many of the women he has loved.

~*~*~

Then, gently the steady candle flames began to flicker again. A cool breeze moved through the church. Each of the three friends realized that the light, sounds and smells that had engulfed the church were fading. The moment of transcendence had ended.

The air was suddenly colder. The church had provided its most intense hospitality as long as it was able to do so. Now the church needed calm and darkness to muster energy for Sunday's services. Father Gallapo realized that his church wanted them to leave.

Softly, with exaggerated motions, Father Gallapo blew out each candle as Coyote and the Mexican Cowboy walked to the back of the church. The Priest came to them in the sudden darkness, took each of them by the back of the neck and steered them through the door. After locking the door and hanging the key on the back of the cross where it had come from, he said with concealed passion, "Coyote may be ready for his first confession now."

Surprised to hear himself saying this, Coyote replied in a voice both meek and strong, confident yet timid: "Yes. It is time for me to confess now."

Father Gallapo and Coyote left the Mexican Cowboy without any further words and walked away toward the trailer behind the truck. With his legs aching, Father Gallapo climbed onto the trailer and opened the doors of the porta-confessional. A rank smell came out the doors. Coyote leaped up on the trailer and the Priest helped him get into the penitent's side of the confessional. The Priest shut the door and went into the other half of the porta-confessional. The Mexican Cowboy heard a door bolt slide into place. Then there was silence in th parking lot.

Alone, and starting to feel the remorse that comes with being abandoned, the Mexican Cowboy wondered what Coyote needed to confess. Blasphemy? Disbelief? Nah. How about fornication? Coyote had in fact sired many pups without marrying their mothers.

The Mexican Cowboy walked over and sat shivering under a small, pathetic tree, wishing he'd brought his winter coat. He was tired, he was unsettled, and he was anxious. Bored with his surroundings, he looked up. He could see a bright star-lit sky through the tree's few branches. He looked around the parking lot. There was nothing to see. He strained to hear what was happening inside the porta-confessional. He heard nothing.

His eyes seemed blurry. He looked up at the sky again and blinked. He was having trouble focusing on the stars. Maybe it was hard to see them, he thought, because the moon—a little past fullness—was so bright. He blinked a few times more. The stars seemed to be moving. The Mexican Cowboy blinked and blinked. The pouches under his eyes were getting damp. Were the stars trying to say something to him? He stared and blinked. There seemed to be a word forming near the moon. He couldn't make it out. He rubbed his eyes and blinked again.

Instantly the word was as clear as a neon sign. The word was **GRACIAS.** His heart raced. He knew the word was meant for him. He looked over at the moon, which was right at the end of the word in the sky. He laughed. The moon had become a yellow Smiley-Face.

"Thanks for everything," the Mexican Cowboy said gratefully back to the sky. The Smiley-Face appeared to wink. Then it turned back into the moon again. The word in the sky vanished also.

With a mix of satisfaction, joy, gratefulness, and a new kind of longing occupying him, the Mexican Cowboy walked back to the truck and climbed into the passenger side. He wasn't tired, cold, or impatient anymore.

Minutes later the doors of the porta-confessional opened. Father Gallapo hopped off the trailer with surprising agility, and climbed into the truck behind the wheel.

"Let's go," he said.

"What about Coyote?" the Mexican Cowboy asked.

"He wants to make his own way back," the Priest said.

Father Gallapo started the engine and drove the truck out of the parking lot and kept going slowly through the almost-one-street little town. He drove slowly because he didn't want to wake up anyone.

But just as he neared Mrs. Whitenose's two-story house, a small gust of wind hit one of the porta-confessional's doors. It banged shut loudly.

That woke Mrs. Whitenose, who always slept poorly. She looked down from her window to see what made the noise.

She recognized Father Gallapo's truck and trailer crawling up the street toward her. She was astonished to see a coyote crouching on top of the Priest's swaying porta-confessional.

The coyote looked as if it had been painted orange and green, with black spots.

The coyote was wearing a crazy Aztec-looking headdress.

Just as the trailer crept to her house the coyote put its head back and emitted a sustained, vibrant, eerie, coyote howl.

"I'll be damned," she said. "That scabby old Priest has really gone nuts. I'll tell the Bishop about this."

As he passed her window Coyote stopped howling and turned and looked her squarely in the eye.

"Maybe I'd better not tell the Bishop," Mrs. Whitenose mumbled to herself, as she crawled back into bed.

Communion

Back at the ranch house, the friends sprawled on the porch. The moon was setting and the night birds quieting down.

"Why did Jesus Christ come to earth?" Coyote asked suddenly. He was musing about why his own god hadn't bothered to come at the same time. Or had he?

"It was necessary that Jesus Christ come to earth to make it understood that all members of the human species are naturally alike and equal," Father Gallapo answered, turning philosopher on them.

"Then who will God send to earth to make it understood that members of the coyote species are as equal as humans?" Coyote asked him.

"We are working on that now. Religion is the great equalizer," the Priest replied.

"Religion can be toxic," the Mexican Cowboy said.

"Religion doesn't have to be toxic, but for the good of all it is important that some people possess it," Father Gallapo said.

"Religion hasn't helped coyotes," Coyote said.

"Wait and see," the Priest said.

"We've waited and we've waited. We've seen nothing yet that keeps us from getting kicked around by you guys," Coyote said.

"Pretty much true of Hispanics in this country too," the Mexican Cowboy said.

"Priests don't have it so good either," Father Gallapo said.

The amigos sat quietly, not dissatisfied, but thinking about what to say next.

"Do you believe in an afterlife?" Coyote asked.

"Sort of," the Mexican Cowboy replied.

"Maybe in my next life I could become a man," Coyote said.

"And maybe in my next life I could become a coyote," the Mexican Cowboy said.

"Becoming something else in the next life is called 'metempsychosis'—the transmigration of the soul," the Priest said, continuing to be philosophical. "By shifting souls around God helps his creatures to understand all of his creation."

"That's a mouthful," the Mexican Cowboy said. "I don't understand that philosophy stuff."

"Maybe I do and maybe I don't understand philosophy. But I'm hungry. I want a mouthful and I can't eat philosophy," Coyote said.

"Let it be then," Father Gallapo said. "Let's eat."

The three of them went into the kitchen, took down from the dusty shelf the 'new' hand-painted and chipped pottery bowls. Over the low-burning propane stove, bumping into each other, they cooked up the Mexican Cowboy's usual Anglo-Mex meal: tamales, tacos, enchiladas, tortillas, salad, rice, and beans.

"I want to eat on the table tonight instead of going outside," the Mexican Cowboy said.

Smiling, feeling very good about how their time together was going, the three friends sat down at the kitchen table next to the turquoise-colored screen door that led out to the patio.

The Mexican Cowboy poured glasses of cheap California red wine from the gallon jug the Priest had brought with him. "Shall we have a toast?" he asked.

"Should we have a prayer first?" Coyote asked.

"Okay with me," the Mexican Cowboy said, and motioned to the Priest to lead one.

After a moment's thought, Father Gallapo said, "Bow your heads and repeat after me..."

They bowed their heads.

"Oh Lord, we thank you for what the three of us have here. What we have gotten is True Communion," the Priest said with a surprisingly authoritative voice.

"This **is** true Communion!" Coyote and the Mexican Cowboy repeated with grins on their faces.

"*Amen,*" said the Priest.

"Nope," said Coyote. "Not all of us here are men." He winked and began to wolf down his food after giggling at his word play.

"Blessed are the cheap wine makers," the Mexican Cowboy said, after pouring half a glass of wine down his gullet. He started eating too.

Father Gallapo took a sip of his wine, nibbled a bite or two from his plate and, looking at his friends, said prayerfully to his Master, You do great work, God. You really do.

Outside the house, all the coyotes in the vicinity were congregating and listening. Joyously, the audience of coyotes burst into howling. While the grownup coyotes were celebrating, the coyote pups were sneaking over to the patio door, thinking about the leftover handouts the Mexican Cowboy would soon be putting out for them.

The Flood and the Furor

I t was an early September evening. Just at dusk Coyote stopped by his friend's house to tell him that he wouldn't be coming for dinner tonight.

"Why not?" the Mexican Cowboy asked.

"I'm tired of human food because there's too much agriculture and not enough fresh meat in it," Coyote answered.

"So you are going hunting tonight?"

"Yes, I'm going to the Bosque tonight. I haven't eaten a goose or a duck for a long while."

"Geese don't get here until November usually."

"I'll take any water bird I can find."

"Take an umbrella. Weatherman's saying a hurricane hasn't passed over the river since 1965. It is going to rain like hell."

"Great. That will make it easier to sneak up on them."

"Eat well," the Mexican Cowboy said to his friend.

"You too. If it's pouring, put out extra food for the animals so they can eat well too," Coyote replied as he slipped away.

In the adjacent, crowded godly dimension 'above them,' local deities watched Cyclone Hermione loop up the west coast of Mexico and curve inland over the Sonora desert. Pestered by weather planes, and hearing she is about to be demoted to just a heavy rain storm, Hermione stubbornly pledges to hold herself together until she's gone further inland than any of her cousins and dumped a downpour which weather record keepers will never forget.

"She wants to be remembered," El Latrano, the Coyote God, said to nearby mammal and bird gods.

"Looks to me like she is going to drown Albuquerque," the Goose God said.

By sunrise, Hermione raged near the Rio Puerco, a meandering riverbed normally as wet as a dust storm. Finding it impossible to keep herself together, Hermione decided to give this sparsely populated landscape her all. "There hasn't been a flood down there since 1941," she said to herself, as she began to disintegrate. Straining over the next six hours, she spewed eight to eleven inches of rain on the mesa west of Albuquerque. Her last mental words were: Flood 'em out.

Up in the gods' realm, after keeping track of Hermione all night and growing worried about his creatures along the verdant river the Puerco flows into, the Coyote god El Latrano summoned colleague gods in the sky and said, "We'd better stop fooling around and get ready to do some work to help the creatures we are responsible for."

Other gods looked at him indifferently.

"You sure about that?" the Crow God said.

"Count me out," said the Duck God. "Wetting up this dry region is good for my guys."

"I'll help," said one of the small bird gods. "Human birders are feeding the heck out of my songbirds."

"Humans aren't helping hawks," said the hawk god.

"What's in it for us?" one of the rodent gods asked.

"If we start working together up here," the Coyote God said, "it will be better for all our creatures down there."

"You sound like you are getting religion," the bobcat god said.

"Have you figured out a way to get the humans out of the picture?" the whooping crane god asked.

"No, but I've got a plan to get humans to start working with us," El Latrano answered.

"I'd rather see them all get the plague," the Buffalo God said.

In the early morning hours Coyote lay on his belly on grasses and lichens in the partially canopied Bosque with remains of a mallard—who put aggressiveness ahead of self protection—and two other water fowl beside him. He noticed that the light drizzle that wrapped him with a comforting but distracting mist, and made meal hunting easiest for him, was turning into heavy rain. Confident he could kill more waterfowl when he got hungry again, he abandoned the remains of his big meal and curled up against the trunk of a still-leafy cottonwood tree where it was drier.

An hour and a half later he awoke to the sound of a truck on the other side of the river. He was surprised to see his mentor, Father Gallapo, pulling into an off-road parking spot near the swelling river. The Priest's battered sand-colored Ford truck seemed to be running well and his porta-confessional—formerly a two-door outhouse—was loosely tied onto the trailer behind the truck. Appearing weary and meditative, Father Gallapo sat inside the truck, wipers trying to keep the windshield clear, and looked out at the muddy blue-grey rising river with concern on his face. "He'd better get away from there," the Coyote thought, before putting his head down and going to sleep again.

Meanwhile, over at the Mexican Cowboy's ramshackle house, it was raining like hell. Rain pounded on his tin roof, puddles widened in the yard, and the Mexican Cowboy was peeved because he had to drive into town and pick up a load of groceries to feed Father Gallapo, who was supposed to be driving up from his Texas parish that afternoon. "Nothing to do but do it," the Mexican Cowboy said to himself, as he hunted for his slicker in a pile of clothes in a corner of his bedroom.

In Cordoba, the mostly one-street town economically deprived by the twenty year old freeway a mile away, he parked outside City Hall, a squat, yellow-painted, six-room, concrete building with an evaporative air conditioner on its roof. Inside, the Mexican Cowboy's sometimes friend, most often enemy, Mayor Howie, stared at the screen of an old computer on his desk. With an annoyed glance at his visitor he hurriedly switched it off.

"Good movie?" the Mexican Cowboy asked.

"Just porn," the Mayor said.

"Where's my groceries?" the Mexican Cowboy asked, wanting to get out of there.

"I haven't gotten them yet," the Mayor replied. "Tell you what. Here's a deal. I'll give you money to do the shopping and buy you a lunch too. Will you do it?" Instantly the Mexican Cowboy felt victimized again by the Mayor, who was always making, then breaking, deals with him. Still, getting a free lunch appealed to him.

"Okay, IF we have that lunch first," the Cowboy said. The Mayor looked cross but got up and went to get his coat.

Over at Jessica's Café, with plates of steak and fries before them, Mayor Howie told the Mexican Cowboy about a Tea Party meetup taking place that day on Joe Eden's old ranch down the river.

"The county bought it and is turning it into a bird-watching park. Not much there now,"

"What's the Tea Party doing there?" the Cowboy asks.

"Folks from around the state thought it would be a good place for a meetup. It's just off the freeway and nobody's going to bother them there." The Mayor ate another chunk of the big, overcooked steak on his plate and sipped half a cup of coffee, then said reflectively: "They are my kind of people; principled, good leaders, and good with each other. Real fine Americans."

"As long as they stay on Joe Eden's old ranch, they'll be fine with me," The Mexican Cowboy replied.

"You a Democrat?" The Mayor asked.

"I vote for anyone who gives me ten thousand dollars. I guess that makes me a Republican," the Mexican Cowboy said.

"How 'bout voting for me for ten bucks?" Mayor Howie asked.

"Could be you're my man," the Mexican Cowboy answered. "No one I ever voted for has ever done anything for me."

Coyote Dives In

Back at the river, rain had driven all animals in the Bosque under cover—except for waterfowl, which were enjoying every drop. Coyote slipped down to the riverbank and lapped water. The river was rising, he noticed, and on the other side he saw water stealing up the nearly flat bank toward the trailer's wheels. The Priest, wearing jeans and a rain shell, obviously worried now, had gotten out of his truck and was retying the ropes holding the porta-confessional to the trailer. All but one of the ropes connected to the two-door wooden structure were lying on the ground. Father Gallapo was on the trailer trying to shove the porta-confessional nearer to the truck. Holding the remaining rope, the Priest climbed down from the trailer and into the cluttered truck bed, his old knees cracking and hurting.

Turning his head to look up the river, Coyote saw a flood wave several feet tall and very wide, approaching quickly. Alarmed, he shouted at the Priest, "Hurry up! Tie that rope to the truck now!"

Looking up, the Priest's eyes skimmed the opposite bank searching for the owner of the commanding voice.

"Who was that?"

"Me," Coyote shouted back, moving into a more seeable position. "Hurry up! Tie that rope now. A flood wave's coming."

"How big's the wave?" The Priest shouted back.

"Big enough to take the Confessional," Coyote yelled back and plunged into the river paddling frantically toward the other side.

"Let me throw you a rope," the Priest shouted, starting to climb out of the bed. "Tie the Confessional down," the Coyote screamed.

His knees cracking and hurting, Father Gallapo got back in the truck bed, picked up the rope around the porta-confessional, and pushed it into a ring on the truck's side. He was about to pull the rope tight and tie a solid knot when the wide, almost fender-high flood wave swept over the bank.

"Hang on," Coyote shouted.

The huge wave rocked the trailer back and forth. The swaying Confessional bowed and leaned, then grandly fell on its side into the water. The one rope attached to it yanked loose. Father Gallapo grabbed the rope and tried to keep the floating former outhouse from drifting away. It was a tug of war the Priest was losing and he tired as he hung on. The flood wave dragged the Priest across the clutter in the truck bed.

Afraid his mentor would be pulled out of the truck bed and drown, Coyote—getting close to the shore—shouted: "Let go of the rope." Fearful now of being dragged into the flood, the Priest let go his hold. The big wave pushed the confessional away from the Priest and the battered, but significant, edifice floated down the flooding river.

Swept away himself, but determined to rescue the itinerant Priest's important porta-confessional, Coyote swam toward the bobbing former outhouse, dodged the heaving, slowly spinning structure, and stalking like a skilled hunter, went after the trailing rope. With a splashing lunge he bit onto it.

The heavy end of the Confessional was low in the water. Working his way up the rope with his mouth like a hand-over-hand climber, Coyote was able to climb aboard the porta-confessional. "I rescued it!" he said to himself. As his shook his fur and reason returned to him, overcoming his automatic responses, he realized that both he and God's instrument were in a fine mess. What to do now? He wondered.

Mayor Howie Finds a New Excuse to Avoid Paying a Bill

In Cordoba, meanwhile, Mrs. Whitenose was standing with twenty-five others on the little city's sturdy bridge watching the furious flood develop. Startled, Mrs. Whitenose saw Coyote float by on top of the Priest's treasured porta-confessional. Unlike the stern gaze he

wore last time she saw him, this time he looked at her pleadingly. She decided she must tell the Priest what just happened when he arrives. He'll want to find his beloved confessional.

Several blocks away at Jessica's Café, Mayor Howie's cousin Frank Corsa, the only policeman in Cordova, had just come into the restaurant to tell the Mayor about the flood.

"Highway Patrol's sent out an alert that the freeway may be flooded near Joe Eden's old ranch. If the water is more than two or three inches deep the freeway will have to be blocked."

"We'd better go down there and see what's up," the Mayor said to his officer.

"Why?" the Mexican Cowboy asked.

"If the park's flooded I want to persuade the Tea Party guys to come up to Cordoba."

"Because they are your kind of people?" the Cowboy asked.

"No, because our town needs their business," the Mayor replied.

"OK, give me my dough and I'll be on my way," the Cowboy said.

"I'll give it to you when I get back," the Mayor answered.

"No deal," the Cowboy said. "You promised to pay me to get the groceries now."

"I haven't got the money with me," the Mayor said.

"Then I'll stick with you until you get some," the Cowboy answered. "I'm coming with you."

The policeman raised an eyebrow, but the Mayor said,

"Let's go."

They left Jessica's without paying the bill. In the kitchen, Jessica added another sum to her long list of the Mayor's unpaid meals.

Coyote Floats from One Danger to Another

Downstream, Coyote rode the porta-confessional like a bucking bull. Holding on to the girding rope with aching teeth, leaning one way, then another, he kept the floating outhouse 'upright,' its twin doors facing the overcast spitting sky. Jumping its banks, the flooded river was moving as fast as a city school bus between stops. Every few hundred yards the porta-confessional bumped against a sandbar or other underwater obstacle, or smacked into a higher bank and slowly spun around. It was a tough ride for Coyote. Eight or nine miles downstream, as the crow flies, the twisting river shallowed slightly because flood waters were pouring west toward the nearby freeway over almost non-existent banks. The current pulled the outhouse toward the shore and Coyote was alarmed to see it heading toward a small crowd of humans, many of them carrying long, thick-barreled guns. Frightened, he slipped off the bottom-bumping porta-confessional, and swam diagonally across the river to the steep, brushy east bank. Soaked and silent, he crept up the bank as stealthily as he could.

On the west side of the river, close to where the Tea Party was meeting, the outhouse sank upside down. Only the end with the composter was sticking out of the water and, brown, poisonous muck drifted downstream from the closed door of the penitent's side of the confessional. Under that seat was a composting toilet, Coyote remembered.

Some nearby human voices startled him. Tea Party hunters in rain gear were clustered in a lean-to by a small camp fire a half minute's trot away in a large clearing in the Bosque.

Alarmed, Coyote skulked into the thicker brush nearby. One of the hunter's chained dogs smelled him and began to bark furiously.

"Something big's over there," a hunter said. "Shall we go see what it is?"

"It's raining too hard for hunting," another said. "Let the dog loose."

"Then I got to chase him," the dog's owner said.

"Why don't we just fire a few shots into the bushes over there? If we are lucky we'll kill whatever the dog's smelling," another hunter said. With nods and 'Okays' all around, the men picked up their guns, aimed at the dense brush, and fired several shots each.

"I didn't hear anything jerk around," one of the shooters said.

"The dog's still barking," another shooter says.

"Make him shut up," another hunter says. The dog's owner went over to the dog tied to a stake in the rain away from the fire and cuffed it to be quiet.

Thirty yards upriver from the dense underbrush the hunters had aimed at, Coyote lay on his belly peering at them from behind a blue palo verde bush. Why dogs put up with slave crap I'll never figure out, he thought as he backed silently away from the camp. Slinking, moving silently, trying to get more downwind of the dog pack, he heard a shout from the other side of the river.

Some guy wearing a three cornered hat and a rain suit over a Revolutionary soldier's costume his wife made for him was trying to get the hunters' attention.

"Other cars are coming into the parking lot," he shouted. "Lots of them. Something's going on."

"Protesters?" one of the hunters shouts back.

"Looks like all different kinds of people. You guys better get back over here now," the shouter on the opposite bank replied.

"Okay, guys, let's get back to the Party," the most authoritarian of the hunters said. "We can come back and get our stuff later." Just a few yards down river there was a rope tied to stakes on both sides of a sandbank, just under water. Stopping a moment to pull on hip waders they had left well above the water line, the hunters waded in one by one and, clinging to the rope, pulled themselves across the flooded river. The leashed dogs were forced to swim alongside them.

"Good riddance," Coyote said to himself. "Now I can get back to figuring out how to let the Priest know where his confessional is."

Another Thing in the Sky

Meanwhile, back at the riverside car park north of Cordova, the crestfallen Priest struggled to pull himself together. I've got to get my confessional back, but how to do is the question, he thought to himself. Coyote will ride it until it either sinks or gets stuck by the shore. Either way he will figure out how to let me know where it is. But I've got to do my part. I've got to go downstream and look for him. Too sore-kneed to kneel, the Priest sent off a hurried prayer to his Lord: Please help me deal with this.

"Do your part and I will do Mine," was his Lord's instant reply.

The ropes picked up and stowed in the truck bed, the rain letting up slightly, the Priest climbed into the truck, gently pulled the trailer out of the ebbing flood, and drove into Cordoba. He decided to stop by Mrs. Whitenose's house and ask her to make a bag of sandwiches, put in some fruit, and let him have several bottles of water to take with him on the possibly long search for his treasured confessional.

Waiting expectantly for his arrival, Mrs. Whitenose hugged the stunned Priest and eagerly told him about seeing Coyote look pleadingly at her as he floated under the bridge on the porta-confessional. She asked her Priest if he would like her to go with him to help him find his porta-confessional. He hesitated, but accepted. Another pair of eyes might make a difference.

Mrs. Whitenose hurriedly packed several large plastic bags with snack makings, and added water bottles and several other things she thought they might need. Oddest of these was a pink dog collar with licenses and an ID-tag dangling on a clip, which belonged to her departed dog Jedthrow. The dog was given that name because he cared only about getting her former husband Jed to throw things for him to chase, catch, and retrieve. In less than an hour they were ready and departed.

Downstream, Coyote had been thinking about ways to notify the Priest, who he was sure would search for him. Looking around him in all directions Coyote noticed the campfire, which the hunters abandoned without putting out, had gotten very smoky. An idea came to him. Coyote lay on his belly again, his snout to the ground, and asked his god, El Latrano, a question.

"Are you thinking the same thing I am?"

"**Do it,**" the Coyote's god answered a moment later.

Coyote got on his feet, and wary as any wild animal can be around hunters, he wriggled through the wet brush toward the smoldering fire. Looking across the river he saw that none of the Tea Party members were looking his way. Most of them were over by the parking lot, trying to figure out where all those vehicles were coming from. Taking a chance, Coyote dashed across the clearing into the abandoned lean-to, which protected him from being seen from the other side of the river. Up close to the fire on his belly now, he blew as hard as he could into the smoldering wood for several minutes. The fire took hold once more, but it smoked worse than ever.

Then Coyote used his tail like a brush to shape the smoke into an immense flat slab that rose into the sky without changing shape. A small way from the top of the slab, with a jab of his tail and a smooth half-circle swoop in the smoky slab, he made a recognizable cutout and let the slab rise into the sky. Working in another dimension barely brushing against the earthlings', the Coyote god El Latrano cleared a mile-wide circle in the low clouds over Coyote's head and commanded the giant gray-black slab to stay in place.

Coyote Makes a New Friend

Ten minutes later Father Gallapo, who had been driving south on the freeway with Mrs. Whitenose beside him, was just a few miles from Joe Eden's former ranch.

"I wonder why we aren't seeing any cars coming the other way," Mrs. Whitenose asked.

"I don't know why," the Priest answered, "but keep your eyes moving around. We don't want to miss anything"

"All right," she said, "but there is something I'm wondering about."

"Which is?"

"Why don't you ever call me Thelma? You know it's my first name."

"Because you never asked me to," the Priest replied.

Ahead of them the sky was brightening dramatically.

"Look over there!" said Mrs. Whitenose suddenly. "There's a smoke column going straight up in the sky."

The Priest looked out the window and immediately slowed the truck and parked off the roadway.

"Why did you do that?" Mrs. Whitenose asked.

"Because that smoke is the Coyote's signal."

"What makes you think so?" she asked.

"What does it look like to you?"

She thought a moment and answered, "It's like a tall flat monument."

"Do you see anything about two-thirds of the way up the slab?"

"Yes," she answered, "it looks like a crescent. With a couple of circles."

"And you still don't know what it is?"

"No," she said. "Tell me."

"It's an outhouse door!" the Priest exclaimed, beaming. "See the crescent and the holes on either side? That's two stars and the moon. Most outhouse doors have a crescent moon and two stars."

"You are right," Mrs. Whitenose said, after staring at the slab a moment. "How in heck did the Coyote do that?"

"His god must have helped out," the Priest said.

"His god? There's more than one god? If you believe that are you sure you're a Catholic?" she asked, worried about heresy.

"Yep, I've met him. The Coyote's god has even been in our church with me."

"I've got to hear more about this," Mrs. Whitenose said, with growing doubt in her voice.

"Later," the Priest said. "Now we've got to save the confessional."

Taking a map out of the glove box the Priest spotted a road going east from the exit they had just passed. It was not a major highway but it did cross the river.

"We'll try that way," the Priest said, giving her the map to hold. When there was a big break in the vehicles passing the stopped truck, he turned sharply left, crossed the very rough median with the trailer bouncing left and right, and started back toward Cordoba. When they left the freeway at the next intersection, the badly paved, narrow road they were taking quickly came to the flooded river. The concrete ford was well under water. The Priest got out and looked at it. The water didn't look much deeper than the truck's hubcaps. He decided to chance it and with the truck in 4-wheel drive he steered into the water. Gripping the steering wheel tightly, he could feel the river pushing against the front wheels. He kept moving steadily and slowly because he worried about water splashing over the engine and killing the old truck's electrical system. Mrs. Whitenose, who had been clutching her hands together tightly, breathed an audible sigh as the truck neared the other side and started climbing out of the water.

"Made it," the Priest said.

A few hundred yards further along the road they saw a very rough road going off to the right along the river. The muddy road appeared on no map, but the Priest guessed this might be the only way to drive to the Coyote. Slipping the transmission into 4-wheel drive again, he turned onto the barely drivable road.

A few minutes later, tending the fire, Coyote heard the Priest's truck crawling toward him long before it came into sight. Looking under the lean-to's bottom edge, he waited until nobody on the other side of the river was looking his way then dashed across the clearing into the brush. Going east several hundred yards he came to the muddy road the Priest traveled on and started trotting toward the truck. He was surprised to see an elf owl in the cottonwood tree on the other side of the road shaking its wings to dry out. As the truck neared him, Coyote hid in the Bosque brambles and waited until it went by. Seeing Mrs. Whitenose riding in the front seat, he jumped out of the bushes and loped after the truck. The Priest had been keeping his eyes open, spotted him in the rear mirror, and stopped the truck. Coyote stopped too, several yards behind the truck, and stood still, waiting to see what the Priest was going to do.

"Come over here," the Priest shouted.

Coyote shook his head.

"Are you afraid of Mrs. Whitenose?" the Priest asked more softly. The coyote didn't budge.

"Okay, stay here," the Priest said, and went around to the right side of the truck to talk to Mrs. Whitenose.

"Thelma, I need you to come out here and bring one of those chicken sandwiches with you." Mrs. Whitenose grabbed the food bag from the back seat and stepped out.

"Does he understand what you are saying?" she asked.

"Coyote can do more than understand," the Priest replied. "Thelma, I want you to hold the sandwich out in front of you and go slowly halfway toward him. Then put the sandwich down, unwrap the plastic, and come toward me."

Looking puzzled and a little frightened, Mrs. Whitehead complied.

"Now Thelma," the Priest said, "I want you to tell Coyote what you put out for him and why you did it." Mrs. Whitenose thought a moment then turned and shouted at the coyote,

"It is a chicken sandwich and I put it there because he told me to." Coyote remained motionless.

"You need to give him a better reason, " the Priest told her.

"All right," she nodded. She turned and said more softly to the Coyote, "Honey, I put that sandwich out there because I want to get to know you. I think you are special and I believe you and I can become good friends."

"Good," the Priest said. "Ask him if he can understand people."

"Do you know what I'm saying?" Mrs. Whitenose asked.

"I know what you are saying, but I have my doubts about why you are saying it," Coyote answered. Although Mrs. Whitenose was shocked to hear a coyote speak perfect English, she was still able to answer him. "I really meant what I said. I really do. Eat the sandwich anyway."

After a moment of hesitation and appraising, Coyote walked over and—with his gaze fixed on her—did what she asked.

Mrs. Whitenose said to him: "I understand you've got a god of your own."

"We all do," Coyote answered.

"Okay, you two can get along," the Priest said. "Now tell me what's happened to the confessional."

"It is a little ways downriver on the other side, mostly submerged against the bank. There are a lot of people nearby and more cars arriving," Coyote answered.

"That's got to be the Tea Party gathering at Joe Eden's old ranch," the Priest said. "Let's go get the confessional."

"Count me out," Coyote replied. "Those guys tried to kill me. I'm getting out of here. You can get them to help you. They are humans, like you."

"You got to come with us," the Priest said. "I don't know why, but I know you've got to."

"Those people over there may have guns," Mrs. Whitenose added, "but they won't shoot you if they think you are a dog."

"I'd rather be shot than turned into a slave dog," Coyote said.

"We're not going to enslave you," the Priest said, "but we got to protect you when we go into that anti-vermin bunch."

"Let me go back to my coyotes," Coyote said.

"Sorry," the Priest answered. "Someone higher up tells me you are going to be needed here."

"Your god?" asked Coyote.

"Yes," the Priest answered. "My God relayed a message from your god."

"What did he say?" Coyote asked.

"Put Coyote in the truck."

"You are not lying?" Coyote asked.

"When have you caught me lying to you?"

Hating this decision, Coyote made up his mind. "All right, I'll go with you," he said.

"I can see why your god made you his Prophet," the Priest replied.

"His choice is bad for me," Coyote replied.

When they were all inside the Ford truck's cab, Mrs. Whitenose insisted on putting the jingly, pink, slave-dog collar around Coyote's neck.

"I hate this," he said.

"Think about it as a disguise," Mrs. Whitenose answered. Coyote whimpered, put his head down, and stretched out on the truck's back seat.

"I'll stay out of sight."

"Don't bet on it," said Father Gallapo. And he started the truck and began carefully driving back to the other side of the flooding river.

Everyone Comes to the Party

Back on the freeway, traffic in front of the truck slowed. Looking up the road the Priest saw a backup at least a mile long with almost no cars coming the other way. Impetuously, the

Priest decided to cross the median again and drive up to the park entrance going the wrong way in the opposite lanes. He could see highway patrolmen had the road blocked and were forcing vehicles to turn around or drive into the park. Because the freeway was flooded, State Patrol officers had blocked all northbound and southbound lanes, and steered stalled traffic going both ways through knocked down wire fences and across the muddy mesa to the rapidly filling car lots at the still developing county park which used to be Joe Eden's ranch. Slowing to turn into the park, a patrolwoman stepped in front of the Priest's truck, waved him to a stop, and came over to his window, ready to arrest him for driving against traffic on the freeway.

Father Gallapo showed her his driver's license and Priest credentials. Holding up his cell phone he told her, "I've been summoned. A woman's dying in there and I must perform last rites. Let me through." The patrolwoman doubted the story, but too much was going on around her to investigate it now.

"All right, we'll check this out later," she said, and motioned him to drive into the park. Lights flashing and horn honking, he squeezed the truck and trailer past vehicles in the stalled line. From the back seat the cowering coyote said,

"I thought you said you didn't lie."

"Sometimes Priests have to," Father Gallapo replied.

With uninvited people pouring into the new park, the Tea Party's program had to be put on hold. Men and women in Colonial and other period costumes were walking around trying to get the people crowding into the park to go away.

"We rented this place and you don't belong here," they said to anyone they didn't recognize. Reporters and TV crews phoned their bosses to learn whether they should leave, now that the Tea Party convention had been interrupted. Most of the uninvited persons who came to listen and watch, as Tea Party organizers put on a lengthy program of talks and activities—sponsored by discreet Republican behind-the-scene manipulators—were annoyed also about the other uninvited persons pouring into the lots. Seven liberal Democrats were there to present the other side of each argument and help these misled and possibly loony Tea Party people get sensible again. They were debating what to do now. The liberals had accomplished little so far because they were too polite to interrupt scheduled activities—and also because they spent time discussing problems rather than acting. Several Tea Party members continued reasoning with the liberals, trying to make them see the follies of their political ways."

A small group of animal rightists had shown up at the beginning also to keep an eye on the Tea Party crowd and the shooters. Hunters were debating with them.

In an enormous muddy lot adjacent to the county park, there had been only forty or so pickup trucks with gun racks across the back windows and NRA stickers and slogans smeared with mud on bumpers. Now vehicles diverted from the freeway were jamming the lot and spreading out into the fields around it. With the Ford pickup's horn honking and lights still flashing, Father Gallapo steered his rig through the growing mass of people by the large tent the Tea Party folks had pitched. Clear at last he pulled up at the north end of the park alongside the river's edge.

Relieved, the Priest saw his porta-confessional mostly submerged a few yards north of him next to a mesquite tree, the rope still tied around it moving sinuously like a swimming snake.

"We found it!" the Priest said to Mrs. Whitenose. "Now we have to figure out how to get it on the trailer."

"Get the Tea Party people to help," Mrs. Whitenose said, "I bet they will."

"Do you want to go get a few of them while I grab the rope and check out the situation?" the Priest asked.

"Sure, I'll do that," she said, and looked at the mirror on the visor in front of her, running her hands through her hair before climbing out of the truck.

Raising the Porta-Confessional

Father Gallapo got out and went over to the bank. His confessional looked intact, but brown goop leaked out of its submerged bottom end. He was still trying to figure out what to do when Mrs. Whitenose returned with six or seven hefty men and a couple of powerful-looking women. "I've told them who you are and what you need," she said to the Priest.

"We'll take care of this," the most muscular of the women said. Without taking off anything she wore, the beefy woman waded into the river and grabbed the rope. Wading back to the bank she gave the rope's end to the biggest of the men and told the others, "Get in guys and we'll lift this out." Hesitantly, and more carefully than she had, the men and other woman climbed down the bank and waded into the river.

"Okay, three of you on each side, and two at the end," the directing woman commanded. When everyone was in place she ordered,

"Now lift!"

A man at the end of the confessional interrupted: "Muck is leaking out of this thing," he complained.

"You've been up to your neck in muck all your life. Shut up and lift," his commanding officer told him.

Several more Tea Party members had shown up and they also took hold of the rope wrapped around the upper end of the confessional. Straining together, the squad in the water rocked the confessional loose, lifted it waist high, and heaving, pushed it up on the bank. Guys on the bank grabbed hold of the roof and sides and pulled it ashore. The others waded out of the river and collectively stood the porta-confessional upright. Brown muck still leaked out of the bottom.

"'The Tea Party has lots of pull," Mrs. Whitenose whispered to the Priest.

"What do you want us to do with it?" the commander asked the Priest.

"Can you put it on the trailer for me?" the Priest asked her.

"There's nothing the Tea Party can't accomplish," she replied.

"Do what he wants," she told her squad.

Working together they swiftly got the porta-confessional positioned back on the truck and started to tie it in place.

"How did your outhouse get in the river?" the capable woman asked the Priest.

"It is not an outhouse. It is a portable confessional," the Priest told her.

"I've never seen crap like that leaking out of the bottom of a confessional," the woman leader responded. The Priest's face reddened, but he said nothing back to her.

The Party Heats Up

With the confessional rescue underway, different groups of stranded, frustrated, and restless motorists left their vehicles and tried to stake out territory for themselves. They also looked for something to do while they were stuck. Lines formed outside the restrooms. Tea Party members tried more aggressively to get motorists to leave, and squabbles started. Cell phones kept ringing. So many people were texting and shouting into their phones that signal strength bars on smart phones rapidly plunged to zero, particularly on the AT&T network.

Over at the Priest's rig, a ten-year-old boy with a buzz cut, wearing a leather jacket with 'America is Home of the Brave!' painted neatly on the back, stood on the truck's running board, peering in at Coyote stretched out on the rear seat.

"Can I pet him?" he asked Mrs. Whitenose, who warily stood beside him.

"No, he's vicious," she answered.

"What kind of dog is it?" the boy asks.

"He's a merrzrnodgicp," Mrs. Whitenose mumbled.

"Where's that breed from?" the boy asked.

"The steppes of Bulgaria," Mrs. Whitenose answered.

"There are no steppes in Bulgaria," one of the confessional rescuers standing behind them said sternly.

Back in the rapidly filling parking lots, two vans of Republican leaders on their way to the state capital from Las Cruces were escorted into a jammed parking lot by a State Patrolman on a motorcycle. With laptops and cell phones in hand they took over a picnic table. Sitting on, and standing around it they continued devising strategies to take control of government, ban more substances and practices, put more people in jail, and put more money in overfilled accounts of the very rich, while providing opportunities for illegal small businesses to do well by selling banned substances and products underground ... all in God's name. A bearded guy with sandals, baggy pants, a Karzai hat and a goatskin coat, made with the fur on the inside, passed by carrying a sign in Pashtun saying, *If you don't want terrorists to attack you, stop attacking Afghans.* Some of the Republicans nodded as he passed by. Trying to keep as far away from him as possible, an Egyptian business student who attended a nearby state university carried his own sign that said: *Israel is Anti-Semitic.* Passing the clustered liberals, one of them read his sign and said,

"You are pro-Palestinian, aren't you?" The seated liberals then began discussing whether being pro-Palestinian could legitimately be termed 'anti-Semitic.'

Meanwhile, two huge trucks pulling flat bed trailers, owned by a wild animal transporter firm, lumbered into the most distant parking lot. The trucks carried giant canvas-covered animal cages on the beds. The crews got out and put tall red plastic cones around the trucks and attached rolled up mesh nets from cone to cone. A 'secure' perimeter established, crew members climbed onto each trailer and rolled up the canvas covers on one side of each cage.

Watchers were startled to see a young elephant in one of the cages and three lions in the other.

A food van driven by Indians from the Navajo Nation parked close to the wild animal transporters' trailers. The diverted van was returning from the Hatch Chile Festival and heading up to Santa Fe to sell Navajo food to tourists there. The three *Diné* cooks inside it knew where customers could be found. They started warming up their stove and oven to make over-the-counter food to sell to the diverted people: boiled mutton, tortilla-like corn cakes, cedar berries, and honey-laced fry bread.

On the sidewalk near the restrooms, two teenagers set up mikes and battery-powered speakers and got ready to perform *Norteño* music as the novice duo, *Los MiniTigres*. Back on the pathway toward the main parking lot an accordion player unfolded his chair and placed an open paper bag in front of him. Music spouted from earpieces and mini-speakers everywhere in the park. Bosque birds joined in, quacking, squawking, and cawing. Many birds were flying around now that the rain had ended. Knowledgeable birders carrying binoculars and note pads were pointing out to one another black-chinned humming birds, olive sided flycatchers, northern mocking birds, curved-bill thrashers, grosbeaks, swallows, tanagers, red-winged blackbirds, western meadowlarks, and other species whose numbers made the county willing to turn this former ranch into a tourist-bringing, bird-viewing park. A man lugging a scope began setting it up on a small rise on the crowded grass. His wife warned, "Soon you won't be able to see anything except people's faces and heads."

"You can ask them to move out my way," he replied, his eye in the rubber cup.

The Conversation Heats Up

Over by the river several well-dressed black men debated with Tea Party women and men, trying to get them to support a countrywide push for federal assistance for programs to get more black males through high school and college. "America is being shamefully neglectful about this," one of them said. Two of the Tea Party women, both white and evidently educated and affluent, pushed back at the blacks.

"Get your own kids educated, like we do," one of the women said;"I know it isn't easy but you can do it if you try."

Holding a young daughter's hand, one of the black men replied, "How can we make our kids stay in school when they know you whites won't give them jobs."

"Do like we do," the other Tea Party woman said. "You start your own businesses. You can get loans, same as we do."

Another one of the well-dressed men replied: "You don't know what it is like to be poor and black in this country."

"And you guys don't know what it's like to be poor and white in this country," the second Tea Party woman responded. The first one added,

"African Americans will be better off if they join the Tea Party."

Several Hispanics butted into this debate. "Mexican Americans have it bad too," one of them said to the Tea Party women. Getting steamy, the blunter of the two women responded:

"Many of you aren't Americans. You can go back to your homeland."

"This is our homeland and we were here before you," a Hispanic woman said angrily. An Apache crowding by added: "And WE were here long before YOU"—pointing at the Hispanics.

"But whites made this country!" a man carrying a book by Glen Beck joined in saying. "We're mightier than you," he added, pointing at the Apaches. "You know that Obama hates white people," he said pointing at the well-dressed African American men. Stepping into this debate a Democrat from Chicago shook a fist at the radical conservative and said stringently, "You are the wrong kind of white person. Being white is wrong when it is like you."

"Mind your English," the Glen Beck toter said back. A young, very conservative Christian joined the argument and said with absolute faith, "God is white, you know."

Meanwhile over closer to the river, an internationally-known graffiti artist, who looked like a hippy, was messing up a picture of Glen Beck someone had taped to a tree. Along the paved walkway from the main parking lot to the restrooms, an anti-abortion quartet was setting up a booth and getting ready to distribute pamphlets and show mind-numbing pictures. People passing by moved to the other side of the walkway when they came up to the booth.

Weary travelers who hadn't intended to be there filled every chair in the large tent where Tea Party seminars were being held. Angry at first about their meeting hall being taken over, Tea Party leaders quickly realized that they had a captive audience and brought out Tea Party speakers to address it. The first one introduced himself saying, "Welcome to our T-Partee! Let me tell you what we are up to." He noticed yawns and pained looks from the frustrated audience he was speaking to. Reactions were mixed after two speakers spoke briefly. Several people in the room cheered and clapped when told that the federal budget must be severely cut to save the economy and make America great again. Most people scowled. An older guy in the audience, who looked like he should be a Tea Party member, shouted when the party's objectives were laid out: "Don't let the government snoop into gun ownership records!" Many people in the audience hissed at him and a couple sitting next to him moved away, afraid that he had an illegal concealed weapon on him. Ten minutes later, when a fundamentalist preacher started to tell about the relationship between God and the Tea Party, a woman with a fuzzy lap dog interrupted saying loudly, "Religion is for ignorant people."

"What do you think of Obama?" a tourist from Seattle asked the speaker. Before he could answer a man in the front row turned around and shouted back, "Obama is made of dark matter and dark energy." The crowd seemed stunned by that thought. Breaking the silence, a conventional looking middle-aged woman rose and asked.

"Are you guys willing to legalize marijuana?"

"Drugs are not good for this nation," the speaker answered.

"Then to hell with the Tea Party. I've got cancer and pain killers aren't working," the suffering woman said and walked out of the tent. About a third of the audience applauded, half for what she said, half because she left the tent. An older man stood up and pointed a finger at the meeting's chairman.

"If you kill Medicare, you'll kill us," he said.

"Don't worry," the chairman responded. "We're going to just take money away from socialized medicine and put it into private hands."

"You want to steal that money! You'll kill us to make big businesses more profitable," the older guy replied, his voice raised. He was about to say more when a younger, very determined woman with red hair and hiking boots rose and interrupted,

"We've got to make oil companies pay their share of taxes. And use that money for wind power."

"And solar power!" said a guy in front of her, turning.

A slim and aesthetic woman got up next and turned to face the audience.

"We need to stop killing animals and eating their flesh. The government should require schools to teach vegetarianism to students."

A woman eating a roast beef sandwich on the other side of the room booed her with her mouth full.

"Are you guys pro- or anti-gay marriage?" a middle-aged woman with short hair asked the speaker.

"That should be up to each state," the speaker replied.

"You mean then that lots of us got to move if we want to get married!" the woman said, and sat down.

There was a moment of quiet as audience members chewed on that. The lesbian looked smug, having scored.

A woman near her said determinedly, "We need better laws to stop men pushing women around."

A man in the center added, "And laws to stop women pushing men around."

A social scientist standing in the back of the tent listening to this exchange of heated views said to his friend, a female professor of constitutional law: "All this shows us something. The Constitution is broken. The system we've got now drives people apart instead of helping them work together."

"Can't be helped," his friend succinctly replied;"this is how Americans want it." They left the tent.

Walking around outside, the professors noted minor conflicts heating up. Evangelists, libertarians, survivalists, greens, and other American factions fought for attention. A uniformed Arizona militia group on its way to the Santos Canyon Machine Gun Shoot, dodged around the unarmed arguers. An eight-year-old boy holding hands with his dad, a thirty-year-old wearing a Sierra Club T-shirt, pointed his finger at the militiamen and shouted: "We are righter than you!"

"That kid's never going to shoot straight," a militiaman said to another. "His father leaned down to the boy and said, "You mean we are more *correct* than you."

A group from Planned Parenthood and a group of anti-abortionists from Kansas stood talking. The Planned Parenthood people seemed pleased by the murderous expressions on the faces of the Kansans—pleased to have angered them.

The Flood Recedes and the Furor Worsens

Everywhere in the park, individuals and groups were becoming more restless and angry. With voices raised in argument, people squabbled and shoved. Factions of every ilk, which usually avoid each other, were squeezed together by policemen and on the verge on fighting. Emotions became predominant and contrasting natures, and variant beliefs and philosophies, came to the fore. People with different intents and purposes packed so closely together could not bear one another for long.

Meanwhile, around the planet the whole world of humans, alerted now and following satellite broadcasts by on-site network cameras, radio reporters, bloggers, texters, tweeters, Facebook users, and transmitted smartphone pix and videos, watched the mob of different sorts of Americans head towards violence. "Every one of the tangled cross-threads in American politics is visible here today," a reporter who sometimes contributes to *The New York Times* wrote in his notebook. A woman on Fox News being watched on a smartphone said: "Every kind of bitterness in America is showing up at this park...."

Not everyone felt antagonistic, to be sure. Real estate agents peddled houses, telling prospects to hurry up and buy before the end of the Great Recession. Seven female theosophists offered healing touch to a sunburned woman lying on a blanket. Pairs of gay bisexuals lined up waiting their turn to get into stalls in the bathrooms. Several copper-skinned, black-haired, and very athletic Mescalero Apache males worked the crowd, passing out cut-rate coupons and invitations to come to the Mountain Gods Resort & Casino. Four women from the Jemez Pueblo sat on a blanket selling lovely pottery.

So many people were squeezed into the park it was hard to move around. Walking toward the restrooms, leaving Coyote locked in the truck, Father Gallapo and Mrs. Whitenose passed twenty-five or so Hispanics sitting in a tight bunch on the wet grass, leaning on bundles, bags and backpacks that looked suspiciously over-stuffed. "I bet they only speak Spanish," the Priest said to his companion while nodding warmly to the men on the grass. Walking past the Mescaleros he heard one Apache say to another, "Their country is falling apart. That's going to be fatally bad for our resort and casino." The liberals still sat in their circle, each raising a hand and being acknowledged before speaking. As he went by them, the Priest noted that the liberals at least still exchanged views calmly and listened to each other attentively.

A little further along the path, a pair of Muslim men from an Albuquerque mosque argued with Tea Party members about why America should provide huge financial support for Egypt and Tunisia.

"So you don't think America sucks?" a Tea Party member skeptical of Muslims asked.

"No! Supporting the Arab world will be great for this country," one of the Muslims said.

"And who is going to pay for it, you guys or us?" the Tea Party members asked.

Further along the path petitioners with clipboards circulated through the crowd trying to get signatures from registered voters on a petition to ban the Constitution and run the country the way the Bible said it should be run. Several children asked to sign the petitions.

Crossing over a small bridge that embraced a widening, fast running stream, the Priest and Mrs. Whitenose elbowed their way to the edge of the main parking lot. They spotted a Christian delegation from a small church in Florida, delayed by the flooded interstate, unloading boxes of Korans and starting a bonfire on the asphalt at the end of the lot. In a reserved parking space near the restrooms, Mexican-American Border Patrol officers, just getting out of their vehicles, suddenly had to defend themselves from verbal attack, with rising agitation, by 'real Hispanics,' who charged them with targeting their own people.

Looking back over his shoulder, the Priest saw dealers working the crowd selling cocaine, crystal meth, and low-grade marijuana. Every group was buying. On the edge of the park, close to the Priest's truck and trailer, two chauffeured limousines with suited and polished British Petroleum executives aboard edged over the wet bunchgrass and cholla cacti. Chauffeurs with their heads out the window yelled, "Move your asses out of the way!" The masses looked like they were about to start beating on the cars.

Looking in the opposite direction now, the Priest saw self-forming pet rescue teams in the most distant parking lot breaking into locked cars to wrestle with pets who didn't want to be 'freed' from dry vehicles. The animals fought back and bit more than one 'rescuer.' Father Gallapo saw an animal rights activist swearing and wrapping a handkerchief around her bleeding hand. Looking off to his right, he saw a broken down fire truck blocking traffic on the muddy road coming into the parking lots. He recognized two of the frustrated crew members, standing by the truck speaking on their phones, who went to his church in Cordoba. The Priest imagined that the guys were swearing at the city council and Mayor Howie for sending them out in a truck they weren't given enough money to maintain. Looking back up the paved path toward the restrooms, the Priest saw that natural foods marketers had set up stands and were raking in dough. Standing beside them he heard several economists rationally explaining and proposing mathematical models whose factors cause this unanticipated furor.

"What can you explain with mathematics?" Mrs. Whitenose whispered in his ear.

"Pretty much everything, they believe," the Priest whispered back.

Governments Take Notice and Lawmen Are Sent In

More TV crews arrived by helicopter and several newspaper reporters on bicycles tried to bypass the stalled, jammed traffic, urgently trying to get to the chaotic and potentially dangerous situation emerging. Light planes circled overhead and nearly collided. Higher up, pilotless drones and satellites turned cameras and radar on the roiling human mass now crammed onto Joe Eden's former ranch. The Federal Aviation Administration in Oklahoma considered whether to rush a controller out to direct air traffic.

Federal and state agencies, worried about what is going on so publicly, scrambled agents and police to the festering site, some uniformed, some in plain clothes, from Homeland Security, the Treasury Department, U.S. Immigration and Customs Enforcement, the FBI, and probably more secretive agencies. Border patrol agents were warned by commanders to watch their step because so many plain-clothed law-enforcement and security agents were in their midst.

No one in the park knew it, but a third of the world away, on an airbase not far from Moscow, Russian spy satellite operators downloaded images of the human-packed scene. They viewed pictures resembling brightly colored pixels of swirling dust motes airborne by mating thunderstorms. "There must be patterns here," a spy boss said.

"This can't be as random as it seems."

"Could this be a natural disaster?" an underling asked.

"No, there is nothing natural about America's disasters now," came the reply.

"Let the President know what's going on over there," the spy boss ordered.

"Why?" his underling asked.

"Warn him that something big may be starting in the States."

The Mexican Cowboy Gets Arrested

Back in the park, the Priest heard a loud siren behind the line of cars still trying to get into the muddy lots. The wail sounded scratchy and oddly pitched. "That's the Cordoba police!" Mrs. Whitenose said to the Priest. A minute later Cordoba's only police car, an old Ford, bounced across the field around the stalled cars, driven by the Mayor's paunchy, uniformed cousin, Frank Corsa, the city's only policeman. Mayor Howie sat in the front seat and leaned out the window to shake hands with people he knew. In the back seat, penned in like a prisoner, the Mexican Cowboy was clinging to the mesh in front of him while the squad car bounced and jarred. Mayor Howie got out of the car and, walking like an emperor—shaking hands and posing for pictures—headed for the restrooms, the center of this widening fuss. Sucking his tummy in, Patrolman Corsa stuck by his side. Angry and despondent, the Mexican Cowboy trailed the pair far enough back that no watcher would associate him with Mayor Howie.

On the wide curved pavement outside the restrooms, officers from several federal and state agencies held a handsome, dark-haired young male 'suspect' while their commanders debated who got to keep him, and thus whether he would be arrested, recruited, deported, or promoted. A huge party of milling watchers also appraised the handsome young male and began to think that here finally was a candidate they would want to vote for and see elected.

Standing to one side and watching, the Mexican Cowboy was approached by two border patrolmen, who asked to see his ID. Resentful, the Mexican Cowboy dug it out and showed the interrogator his driver's license: Expired.

"Have you a birth certificate or passport?" the border patrolman asked.

"You show me yours and I'll show you mine," the angry Mexican Cowboy replied.

"Anybody here who can vouch for you?" the female officer asked.

"Sure," the Mexican Cowboy replied and looked around for the Mayor, but Howie had moved away. The crowd focused on the border patrolmen and Cowboy.

"Can I pat you down?" the male officer asked.

"I don't like to be touched," the Cowboy said and tried to back away.

"Grab him," the woman officer said. The Cowboy tried to edge into the surrounding crowd but he couldn't get through. The Border Patrol officers nabbed and handcuffed him.

Following the action from way back in the crowd, Mrs. Whitenose asked the Priest, "Is that the man you are staying with now?"

"It's him," the Priest answered.

"We've got to do something about this." Looking around, the Priest spotted Mayor Howie pushing his way into the group over at the picnic grounds. He and Mrs. Whitenose headed that way. The handcuffed Mexican Cowboy saw them spot him and then, walking away, became angrier and more dejected than he had ever felt in his life.

Squeezing in close to the Mayor, the Priest tapped him on the shoulder and said, "The Mexican Cowboy's been arrested for not being American."

"Maybe he **isn't** American—I've always wondered about him," the Mayor instantly replied. "I've never seen his birth certificate."

"You've got to vouch for him," the Priest insisted.

"Can't do that," the Mayor responded. "If the Cowboy's not American it would be politically bad for me to fight for him."

"So, you are not going to help the guy you fixed up for me to live with when I'm in Cordoba?" the Priest asked.

"I've done plenty for him—and for you," Mayor Howie snapped, and turned around and went back to shaking hands and posing for pictures.

"I guess we've got to do something for the Cowboy on our own," Mrs. Whitenose whispered to the Priest. He nodded as they walked away toward the river talking about what to do.

A Plan to Get the Cowboy Released

Back at the truck, Mrs. Whitenose opened the door, leaned in and asked Coyote if he would like to come out.

"Anybody around?" Coyote asked, looking very scared.

"Just a few people," Mrs. Whitenose answered. "And most of them are over by the restrooms." Leaning over her, the Priest said:

"Something bad's happened. The Mexican Cowboy just came here with Mayor Howie and got arrested by the Border Patrol. The Mayor refused to help." The frightening emotion Coyote had been protecting vanished. Hurriedly getting to his feet, Coyote said with determination, "Let me out. I'm going to do something about THAT. He's my only human friend, he's decent but peculiar, and I'm not going to allow him to be arrested."

"So, what shall we do?" Mrs. Whitenose asked.

"Let's talk about it," the Priest said. With the Coyote still in the truck, she and the Priest climbed in and the three of them made a plan to rescue the Cowboy.

Ten minutes later Father Gallapo, leading the leashed Coyote wearing the pink collar, was back in the crowd surrounding the worried Border Patrol agents holding the Mexican Cowboy. One of them talked with her supervisor on her hand-held radio. Around them people in the crowd stridently argued about what should be done with the angry handcuffed man. A lefty Arizona Hispanic shouted, "Free the illegal immigrant." Another Arizonan not far away said, "Put chains on his feet and drag him across the border." A lawyer said: "Get him a lawyer." A so-so liberal who had split from his dysfunctional group proposed, "Turn the guy over to the Immigration Bureau and let them deport him." A Tea Party member yelled: "These illegal immigrants are out-breeding whites. Soon they'll be the only Americans left." Coyote rubbed against the Priest's leg and Father Gallapo leaned down to hear what he had to say. "If whites need help breeding, coyotes can teach them how," Coyote whispered. The Priest nodded and got back to listening to the enveloping arguing.

"Let's progress beyond confrontations," a liberal said.

A Tea Party attendee shot back at her: "You liberals got nothing between your ears but diplomas."

A liberal (finally getting steamed up enough to stand up for his beliefs) said: "You Rednecks are deluded and mis-educated savages."

A Tea Party attendee: "Maybe, but we talk straight and shoot straighter!"

Liberal: "You are fools, chumps and unemployed high school dropouts!"

Tea Party: "We know the Bible and the Constitution backwards and forward and you guys haven't read either!"

Liberal: "Your understanding of both of these is cock-eyed!"

Tea Party: "You liberals tax us to death to bloat the bureaucracy!"

Liberal: "You Rednecks won't even vote for a Republican unless he wants to invade some country!"

Tea Party: "You liberals don't give a damn for Liberty and Democracy!"

Liberal: "If you Rednecks take over Congress you'll use the government to wipe out democracy and liberty!"

Tea Party: "We've got the NRA on our side! You won't eat meat!"

Liberal: "You are over-heating the planet!"

Father Gallapo wished he could put his fingers in his ears, but he couldn't let go of Coyote. Over at the picnic area Frank Corsa, Cordoba's one policeman, pulled his attention-seeking Mayor aside and said in Howie's ear: "There's an escalating word battle going on around the Mexican Cowboy. It is going to be bad for tourism if someone starts shooting and people die here. You need to stop showing off and get over there. This is bigger than the Mexican Cowboy now."

"Alright," the Mayor replied grumpily—not too upset about leaving because the racket from the crowd in front of the restrooms drowned out what he was trying to say to people he was greeting.

The Mayor hurried back to the mean crowd with his policeman behind him and started pushing his way to where the Mexican Cowboy and the Border Patrolmen were surrounded. Talking on her handset, one of the officers told her supervisor what was going on. She asked what they should do.

"The whole world's watching this," he said. "Border Patrol officers must not be seen holding a possibly innocent Hispanic handcuffed in the middle of an angry, arguing crowd. Confirm the suspected alien's address and let him go."

The Mayor and his uniformed cousin broke through to the center of the angry mob just as she put her handheld away. The policeman introduced the Mayor. Mayor Howie showed one of the officers his credentials and pointed at the handcuffed Cowboy saying: "He's okay. I've known him all my life. He votes for me. Let him go." Very relieved, one of the officers copied down the address on the Cowboy's expired driver's license while the other officer unlocked his handcuffs.

Many watchers in the crowd were angry about the Cowboy's release and the back and forth shouting resumed. At the crowd's edge, the Priest and the leashed coyote slipped away, hoping to get back to Thelma Whitenose before she carried out her part of the plot to free the

Bruce Saunders

Cowboy. But it was hard to get to her. Mixing and melding sign-wavers, shouters, and others with adrenalin maxing out, blocked the way and demanded attention.

Thelma Takes Off Her Clothes and Dons a Mop

Back at the trailer by the swollen river, Thelma Whitenose prepared to carry out her part of the plan. She'd taken from the truck a filthy mop the Priest used to scrub the inside and outside of his porta-confessional. She unscrewed the mop head from its handle and draped it over her hair. With a piece of string, she tied the mop's dark strands behind her into a ponytail. On the river side of the truck now, she took off most her clothes and, with her glasses on, jumped into the chilling river and began screaming. Though she was standing on the bottom, she splashed wildly and attracted instant attention.

Two women on the bank ran over to her. Looking down at the screaming, nearly nude female, one of them said, "She looks like Sarah Palin." The other woman shouted over her shoulder to her husband, running toward them, "Ronald, get over here. Sarah Palin is drowning!""Sarah Palin's drowning!" Ronald shouted over his shoulder toward the crowd.

Word passed around the park almost instantly and hundreds of people started running toward the river, including the Border Patrol officers, who had forgotten all about the Mexican Cowboy.

"If that's Sarah Palin, let her sink or learn to swim!" said a bearded, left-leaning ex-college student to his stoned girlfriend from the riverbank looking down at the now genuinely floundering 'Sarah Palin.' Hearing that comment angered a local rancher standing beside him. Being ordered by police to leave the highway and mix with this wild mob was bad enough. The anti-Palin comment really set him off. "Throw that Lefty Goon into the river," the rancher ordered the two workers with him. Obediently they tackled the anti-Palin Lefty, picked him up, and heaved him into the water. The splash almost blinded Mrs. Whitenose. And it didn't help that one of the workers slipped on the muddy bank and fell in himself.

A Navy SEAL—whose presence at the Tea Party gathering may not have been accidental—waded in to rescue the splashing, shouting Thelma Whitenose who still held the dirty mop on her head with one hand. With her free hand Mrs. Whitenose thoughtfully reached out and took the hand of the very frightened Lefty who had gotten himself pitched in. Watchers on the shore applauded her for doing that. Cursing, the rancher slid down to the water and waded in to help his own man come ashore. "You were born clumsy," he said angrily to his flailing employee.

It is Time for the Gods to Do Their Part

'Overhead,' in a different but adjoining dimension, El Latrano, the Aztec-looking Coyote God, keenly watched the intensifying conflict, which had spread into the river too. Seeing an opportunity he had longed for, El Latrano sent an impulse to his furry prophet, leashed and wearing a pink collar by the Priest's side, to get unleashed and cross the river.

"NOW is the moment we've been waiting for."

"Turn me loose," Coyote said to the Priest.

With everyone's attention diverted by events in the water, the Priest unleashed Coyote, who raced for the river like a dog going after a rabbit. Speeding through the melee and nipping at hands that tried to grab him, Coyote ran south along the bank and jumped into the ebbing river at the spot where hunters and their dogs crossed earlier. Seeing Coyote go into the river, Mrs. Whitenose realized she had done her part in the plot they hatched. Gladly she let go of the mop and accepted help getting out of the river. A conservative lawyer courteously offered the nearly naked woman his coat and helped her put it on—while hundreds around her were taking pictures and videos.

Watching from the other bank now, Coyote thought to himself: This shrinking river is going to get tossed full of wetbacks if the humans here keep fighting. At that moment an argument between ranchers and Animal Righters broke out. The discussion over whether it was legally and morally okay to kill animals which the ranchers call 'vermin' became concrete. Coyote was spotted on the other side of the river. "A coyote's over there," a rancher shouted. "Shoot him!" Fearing for his canine colleague's life, the Priest hurried over to the rancher. Standing between the rancher and Coyote, the Priest rapidly explained that the apparent *canis latrans* watching them from the other bank was really just his washed-away dog.

"See the pink collar?" he said.

"He still looks like a coyote to me," the rancher said, doubting the Priest's claim. Coyote overheard the Priest's lie and hated it.

"A slave dog I'm not and will never be," Coyote said to himself. While the Priest tried to smooth things over between ranchers and animal rights advocates, Coyote slipped into the brush and started up the low hill that overlooked the park on the east side.

On top of the hill now, lying on his belly, his head to the east and his tail pointing down at the infuriated mass of outraged persons with different philosophies, beliefs and religions, Coyote prayed to his god. "Are you sure about what you want me to do next? Coyote asked. "**Absolutely!**" El Latrano answered. "You are MY Prophet. I want you to summon every coyote in the vicinity and instruct them to herd all flood-harmed, nearly dead animals and birds within a several mile radius toward the human war zone." Coyote lowered his head and assembled his courage.

Coyote stood on the hill and howled, summoning all the other coyotes in the vicinity, as his god ordered. Across the river, many in the crowd turned to watch and listen, confused and fearful for their lives, as tens of nearby coyotes obeyed the call. Driving wildlife into humans' company cannot be life enhancing for them. Does, maturing fawns and a stag or two, calves swept downstream from their herds, stray dogs and cats, loose chickens, several piglets and a fattened sow, a few skunks and armadillos, lizards, and many rabbits on both sides of the river were surrounded and firmly herded inwards by coyotes, toward the feared humans. It was turning out to be a very bad day for animals too.

'Overhead,' meanwhile, the coyote god negotiated with bird gods to help him with his plan.

On the other side of the river, the Priest had rejoined Mrs. Whitenose. The now mopless—and very wet and shivering—woman, asked what Coyote was doing. She had watched him suddenly run away, swim the shrinking river, climb the hill, lie down for several moments, then rise and begin howling to other coyotes.

"What's this about?" she asked. Father Gallapo answered:

"He's working with his lord and carrying out the plan, I imagine."

"Is that our plan too?" she asked. "Not necessarily," the Priest replied.

"Gods have their own ways and even when they are working with us they may have plans and intentions of their own."

"Do they take advantage of us?" Mrs. Whitenose asked.

"Probably," the Priest answered. "Where does it say that creating creatures is done only for the creatures' good?"

Getting Every Being to Come Together

Just then without premonition, a powerful urge that could not be ignored came over the Priest. He waded recklessly across the slowing river and climbed the hill where Coyote howled. The sun was coming out and, with his white collar showing, the Priest waded across, praying to his Lord for help and guidance. '**All right**,' God said to him in his softer voice, '**I'll get involved.**'

To the east the sky lightened and a magnificent arching rainbow appeared, slowly rotating in the sky above the hill the Priest and Coyote shared. Across the stilling river *Los MiniTigres*, lit by beams of light coming through the clouds, began playing softer, hymn-like music.

Bedraggled animals arrived in the camp from all sides, not many but enough to be noticeable. Some hunters in the calming crowd took out their guns... and then put them down when they saw the police reach for theirs. Women and children rushed to pet the few young deer standing trembling in their midst. Teenagers put away their smartphones and began talking to each other. Stray cats and dogs driven by a compressing circle of snarling coyotes attracted nearly everyone's attention. Pets running loose and locked in cars were strangely quiet and filled with longing. Armadillos were picked up and examined. Chickens pecked around people's feet. A sow lay on her side, nursing piglets, while other pigs rooted for dropped food in the park.

Moving around the park excitedly, a mammaler hurriedly noted every mammal she saw driven into the park by the coyotes. Raccoons; striped skunks; western harvest, white-footed and deer mice; hispid cotton, kangaroo and pack rats; beavers; a bobcat; mule deer; muskrats; desert cottontails and black-tail jackrabbits; valley pocket gophers, and even a soggy brown bat who landed and hung upside down on the low branch of a willow. Children ran to the animals, the parents following. Warmth, excitement—even love—arched through the park now.

Over in the wild animal transporter's uncovered cages one of the lions put her paw through the bars, reaching out to watchers. A small girl who had been standing, watching, and adoring, crawled under the mesh and took the lion's paw in her hand. The lion began purring maternally. Unbelievably, the girl's mother stood behind the fence watching with a sweet smile on her face. The young elephant in the other cage appeared to be humming along with the semi-religious music everyone could hear. The elephant trumpeted and smiled as it accepted bananas from three Tea Party women. On the grass behind the restrooms, liberals had gotten out of their chairs and stood in a half circle around a medley of noisy waterfowl. They took turns feeding the birds.

A small flock of Sandhill Cranes landed in the calming river alongside the humans, who suddenly felt cooperative and loving. The cranes sensed somehow that the humans didn't want to hurt them. Birds of many varieties appeared in the park's trees and began calling and singing. People took pictures and tried to feed them.

Electronically present, people everywhere on earth sensed a multi-species peacefulness in the park. The satisfying feeling of peace spread rapidly throughout humanity. For many minutes humans and the wild animal kingdom conjoined. Happiness and a sense of universal security vibrated warmly as food and drinks appeared and were shared among persons, and with animals and birds. Touching and nuzzling within and between species happened everywhere in the park. Glen Beck, watching from his TV studio, said with genuine feeling: "This is an inspirational moment."

Father Gallapo and Coyote (unleashed but still wearing the pink collar—which had become, he realized, his Prophet emblem) crossed the river once more side by side.

Several of the formerly most combative opponents took turns going into the two doors of the porta-confessional and sitting side by side. After a short while they came out with calmer looks on their faces, although several complained: "There is no toilet paper in there." The Priest remarked: "Religion can be calming, but so is pooping."

And then.... The warming, inspirational, universal sharing moment began fading, as all inspirational moments will.

Reflections Afterwards

Water levels across the highway lanes fell to no more than hubcap depth. Highway patrolmen used their car's loudspeakers to tell drivers they were free to leave. People in the drying park site packed up, exchanged phone numbers and email addresses, hugged, shook hands, waved goodbye to each other and, feeling genuinely uplifted by this day that began so frustratingly for them, slipped regretfully into their vehicles and started on their way again, returning to their ordinary lives via the park's muddy roads.

As the crowd thinned, Coyote and his mentor the Priest, Mrs. Whitenose, Mayor Howie, and his cousin, and the still miffed Mexican Cowboy—all feeling enormously tired now—made their way to the large picnic table deserted by the departed Republican political elite. Bottles of beer and wine, paper cups and plates, napkins, plastic utensils, and unopened bags of snacks had been left behind, and the friends sat down, opened, sipped and drank, and talked.

"What has this been all about?" Mrs. Whitenose asked the quiet, small, meditative group. "It is about a Return to Eden," the Priest answered. "This was an experiment to see what our world might be like if all species once again might interact freely without harming others."

"If this was a Return to Eden, does my being nude before so many people turn me into the New Eve?" Mrs. Whitenose asked.

"If this was truly a return to Eden, all you humans would have been naked," Coyote said. "But the Priest is right. My God wanted to know how a reunification of animals and humans might work out," Coyote continued.

"I think this business was more about politics and negotiations between gods than a return to Eden,'" the Mayor said, speaking more honestly than usual. "It looks like the animal gods are trying to copy our political system. This doesn't surprise me. Gods are political beings too."

"Politics," the Priest said, "gets in the way of religion."

"Religion," the Cowboy said, "is better experienced indoors than here."

"That's not true for coyotes," Coyote responded.

"Our God is all colors," Mrs. Whitenose said, reflecting on the racism she had just witnessed.

"And furry too," Coyote added.

"This mess was about kicking Hispanics around," the Mexican Cowboy claimed, still feeling furious and abused. Coyote got up and gently moved beside him. Unconsciously, the Mexican Cowboy put his hand down and Coyote started licking it. In return he patted Coyote's head and rubbed the fur on his neck. A small smile started to appear on the Cowboy's face. Songbirds in the trees around the party sang more ecstatically and ebulliently than usual. Overhead, the spectacular rainbow dimmed. The park emptied. Even Tea Party members were leaving.

Did this work out the way You wanted? The Priest silently asked Jesus.

"You and all humanity get to be the judges of that," his Lord immediately answered.

"Coyotes and my God will be judges of that too," Coyote whispered to the Priest.

"And the animals' and birds' view of this mess?" Mrs. Whitenose asked Coyote.

"It was a meaningful day for them," Coyote answered. "They got fed, watched, petted, and weren't killed."

"And now if you will excuse me," Coyote went on, "we've got to get back to our own lives." He turned and trotted away, his coyote followers who waited on the perimeter of the park leaving with him.

"Good hunting!" the Mexican Cowboy shouted to his departing friend. "Put extra food outside your door for animals to eat tonight," Coyote shouted back.

"See, you got to give me more food, Howie," the Mexican Cowboy said to the Mayor. "More food to waste?" Howie replied. "Feeding animals isn't a waste," the Priest said, before taking his leave with Mrs. Whitenose.

A short while later, driving back to Cordoba with the Mexican Cowboy again in the screened back seat of the rickety squad car, Mayor Howie turned around and asked him: "Don't you love this country!"

"Only if I can get away from the people in it."

"You want to be by yourself all the time?" the Mayor asked.

"No. I want to be with Coyote."

"There is something to be said for that," the Mayor replied. They were silent all the rest of the way back to Cordoba.

Politics in the Gods' Realm

In the Gods' adjoining universe, the Coyote God's 'Return to Eden' experiment was under discussion.

Coyote God: "That worked out pretty well, I think. If it wasn't for Hermione we couldn't have done that."

"At least none of my creatures got killed," the Deer God replied.

Coyote God nodded and said: "And they were fed and petted."

"But skunks weren't," the Skunk God said angrily.

"What's so special about your coyote?" the Pig God asked El Latrano.

"He's my prophet."

"Animals don't have prophets. That's a human thing," the Lizard God said.

"Having religion and prophets is the thing that took humans so far beyond us. Their god is progressive," the Coyote God responded.

"Why would a god want to change a system that is millions of years old?" a Rabbit God asked.

"Their God wants humans to develop. He believes in evolution," El Latrano answered.

"What have prophets to do with that?" the Owl God asked.

"They communicate, steer, raise expectations, teach, mold awareness by building links to their God," the Coyote God replied.

"We want to keep things as they used to be. How do we make humans go back to where they were a few thousand years ago?" the Antelope God asked.

"You can't do it. And that's our dilemma. Animal gods have to begin working together to help our creatures catch up with humans. And we need humans' help to do it," the Coyote God said back.

"Humans don't help animals," the Bear God said.

"They can and will if their God works with us. And he is willing to," El Latrano answered.

"What are we supposed to do?" the Beaver God asked. El Latrano reflected a moment and answered: "You have got to pick your times and ways to work with humans and be prepared to always try something different. And keep trying. Gods need to evolve too. And theirs has," El Latrano said.

"You are trying to turn us into the human God. We don't work together," the Badger God complained.

"If we don't work together, nothing is going to change," the Coyote God replied. "It is the same with us as it is in the human realm. And we do work together—sort of—when we play soccer."

"We'd rather just keep playing soccer. We like things the way they are," several of the Gods said.

"Your creatures don't," Coyote's Master replied.

"Tough. We're doing Okay," said the Mountain Lion God.

"Yeah, but you won't last if your creatures don't," El Latrano replied.

"You got a point," the Bear God said. "We'll think about it. Now, how about another game of soccer?"

Coyote Writes a Christmas Poem

I t was a windy day, cold and troubling. The Mexican Cowboy stood coatless on his porch, shivering and pondering, sadness tormenting him.

Looking over the bank of a nearby arroyo, Coyote saw that his human friend was not in a good mood. The Mexican Cowboy's gestures and expressions suggested weariness and sadness.

Wind blew Coyote's way and conveyed a mix of scents and words that Mexican Cowboy didn't realize he spoke aloud as he thought. Coyote turned his head sidewise. Sniffing, ears pricked toward the porch, Coyote followed what was going on in his friend's mind.

"Sadness doesn't often overcome me... So why can't I escape?"

What's missing in my life?

Other people!

But then why am I alone?

Because I am a loner.

But not a complete loner. I help other people. I reach out to them. Why don't they reach out to me?

Because I don't ask?

But can't they ask me? I guess they can't.

What should I do then?

I don't know. Stop feeling lonely?

How do I make myself do that? How can I make myself stop feeling sad and lonely? I don't know. I DON'T KNOW.

And damn, it is almost Christmas too."

Suffering, the Mexican Cowboy went indoors, took a jar from the fridge, spooned cold *frijoles* onto a plate and sat at the table. He knew he should eat, but he wasn't hungry. Another lousy Christmas, he thought. I can't face it. I should hibernate in December like a bear. It's the worst month of the year.

The Mexican Cowboy lay down on his bed and stared at the ceiling, too upset even to pull his blanket over him.

Sympathy and Resistance, Prayer and Guidance

Standing in the arroyo near the Cowboy's rusty water pump, Coyote's face was lit by dim reddish rays from a setting solstice sun.

"Crap," said the Coyote. "What am I supposed to do about this?"

Coyote smelled his friend's mood, and figured out what was going on, but had no idea how to help the Mexican Cowboy.

"Not my problem," Coyote said to himself, and trotted off to search for his dinner.

Two hours later, with a bright moon rising over the Manzano Mountains east of him, Coyote finished his meal—a sick rabbit he had tracked and caught easily. Coyote was full and would have felt content if the Mexican Cowboy's dejected mood weren't haunting him. Coyote couldn't get his friend's sadness out of his mind. Musing, he could think of only one thing to do about it: Ask for guidance. And go where it might be given.

Afraid of the effects another encounter with his god would have on him, Coyote trotted up the highest hill in his territory. An ancient pine tree stood at the top. In front of the tree on a flat rock lay remains of small animals he had killed and left as sacrifices to his coyote god, El Latrano. Facing his altar was a small, carefully excavated hollow in the concrete-hard caliche soil: the Coyote's place of prayer.

The moon high now, Coyote turned around, squirmed, and settled into the exposed depression he called his 'prayer den.'

Coyote had a hard time focusing on praying because tens of coyotes on nearby mounds were yapping, howling, exchanging news, reaching out to one another—by long-distance because territoriality prevented them from doing so in person. Coyote intensely wanted to join them.

Coyote's wandering attention locked onto the owls, bats and nighthawks flying over him, speaking in their unique tongues. Coyote heard the scurrying sounds of rabbits and ground squirrels and the scraping noises of night-hunting reptiles. A cold night wind carried scents of nearby badgers, possums, and skunks. The sky was lit with stars and Coyote could not shut out the numerous animals around him. It was like a human trying to pray in a parade of people, Coyote thought. Coyote's ears prickled and involuntarily pointed in the direction of the Manzanos, picking up the soft growls and grunts of hunting bears and cougars there.

It was an ordinary night in early winter.

Anxiously, reluctantly, Coyote put his head on his paws and tried harder to pray to his god, El Latrano. Oh God, God of Coyotes. God please help me. Help me to help my friend, the Human who is good to coyotes.

For a dreadful long time, sounds and odors of activity surrounding him burst into his consciousness and there was no response from On High.

Coyote waited. And waited.

Doing this was a mistake, Coyote decided. Feeling abandoned by his Coyote God, El Latrano, Coyote made up his mind to give up...

The busy sky above him dimmed in Coyote's gradually focused consciousness. Sounds and scents fell away. The pine tree before him was brighter, more central in his transforming awareness. A holy, familiar smell filled his nostrils. Un-earthly sounds moved majestically into his ears. Glancing timidly, Coyote saw El Latrano appear before him... looming, multi-colored, spotted like a leopard, an Aztec headdress topping him, a god of overwhelming presence and overwhelming power. Awed, fearful, yet profoundly grateful, Coyote burrowed deeper into his prayer den and waited for the instructions that would be indelibly his.

Worshipful and very frightened, Coyote planted his snout deeper into the shallow pit he dug to pray in. He shut his eyes and fearfully accepted the instructions rammed into him by his God.

Quickly, decisively, bluntly, his god gave Coyote the guidance he was seeking.

"Must I?" he whispered.

"You have no choice," his god said.

Coyote did not raise his head until the brightness in front of him dimmed and the sounds and smells of winter nightlife resumed around him once more.

Reluctantly, feeling resentful and heavily taxed but still grateful, Coyote rose from his prayer hollow, shook dirt and pine needles from his fur, and sullenly trotted down the hill.

At the bottom he turned southward and began to lope over the mesa toward the little town whose lights he saw in the distance. Its smells and sounds came faintly toward him.

"Guidance is a pain under the tail," he said aloud to no one as he trotted along.

Pushy Visitors

Next afternoon, the day before Christmas, Mayor Howie pulled into the Mexican Cowboy's front yard in his old, polished Cadillac. Obviously rushed, Howie leapt out, marched onto the porch and went inside without knocking.

With no polite preamble, he said to the morose Mexican Cowboy, sitting at the kitchen table, a cold plate of refritos and two empty beer bottles beside him, "Come on. Get up. I need your help."

"You always demand something from me and never give me anything in return," the Mexican Cowboy said back.

"Keep complaining," the Mayor said, urging him out the door. "Complain and you shall receive."

Mayor Howie opened the nicely curved, black trunk-lid of the old Cadillac. The trunk was packed with folded metal chairs, and there were more inside the car.

"Take them. Keep them safe. And don't forget to bring all the chairs back to City Hall," Howie said.

"Why?" asked the Mexican Cowboy.

"Shut up and do it," the Mayor told him.

"I'll do it if you stop pushing me around."

Hating the Mayor and hating himself for complying, the Mexican Cowboy made nine trips back and forth to stack all the chairs against his porch.

The Mayor drove off without a word of thanks or explanation.

Forty minutes later the Mexican Cowboy sat again at the kitchen table, anger boiling inside him, a half-filled bottle of beer and last night's ignored frijoles beside him, reheated twice but cold and waxy now, when he heard a loud siren coming up the dirt road to his house.

"Now what?" he said. "Are the cops coming to arrest me again?"

Going out on his porch, the Mexican Cowboy saw Cordova's only fire truck pulling up in his yard. Six volunteer firemen hopped off and, without a wave or hello, begin unloading the half cord of firewood piled neatly on the truck's back.

The firemen carefully stacked the wood into five crisscrossed piles in a broad curved circle about fifteen feet away from the porch. After putting cans of charcoal lighter beside the stacks, the firemen climbed back into the truck and drove away without so much as a wave goodbye.

Now the Mayor's dumping Cordoba's leftovers on my property, the Cowboy thought angrily.

Furious, he went back inside, where he felt even more lonely.

Pushy Guests with Pizzas

As the just-past-solstice sun hurriedly plunged toward the southwest horizon, Mayor Howie drove up again with his police chauffeur, Frank Corsa, and Mrs. Whitenose. She hopped out and carried a small evergreen tree into the house without knocking. The little cedar was decorated with a dozen red & white peppermint candy-canes, and had a seven-pointed star made of aluminum foil pressed onto the top of its trunk. It actually looked pretty good. Intent on what she was doing, Mrs. Whitenose tossed a hello the Cowboy's way, patted him on the shoulder, and began hurriedly unpacking a box the chauffeur carried in.

It was plain to the Cowboy that she had taken over his kitchen.

Mrs. Whitenose covered the scarred and stained kitchen table with a red and white cloth and set the table with silver, napkins, wine glasses, and two half-burned white candles—which had been lifted from the church where Coyote was baptized.

Frustrated, the Mexican Cowboy heard Mayor Howie on the porch shouting into his cell phone. Instead of paying attention to him, the Mayor was making one call after another. Why did he come out here to make all these calls? Cowboy thought angrily.

"What the hell is going on?" the Mexican Cowboy asked insistently. No one bothered to answer. Instead Mrs. Whitenose gave him a broom and told him to sweep the floors. "And go get a bucket of water when you are finished."

Resigned, the Mexican Cowboy swept up, gave the broom back to Mrs. Whitenose who was opening wine bottles, and went outdoors with a bucket to get water. Before filling the bucket at the pump, he looked into the arroyo hoping to see Coyote. He wasn't there. Feeling abandoned even by his best friend on Christmas Eve, the Mexican Cowboy trudged back to the house, water spilling like streams of tears from the full bucket he was carrying.

As he lugged the heavy bucket onto the porch he saw a pair of headlights coming toward the house along the dirt road from the highway. More pushy visitors, he thought.

Mayor Howie was still on the porch yelling into his cell phone. The Mexican Cowboy slid past him into the kitchen and put the bucket of water beside the sink. Mrs. Whitenose told him to make a pot of coffee with the sack of ground beans she handed him. While he got the coffee percolator ready to put on the stove, he heard a truck parking on the north side of the house.

"Now you guys are turning my place into a parking lot," he said loud enough for her to hear. Mrs. Whitenose ignored him, which hurt his feelings more.

The coffee maker bubbled on the stove, and the Mexican Cowboy started to sit down at his usual place at the table. At that moment the front door opened and Mayor Howie's chauffeur arrived carrying four large, steaming, flat boxes. Hurrying inside after him came Father Gallapo, carrying a large bakery box and a heavy shopping bag.

"You got all the stuff?" Mrs. Whitenose asked him.

"We've got it," the Priest replied. "Salad makings, cans of cranberry sauce, two turkey pizzas, two ham pizzas, and a box of pumpkin cupcakes. And stuff for the kids and animals too."

"Good," Mrs. Whitenose said. "Get the Mayor. We've got to start eating."

"You sit there," she said to the Mexican Cowboy, pointing at the end of the table.

As he walked to his chair the Cowboy noticed how nicely Mrs. Whitenose had fixed up his kitchen. The small tree, the brightly lit candles, the tablecloth and silverware, the swept floor, the bubbling coffee pot, the bottles and wine glasses pleased him and kindled a little Christmas Spirit inside him. Feeling better now, he sat at the end of the table and watched Mrs. Whitenose speedily make and dress a salad, pour the cranberry sauce into a nice dish with a silver spoon, and set both on the table along with the pizzas she had taken out of the boxes and put on large platters. Just as she finished, the Priest pushed Mayor Howie into the kitchen.

"Put the phone away, Howie," Father Gallapo said sternly. "Sit down everyone. Eat. Celebrate. This is going to be a very special Christmas Eve." The Mexican Cowboy was not so sure of that.

Still, a glass of wine in his hand, turkey pizza and cranberry sauce on his plate, his friends raising their glasses to him, Cowboy realized he might have a joyous Christmas after all. Yet the conversation was stilted and he felt tension rising in the room. Is that because they don't want to be here? He asked himself. "I wish Coyote were with us," he said to the others. He felt hurt when no one replied.

Half an hour later Mrs. Whitenose cleared the table. Salad, pizzas, and cranberry sauce eaten, the men at the table drank coffee and ate pumpkin cupcakes. They heard the rumble of a large vehicle pulling up outside.

"I gotta go," Mayor Howie said and got up unexpectedly.

"Me too," Father Gallapo said, following him outside.

"Come over and help me do the dishes," Mrs. Whitenose told the Mexican Cowboy.

"The other guys leave and I've got to do the dishes," the Cowboy said, resenting again the things he'd been made to do this day.

"How about taking off your hat?" Mrs. Whitenose asked after bumping into its brim.

"Not even on my dying day," the Mexican Cowboy answered stubbornly, rolling up his sleeves and pouring water into a large pot on the stove. While the water heated, he slid plate scraps into the food bucket he would take out to the horse trough and leave for the animals.

When the dishes were dried and put away, Mrs. Whitenose got the Mexican Cowboy's coat off his bed, cornered him, and made him put the coat on, telling him: "Go on. Get out of here. Go see what the men are doing."

"You are kicking me out of my kitchen?"

"I've got stuff to do and I don't want you hanging around here. Go on. Beat it." Feeling really pushed around, the Mexican Cowboy went outside.

As soon as she was sure he'd gone, Mrs. Whitenose opened the bag she brought and took out a faded red rebozo, a long white robe, and a makeup kit. Anxiously, she explored the house looking for a mirror.

Christmas Events are Orchestrated

A school bus pulled up outside. Kids with band instruments and teachers and parents from the small K-12 school in Cordoba climbed out. The town's fire truck parked behind them and the same six firemen who had delivered the wood started lighting the fires they'd laid.

Stunned and bewildered by the events unfolding in his yard, the Mexican Cowboy melted into his faded green rocker on the porch. He watched the music teacher help the kids put folding chairs into a three-row semicircle facing the porch and carry music stands from the bus and put them in place on the uneven ground.

With sheet music on their stands, fires providing illumination and warmth, and parents standing behind the musicians, the school band began playing Christmas music with cold lips—gloves and mitten on their hands. A chorus of a dozen students, parents, and teachers stood on the Cowboy's left, near the porch.

Happier now, the Mexican Cowboy rocked in his chair listening to traditional songs performed by a surprisingly good band and chorus outlined by the fires—"Oh Little Town of Bethlehem," "Silent Night," "Away in a Manger," "Oh Holy Night"—music appropriate for a lonely man on Christmas Eve. Looking behind him the Cowboy was surprised to see that not one of his friends had come to be with him. Sadness began to steal into his heart again.

Las Posadas

The musicians stopped playing. In front of the Cowboy three teachers and some parents quickly constructed a small wall out of folding chairs angling away from him. A 'doorway' was left in the wall. Three of the older band players stood up and lay their instruments on their chairs. Parents handed them a push-button accordion, a guitar, and a violin as they walked inside the wall. The chorus broke into two groups, one inside, one outside the wall with small, lit candles in their hands. The giant fires dying down behind them now, the performers waited.

The Mexican Cowboy waited patiently too. Something important must be about to happen. He noticed band members, parents, and teachers looking off to their right in the direction of the arroyo. Do they see Coyote? He wondered. It is dark out there but the Mexican Cowboy can make out a small party coming slowly toward the enclosure.

When he realized what was coming toward him, he was surprised. The students and adults sat in reverent silence as an old man wearing a worn, blue tunic slowly led a donkey toward the wall. Slumped on the donkey sat a shivering, exhausted woman with a large red shawl partly covering her body and head. Cowboy could see in the dying firelight that her hair and skin were dark. Streaks of soft multi-colored light reflected from her face and hands in a way that made it plain that this was no ordinary woman.

The old man tied the donkey to one of the chairs at the enclosure's entrance and slowly walked to the 'doorway.'

With guitar, accordion and violin introducing the piece *a travo* style, a musical duel began between those outside and those inside the enclosure.

The old man said loudly, knocking on the wall near the door, "In the name of heaven I ask you for lodging. My beloved wife cannot walk."

As he spoke, the half of the choir standing near him sang in Spanish the *Outsiders* part of the famous Christmas song"Las Posadas."

En nombre del cielo as pido posada ...

Inside the enclosure a short, rumpled man stepped out of the dark and responded angrily, "This is not an inn. Keep going." The half of the chorus beside him who were playing the '*Insiders*' sang: *Aqui no es meson, sigan adelante....*

The older man, backed up by the *Insider* choir pleaded: "We come very tired from Nazareth. I am the carpenter named Joseph."

The grumpy man inside with his choir responded: "I don't care what your name is. Let me sleep."

Older man: "We ask for shelter, just one night for the Queen of Heaven."

Grumpy man: "Well, if a queen is asking why is she so alone?"

Older man: "My wife is Mary Queen of Heaven and she is to be Mother of the Divine World."

Grumpy Man: "Come in pilgrims! I didn't recognize you."

With Mary still collapsed on the donkey, the couple went through the door into the Inn as idle band members, parents, teachers, fireman, *Insider* and *Outsider* members of the chorus, and the Mexican Cowboy too join in singing:

Entren santos peregrinos, peregrinos,
Reciban este nincon....

"Come in holy pilgrims. You are welcome though this dwelling is humble. We offer you our hearts."

"Let us sing with happiness, that today Joseph and Mary have come to honor us."

The song was over. Everyone before him stood quietly, waiting to hear the Cowboy's reaction. Without thinking, the Mexican Cowboy leapt up, stepped forward and shouted impulsively, "Viva! Viva!" Parents and teachers burst into applause. Firemen shouted their approval while the fire truck driver rang the truck's bell and tapped the siren. Musicians and choir members bowed in three directions. The band's drummer banged his cymbal. With a roar, a barrage of "Thank You," and "Merry Christmas," echoed back and forth among the pleased crowd of grownups and students.

Then, impatient to leave, students began giving their music to the band teacher, folding stands, and putting away their instruments. The concert had gone well. Now they were eager to get on the bus.

Still applauding and cheering, the Mexican Cowboy's eyes moved gratefully from person to person before him. Looking into the Inn, he saw that the donkey was still tied up, but Joseph, Mary, and the grumpy innkeeper were gone. An older girl hurried over to the donkey, untied him, and led him around the corner of the house.

As adults and students began to leave his yard, Mayor Howie, Father Gallapo, and Mrs. Whitenose came out of the house behind the Mexican Cowboy. Mrs. Whitenose hugged him and the Mayor hastily led them down into the crowd.

Hurrying to get in front of the departing people, congratulating and shaking hands as they pushed forward, Mayor Howie and the others reached the school bus door before anyone climbed aboard. Frank Corsa, the chauffeur and policeman, had set up folding tables laden with bouquets and stuffed Christmas stockings by the door of the bus.

As students climbed into their school bus, Mayor Howie, Father Gallapo, and Mrs. Whitenose, gave each youth a Christmas stocking filled with candy, a pair of socks, a toothbrush, and a multi-colored piece of paper with the Mayor's Santa-capped picture and a list of ridiculous promises he would carry out for the school in the coming year. Students grabbed their stockings, nodded or said thanks, and hopped aboard the bus.

Mayor Howie's chauffeur Frank stood beside him and took over handing out Christmas stockings so the Mayor could personally give parents and teachers bouquets of red and white carnations he had purchased from a hothouse in a nearby town. The cheap flowers were bunched in plastic-wrap tied with a green ribbon. Stuck in the top of each bouquet was a Christmas card with a picture of the Mayor wearing a Santa hat and a vote-for-me message.

Parents and teachers were as eager as the students to get home. With thanks hastily delivered they passed the Mayor's polished old Cadillac and climbed into the bus. With everyone aboard, the fire truck and bus backed up, turned around, and drove away. As the bus jolted along the dirt road toward the highway, students threw toothbrushes and the Mayor's junk promises out the windows.

Waving goodbye until the bus jounced out of sight, the Mexican Cowboy followed the Priest, Mrs. Whitenose, and the Mayor, back into his house.

Aftermath

Sitting around the kitchen table now, the Mexican Cowboy and his guests relaxed. The short white candles 'borrowed' from the Priest's church in Cordoba were blown out. A plate of pumpkin cupcakes was put on the table, and coffee and wine was sipped. Talk centered around the band and choir's superb concert.

"But two things I don't get," the Cowboy said. "Who put all this together? And who played Joseph, Mary, and the innkeeper? Some of the parents?"

"You'll find out sooner or later," Mayor Howie said tersely.

"Why does it matter to you?" Mrs. Whitenose asked softly.

"Because I wanted to thank persons who did all this for me. I'm grateful so many people turned my Christmas around and made me a happy man. Also I want to thank you guys for all you did. I'm sorry I was so angry. I didn't know what was going on."

"We didn't want you to." Father Gallapo said. "A Christmas without surprises is no Christmas at all."

"You are pushing me towards joy?"

"Trying to," the Priest answered.

"Then I thank all of you. Merry Christmas!" said the Cowboy with a smile, and raised his wine glass.

The others clinked glasses and cups with him, but said nothing back.

The Mexican Cowboy chewed on a cupcake and started to feel ignored again. He wondered why such a festive evening looked like it was going to end without the shared joy he wanted so desperately.

Hearing sounds in the yard, Mayor Howie pointed at the door and cupped his ear.

Rustling, gibbering, growling, flapping, meowing, grunting, hissing and other sounds were coming through the door.

"What next?" the Mexican Cowboy asked.

"I honestly don't know," Mayor Howie said, being more truthful than usual.

"Let's go see," Mrs. Whitenose said. Led by her, the Mexican Cowboy, Father Gallapo, and the Mayor went outside.

Presents for the Cowboy

About ten feet from the porch, Coyote sat on his haunches, a red hat on his head, a very phony white beard hanging under his snout, a bell with a wooden handle on the ground. Bright moonlight helped the Cowboy and his friends see the Coyote, outlined by the fires' dying embers. Over the house to the northwest Sirius shone steadily, like the point of an LED light.

"Merry Christmas. Please be seated," Coyote said. He waited for his audience to sit, then took the bell handle in his mouth and—jerking his head back and forth sharply—rang the bell three times.

Nothing happened.

He rang the bell three more times, impatiently.

Nothing happened.

Growling, he dropped the bell, barked angrily, and emitted a short, wavering, commanding yelp. At the edge of the darkness beyond the fires' embers, Cowboy and his friends on the porch saw a dozen or more coyotes escorting a mix of small and large animals into the yard. Individual animals in the small mob, wary of one another, tried to keep their distance, yet were shepherded closer together in front of the little audience by flanking coyotes, who barked and nipped like sheep dogs.

Watching the animals coming toward her Mrs. Whitenose whispered to Father Gallapo, "I don't see any house cats."

"No housecats here," Coyote said. "We can't herd them."

"Why are all these animals here?" Mayor Howie asked.

"To give the Mexican Cowboy presents," Coyote answered.

"Why do they want to give him presents?" Mayor Howie responded.

"Because he's been putting food out for them for years," Coyote said.

The Mexican Cowboy stood up and looked in several directions. One of the snakes living under his porch had crawled into the chilled air and coiled. Bats and night birds circled overhead. Beyond the dying fires he could see an antelope, two stray dogs, a small black bear, a bobcat, raccoons and rats, deer, a porcupine, a lean, tusked peccary and even one of the river otters that people from Seattle had dumped into the nearby river.

Herded by the coyotes, several animals were brought forward to give the Mexican Cowboy his presents. Without being asked, the Cowboy moved down to sit on the lowest step of the porch to accept their gifts.

Coyote shook his bell.

Three chipmunks ran up to the Cowboy and each dropped several hoarded pine nuts from their cheeks. As he bent over to pick up the nuts the chipmunks scurried around the side of the house, herded by two coyotes, before he could thank them.

Coyote shook his bell again.

A chicken walked over, squatted down next to the Cowboy and began straining.

After another bell ring, a white-tailed skunk, zigzagging as though its vision was poor, came slowly toward the Cowboy, its tail lowered passively. The skunk offered the Cowboy a tattered red and white cotton scarf she carried in her mouth.

"Thank you," Cowboy said, tipping his hat to the skunk. Holding his gift to his nose he said, "May I ask where this nice scarf comes from?"

Coyote answers for the skunk. "A camper ran away holding it to his face after a skunk had to spray him. The stinky scarf was left at the camp site."

"How did you get it clean?" the Mexican Cowboy asked.

Coyote pointed at the arroyo with his nose. Squinting, the Cowboy saw a dark blob near the bank, light reflecting from its eyes and big flat teeth. "Beaver tried to clean it for you by dragging the scarf underwater upstream from his dam. He hung the scarf over a low branch and smacked it with his tail."

"Give my thanks to the beaver," the Cowboy said.

A coyote began escorting the skunk around the side of the house. The Cowboy noticed the beaver headed that way too. As it passed by him the beaver looked at the Cowboy without expression on its face.

"Coming so far from his pond must have been terrible for the beaver," Cowboy said to his friends above him on the porch. "I wish there were something we could give him in return." Now the remaining animals cowered as a mountain lion padded forward and sat only a foot away from the Cowboy. The lion bared its fangs and with an indescribable screech/yowl/purr, it reached forward and swiped the air in front of the Cowboy's nose. The Cowboy did not flinch.

"That," said Coyote, "is the 'safe-word' for mountain lions. If you ever get attacked by a mountain lion, use it."

"I'll try to remember," said the Cowboy, trying to mimic the sounds and swiping gesture. The lion looked exasperated.

"I'll get her to do it again," Coyote said. "Pay attention." He growled sharply at the big cat.

This time the lion's paw grazed his cheek, leaving a faint scratch. "I've got it," the Cowboy said. "I won't forget. Thank you." Then to his friends surprise the Cowboy rose, stood in front of the lion, put his arms around her head, and scratched her neck behind her ears. The lion seemed to like that. A few seconds later four coyotes came to escort her around the side of the house.

Over by the woodpile a bull pulling a small cart heaped with dung appeared out of the darkness. Looking his way, the animal twisted his horns in the Mexican Cowboy's direction, bellowed, jerked forward and, turning suddenly, he upset the cart, spilling dung beside the stacked wood.

"That's in case you run out of firewood," said Coyote.

"Thank him," said the Cowboy. "I'll put it to good use."

"Your next gift will give you another good reason to have the dung," Coyote said. "Look over there."

On his right, a few feet in front of the folding chairs stacked against the porch, Cowboy saw several wobbly, narrow trenches being dug by a badger, a gopher, and a prairie dog. When the Coyote rang his bell they stood aside.

Immediately a flurry of small birds dived at the trenches from the star-lit sky. Each bird dropped one or two seeds from its bill into the cuts. Mrs. Whitenose, a birder, thought she saw sparrows, flycatchers, blue jays, chickadees, nuthatches, wrens, and starlings seeding the trenches.

When the birds flew away an armadillo used its shell like a road grader to push the displaced earth back into the trenches. The donkey that had carried Mary earlier came around the house by itself and walked delicately back and forth over the filled trenches, lightly packing the soil.

"That's Gus, my horse Turco's friend!" the Cowboy said. "How did he get here?"

"He got driven over," Coyote answered, being deliberately vague.

"What are the trenches and the birds about?" The Mexican Cowboy asked.

"Flowers and vegetables for you," Coyote answered.

"It's night and it's winter!" Mrs. Whitenose said to Coyote. "How did you get so many birds to do this for you?"

"My god worked with their gods," Coyote replied. "The deal they made will be hard on coyotes. We promised to eat only half as many small birds in the next three months."

"The coyotes' gift is unfair to the givers! I wish I could give it back," the Mexican Cowboy said with genuine regret.

"You deserve it," Coyote said. "And there is more."

A whitetail doe led her seven-month-old fawn to the porch for petting. Mrs. Whitenose gingerly came down the steps and lightly stroked the fawn. She was excited. "I've never touched a live fawn before," she said.

"You could if you shot its mother," said Mayor Howie, a hunter.

Next, two pack rats with long bushy tails took turns carrying a shiny, gold-tinted Elgin pocket watch across the yard. The watch had a dented case and smashed crystal and had, perhaps, been thrown away by a disgusted camper in the late 1960s.

The Cowboy took the watch from the rats, admired it, touched his index finger to his lips to wet it, and put the finger near the ground for the rats to smell. Sensing his gratefulness, they began to back away. Quickly the Cowboy pulled two dimes out of his jeans and dropped them near the pack rats. Excited, they studied the coins for a moment, then picked the dimes up and ran around the side of the house.

Hearing excited clucking at his feet now, the Cowboy looked down at the chicken he'd forgotten about. She'd laid an egg for him and obviously wanted him to take it. He was about to pick the egg up when a raccoon dashed out of the darkness and seized it. There was a quick growl from Coyote. The ringtail raccoon hesitated for a moment, then came over to the Mexican Cowboy and handed him the egg. The raccoon had a disappointed look on its face as it watched the chicken run as fast as it could around the corner of the house.

A Present from the Coyote

With only a few coyotes remaining in the front yard, Coyote dropped the bell from his mouth and walked over to the bottom step of the porch, the coyotes behind him. Father Gallapo carried the wide chair he'd been sitting on down to the Coyote, who hopped onto it. The Priest sat beside the Mexican Cowboy on the steps and looked up as Coyote began to speak.

"All this gift-giving was easy to arrange compared to what is coming next. I wanted the gift I am giving to the Mexican Cowboy to be the best gift of all. Fortunately I had some help deciding what it should be. Unfortunately, making the gift I was told to give is the most difficult thing any animal has ever done.""What was that?" the Mexican Cowboy asks his best friend sympathetically.

"I wrote a poem," the Coyote said quietly.

"What's it about?" Mrs. Whitenose asked.

"How all the things that happened this evening came about."

"Get on with it," Mayor Howie said, looking at his watch and holding up his cell phone.

"Father Gallapo wrote the poem down for me so my friend would have a copy to keep."

Father Gallapo handed a scroll of paper to Coyote who unrolled it and said, "Here is my poem."

Squirming, looking abashed and uneasy for the first time that night, Coyote said, "All right. Here goes."

And he began to recite in a deeper voice than his friends had heard before.

Starry night and still, after a
Day short, cold and sunny.
My fur is thick, my nose is runny.
I just killed and ate a bunny.

Yes a night to bark and howl with friends,
A night to muse, receive, and send, an
Eve of coyote delight, long to end.

But then I heard your words—sad and gloomy.
You aren't feeling as you should, you're moody.
Your Holy Eve you sit alone, consternate and moan.

I pray for you and am told to trot away, not scared but bold,
To consult your friend the Priest who made me atone
Baptized me, confessed me, put me on the Prophet's Throne,
Led me to love some men, but YOU good friend to enfold.

The Priest was locking the church when I arrived,
Heading to his truck unfriended. 'Howdy,' I said,
'It's me again.' The itinerant Priest pretended
He's pleased, but I could smell his doubt and wish that
Our meeting won't result in more hours
Spent on creaking knees. He didn't look surprised.

My god I said demands that for the morrow,
We must plan, prepare, and undo the sorrow
Of our Unbeliever friend, the Mexican Cowboy,
A Holy Atheist who gives and does not receive,
Who yearns to be loved and cannot believe joy
Will come with presents for him on Christmas Eve.

Father Gallapo leans against his truck,
Thinks, beams and shares his plan.
"You are in luck. I'll do what God instructs.
Humans are my responsibility
And I'll do what's needed, see.
But Animals are yours, you understand?'

'All right!' I said. 'You bring the people, music, food and drink.
I'll bring presents with creatures that fly and walk and slink.
You must bring foods of different kinds for all our Guests
Who gladly put a night aside for a Cowboy so distressed.

'Get me a white beard, red cap and bell
I'll M.C. and think of things to tell.'

'A deal,' he says. But one thing more as well.
'You too must have a gift if you expect to remain an equal and hope to quell,
Not widen, the giant rift between clans coyote and human.
If you don't know what to give, just sit down and write a poem.'

And so I have, and bad it is, as all who hear will know.
Cowboy Friend, let me—Your MC—convey
With my poem and our creature show
The animal kingdom's wishes on your Christmas Day

I bring warm sentiments from Gods above,
Love from animals that love,
Respect or thanks from those who can't, but
Nothing from humans, straight or bent.

One final phrase, before the poem's past. Here is
Humans' favorite wish: Merry Christmas!

And please, one thing more:
Keep putting food outside your door.

The human listeners smiled and formally applauded the Coyote's poem. Other coyotes looked at their leader with puzzled expressions and cocked heads. Coyote rolled up the scroll and ceremoniously presented it to the Cowboy.

"Around to the back," Mayor Howie ordered.

Christmas Eve Feast

As humans and coyotes rounded the corner of the house, a moonlit scene of satisfaction and pleasure opened before them. Wary-eyed, and staying as far as possible from other species, animals and birds feasted happily on widely separated piles of foods. Food gifts included seeds, nuts, alfalfa and oats, cheese, meat and fish scraps, and other goodies collected from the city dump.

A Cordoba city pickup truck was parked by the kitchen door next to the flagstone patio. Mayor Howie's chauffeur Frank Corsa and his wife Luisa lifted out garbage bags containing sorted food scraps. As each creature ate, and more birds and animals gathered, Frank and Luisa placed more food before them. Thirsty birds and animals drank from large, widely separated bowls of water set on the ground. The Cowboy noticed the beaver busily chewing on large pieces of a downed aspen tree. Gus, the donkey that carried Mary, was eating a small pile of hay, placed far away from the lion, off by herself vigorously eating a road-kill deer.

"So many birds, so many kinds of animals eating together. I've never seen anything like it," said the Priest, obviously impressed with the feast he helped plan. "It is like a feast of many persons with different faiths."

"It is like a *National Geographic* special," Mrs. Whitenose said.

"Frank Corsa is a mammaler," Mayor Howie told them. "His wife Luisa is a birder. That's why they are doing this."

"And why did YOU do all of this," Mrs. Whitenose asked Mayor Howie.

"Because coyotes are moving up the political chain. Either I go after their votes—or they go after me. Coyotes are getting birds and animals behind them. In politics it is either divide and conquer or cooperate and share. I do a lot of both."

"It is that way with religion too," Father Gallapo added.

The Mayor looked at his watch and nodded. "I have to go. I still have a lot to do in Cordoba before I can sleep."

"We'll vote for you," Mrs Whitenose and the Mexican Cowboy said.

The Mayor raised his voice to a campaign level and, waving, said to the sea of feasting wildlife before him on the dry mesa, "Merry Christmas to all of you."

The animals and birds looked up at him and voiced a brief cacophony of replies.

"What did they say?" the Mayor asked Coyote.

"They said, 'We are all having a good night. Thanks for the feast.'"

The Mayor turned and started to walk away. Mrs. Whitenose hugged the Cowboy, scratched Coyote's head, and said goodnight to Father Gallapo. "I'd better go too. If I can use your truck I'll take Gus back to the barn on my way home."

"Please do that for me," Father Gallapo said, and gave her his key. Moving close to Mrs. Whitenose, Father Gallapo said softly,

"Merry Christmas, Thelma."

She grinned. Their relationship had its trials, but this night had gone well.

"Thanks for feeding all of them," Mrs. Whitenose shouted at the hard-working Corsas as she walks away.

"We'll keep shoveling," Luisa Corsa replied.

"I think we should say goodnight too," Father Gallapo said to the Cowboy. "I'm tired. Let's go to bed."

As they walked toward the kitchen door, Coyote followed behind looking expectant. Without bothering to say goodbye or thanks for all that Coyote had done for him, the Mexican Cowboy went into the kitchen.

Even though the Priest patted him and thanked him and said how glad he was that Coyote made all of this happen, Coyote felt angry and let down. "I did all this terribly hard work for nothing," he almost said to the Priest.

The kitchen door opened and the Mexican Cowboy came outside carrying two large buckets he'd hidden in his bedroom. Coyote's nose twitched with delight at the odors it picked up. The Mexican Cowboy walked around to the front of the house with the Priest and the other coyotes following. Cowboy opened the large bucket and spread a trail of meat scraps he'd bought at a slaughterhouse that morning all over the ground. Without asking permission, the other coyotes ran to the meat and buried their snouts in it. Coyote sat patiently near the porch.

The Mexican Cowboy climbed the steps into the house and returned a few seconds later carrying a large plate decorated with an image in the center of a coyote on a hill howling at the moon. He put the plate on the ground, opened the smaller bucket, and began arranging much nicer pieces of meat for his friend the Coyote: steak, lamb, ham, chicken, turkey, and quail. Coyote watched him gratefully.

"Eat up," said the Mexican Cowboy. "I bought the best for the best."

"You didn't forget me!" Coyote said.

"You didn't let me down either!" the Mexican Cowboy replied. "Now feast."

With other coyotes looking at him enviously, Coyote began leisurely enjoying the fine meal prepared for him. The Mexican Cowboy went inside again and returned with a bowl of water for Coyote.

"It's past your bedtime," Coyote said, looking up at his friends.

"We'll say goodnight then," the Priest replied. "Merry Christmas."

"And Merry Godsmas to you Father," Coyote answered. "Thank you for putting all this together with me."

"When creatures work together they get things done," the Priest said before he walked up the steps.

"When humans and animals spend time together they get to like one another," the Mexican Cowboy said while scratching the Coyote's head. "Thanks for everything you did for me and the others."

"What did you think of the poem?" Coyote asked, as his friend started up the steps.

"Both of us have a lot to learn about Poetry," the Cowboy said obliquely. "Thanks for getting us started."

"Writing poems is a lot harder than catching rabbits for supper," Coyote said, putting his snout down toward the plate again.

"Creating is never easy. Keep at it," said the Mexican Cowboy before going inside. "Good night."

"Sleep tight," Coyote replied as the door closed behind the Cowboy.

Finis

Before he started to get ready for bed, the Mexican Cowboy realized he had a question he had forgotten to ask anyone.

"The Mayor said that his chauffeur Frank is a 'mammaler.' What did he mean by that?"

The Priest answered him. "Frank says that humans are too tidy, and too neat and health conscious with their garbage. We control most of the Earth's land. We raise, harvest, or kill most of its food, and what we don't eat we lock away, bury, compost, or burn to keep animals, birds, insects, and sea life from eating it."

"We only feed pets, animals, and birds we are going to eat, zoo animals, horses we own, or a few species of small birds. Bird populations are coming back because we are feeding them, but mammal species are shrinking and dying out because we've taken away their food."

"So Frank feeds them?" the Cowboy asked.

"Every chance he gets. He wants mammalers to become as numerous as birders."

"This makes something clear to me I hadn't understood," Cowboy said, yawning. "'Saying 'Merry Christmas' isn't just an empty wish. Hearing 'Merry Christmas' so often reminds us to make Christmas merry for people we care about. But what you, the Mayor, Mrs. Whitenose, the Corsas, and Coyote did tonight taught me that Christmas is also about working constantly with others to improve all creatures' lives."

"Coyote understood that already," the Priest said, yawning too. "You are getting there, but you've got a long ways to go."

"I've got time," the Cowboy said.

"Less than you think. There is more to the Christmas lesson than giving."

"What's that?"

"Getting something very important that we humans cannot give to ourselves."

"Night," said the Cowboy.

The Priest didn't answer.

Ursula Hugs Celesto

An evening in March. Snow was on the ground in scattered patches and the Mexican Cowboy and his tenant Father Gallapo were sitting in the kitchen of the Cowboy's crummy house. Gusts of wind whistled through the non-weather-stripped windows and doors. They had eaten, and Cowboy was facing a task he kept postponing—telling the Priest that he wanted him to move out.

"Something's been going on," he said as a fumbling starter.

"Tell me about it," the Priest said.

"It is complicated. It'll take a while."

"I've got all night. Let's open a bottle of wine, get comfortable, and hear about it."

With filled glasses in front of them, the Mexican Cowboy said: "I wish Coyote were here. A lot of this story is his."

"Well Coyote isn't here. He probably wants you to tell me his story. He trusts you."

"I never understood why he trusts me," the Cowboy replied. "But okay. Get comfy. This will take a while."

Squirming to get comfortable on the kitchen's hard wooden chairs, the Cowboy said, "First let me tell you how the Coyote and I met up. You'll need to understand that—and how the Coyote was made—before I can tell you what's on my mind that we have to talk about."

"How the Coyote 'was made?'" the Priest asked. "By his momma bitch and his daddy, no?"

"No," said the Mexican Cowboy. "It is all a long story. Let's get at it."

"Go for it," the Priest said softly. "My ears are all yours."

"I'll fill 'em up then," the Cowboy said, and wriggled some more and took another sip of wine and began telling the story of his meet-up with Coyote.

Turco Finds Celesto

"This is about my wonderful stallion, Turco, hearing a bear cub crying," Cowboy began, and went on telling his story:

Nine-year-old Celesto lived near the mouth of Salerno Canyon on the edge of the Manzano mountain range. It was February—the coldest month—some years back when Celesto decided he'd rather do his learning by exploring the mountains that day than going to school. Mirella Montagna, his mother, had gone to Cordoba to clean homes, her way of supporting them. Celesto dressed warmly, sat in his mother's new green rocker putting on boots, packed a water bottle and a couple of plastic bags of food, and left. He walked swiftly up the rough, windy jeep road that was little traveled except by hunters in the snow season.

Several hours later, and further up the road than he'd walked before, he noticed what seemed to be an animal 'trail' going up the canyon wall. Thinking he'd climb up and find a place to sit and eat, Celesto started up the rocky hillside. There were patches of snow on the barely distinguishable path and Celesto slipped several times, nearly sliding down the very steep hillside. A little higher than he meant to climb, the boy spotted a large rock with what looked to be a top flat enough to sit on. "There's my place," he thought as he struggled the last ten yards up the steepening path.

Celesto was surprised to see a small flat area behind the rock shielding the mouth of a little cave. It was early afternoon, warmish, and sunlight was lighting the inside of the cave enough so he could see rocks up against the back wall. He thought about exploring the cave but worried about rattlers, though he'd be told rattlesnakes don't live in caves. Pondering this, he sat on the rock, basking in the wan sunlight, looking at the canyon below and the mesa beyond stretching over to the river. Celesto could make out his house, and far off to the right, the house and stable where his mother's friend the Mexican Cowboy and his horse Turco lived. He remembered the Cowboy teaching him to ride on Turco—who wouldn't let most humans near him.

With his hand shielding his eyes from the lowering sun, Celesto scanned the canyon beneath him and the nearby mountains rising above him. He spotted a rare Gambel oak, the usual willows and ponderosa pines, a few small aspens, and nearer to him stems of numerous wild flowers including asters and wild strawberries. He was hoping to see a deer or elk, a bobcat or a coyote, or even a *gallo*, the local word for a wild turkey. It was a satisfying moment for the boy who loved these mountains. Young, sensible, brave, more eager to explore and learn about this part of the world than be afraid, Celesto made up his mind to go into the cave for a minute before he started down the trail and back to his home. He knew he had time to get to his house before his mother Mirella returned from her labors. He worried now only that he might slip and hurt himself on the way down.

Bending over with his palms out and his knees near the ground and with his head brushing the dangling—and perhaps loose—overhead rocks, he waddled into the cave. His body blocked most of the sunlight coming in behind him and Celesto could just make out a small rightward bend about four yards in front of him. Celesto's sense of smell wasn't good but he was picking up a strong odor he'd never smelled before: musty, warm, slightly like both berry bushes and rotten meat. Crawling into the darkness around the small bend he started to feel afraid now. Celesto promised himself he would only crawl another yard or two before he backed out of the cave.

It was very dark in there. Reaching out with his right arm after one last waddle forward, Celesto suddenly felt soft, matted fur against his open hand. Instantly he realized he was touching a hibernating bear. Or maybe not hibernating—because before he could back away quietly the bear rolled on its side and with a soft paw pulled him to its stomach. Lying against the bear Celesto felt warm and cuddled, but he didn't dare yet to try slipping away. His uncle had taught him to figure out what to do in any rough situation before attempting anything. Afraid of awakening the slow-breathing bear he rested, wondering what he should do. A wave of fear passed through him when he realized how his mother would feel if she came home and found him missing. Determined now to get away, Celesto squirmed, trying to gently slip away from the bear's loose grasp. But the sleeping bear sensed his movement and tightened its grip on him each time he tried to move away. It was a female bear, Celesto realized, certainly pregnant, and he remembered learning in school that hibernating female bears give birth and suckle cubs while they are still semi-hibernating. The bear's automatic responses were not under its control. Its nervous system had mistaken him for a newborn cub and wasn't going to let him be free until spring.

Crap, he thought, how am I going to get out of this? But he was comfortable and warm, he had food and water in the small pack on his back, and the sun was setting, so he relaxed, closed his eyes and rested. "Being mothered by a bear is not such a bad experience," he thought. Several times that night he awoke and tried to slip away and the future mother-bear clamped hold of him tighter each time. When he stopped struggling she relaxed her hold. With the new day's light just beginning to probe the small cave's depths, Celesto made one heroic effort to escape. He pushed the bear's paws away gently and tried to push himself quickly out of the bear's reach. Sensing his intent, the bear twisted her body and trapped him against the cave wall. He was its prisoner. Celesto began to cry. The bear gently cuddled him. The hibernating bear seemed to actually be trying to soothe and comfort him. She loves me, he thought. I'm a prisoner of love.

Meanwhile, Mrs. Montagna had gotten the Sheriff's deputies to set up a search party. Team members were exploring all the nearby roads and trails, looking for signs of the missing boy. Celesto even heard a pair of search-party 4x4 pickups stopping on the jeep road below. He could hear voices discussing whether to climb up the canyon walls next. Speaking loudly in a whispery voice, Celesto tried to get their attention, but he was too scared of what the bear might do to him if he shouted or screamed. The search party passed him by. That night it started to snow.

Back in Cordoba, after hours of scrupulous searching near Celesto's home and in the mountains—with ground parties and helicopters—the Sheriff's search organizer decided that the boy they hadn't found must have run away toward town. Or been kidnapped. The search effort turned away from the Manzanos and moved west toward the river and settlements. Mirella Montagna however was sure her son had gone into the mountains as he often did and something bad had happened to him there. Desperate to get more help now, she drove over to her former lover's house to ask the Mexican Cowboy to help her. Their connection dated back ten years, when the Mexican Cowboy—and his horse Turco—were fitter. Holding his crying friend, the Mexican Cowboy instantly decided to help find Celesto. He sent Mrs. Montagna home and went to his bedroom to dig ragged, long woolen underwear and thick wool socks out of his stuffed dresser. He rummaged in the back of his closet until he found his double-legged work pants and heavy, green plaid shirt, switched clothes and sat on the edge of his bed pulling on his heavy winter boots. Dressed warmly, with thick-lined coat zipped to his neck scarf and faded yellow hat pulled low over his head, and with his Winchester rifle and a blanket and supplies he packed up in the kitchen, the Mexican Cowboy went outside to his decrepit barn to saddle up Turco.

The intuitive mustang seemed to be expecting him and eagerly greeted his sole human friend. Turco was barely able to stand still inside the barn while the Cowboy hurriedly brushed the mostly brown pinto with the white blaze, rich black mane and thin curvy white marking on his right side that looked like a wavy stripe swiped by a three-year-old playing with a wide brush and house paint. Turco was excited to be going out and listened restlessly to the Cowboy's explanation as the only human he trusted hurriedly picked his hooves, put the small worn wool rug bought years ago at Ortega's in Chimayo over his back for a saddle blanket and swung the battered Mexican saddle he'd inherited from his father onto the horse, tightened the girth and fastened the loose flank cinch under him, and bridled him. With his rifle in the saddle's cracked leather holster and a rope hooked to the tie strap holder, and with supplies tied on behind the cantle, the Cowboy led Turco out into the light snowstorm. He put his left foot in the stirrup, swung up and with a rub against Turco's powerful neck, he and his best friend rode off toward the mountains east of his run-down house.

It was snowing lightly and the Mexican Cowboy hunkered down on his saddle seat and tried to stay warm as Turco gingerly walked up the slick canyon road. His eyes constantly moving, the Mexican Cowboy looked for signs of the boy's visit. He paid particular attention to tracks in the snow on his way up the canyon, fearing that an animal may have killed and dragged Celesto away. What he dreaded seeing most were mountain lion tracks. Passing a junction where a side-canyon joins into Salerno canyon road the Mexican Cowboy spotted several hunters in camouflage gear standing around parked vehicles talking and perhaps drinking. The only one he recognized was his least favorite human, the arrogant and selfish Howie Waters, who had caused him trouble many times in the past. He guessed the others were local businessmen. The Cowboy raised his hand in a 'howdy' gesture as he passed by but none of the men seemed to notice him riding past on Turco.'

Further up the canyon the Mexican Cowboy spotted animal footprints in the snow crisscrossing the road and going the same way he and Turco were headed. He dismounted and inspected the tracks carefully. They were about two and a half inches long with hind prints smaller than front ones, outer toes tucked in neatly behind the two front toes, and heel indentations compact and connected. He saw the claw marks, which are small dots ahead of each toe, and observed the line of footprints was narrow. The tracks weren't those of a bobcat or dog. They were a trotting coyote's. A few yards further up the road he saw a spongy, rope-like tapering scat deposit. Leading Turco to it he recognized the fur and rodent bones he used to identify coyote poop. The Cowboy got back on Turco and started up the road again. Nothing to worry about here.

Seeing coyote tracks caused him to momentarily remember the coyote with an exceptionally big head, exaggerated bulgy throat, gray coat with unusual brown streaks, and smallish ears and tail, whom he saw occasionally around his place surreptitiously sneaking off with food he put out for animals. He didn't mind the coyote doing that. Odd looking coyote though. And cleverer than most.

Half a mile further up the canyon Turco stopped abruptly and jerked his head upward to the left several times. The Cowboy looked up the snowy slope and saw nothing. "Come on, Turco," he said. "We can't stop here." But Turco wouldn't move. This was unlike him. Reflecting, the Mexican Cowboy got off the pinto stallion and looked around, wondering if Turco was trying to tell him where the boy might be. He scanned the canyon walls and saw nothing. Snow covered the ground on both sides of the road and there were no tracks visible in it. He walked several yards up and down the canyon looking for tracks along both edges of the road. Turco impatiently pawed the ground while his friend walked back and forth. Frustrated and about to get back on and see if he could persuade Turco to move up the canyon further, the Mexican Cowboy crossed in front of his horse. Instantly he was shoved in the small of his back and almost lifted into the bushes beside the road. Turco had put his head down and pushed hard on him. Momentarily angry at his horse, who'd never tried to hurt him before, then suddenly sure that Turco has heard something up there and was doing his best to make it plain the Cowboy needed to climb that slick hillside and check it out, the Cowboy put his gloved hand under Turco's lower lip and said, "All right, damn it, I'll go up there." The horse jerked his head to the left again and stood still with something like a human smile appearing on his lips and cheeks.

Climbing the slippery slope the Mexican Cowboy grabbed onto anything he could find to keep from sliding back or falling down. He tired rapidly going up the steep slope and he wasn't sure the route he was taking was ever used by anyone. Breathing heavily, and his legs hurting badly, he looked around for a place to sit. Uphill and a few yards to the right of him he spotted a fairly flat rock. Panting, he struggled up to it and worked his way around the giant rock, hoping to find a place to stretch out. He was startled to notice the small cave entrance he discovered behind the rock. And just at that moment he heard a commanding whinny from Turco. Turco was trying to tell him something important. Better check out the cave before I rest, he thought. Taking off his hat, the Mexican Cowboy got on his knees and peered inside the cave with his flashlight. He smelled the pungent odor of a hibernating bear and heard a voice softly asking him, "Can you save me please?" Crawling a few yards into the cave he saw the boy's foot sticking out from around the bend.

"Celesto, that's you, isn't it?" the Cowboy said softly. "Are you alone?"

"A bear's got me," Celesto replied.

"Did she hurt you?" the Cowboy asked, wishing he'd brought his gun uphill with him.

"No. She loves me. She thinks I'm her cub. That's why she won't let me go," Celesto said softly.

"You can't slide away from her?"

"She pins me down every time I try."

They whispered back and forth for a minute while the Mexican Cowboy used his flashlight to see the bear's position. It lay on its side, legs blocking the exit, and the Mexican Cowboy sensed it was not fully asleep. Determined to rescue the boy, the Cowboy warned Celesto to stay quiet and still while he went back down the steep trail and brought up a rope to silently pull the boy a few inches at a time away from the bear.

"How'd you find me?" Celesto whispered.

"Turco found you. He must have heard your soft cries. He made me get off here and climb the hill."

"He'll be my friend for life," the boy whispered back.

"Good. He needs more friends," the Cowboy answered as he began to back out of the cave, his head bumping against the ceiling.

Outside the Mexican Cowboy started down the hill, making each step carefully and hanging on to anything that would keep him from sliding. But he was hurrying also. He felt afraid of what the bear might do to Celesto if something he did awakened her suddenly. On the other hand he believed he recognized the bear as one he had fed occasionally, and who had been easy to get along with. Slipsliding down the slick hillside, with the bottom nearing, the Cowboy stretched out his arm to grab a tree branch in front of him. His action was planned but it was a big stretch. Reaching forward as far as he could, he let go of the branch behind and grabbed for the next one. The icy branch

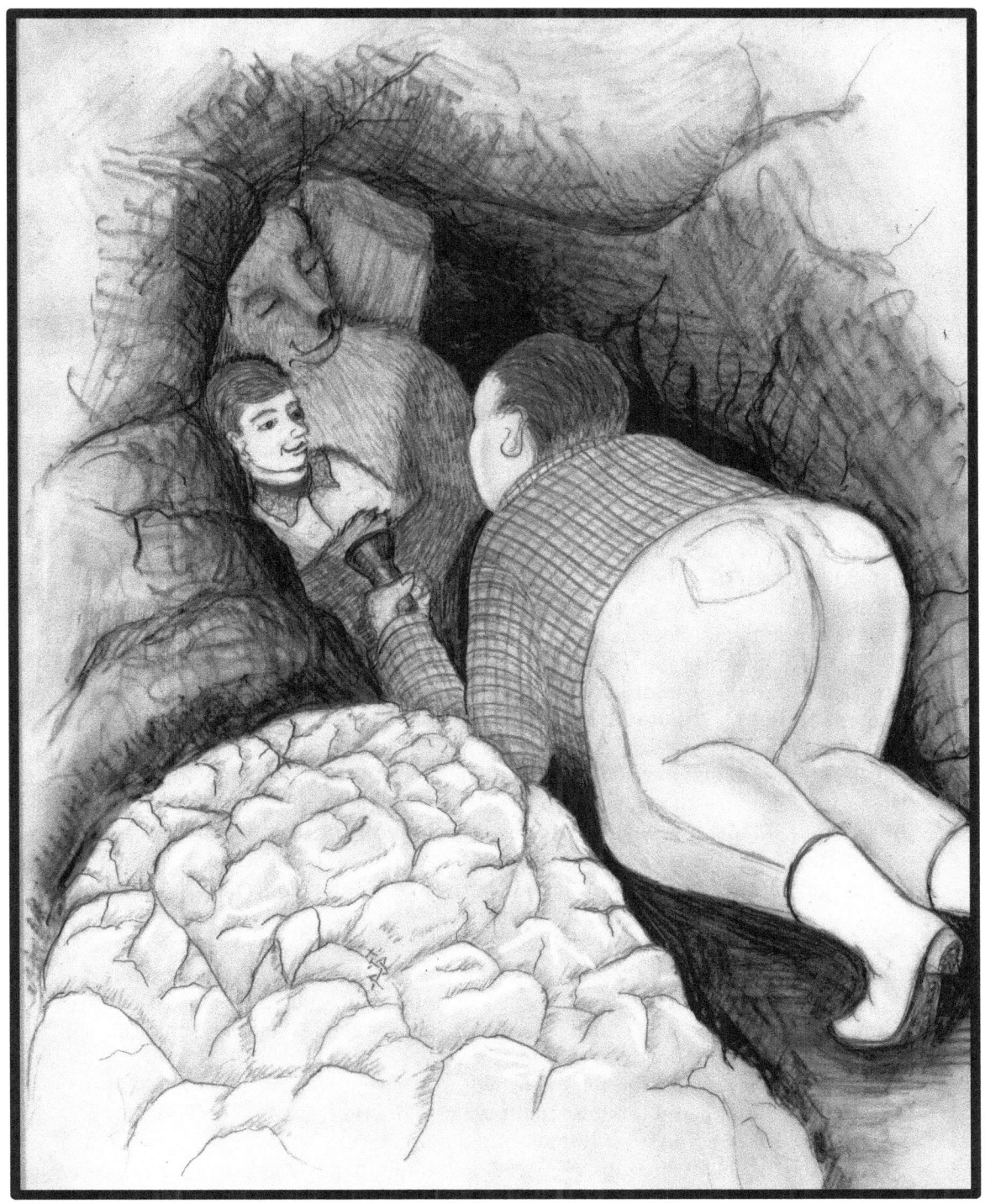

slipped through his gloved grip and the Cowboy pitched forward and slammed his face into a small rock. With gathering momentum he slipped, twisted, rolled and slid down the hill trying to grab onto something that would stop him. Bumping into rocks and trees, he knew he was getting seriously injured. Turco watched him tumbling down in panic. Only seventy feet above the road the Cowboy landed in a bush and held on to it as he slid through. Laying in the bush, bleeding profusely and semi-conscious, he heard the boy's faint calls and saw the frantic Turco trying to get to him before he passed out.

Lying there for over an hour and drifting in and out of consciousness, the Cowboy struggled to move out of the bush holding him. Furious pain in his bleeding limbs warned him that bones were broken. "I may never get out of this by myself," he realized. He wondered if he could make Turco come to him and let him use the reins to pull him the rest of the way down. Looking at his slick bloody hands with a twisted finger on each, he knew he wouldn't be able to hold onto the reins enough to be yanked out even if Turco did climb up to him. Despairing, he slipped into unconsciousness again.

But help was near. Coyote had been hunting game further up the canyon and was returning to his pups with a turkey in his mouth when he came onto the scene. Avoiding the dangerous horse by going up the hillside to get around it, he smelled and heard the breathing of a human in front of him. Coyote, who hated and feared humans generally, sneaked closer to the fat, shabbily dressed, unconscious man with his thinning hair showing and his prized yellow hat laying ten feet further up the mountainside.

Holy El Latrano, Coyote said almost aloud when he was closer to the prostrate fat-bellied human with clothes-staining wounds. "I know this **two-legged, tailless, bad-smelling rectum.**" (Actually that thought wasn't put into human words. He expressed the notion with coyotes' left-ear down, right ear up, snout pitched into a half snarl, fur on neck upright, growly with a rising then dipping note—the way all coyotes express their concept of hated humans in general). "**This two-legged, tailless, bad-smelling rectum carries food out of his** (small growl, raised eyebrow, indescribable scent puff from his rump, which is coyotes' way of 'saying' *house)* **to feed animals**."

Coyotes, he momentarily reflected, hate the idea of living **inside.** Sure you have to be in a den when you whelp and raise young, but otherwise being **inside** isn't being in The Real World. Humans, coyotes figured out thousands of years back, construct super-networks of non-livable places to hide away in. Humans are scared of the world. "If they lived with us we'd eat more of them," Coyote thought, then dropped the subject.

Staying out of sight (he hoped), Coyote slithered from rock to rock nearer to the prone human and thought about what to do. If I leave him he'll die and a lot of animals are going to go hungry and stop hanging out at his place where I easily catch meals for my pups. I guess I should help him, but how? Pondering the problem, Coyote realized the only thing he could do to help the unconscious human was to lead other humans to him—and that was as risky as trotting through a pile of mating rattlesnakes.

At that moment, concussed and semi-conscious, bruised and bleeding in the bush holding him, the Mexican Cowboy opened an eye and caught a glimpse of the coyote stealing toward him from rock to rock. "Coming to see if I'm dead and eatable yet," he thought struggling to stay conscious, then passed out again.

"I've got to risk it," Coyote decided. He dropped the turkey he was taking to his pups and started downhill away from the path, intending to avoid Turco who surely would try to kick him. Coyote was passing between two rocks by the bush when the Mexican Cowboy woke briefly, saw him and said unexpectedly, "Help me coyote. Please... help.... Me."

"I am," Coyote replied in English—without realizing he'd just violated his most essential law: Never Speak to Humans.

"Thank... you," the Mexican Cowboy answered and passed out again.

"El Latrano, God of all Coyotes, why in this hellish planet of humans did I do that?" Coyote said to himself as he trotted down the canyon to find help. Not only had he broken his personal law about never speaking in the presence of humans, Coyote had also decided to do something his mother taught him never to do: connect with humans. "This is going to get me killed," he figured.

Hurrying down the road now with his ears up and nose searching for human smells, Coyote approached the canyon junction where he easily picked up the hated smell and heard human voices. Crawling up the canyon wall into a grove of cedars, Coyote studied the deadly hunters further up the side canyon under him. He was appalled. It was the worst possible group he could find. Seeing the guns, the camouflage clothes—Why do humans wear clothes? He wondered momentarily—the dogs in the jeeps and trucks, he realized that these guys had been hunting cougars and were packing up to leave. He'd been taught to plan carefully but he couldn't think of what to do here that would be good for the wounded Cowboy and safe for himself. Frustrated, and with the men starting to get into their vehicles and leave, he blurted out loudly, "Help! There's a wounded man back up the road!"

The hunters look around trying to see who called to them. The dogs, smelling Coyote, started barking. "Help!" Coyote shouted again and, crouching as low as he could, sneaked back along the hillside. Looking over his shoulder he saw the men discussing what to do. What he didn't realize is that one of the hunters had seen him. As Coyote moved quickly into the open between two big rocks, one of them shot at him, hit a nearby rock, and the chip flew at him and nicked his ear. That made Coyote very angry. He'd kill those guys if he could. But an unfamiliar stubbornness had risen in him and Coyote couldn't make himself quit trying to save the downed human. Trying to remain invisible in the rocky, mostly barren canyon, Coyote continued shouting at them from hiding places and kept the rescuers moving up the slick road after him.

Around a small bend they come upon Turco, who was immensely glad to see them. Reins dangling, Turco was still trying to get up the steep icy trail when the hunters arrived.

Howie Waters, tired and wanting to get home, was furious about being dragged up the snowy canyon by that invisible voice. Seeing Turco though calmed him slightly and gave him a false insight into what might be going on. Looking at Turco from behind, Howie said, "Careful guys. This pinto is all boy! He used to be wild. His owner is that crazy animal-feeding jerk, the Mexican Cowboy. He wouldn't leave his horse untended. I bet the horse ran away... I would if the Cowboy owned me." Howie grabbed the reins and tried to calm Turco.

But Turco wouldn't stop thrusting and jerking his head up toward where his owner lay semi-conscious. Suddenly one of the hunters began to understand the horse's helpful gesturing. "The horse is telling us something. His owner must be nearby and in trouble. Let's try to keep the horse still while we search for him."

"He's probably up there!" another hunter said, and pointed toward the bush where the Cowboy lay.

Howie groaned impatiently. "I doubt that very much. I think the Cowboy's back at his shabby cabin rocking on the porch. But if you believe that he's up there, you go get him," Howie said. "I'll stay with the horse."

Watching from behind a rock high on the opposite canyon wall, his ear still bleeding, Coyote saw three of the nimblest hunters climb the slippery path to find the moaning Cowboy. "We've got him!" a hunter shouted to Howie.

"Well bring him down, then. And hurry up, dammit," Howie shouted back.

"He's got broken bones and is bleeding bad," a hunter shouted.

"Well you can't fix him there. Drag him down," Howie shouted up. The hunters at the Cowboy's side looked at one another. One of them said, "You got a better idea?" The other two shook their heads. "Okay, pick him up, here we go," the first hunter said. Holding him by the belt, his boots, and his shoulders, the three men carried and dragged the crying Mexican Cowboy down the hill and put him on the road. Turco moved over him, nuzzled him, and looked up at the hunters with a very frightened expression.

"Speed it up, we haven't got all day," Howie said angrily. "You guys heave that Mexican on the horse." Turco stood still while four hunters tried to boost the flaccid Cowboy into the saddle, but the Cowboy was too heavy. Angrier still, Howie joined them and told them to hold the crying man as high as possible. Then he flung the Cowboy's broken right leg over the saddle and furiously pushed the wounded man onto the seat. He pointed to the rope and said to the guys, "Tie him down and let's get out of here." In a couple of minutes this was done and Howie started walking back down the road, leaving the others to lead the horse and wounded man after him.

One of the hunters grabbed Turco's reins and tried to turn the stallion around. Turco jerked the reins out of the guy's hands with a gesture and look that threatened an assault if the reins weren't dropped. With the Mexican Cowboy on his back Turco started trying to go up the trail again. One of the hunters yanked on him while others pushed his flank, but Turco wouldn't give up. More frustrated than ever, Howie turned around and walked back. He was about to slug the horse when one of the guys said, "Hey, I wonder if there is someone else up there."

"If you believe something that stupid why don't you go up and find out," Howie replied angrily.

"I'll do it," said Hirshy Dismas, a former Marine, and the most able of the hunters, and started to run up the steep slippery path, holding on to rocks and trees to keep from sliding or falling. Following footprints in the snow Hirshy speedily reached the cave. Having a keen sense of situation awareness after having been in combat, Hirshy instantly noticed the odd marks on the ground going into the cave. "Knees, elbows, toes and bellies?" Hirshy asked himself. "Someone's been in there. Why would the Cowboy go there?" Pretty sure he can handle whatever's in the cave, Hirshy took out his flashlight and crawled in himself.

"Is that you?" Celesto asked softly.

"Who are you?" the Marine replied, loudly.

"Shhhhhh," Celesto said. "Don't wake the bear."

"Bear?" the Marine wondered. Senses alert and very hushed now he wriggled up to the boy ankles. Could this be the missing boy?

Without thinking about what he was doing, he grabbed the boy's feet and yanked Celesto backwards.

The hibernating bear instantly started to roll on top of the boy to pin him down. No coward, Hirshy responded by scrambling into the cramped den and tring to lift the bear off the child. He could feel Celesto pushing against the bear too. The bear yawned and began to wake up. The Marine put his feet against the den wall, and his back up against the bear's chest, and with a giant heave, pushed the 250-pound black bear toward the other wall. The bear whimpered, opened a sleepy eye, saw the Marine, and was visibly frightened. She tried to back away from him. The Marine turned and with impossible effort rolled the sleepy bear on her back. "Get out of here!" he said to the boy.

Celesto was already halfway out of the cave, but he was afraid the bear would hurt his rescuer. Or that the Marine might kill his mothering protector. "I won't move until you come too," Celesto said, defiantly. "Don't hurt her."

"I don't want to hurt her. I just want us to get out of here," the Marine replied. With the bear waking and yowling and possibly growing more aggressive, the child and Marine backed out of the cave as fast as they could.

Outside again, the Marine picked up the boy and started to slip and slide down the snowy trail with him over his shoulder. "Put me down," Celesto screamed.

"Can you get down to the bottom without hurting yourself?" the Marine asked.

"I can go up and down snowy trails better than you!" Celesto said. The Marine stopped and put the boy down. Celesto looked over his shoulder, expecting to see the bear racing down the trail after them, but there was no sign of her. "She going back to sleep," Celesto thought. "It's weird, but I'll miss her."

With Hirshy leading, the two held on to each other and carefully made their way toward the bottom. "Look who I found!" the Marine shouted at his friends.

Howie saw them coming and instantly knew whom Hirshy had found up there. The Marine would be the star of media stories all over the country tomorrow. "This is a big deal and the Marine is going to take it away from me," Howie said to himself. While Celesto and Hirshy carefully took their last steps down the snowy hillside, Howie began thinking how he could make something for himself out of this mess. First he needed to get credit for finding the boy, Howie figured. And that depended on taking credit away from Hirshy and the Cowboy. A plan started to form in his head. First, I'm going to turn the Mexican Cowboy into a villain instead of a child finder. I know how to do that too.

Before Hirshy and the child joined them, Howie looked up at the other guys and said—pointing at the unconscious man tied to Turco: "I bet the Mexican Cowboy kidnapped this boy. Let's nail him. All you guys tell reporters what that child molester up there's done."

The others nodded with quirky looks on their faces. With the Marine and boy alongside him now, Howie continued, "Okay. Now let's get out of here. I've got to take the kid to his mother and tell the Sheriff about his rescue."

Now that the rescued youngster was with them, Turco was eager to leave the canyon and get the Cowboy to a hospital. He would have raced off with his wounded friend aboard if Celesto hadn't grabbed his reins and started leading the group rapidly down the snowy road. Watching from behind a tree high over the departing humans Coyote realized how gingerly the horse walked to avoid jolting and giving pain to his injured human friend. "Why would a horse slave be so kind to its master?" Coyote wondered. With no humans in sight now, Coyote trotted over to where he had dropped the turkey he'd caught for his pups. It wasn't there. One of the hunters must have found it and carried it away. "So I get shot, have a bleeding ear, and humans steal my pups' dinner. I shouldn't have done what my mother always warned me about: **Never get mixed up with humans**!" Angry with himself and repenting, Coyote trotted off toward his pups' den with an empty mouth.

Down the road Celesto proudly led Turco and the hunters back to their cars. While the men were at the parked cars discussing what to do with the horse and wounded Cowboy, Celesto dropped Turco's reins, slipped away, and walked hurriedly toward home to surprise his grieving mother. One of the men wasn't struggling to get the unconscious Mexican Cowboy off Turco and into one of their trucks to drive to a hospital. Standing apart from the other hunters, Howie Waters suddenly realized that the boy had disappeared. "Damn it. He's run away again. He's probably walking back to his mother's. If I don't catch him and drive him home I'm going to lose a lot of credit for saving him," Howie reasoned.

"I've got to run," he said to the others. "You take care of the kid and the Cowboy," and he got in his vehicle and drove away. His friends watched him go with hatred showing on their faces. And then they too noticed that the boy was gone. "Howie took him," Hirshy said. "He's going to steal the credit for this rescue from us. Well, let's get on with it. There's nothing we can do about that at the moment." Meanwhile, down the road in the fading light, Celesto heard a vehicle coming toward him from the canyon. The boy stepped back into the brush, lay down, and watched Howie drive slowly past him, head turning back and forth, obviously looking for him.

"No one's going to drive me home," he said proudly to himself.

Coming upon Mrs. Montagna's house without bringing her son, Howie decided not to stop and tell her about the rescue and how he let her boy run away again. His mind was made up to race to the Sheriff's office and tell the world he'd located the boy and left him with the other hunters while speeding off to let everyone know the boy was safe. Still, he was angry that Celesto hadn't stayed around so he could drive the lost child to his mother, get the Sheriff out there, and have pictures of him with Celesto and his mother in the background on every news broadcast and paper in America. "At least I'll be the one to tell the Sheriff the boy's been rescued. I'll take the Sheriff with me to his mother's house and get the credit that way." Coming onto the paved road at last, he gunned the car and sped toward the Sheriff's office. Howie had completely forgotten about the wounded Cowboy.

"And that's how Coyote and I met up," the Cowboy told the Priest. "I was in the hospital for weeks afterwards and only Celesto and his mother thanked me for finding the boy."

"Howie got the credit then?"

"He did. He lied to the Sheriff and the press and used his false fame to win an election and become mayor."

"Celesto and Hirshy Dismas didn't expose him?"

"Celesto tried but the Sheriff and press treated him like a fibbing child after Howie grabbed the headlines. Hirshy Dismas is a good guy who keeps stuff to himself. Howie made him deputy mayor and wouldn't let him talk about finding the kid. Last year he quit Howie and went to work for the government. I haven't seen him since."

"What happened to Turco that day? Did he get any credit?" the Priest asks the Cowboy.

"Dismas rode him to Hank Godding's stable and persuaded Hank to look after him. That's where Turco met the donkey who became his best friend. I was just getting well enough to be on my own again when we had a terrific windstorm that blew my old barn down. I had no place to put Turco, so Hank's been keeping him for me since."

"What happened to the bear?" the Priest asked next.

"She's dead now. An out-of-state-hunter got her. But she became famous after caring for the boy. Her name was Ursula. She got in the habit of bringing cubs out of the mountains and down to my place for the food I was putting out when there wasn't anything to eat up there. During a bad drought years ago Ursula came down onto the mesa with a cub looking for things to eat. Several worried mothers spotted them and called the Sheriff's office. Back then deputies and game wardens used dogs to track bears that had come onto the mesa, and they tranquilized them and hauled them back into the dry mountains. This time the scent trail went up to my house and stopped there. I invited the trackers into the kitchen for some coffee and told the guys I'd seen the bear going past the window and down the road toward Cordoba and the Bosque. Since they and a lot of others had been driving back and forth on that road they weren't surprised their dogs couldn't pick up the scent beyond my place.

"They thanked me, wished me well and drove off to check out the Bosque. After waiting half an hour to make sure they weren't coming back, I opened the kitchen door, spread out a bag of food on the flagstones in the patio—mostly vegetables—went back indoors and opened the bathroom door and told Ursula it was safe to go outside again. I led her and her curious cub onto the patio, showed them the food, and told them to eat up fast and hurry back up the way they'd come from the mountains. Ursula and I trusted each other after the thing in the cave, and in hard times she'd bring her cubs down with her for emergency feeding.

"Unfortunately she was seen doing this by many people—and most of them wanted her captured and hauled miles away from here. People around here are scared to death of bears. I told everybody who would listen that Ursula was the bear who mothered the runaway child in the snowstorm, but I couldn't do anything else to save her and I figured she was a goner until one day, when she was here, the press showed up and began taking videos and pictures of her and the cub feeding at my place—which made the national news—and next day tourists started coming to Cordoba to see the famous bear who had mothered a kid. Ranchers wanted her shot but local businessmen worked the story for all it was worth and made a lot of money out of Ursula and her cubs. I had to do the work of feeding them though and I didn't get any credit for that. But Howie helped out by keeping food coming my way. Ursula became a celebrity and the town's few animal rights folks began publicly helping me feed her. The Sheriff's department would even call to warn me when the game wardens or press were headed my way. Ursula became a celebrity and welcome visitor. And a lot of tourists rented horses to ride around on over at Hank's stable and asked to see and pat Turco when word got around he'd spotted the boy. Hank made pretty good money out of that."

"So that's the story of how you and Coyote met up?" the Priest said.

"Not quite," the Cowboy answered. "I was pretty out of it when I got banged up so badly on the hillside. I remembered the coyote talking to me but because meeting a coyote who could talk seemed so crazy I was pretty sure the bangs on my head made me dream that. I didn't trust the memory. Our real first meet up occurred when I was recovering and resting on the porch in the spiffy green rocker Celesto's mother gave me for finding her son. It was sometime in April, just after dusk, it was warm still and the stars were out. I was drinking coffee and rocking contentedly when suddenly Coyote appeared at the bottom of the steps."

"'Thank you!' I blurted out to the super-cautious beast. 'I'm really glad to see you! You saved my life. And my son's.'" Whether he could talk or not, I had to thank him when I saw him again.

"Coyote stood there for over a minute, looking at me, sniffing, his ear's sticking up. I kept still. I didn't know why he was there but I knew something was going on inside his head. It was like he'd made up his mind to do something, but now couldn't make himself do it."

"Can I get you something to eat?" I asked him. He just sat there so I got up very slowly with my hands in my pockets and told him, "Wait a second. I'll go get you some food." I went into the kitchen and brought out a chunk of raw beef I'd been saving for myself and threw it off the porch away from the coyote, then sat down again, hands in my pockets. "That's yours," I said. Coyote just sat there and I couldn't figure out what was going on in him. "Anything on your mind?" I asked.

Rocking, looking at him, waiting, I was stunned when Coyote seemed to make up his mind and suddenly said to me: "That was your cub in the cave? I didn't know humans could father a bear cub pup."

"We can't. And I didn't know Celesto was up there in Ursula's den until my horse Turco heard him crying and refused to go past him up the canyon. That's why I got off and climbed up. Turco found him. And Turco kept working all the humans who showed up there until I was rescued. Hirshy found and saved the boy."

"You didn't save the pup. You fell down the mountain instead of saving him. Why'd you do that?" Coyote asked.

"Try walking down a slippery slope on two legs like humans have to do."

"And you asked me for help," Coyote said.

"I did, and I'm grateful for what you did."

"And that got me shot," Coyote replied.

"You are the bravest and smartest coyote I know. You were the one who got the hunters to rescue me and the boy."

"Which was the dumbest thing I've done. My mother was furious when I told her."

"But it gets you my promise of lifelong help and friendship. Whatever you need, I'll try to do for you. Anything at all."

"You are asking me to trust you? I can't trust humans. My mother made that plain to me."

"She got that right... but a few humans, maybe only me, are trustworthy."

"I know another one who is," Coyote said.

"You want to tell me about him?"

"Some day, maybe. For now, feed me, and my pups. We'll see how trustworthy you are. Keep feeding the animals too. And keep your mouth shut about me. If I need more I'll tell you."

"You got a deal," I said and reached down to pat the coyote like a dog. Coyote reacted instantaneously to a human trying to grab him, backed away and disappeared into the dark warm night.

"Wow. What a meet up that was!" the Priest said. "But what happened to the meat you threw out?"

"Never had a better meet up, that's true, but meeting up with you comes close," the Cowboy said. "And the meat was gone in the morning. I don't know what animal got it."

The Priest smiled, and then a puzzled look came onto his face. "Celesto's your son?" the Priest asked. "I didn't know that."

"That's what his mom Mirella tells me. She was never married, but she had guy friends and I hooked up a few times with her. I don't know if it is really true that Celesto is my boy."

An odd thought crossed the Priest's face at that moment, but Church ethics prevented him from telling Cowboy he intended to put that question to Mrs. Montagna next time he confessed her.

"Any more questions?" the Mexican Cowboy asked, getting up to get some more food on the table and open another bottle of cheap red wine.

"Just one. Where did Turco come from?"

"Ah, that's a long story. Here's a bit of it. Turco was a mustang stallion who got snatched from a wild herd outside the Carson National Forest north of Taos. He was in a trailer with other horses being hauled to Las Cruces to be diced and minced at a pet food plant. The driver parked at a rest stop late at night to get some sleep. While he was snoring, some wild horse advocates sneaked up, opened the trailer, quietly shooed the horses down the ramp, and departed. The herd ran away and I don't know what became of the others. But one showed up at my place and was hanging around the water pump when I found him. Turns out Turco was willing to trade some of his freedom in return for a safer place to live. We got to be best friends."

"Were you the guy who turned him loose?"

"Since when do I confess to you?" the Cowboy replied with a grin.

"Alright," the Priest said. "Is that all you are going to tell me tonight?"

"Can you stand some more?"

"I suppose, but I wish I knew where this was going."

"Hang on. Stick it out. And don't believe you are going to like what I have to tell you. I'm sorry."

"You got me worried," the Priest said. "Okay. Get on with it."

"Okay," the Cowboy said looking tired and strained. "Here's how I found out where Coyote came from. You asked who made him."

The Priest's eyes open wide but he reached for a handful of snacks and didn't say anything.

Bill's Most Successful Creation

The Priest went to the bathroom and sat on the unswabbed potty thinking about why God pushed him into all these un-Christian messes he'd been putting up with since he moved in with the Mexican Cowboy. Wiping his bottom he shivered when a sinister thought popped into his mind. The Devil's got me. Is that what's going on? Feeling drained and wanting to go to sleep more than anything, he flushed, straightened his clothes, rinsed his hands, and hesitantly walked into the kitchen, where the seated Mexican Cowboy looked just as tired and wretched as the Priest felt.

"Want to quit for the night?" Father Gallapo said with a rising tone that had a note of hope in it.

"I do, but we can't quit now. You'll see why if you can keep awake. How about some coffee?"

"Please, " the Priest said with a falling tone, which didn't conceal his tiredness and fears. While the Mexican Cowboy put water on to heat and ground coffee beans, the Priest summoned his fading professional strength and said, "Okay, I've got all that you told me about the meet up with Coyote. But where did Coyote come from? Out of nowhere? Was he created by his god? Is there more to his being able to talk than I can guess?"

Pouring hot water over the ground coffee and refilling the cracked bowl with tortilla chips, the Mexican Cowboy hesitated—obviously worried about what he was going to say, then answered: "It's a complicated story and I don't know it very well. But I'll start by telling you what I know."

He sat down at the table across from the Priest, drank some coffee and began to talk reluctantly. "More than fifteen years ago I met this oddball guy who drove onto my ranch when I was still raising cattle. He was driving an ancient two-door Land Rover with California plates. He wore clothes that looked like they came from Goodwill and hadn't been cleaned. He had buckteeth, thinning hair, which he cut himself, round, thick, frameless glasses, and wore sandals without socks. Your woman friend…"

"Thelma Whitenose?" the Priest asked.

"Her. She would have scrubbed that guy's feet and clipped his toenails before letting him into her house. A crazy looking guy—his name is Bill Lockwood –but I was stunned when he talked. His voice was low and smooth, and he had an accent that was sort of English. And he was smarter than any man I ever met. I couldn't help thinking of him as a giant, though he was a dirty little squirt."

"Where'd he go to school?" the Priest asked, his interest rising.

"Mostly in California. He never could say much about himself but those of us who got to know him figured he'd studied briefly with some of the best scientists at Berkeley, Stanford, and Cal Tech. Or maybe taught them instead? I don't think he had any degrees. Or even finished high school for that matter. His brain's weird. He couldn't read classics, newspapers, or a comic book, but mathematics, lab biology, robotics, engineering, and computer science poured into him like water going over Niagara Falls and stuck in his brain like superglue."

"And he didn't like people. He could figure us out. He knew how to manipulate us, but being around us pained him every moment."

"So why did he come to see you?" the Priest asked.

"He was like a hermit trying to find a cave. Bill needed to get away from people who couldn't teach him anything. It was like you'd want to get away from a cesspool if you were swimming in it. He had money, tons of it, maybe from his patents I think, but I'm not sure about that. He liked the climate here, liked the open spaces, the night skies, the mountains and Bosque. He liked animals too and wanted to be around them. He had detailed maps of the county and wanted help picking a place to buy and live in."

"So why did he come to see you?" the Priest asked again.

"I don't know. Perhaps because I feed wild animals. Or perhaps because my ranch is close to both the mountains and Bosque. Or maybe someone told him I like animals too. I figured him out a little, could stand him more than most people would, and I didn't waste his time. I showed him some places on the map where property was available and we drove out to see several of those in his beat-up Land Rover—which was mechanically perfect. Turns out he was an incredible good driver: fast, unbelievably aware of what was around and ahead of him. It didn't take me long to realize he was a guy who never made mistakes."

"So he bought some property?"

"He did. About 2,500 acres right up against the Manzanos—even stretching into them a little ways where two ridges come together. He picked the place because there wasn't anybody out there who would be living near him. Then just a couple of weeks later trucks and earth-moving equipment from out of state were all over out there, building something that looked like both a house and a small factory. County inspectors couldn't figure out what was going on, but the place met all the rules. On the surface. They figured it might be a secret government facility. The oddest thing about the place was that it was completely off the grids. No power or phone lines, no water or sewer lines. Nothing linking it to the rest of us. Even Mayor Howie doesn't know how that place is powered."

"Why didn't the county inspectors demand more information?"

"Lots of money was suddenly flowing into Mayor Howie's and county commissioners' election funds. That may have had something to do with it."

"Is it fenced in?" the Priest asked.

"Nope. Wide-open. And yet something about the design makes people want to turn away when they get near to it. The place has psychological security. My guess is that there are several unseen automatic security layers, but how those work I can't guess. Remember. This guy is way smarter than I am."

"So what's all this about?"

"Damned if I know. Like I said, I can't figure Bill out. But I know he feeds the animals and coyotes who always hang around his place."

"Our Coyote too?"

"Yep. He came from there. He told me that Bill kept coyote dens and he was kind of like a father to pups. But he also messed with them. He'd put them to sleep, take them inside and mess with them, sometimes in ways that left them bandaged or with scars. But he didn't kill them and they liked being around him. And each new generation of pups seemed to be smarter. Somehow he messed with their genes and brains and voice boxes. I don't know this stuff but somehow he created Coyote."

"Jesus, God Almighty!" the Priest said softly, crossing himself. "And Coyote knew about this?"

"Sure. Bill was Coyote's dad, his teacher, his friend."

"So Coyote wasn't a lab animal?"

"He never thought about himself that way. He lived like a coyote outdoors, but inside he wanted to be with Bill. He enjoyed learning with him—still does for that matter—but Bill's not there anymore."

"Why's that? What happened to him?"

"He had a stroke. Coyote came over there one night—he knows how to get in the house—and found Bill semi-conscious. Coyote didn't mess around. He called for an ambulance."

"He called? How? Coyote can't use a phone."

"Sure he can. Bill made him a voice-operated media setup with controls designed to work for coyotes. The pups grew up with one too. They were online all the time. Coyote called the ambulance and set up the security system so the paramedics could get in and take Bill out—but couldn't get into the rest of the complex. They probably didn't realize how much more really's there. Most of Bill's place is hidden underground in the mountains. Coyote watched them on security video cameras arriving, being let in, checking out Bill, and taking him away, talking to them all the time and pretending he was an employee of Bill's a thousand miles away. He even showed me the videos."

"You've been there?"

"A few times. With Bill now in a rehab facility in Socorro, Coyote's looking after the place. He's doing a pretty good job of it too. But now and then he wants me to help him figure out some human thing."

"Like banking and bill paying?"

"No. That stuff is automatic at Bill's place. Even feeding the animals outside is automatic. No, Coyote needs help figuring out where to go from here and how to raise the pups that keep being born there."

"Is Bill coming back?"

"He may someday. He's not making progress. But who knows."

"Jesus, what a story! I never thought anything like this could happen. I always thought that Coyote was a freak of nature, or a creation of his god."

"Could be that he's both. Bill's part of nature too, you know. And the gods may have been using him."

"Hmmmmm. Okay. And why are you telling me all this tonight, but none of it ever before?"

"For the hard part then. I'm telling you all this because I want you to move out of here. And I want you to understand why."

The Priest's face didn't hide the shock and sadness these words caused in him. His perfect world was suddenly dissolving. He drained the rest of his coffee, looking away before turning back and saying, "Okay. Tell me why?" the Priest said, trying not to show feelings he couldn't hide.

"Okay. Here goes. It's the hardest part to talk about. None of this, by the way, I would have told you without Coyote's permission."

"Got you. Go ahead please."

"A few weeks back Coyote called and said he needed my help right away."

"Coyote phoned? Tell me again how he can he do that?"

"Like I told you, Bill set-up a voice-activated system for Coyote—and some of the pups—that is pretty well matched to coyotes' neural, sensory, and manual body systems. His words, not mine. Coyote tried to explain it to me but I'm too dumb to understand a lot of what he was saying. But when he's at Bill's, Coyote can phone and text and pass for a human, as long as he keeps the video camera off. Bill was working on a smart phone for him when he had a stroke."

"Wow! What an engineer that guy was."

"He's a genius. Coyote said the new 'phone' could sense and transmit both smell and hearing that guys like us couldn't pick up. Its touch parts were different too. Anyway, Coyote needed me there. He said some human had broken into the place and he didn't know what to do about her."

"Her?"

"Yeah. She's an escaped old lady."

"Escaped? What did she escape from? And how?"

"From a nursing home in Socorro."

"I don't get any of this."

"I didn't either at the time. But Coyote needed me. I went over to Bill's right away. It was early on a sunny morning at the start of March. Coyote had been out all night as usual. He'd killed several rabbits and put them into the outside wild-food pup-feeder, part of the automated system Bill had devised for caring for the pups."

"Coyote doesn't have to feed them himself?"

"Only if he wants to, and he does. He likes these pups, and not just because many of them are his."

"Coyote's a father?"

"Many times over. But unlike other guy coyotes, he helps to raise his kids. His pups grow up with him and keep in touch with him when they are old enough to be on their own."

"Bill turns them loose?"

"Of course. In his mind the pups aren't lab animals. They are like young kids, people he's trying to help out. In Bill's mind coyotes are more human than humans are."

"That doesn't make any sense to me. Coyotes aren't humans."

"Yes. I said that badly. But I don't know how else to put it. Bill connects with coyotes in ways he can't with people. He is trying to help coyotes become equal to humans. Maybe even superior to us."

"Wow. All this sounds like wacky science fiction. Who'd want coyotes to be superior to us?"

"You know Coyote. You know what he's like and what he can do. If this is some science fiction story, then you are part of it. The author couldn't take you out of it. Her story would be just ink on blank paper without you."

"Then tell her to write this: 'I don't know if I would have baptized and confirmed Coyote if I'd known he'd been made by a mad-genius human to replace us.'"

"And you believe that your God and Coyote's god didn't play any part in this?"

"No. You are right. I'm a mortal and I'm a fool," the Priest said, while hurriedly trying to figure out what was right and what was wrong in all this.

"Coyote knows that you are a big player in this game."

"What's the game?"

"Think about the 'Return to Eden'—what your lady friend called that political war on Joe Eden's old ranch where I got arrested and roughed up. Using animals to calm down fighting humans was really done for the good of animals, and not for us. Animals got great publicity out of their return to Eden, and it warmed lots of human hearts. The animal gods are fighting to save their species... and most of them are in danger. You and your God are a big part of this."

"I don't believe in animal gods."

"Then you don't pay attention to things your god—our God—is trying to get us to do."

"All this is beyond me." The Priest was exhausted. He looked at his watch. It was almost three in the morning. "I can't keep going," he said. "I need to put my head on a pillow, think about all you've told me, and try to make up my mind where to go from here." Without waiting for an answer, he got up, left the kitchen, and went to his room.

The Mexican Cowboy was exhausted too. Barely able to keep his eyes open, he put the leftover food away, dishes into the sink, and went to his bedroom. This isn't working out, he thought to himself. Why do I keep getting put into these messes? And why is each mess worse than the one before? As he stripped, it occurred to him that each of these messes had transformed him and others in important and memorable ways. Hunting for Celesto hooked him up with Coyote. Baptizing Coyote brought him a good friend and roommate. The furor at Eden during the flood brought lots of money into Cordoba and made Howie want to put the great Christmas celebration together for him. But I still feel like I'm being used by lots of people. And maybe by gods too.

Climbing into bed, a spark of religion rising in him made the Mexican Cowboy recall the tragic fates of so many of the early Christians. Still, what they did changed the world, he thought as he pulled the covers up to his neck. "And they paid a huge price for it," he said aloud, scratching himself all over. "Do I want to keep doing this stuff?" he asked himself. "What's in it for me?" He paused then asked himself,"What was in it for them?" Rolling onto his side, he asked aloud: "Why was I chosen to do this stuff at such a cost to me? And why were they?"

Having no answers to these vital questions, the Mexican Cowboy closed his eyes. He was falling asleep when he heard the Priest's aging knees creaking as he got down to begin his night-time prayer. As usual, he could hear clearly what the Priest was saying. Suddenly Cowboy jerked awake as he realized he was also hearing again—only for the second time—the words being put into Father Gallapo's mind by God, Jesus, and the Holy Spirit.

The Priest had asked: "Why did **You** want me to baptize and confess the Coyote if he was made by a human? And why did **You** let me believe that Coyote has a genuine soul?"

God: "**You have forgotten that I didn't order you to do anything.**"

Jesus: "*Coyote wasn't made by a human. He was made by his father and his mother.*"

Holy Spirit: "We don't control what you believe."

God: "**Where does it say in My Book that animals do not have Souls?**"

Jesus: "*I had good reasons for calling humans 'My Lambs.'*"

God: "**Humans are called *sheep* over two hundred times in the Bible.**"

Priest: "Are YOU claiming that humans and sheep are the same beings?"

Holy Spirit: "These questions are more philosophical than practical. Stop screwing around with your dumb questions. Get on with Our Work."

Tears began dripping down Father Gallapo's cheeks. "You never answer my questions," he said.

God: "**We don't prevent you from finding answers.**"

Jesus: "*Your questions may be interfering with leading lambs to salvation.*"

Holy Spirit: "Stop praying and get some sleep, Gallapo. Tomorrow's going to be hard on you."

Priest: "You can see the future?"

Holy Spirit: "Questions, questions. You Priests can't be made to do what we expect of you. You ask questions when you should be acting on Our behalf."

Priest: "We are not Your machines."

Jesus: "*Neither are Bill's coyotes.*"

God: "**If I wanted only Obedience from my creatures I would have created machines.**"

Holy Spirit: "Enough of this crap. Lights out!"

And the light in the room went dark. The Priest pried himself off his sore knees, got into bed and pulled the ratty covers over him. He was wiping tears off his cheek when he fell asleep.

The Mexican Cowboy was appalled by what he'd overheard. "The Holy Spirit sounds like a bullying boot camp sergeant," he said to himself. "I'm glad I'm not a Christian." He was almost asleep again when an angelic voice whispered into his ear, "Things will work out better for you and the Priest than you can imagine."

"I won't bet on that," the Cowboy said and dozed off.

Rising

During the remaining hours of the moonless night, animals outside and under the house were surprised by the intensity of the sleepers' noises. Restless turnings, deep snores, and unintelligible snatches of speech startled and puzzled the unseen rats, raccoons, badgers and bats who lived and hunted nearby. As the sky lightened imperceptibly, and a yellow-green glow began spreading to the east over the top of the Manzanos, robins awoke and began singing and chirping mercurially. Several even tentatively practiced mating calls they'd need to be good at in a few weeks.

Indoors the Priest and the Mexican Cowboy slept on, but more quietly now. It was almost nine-thirty when the Cowboy began slowly awakening. Looking at the click-clacking wind-up alarm clock on the dusty nightstand by his ear, he began thinking about how to handle the day's difficult issue—getting the Priest to go to Bill's house. He knew Father Gallapo was very upset over learning the truth about Coyote's origin. It wouldn't be surprising if the Priest wanted to pack up and leave for a few days to sort things out in his mind, trying to accept that he was being kicked out of a place he had come to love.

In the kitchen making breakfast, the Mexican Cowboy worked more quietly than usual, hoping to let the Priest sleep until he figured out how to persuade him to go to Bill's. With bacon frying and the huevos rancheros almost ready, he was fishing around in the refrigerator looking for fruit when he heard a chair being pulled out and Father Gallapo sitting down behind him.

"Morning," the Cowboy said. "How'd you sleep?"

"Couldn't," the Priest said. "I had too much on my mind."

"I heard you snoring."

"I heard you snoring too."

This is starting badly, the Mexican Cowboy said to himself. "Too hell with it," he thought. "I should just tell him what we've got to do."

"We've got to go to Bill's place today."

"I knew you would be asking me to do that. I don't want to—and you know that too. But I'm a Priest and I can't allow myself to run away from a huge problem one of my constituents has."

"Bill's not your constituent. Are you talking about Coyote?"

"I'm talking about you."

A flash of pleasure brightened the Cowboy's face. His friend's caring remark made him visibly quiver. Still, he said: "I don't go to your church."

"That doesn't mean I don't look after you."

Without realizing why, but feeling very warm inside himself now, the Mexican Cowboy stepped behind Father Gallapo and put his hand firmly on the Priest's shoulder.

"What else can I get you to eat?" he said sweetly.

Driving to Bill's

An hour later the Mexican Cowboy and Father Gallapo were in the Priest's sand-colored Ford pickup bouncing along a very rutted dirt road. The Cowboy was constantly giving directions because there were lots of right-angle turns at intersections of almost invisible roads dating back 140 years. Noon sun beaming in on them, windows open, passing by bunch grass and a cholla cacti with a cactus wren picking at it, the Priest asked, "Why can't Bill get a grader out here and take care of this road?"

"Bill's got reasons for everything," the Cowboy replied opaquely.

The sand-colored Ford pickup bounced all over the place as it topped a little hill, dropped down sixty feet into a dry gully, banged over a rocky flash-flood bed, and started up a steep hill on the other side. "This is crap," the Priest said. "Any road crew could grade a better road to Bill's place." Not wearing a seat belt and holding on to the open window, the Mexican Cowboy kept his mouth shut.

Topping the next ridge, Bill's little house, nestling against the purplish, mostly barren mountain chain, came into view. Father Gallapo was surprised by its appearance. "That looks like a badly painted, wooden Victorian house in Cincinnati," he said, rather accurately describing the place he was looking at. "Why couldn't Bill make a place that the rest of us out here would like to see?"

The Mexican Cowboy said nothing back.

With the dirt road straighter and smoother now, the Priest shifted into third gear and picked up speed. A pair of crows passed overhead. Discreetly, the Mexican Cowboy pulled his seat belt over his chest and latched it down. "Thanks, I was just about to tell you to do that," the Priest said. There were ten-foot high boulders along the road, and just as the speedometer needle began to touch 30 mph, a mule deer doe and her fawn sprang out from behind a giant boulder. The Priest slammed on the truck's brakes and yanked the steering wheel away from the two deer he was about to kill. The truck was headed toward another big boulder on the Cowboy's side and jarred badly when it ran off the road. Father Gallapo got it stopped just in time.

Breathing heavily, his heart racing, the Priest put the Ford into reverse and gently backed up. Getting back onto the road was surprisingly easy. The deer were still standing in the middle of the road. "Are you guys okay?" Father Gallapo asked, leaning out the window. The deer kept staring at him. "Would you mind letting me by?" he asked them. For a few seconds the mule deer didn't move. Then, apparently deciding he was no threat to them, the doe and her fawn stepped around another boulder and disappeared.

"I would have felt terrible if I'd hit them," the Priest said, starting up the road again and driving more slowly. "Hurting animals is not my thing."

Half a mile up the now smoother and straighter dirt road, Father Gallapo saw a hawk with a white breast and red bib standing by the road. As he drove by, the hawk raised one gray and brown mottled wing as though saluting him. The Priest waved back.

"Somebody just thanked me for missing those deer," he said to Cowboy.

Closer to the odd-looking house now, the road broadened out into a wide dirt parking lot with a low, badly made stone fence reaching out several yards on either side of a path leading to the house. "This is crazy," the Priest said as he parked the truck. "Why put up a fence that doesn't go anywhere?"

The close friends got out of the truck and started walking up the path toward the house, which was still almost a block away. Looking again at the house now, the Priest realized he was mistaken about its appearance when he saw it from a distance. The house was larger, more brownish than purple, and the front looked more like an adobe church than he expected. The house's few windows were tall and narrow and he couldn't see inside them as he approached.

The path widened and was covered now with widely spaced, uneven flagstones. Many different kinds of plants grew between the scattered, irregular flat pieces of red stone, some which he'd never seen before in this part of the country. Eyes down, Father Gallapo spotted a winterberry, a Kansas leadplant, some heavy sedge, Red Indian Paintbrush, bear grass, a purple clarkia flower, a speckled thimbleweed coming up between the stones, and even the tiny white flowers of pussytoes in the gaps. Staring for a moment, he thought briefly about where he'd been when he had seen these plants before. And he wondered why these plants were here. "Who is Bill's gardener?" he asked.

A couple of yards closer to the house the path turned into dry dirt again. "What's going on here?" Father Gallapo asked.

"Look over there!" the Cowboy said, pointing toward the mountains. Thirty yards away, up against several giant boulders, the Priest saw a collection of large, closely grouped statues, every one of them smeared with vivid, eye-wrenchingly odd colors. The Priest stared at each one of the art works for several moments.

Nearest to him was a neon-fuchsia statue of a nude, older woman, with ice cream cone droopy breasts. The statue reminded him of a nun he hated in third grade, now ancient and with her clothes off.

The statue of a tractor-red child holding hands with a school-bus-yellow shirtless man reminded him of a Priest he went camping with when he was twelve.

A statue of a Caribbean-green hunter, aiming his gun at the Priest, instantly reminded him of hunters at the Tea Party gathering, which had turned into a world-famous battleground of humans with widely differing views trying to dominate one another. That statue reminded him also of his disappearing Porta-Confessional, Coyote's rescuing it and being shot at, and what he and Coyote and Thelma Whitenose did to bring about the animals' peacemaking in Eden Park.

Looking at another sculpture, Father Gallapo couldn't make up his mind whether the crayola-blue complex metal abstraction vaguely reminded him of an atom, or of a virus he'd seen a picture of in an Albuquerque newspaper.

A multi-colored statue of Tsuku, the round-bellied, nearly bald Hopi Clown—whose tongue always sticks out and curls down—delighted him and roused memories of many moments of laughter and joys, long forgotten.

The figure of the little known Saint Raymond the Unborn, wearing his long, rounded red bib, made him think about the fates of so many saints, and how the Church was losing members in this country.

The statue whose presence he understood least, and which towered above all of the others, was of President Clinton hugging the second President Bush. They held each other tightly while smiling lovingly. Staring at this oddball work of art started the Priest's mind swirling with American politics, government, and people's divisive feelings.

"Bill must have had reasons for choosing each of these very odd statues," he thought. "But what are they?"

"Weird collection," he said to Cowboy as they trudged the last few steps towards the house's porch and covered entryway. Looking briefly to his right the Priest saw something so unexpected that he stopped in his tracks and stared at it for a long moment. It was a chalkboard filled with mathematical formulas, written boldly in different hands. Only a few of the formulas were familiar and known to him. For a moment, he pondered the meanings of several formulas he almost understood. "I was good in mathematics until I went to college. Now most of mathematics is beyond me," he said with regret.

"This math board is art too?" he asked the Mexican Cowboy, who again said nothing in return. "You're quiet today," the Priest said.

Stepping onto the covered porch, Father Gallapo noticed a nicely molded, comfortable, adobe *banco*, its foam cushion covered with faintly purplish wool cloth. Weary, and still jarred by his driving accident, the Priest felt a need to sit a minute and rest before continuing with this hazardous visit.

Sitting in the shade and comfortable, with a superb view of the dense green foliage along the river fourteen miles away, the Priest relaxed. He could see distant Mt. Taylor rising miles off to the northeast. "I wonder if it hates being alone?" he asked himself. Surprisingly, the porch felt like home to him. Suddenly he was glad he had come. "Why this change in me?" Father Gallapo wondered.

"If you are ready now, let's go in," the Cowboy said. The tired Priest nodded, and the Mexican Cowboy knocked on the large, dark-cedar, Santa Fe-style sculpted door. He stepped back to wait for someone to let them in.

In the Waiting Room

After two minutes of standing impatiently at the door Father Gallapo turned and said to the Cowboy, "These guys are slower than Mormons in opening the door for Priests."

There was a loud clicking sound. "That's the door being unlocked for us," the Cowboy said back to the Priest. He pressed down the thumb latch and opened the door. The Priest followed him inside. Looking around, he saw they were in a wide, short hallway with cream-colored walls and uneven red tiles on the floor. Father Gallapo was troubled that the hall's walls were bare. "Bill doesn't like pictures or decorations," he thought, as he followed the Cowboy through a door at the end of the boring hallway.

Looking around inside, the Priest was surprised by the appearance of the large 'room' they had entered. It was filled with things that interested him. There were reproductions of famous Italian pictures and statues of Saints. Intricate multi-colored wool carpets laying on the red tile floor reminded him of rugs he saw being made at Trujillo's store in Chimayo. Against the wall on his right stood shelves jammed with books regularly used by Priests. And on the wall above the bookcase there was a large mural with pictures of Ford trucks built from the 1920s to the present. One of the pictures was exactly like his pick-up. "Throw out the trucks and this room would pass for a vestry," he said to the Cowboy.

"This is Bill's waiting room. Do you like it?" the Cowboy asked, collapsing into a beat-up green rocking chair almost exactly like the one on the porch back at his ranch.

"Their stuff is good. But I wish Bill had also put up some of those small wooden pictures of Santos made by New Mexico village artists," the Priest replied.

"Then look behind you. That wall is covered with Santos art."

Turning around, Father Gallapo was instantly pleased with the religious art he saw hanging on the wall. On a small wooden board, about three times the size of a smartphone, was a folk painting of St. Michael on Feast Day. With gray, orange and black wings, and wearing a short blue gown with dark stripes and borders, the Mighty Saint held a balance scale in his right hand, a sword pointing downward in his left, and he stood in front of a snaky dragon he has just slain.

Next to the portrait of St. Michael, but on a smaller rectangular board, an unknown artist had painted St. Jude, the Apostle sent by Jesus to cure the King of Edessa from leprosy by using a circular cloth impressed with his Lord's image. St. Jude is tall and wears a long reddish and brown robe, he has a well-groomed beard and long black hair, there's a sun-like halo behind his head, and he carries a brown walking stick almost his own height.

Beside St. Jude was a much bigger, squarer image of San Pedro wearing a red and black tailored robe, bearded, with short black hair, and holding a giant key in his right hand, his left hand over his heart.

"Wonderful, wonderful, pictures. I like this room. But, okay. Now, let's move on. What are we waiting for?" the Priest asked.

"I can't say," the Cowboy replied, with a tiny smile.

"I could take that a couple of ways," the Priest said back.

Actually, the Mexican Cowboy knew why they were waiting. The Priest was being psyched-out by Bill's 'Team'—which the Cowboy knew was made up mostly of bio-computers and biorobots rather than humans. The waiting room's setup was in fact illusory and being programmed based on results accumulated from scans of the Priest's views and tastes. Everything unexpected that the Priest had experienced on his first visit to Bill's place was actually programmed to explore facets of his consciousness. Tiny sensors planted in his truck monitored eye and muscle movements and physiological responses during the rough drive and his shocking encounter with stunningly real-seeming biorobotic deer. The non-native plants, the math formulas, the statues the Priest wondered about, all were programmed to investigate different facets of his mind. As its knowledge of his mental states grew, Bill's Team was reprogramming illusion settings to confirm and expand its assessments.

Rocking contentedly while the Priest studied the waiting room, the Mexican Cowboy was happy that his own experience here had been less disconcerting than his friend's. He'd been through this before. Now fully accepted by Bill's Team, Cowboy understood that he could ask them to 'turn' the 'waiting' room into any kind of place he wanted.

In the hallway—without telling the Priest—he had mentally asked Bill's Team to make 'his' waiting room more barren, more rundown, and dirtier than the Priest's 'room.' And he'd asked them to give him a rocker that fit and would feel as good as his favorite chair. He knew he could change what he was experiencing.

To play with the system, he thought about what he'd like to see outside and turned to look out a big glass window that wasn't there a moment ago. A mix of animals was feeding on a luxurious lawn at twilight. Ursula and her cub were near and looked up and waved at him. He turned away, had a different desire, and looked out the 'window' again. Turco and the donkey were grazing, nibbling each other, bouncing around with the mustang energy Turco lost a year or two ago. The Cowboy said under his breath, "Thanks, Bill, you know what I like."

"Glad to help," Bill responded in his head. "Thanks for waiting. You know why it takes us a while to figure out your friend and conform better to his sensibilities."

"No hurry," the Cowboy said. "The show's always good here."

But—the Mexican Cowboy's contented rocking, his staring with rapture out the small dark window, stirred in the Priest's mind a suspicion that both of them were being manipulated to an incredible degree. He thought of a quick way to prove that someone was messing with his mind. The Priest carried a pocket camera, a Canon Digital Elph, in his tunic. Without any attempt to hide what he was doing he took out the camera and snapped pictures of many of the objects that so appealed to him in the waiting room. He checked the pictures to make sure they were good ones, then went over to the small window and took two more pictures of the nearby mountain. Looking at the images again, he was stunned to discover the previous picture were no longer in the camera. "This whole visit is some kind of a put-on," he thought. "Somehow Lucifer's work is being shown to me at last!" he exulted.

"You are perfectly right, this is a put-on; but not Lucifer's," a sweet voice said behind him. "We *have* been checking you out. And you are passing every test with flying colors."

Meeting the Team

Father Gallapo jerked around. Standing in the door was a human-like biorobot who instantly reminded the Priest of Maresa, his younger sister, a large devout woman who became a nun. The biobot's appearance was illusory, the Priest realized, but he couldn't help liking 'her.' Without knowing why this should be, he realized that he expected 'her' to be attentive, bright, comforting to be with, just like his sister. Looking at him with a quizzical expression, then lighting up with a warm smile—just as his sister would—the biobot walked up to him and shook his hand. "We've wanted to meet you for months," 'she' said. "I'm Emma, and I'm going to be showing you around here."

Stunned, but somehow still pleased, the Priest debated with himself briefly over how to treat a soul-less machine who could speak with him like a human. "Everyone I've met has the same question," Emma said with a smile. "I am partly biological, you know."

"That doesn't mean you have a soul," the Priest responded sharply.

"I'm not sure humans know whether they have a soul either," Emma replied. "But I wonder if you would mind postponing this discussion until after I have a chance to show you around and introduce you to more of Bill's Team? I can tell you frankly we want you to join us."

"I can't work for you. I'm a Priest and I'm not going to stop being one."

"I understand perfectly, Emma says with a wave of 'her' hand. "What I meant is we want you to collaborate with us on tasks that will be very important for you as well."

"What are they?" the Priest asked.

"Can we take that up later?" Emma asked. "We have so much to show you first."

"You are the boss here," the Priest said.

"Bill's the boss here," Emma said with a flash of pain passing over 'her' face.

"Bill's not recovering from his stroke?" the Priest asked. "I thought he was being well looked after."

"Can we go into this later?" Emma asked with a spark of impatience.

"Sure. Sorry for keeping you from doing your job," the Priest answered. Inside he realized that he was growing fond of 'Emma.' Typically he was reserved when he interacted with people he'd just met. But in the short while they had been together Emma had discreetly yet rapidly forged their relationship. 'Her' sensitivity and 'her' brevity, like his sister's, was making him like and trust 'her' more than he understood it was possible. "These guys are very good at running a put-on," he said to himself.

"That's true," Emma said with a grin. "But you'll soon discover our faults."

"If I hadn't liked you from the start, would you send in another robot, or could you change before my eyes?"

"We are pretty good at manipulating human perception," Emma said. "Watch." Slowly, Emma's appearance changed as he watched. She became leaner. Her dress turned vividly blue, as did her eyes. Her hands and arms changed into a position like the one women use when they hold an infant. Her voice softened, became Holy and assuring. "Who do I remind you of now?" Emma asked.

"The Virgin Mary, of course," Father Gallapo answered.

"Now watch" Emma said, her voice more sharp-tongued as 'she' became more rough-faced, like his cranky mother.

"I'm glad you faked being my sister," the Priest said. "My mother and I had our problems."

"I know," Emma said, widening, warming and smiling again, looking like Father Gallapo's favorite sister once more. "Ordinarily we would never make such abrupt transformations in front of humans. But we wanted to show you what we can do. If things work out we will have no secrets from you."

"I'll have secrets from you," the Priest said bluntly.

"Of course you will," Emma replied. "You can tell no one what your parishioners confess to you."

"You guys can read my mind," the Priest said.

"And we want you to read ours," Emma replied. "Now, let's see what this place is really all about." Emma motioned the Cowboy to get up, who had been watching this exchange attentively. "I have so much to show you. Let's begin with your Teacher."

'She' went to the door and someone handed 'her' a small object that looked like a smart-phone without a screen that had been made into a necklace. Emma slipped the Teacher over Father Gallapo's neck saying, "Pay no attention to this. It will be working with you, teaching you, helping you understand and get to know us better as weeks go by. But you won't be conscious of what it is doing unless you ask it deliberate questions, which it will always try to answer. Take your Teacher off when you shower or go to bed. Getting wet won't hurt it but it will be in the way when you wash your neck."

"I don't do that very much," the Priest said, with a cocked eyebrow. Emma winced, like his sister would.

"Often in the first weeks you'll 'hear' fragments of what your Teacher is helping you to learn. That will be annoying at first, but you'll get used to it."

"I don't know about that," Father Gallapo said. "Jesus, the Holy Spirit, and God are pumping thoughts into my head all the time. I have never gotten used to this."

"They have more important things to teach you," Emma replied.

"They are lousy teachers," the Priest answered back.

Suddenly a startled look swiped across his face. He turned and looked oddly at his friend the Mexican Cowboy. "There's stuff getting dumped into my head." Looking like he was being taken over, the Priest's mouth opened and he began droning, "...*subjects include designs of bio-material, synthesis biology, synthetic genes, binding proteins made and connected, and neuroinformatics....*"

"You are smarter than I am," the Cowboy said. "They know there is no way to teach me any of that stuff."

"Not true," Emma replied to the Cowboy. "We needed to teach you different things and you learned it all. Now, follow me please," Emma said, walking toward an open door opposite the wall with the Ford truck pictures on it.

"Get rid of those," said the Priest. He was pleased when they vanished.

A Kiss in the Dormitory

Emma led the way down a wide hall past many closed doors. The building was far larger than it appeared from the outside and the Priest began to suspect that it had many underground levels, and probably extended under the mountain as well.

"I want to show you the Dormitory first," Emma said, opening a very wide door. The Priest stepped through the doorway and was instantly greeted by seven biobots who stood and applauded him as he walked in. "These are some of Bill's 'People,'" Emma said. Father Gallapo looked around the huge room. The biobots applauding him had no distinguishing features, and the uniform smiles on their faces struck him as mechanical. Turning his head and glancing in different directions, he saw tables set with silverware and napkins, water pitchers, something that looked like a toilet, a sink, towels, and even a tier of bunk beds.

Emma began to lecture him. "Bill calls his biorobots 'Friends,' 'Folks,' 'People.' He gave us names and wants us to be likable, sensitive, and kind, as well as efficient. We are partially alive, you know. We even have a tiny evolving social culture. That's why we live together and you see the water pitchers, the toilet and places to eat and rest. But we don't have much in the way of brains. We operate with the guidance of a connected system of powerful biobrains Bill designed, which are aware of far more than we need to know. Together we make up Bill's Team."

'She' stopped for a moment and looked at the Priest, who was shaking his head sideways and looking pained. He was distracted from hearing what Emma was saying by word fragments popping into his mind: "...*structures of protein build helical protein scaffolds that collect binders..., fusion peptides..., it is necessary to identify placements for side chains...*"

The Priest started to apologize to her when she interrupted him and said, "Don't, please. We understand what's going on inside your head. Let's go into another room."

The Mexican Cowboy waved goodbye to the biobots as he followed his friend out of the Dormitory. He couldn't help, though, stopping for a moment at the door. Taking off his hat, he bowed to the 'bots. Several of Bill's 'People' ran over and shook his hand and wished him well. One 'bot, turning vaguely feminine, even gave him a hug and a smack on his cheek. "Like 'em," he thought. He blushed as he put his hat back on and closed the door behind him. He hurried down the long, wide hall to catch up with his friend, who followed Emma into a large room.

A Shoot-Up in the Control Room

Walking through a steel door obviously built for security purposes, the Cowboy saw Father Gallapo looking around him in what the Cowboy just heard Emma call the 'Control Room.'"This is where all our Team's members are made to work together," she was saying. The room did seem more sterile and formal than the Dormitory did, but Father Gallapo didn't see the screens, keyboards, overhead monitors, speakers, and tons of other equipment he was used to seeing in 'control rooms' on TV.

"But it is all here. Really," Emma said to him, apparently reading his mind. "I'll show you both how it works. Father Gallapo, please come up with a few questions, and let's see if the Team can get answers for you here."

"All right," the Priest said, after thinking a moment to come up with something tough. "Show me what Thelma Whitenose is doing at this moment."

Emma nodded. 'She' took his hand and led him to a 1950s wooden university-style chair, with legs like ladders, curved backrest, and solidly attached padded arm rests, which had just appeared in the Control Room. Turning him and pushing him gently into the chair Emma said, "Hold on tight," and stepped away

Instantly the chair seemed to rocket out through the roof that was no longer there.

Feeling the fierce acceleration and wind buffeting his face, the Priest gritted his teeth and clenched fingers tightly around the armrests, scared he might fall off. Looking downward and back, he could see Bill's place dwindling below him as the chair arced out toward Cordoba. Then, hurtling downward in an accelerating free fall, the weightless Priest cursed himself for blundering today so badly. "I'm going to die," he thought as he plunged.

He was asking forgiveness from God when the chair slammed onto the top of a kids' slide on a little mound at the city's children playground. Stunned by what just happened, his heart racing, Father Gallapo looked down and saw his bloodless white hands still clenching the chair's armrests tightly. Trying to relax, with the chair teetering under him, he let go and looked around. Timidly leaning over and looking down on his left side, he was amazed to see Thelma beneath the slide talking with a mother from his Cordoba church who brought her two young children to the city's tiny park to play. The Priest was about to climb down from his perch and say hello to them when the chair rocketed up again, arced through the sky, and smacked back onto the Control Room floor in the same position it had been in before it took off. The Priest was stunned. He also felt sorry he couldn't speak with Thelma.

"Why didn't you let me talk with her?" he asked Emma.

"You weren't there," 'she' replied. "But Thelma was where you saw her. We gave you the experience of actually going to see what she was doing. But you were really here the whole time."

"That's true," the Mexican Cowboy said. "You were here, but I could see on your face and body all the movements you were experiencing. They showed me the park images you were seeing on a screen that popped up then vanished. I'm damned if I'd ever let them rocket me over to Cordoba and back."

"We wouldn't do that to you!" Emma said. "But we did want to give Father Gallapo a memorable thrill. And when he asks Ms. Whitenose where she was today, he'll learn that he was really seeing her."

The Priest, looking shocked still, suddenly put fingers in his ears.

"What are you hearing?" Emma asked him.

"...*Compute protein backbone...*, *make improvements over starting designs....*, *create diversity in cells..., design proteins....*" The Priest repeated to 'her.' "Urk. Stop pouring this stuff into my head, will you." Emma looked stern and shook her head.

"Any other questions you want us to answer for you?" she asked.

"God, no! I'll be suffering from my Thelma question for days."

"No you won't," Emma said, slipping her arm around him like his sister used to do. "This was an experience you'll relish and never forget."

"I doubt it," Father Gallapo said. "What else do you want to show us?"

"The Nursery," Emma said. "I know that **you** love to go there," she said, pointing at the Cowboy.

"Just about my favorite place on the planet," the Cowboy replied.

"Lead the way then," Emma said. Motioning them to follow, the Cowboy led them out of the Control Room and down a staircase.

The Filthy Nursery

Two minutes later Emma and the Priest were following the Cowboy into an underground commuter station. Dark tunnels extended in both directions but there were no tracks. Looking overhead, the Priest saw a ceiling rail. Emma held each of their hands tightly as a little tramcar, hanging from the overhead rail, silently pulled up to them. Emma opened the door and the three of them climbed in. The tram speeded down the widening and narrowing tunnel, making sharp turns at intersections of tunnels. Riding face to face, knees touching, Emma said, "This used to be a large mine in the mountain east of the house." Father Gallapo struggled to listen to 'her' as she went on about how Bill's Team turned the mine into a work area and a place to raise coyotes. The Priest's head was getting over-packed with new information. He had to pinch his wrist to pay attention to what 'she' was saying. Suddenly, with pain, his head jerked back and he could not stop himself from repeating parts of what was being pumped into his brain: "..*epigenetic robotics.., metaphors from neural and developmental psychology..., autonomous mental development like humans have.., artificial emotions, self-motivation, and self-organization.....*"

The little tram glided to a halt at a small stop. There were several closed doors around them in the tunnel. They got out and the tram vanished down the dark tunnel as Emma opened a door and led them into what 'she' called the 'Dressing Room.'" The place stank and the light was dim inside the room. Dark, foul-smelling clothes hung on hooks on two of the walls. "Put these on, please," Emma said, choosing the right-sized head-to-toe suit for each of them. "This is what visitors have to wear before they can go into the Nursery."

"These stink. Don't you ever wash them?" the Priest asked Emma as he crawled into a suit that covered every part of him but his eyes.

"They smell good to pups," Emma said. "Now, put these glasses on," 'she' said, handing each of them a pair of wrap-around sunglasses with dark, purplish lenses.

"I can't see a thing with these on," the Priest complained.

"You will in a minute," Emma replied. 'She' pressed a switch and the dim overhead lights went out. Other lights turned on which had a spectrum that could only be seen with the glasses they'd put on. The room was faintly visible again now. "We don't want the pups to know humans are here. They can't see this light," Emma said.

'She' told them to be quiet and, opening a door in the dressing room, led them into a very dark room with two chairs facing a small blank window. "The window is smooth on our side, but rock-shaped on theirs," Emma whispered. "They won't be able to see or hear us." Settling them into the chairs 'she' waited until they were still and ready. Then 'she' signaled the House-Team—the part of the bio-brain that controlled house activities—to 'open' the window.

Lights coyotes cannot see switched on inside the den where five-week old pups were playing, fighting, feeding, throwing up, and emptying their bladders and digestive tracks. The pups—there were nine of them—had different mixes of fur color: brown, yellowish, patches of gray. Their heads were wide, snouts short; they had saggy bellies and small beady eyes. The pups were whining, snapping, yapping and playing. One lay with her back draped over a small rock, front paws in the air. Another pup squirmed on top of its brother, chewing his throat while the bottom pup had its ear in his mouth. Several of them had small bandages on their backs, necks and heads.

The pups' mother was barely visible two yards away, curled up and licking herself.

"I'm going to switch on the smell sensor," Emma whispered. A moment later strong odors from the den wafted up the Cowboy's and Priest's noses.

The Priest squirmed in his chair. He didn't like what he was being made to observe. The Nursery was a dark, filthy, foul-smelling den, which disgusted the childless Priest, because he believed infants should be raised in sanitary circumstances.

But the Cowboy was watching with obvious love and appreciation, which flowed out of him like odors from the Nursery. "That guy is part coyote," the Priest thought.

"Look!" the Cowboy whispered loudly. "There's Coyote bringing food to his pups." The Priest leaned toward the window and saw Coyote squirming into the den through its narrow opening, carrying a large dead hare in his mouth, its ears dragging on the rough den floor. Coyote dropped the hare and backed away as the pups swarmed over their meal. They were ripping at it, snarling and snapping at each other when their mother pushed them aside, lay down, turned the hare on its side, and with a paw on the rabbit to keep it in place, began chewing open its belly. The three smallest pups moved to her side and began suckling their mother. The most aggressive pups were trying to work around their mother and get their teeth into the hare. The Priest hated seeing them chew on its ears, neck and rump. Coyote watched for a minute too, then he turned and began crawling out of the den.

"Time to leave," Emma whispered. With the Cowboy staring longingly through it, the window slowly blanked out. He joined the others silently backing away. Led back into the dressing room and the Nursery door closed, goggles off, lights on again, they stripped off the protective gear.

"That place is filthy! Why in hell don't you guys clean it up? You ought to give that mother and her puppies a nice clean room to grow up in," the Priest complained.

"Whoa. Easy," the Cowboy replied before Emma could answer. "You were in the coyote world then. They don't like to live like we do."

"That's very true," said Emma. "And important too. You were looking into a real den, dug by coyotes centuries ago here in the mountains about half a mile east of the house. Bill wants coyotes to live normal lives."

"Why the bandages then?" the Priest responded with a touch of angry defiance.

"Bill is helping them to evolve," Emma said gently, with a small turned-up smile that reminded the Priest of how his Jesuit teacher had answered and dealt with students' insolent, Belief-challenging questions.

Before the Priest could reply, his eyes snapped shut, his chin dropped onto his chest, his face jerked into a frozen strained expression, and his hands flew over his ears again.

He helplessly mouthed the concepts pouring into his brain. "...*key are ways to promote task non-specificity, environmental openness, sensors for raw signals, and how to do incremental processing—acquiring new skills and values –linked with evolutionary robotics....*"

Emma reached over and touched him gently, warmly, gave him a small hug, waited patiently until the seizure passed, then led them to another tunnel and into another tram car. Whirling down the well-lighted tunnel, she held the Priest's hand until he relaxed. Father Gallapo leaned back on the little seat he and the Cowboy shared.

"God! That was terrible. What are you guys doing to me?" he said like a prisoner being tortured.

"Educating you," Emma responded gently, but with a firm look and a teacher's determined tone.

"Who gave you that right?" Father Gallapo demanded to know.

"Bill's in charge here."

"If this keeps up I'm going away and will have nothing to do with him."

"Fine," Emma said. "You do that after you leave. But now, please let me show you the Classden."

"How much more do I have to put up with?" the Priest groaned.

"About another hour," Emma said with a softer look on 'her' face. "Now behave. We have important things to do together."

The Priest closed his eyes and let the mine's cool air slam into his face and take away some of the pain he was feeling. "Have I ever had it worse?" he asked himself.

Mentally flashing back over bad things that had happened to him in his many years of life, the tram slowed and gently stopped.

"All out, please," Emma said, and led them toward a stairway.

The Human in the Classden

Two minutes later, after they had walked down a long hallway, they found themselves sitting in another viewing room. The glass looked as if it might be two-way. Emma turned the sound and smeller on and began talking about educating groups of adolescent coyotes like ones they saw studying in the Classden. These cubs were nearly grown. They had yellowish eyes, mixes of brown, gray, and tan fur, lean bodies atop very long thin legs, downward curving bushy tails, and all of them appeared to be energetic, eager, happy learners. Their Classden was a very large, but still den-like space. A few 'students' were eating raw food. One was sleeping. Three others were playing and fighting. "Young coyotes have to be allowed to do things that are in their nature," Emma remarked.

The Classden's floor was rough and mesa-like, with three-foot high boulders and real plants. In many places the Priest spotted small, very odd furry objects with screens, which must be learning tools he thought. Several young coyotes were sitting or stretched out in front of these, staring intently, sniffing rapidly, and making mixes of sounds he could not understand. The students had intense, concentrating looks on their faces. Emma touched a tiny switch and odd sounds like growls, clicks, snarls, and howls came from invisible speakers, filling their ears with the furry little teachers' 'voices' on the other side of the window. Emma touched another switch and a mix of intense and very faint smells were blown past the watchers' noses. Artificial noses on the front of the furry teaching tools were sniffing furiously, while something like an artificial gland emitted odors necessary for coyote 'talk.'"That's the 'coyote communication mode' you perceive," Emma said. "Because it isn't just sounds, we can't call it 'language.'

There were biobots also in the Classden. The Priest was stunned when two coyote-like female biobots, four legged and furry, with tails, snouts, and upright ears, and carrying furry Teachers in their mouths, appeared from behind the mounds in the back of the Classden. The 'bots put the Teachers down and separated three students who were playfully fighting. With resigned expressions, the lively pups sat down in front of their furry Teachers—one with an arching tail—and began studying.

"Those 'bots are my People," Emma was saying. "They shepherd, separate and pair, teach and control the pack of pups inside the Classden. They can become either a male or a female coyote teacher," Emma told them, pointing at the biobot coyotes with a look of pride. "Coyotes couldn't evolve rapidly without us."

"Are these Coyote's pups?" the Cowboy asked.

"The students you are watching are two litters from moms with different mates who actually shared a den," Emma said proudly.

"I thought coyote moms always had a den to themselves," the Priest said.

"That's true," Emma replied gently. "Bill is gradually changing coyote culture."

"Does he have any right to do that?" the Priest demanded back.

"That's for Bill to answer," Emma replied. "You can ask him when you see him."

"Are we going to meet up with him today?" the Priest asked warily.

"Sort of," the Mexican Cowboy said over Emma's silence.

"Can those students talk to us like Coyote can?" the Priest asked.

"Only two in there are able to speak some Human. But the others are studying both coyote and human psychology and history. And all the students are learning to protect themselves and other coyotes," Emma said.

As the Priest watched a little fight broke out between two snarling adolescents on the backside of the room. The coyote-like biobot teachers instantly separated them, made them lie down on their backs with legs in the air, and appeared to be telling them they would be made to hold that submissive position for a minute or two now, and longer if they fought in the classroom again.

"I thought coyote males keep apart and do fight if they get close to one another," the Priest said. "Why are you stopping them?"

"That's so," Emma replied. "Bill is shaping a new form of coyote society."

"Trying to turn them into humans, I bet," Father Gallapo said back.

"No," Emma replied with a serious expression on 'her' face. "He's trying to help them turn into a species that can live with humans and still be themselves."

"Sounds impossible to me," Father Gallapo responded.

"You will learn," Emma said with a stern expression. "Now, before we meet Bill, I want to show you one last place that is as important as any you've seen. We call it 'the Lab.'" Emma said.

As they left the Classden, the Mexican Cowboy looked over his shoulder. A tall, older human woman, gray haired with a wrinkled face, and who looked brainy, had just come into the room carrying snacks for the students. Several coyotes stopped what they were doing and trotted over to her. "Oh Lord, there's Cece," the Cowboy said, as he hurried after Emma and the Priest.

Learning In the Lab

The Cowboy followed his friend and Emma down a long flight of stairs to a different tram station. A passenger car with a dozen seats was waiting for them. Coupled behind it were two long freight trams, which biobots were finishing loading with crates, bottles, laboratory tools and instruments, and many other things the Cowboy didn't recognize. Going aboard, he took a seat behind the others. At the back of the car were several more faceless 'bots, quiet and motionless—until he turned around to look at them. Coming 'alive' instantly, smiles appeared on their faces, their heads bobbed, and they waved and said, "Hi" and, "Hello," and, "Hey, it is good to see you again," to him. Smiling back at them, he waved and touched his hat brim just as the door closed. The tram began to accelerate silently.

Suddenly the Priest jerked and put his hands over his ears again. A sentence fragment dribbled out of his clamped mouth, "...*learning and playing games which increase both crystallized and fluid intelligence, ...reverse engineer—not biobrains—but computer science.*" Emma gave him a hug and stroked the back of his head until the Teacher around his neck shut itself off.

When Father Gallapo was himself again, Emma turned sideways in the seat in front of the Cowboy and began lecturing at them like a tour guide once more. "I'm going to take you quickly through the Lab now," 'she' said. "It consists of many rooms underground where research is being done in bio-syntheses, bio-engineering, and iosynthesis fields. Humans do work there as well as my Folks, but you won't see any of them today. Also, many of the Lab's units are maintained sterile and we aren't allowed to go into these."

"I don't want to visit any labs," the Priest said, looking much worn.

"We'll only have one more stop and then you can leave," Emma said to him.

Ignoring them, staring out the window at the unlighted and very rough mine tunnel passing by him, the Mexican Cowboy noted that this underground tram trip was taking much longer than the others. "Probably we are crossing under the mountains," he reasoned. "I wonder if Bill's Team's had a secret access built on the eastern side."

"We have," Emma said to him, obviously reading his thoughts.

"Thanks. I know I don't have to open my mouth around you," he replied.

The tram finally slowed, and the Cowboy looked out and saw they were in a wide cavern and were passing several large freight elevators with biobots waiting to unload the tramcars behind him. The tram stopped without a jerk, the door opened, and Emma and the Priest left. Considerate, as he always tried to be with non-humans, the Cowboy stopped by the door and politely motioned the 'bots to precede him out. "Thanks. No. We are going two more stops," one said, a grateful expression appearing on 'his' face. The Cowboy lowered his chin an inch, touched his hat's brim, then stepped out and spotted Emma, and the obviously impatient Priest, waiting for him in an elevator. The Cowboy went into it, the elevator rose for almost twenty seconds, the door opened and the three of them walked into a small circular room with corridors leading off in several directions. Emma immediately led them down one of the corridors.

For the next twenty minutes the lecturing Emma guided the Cowboy and the Priest in and out of a mix of research labs, which Emma insisted were, at a minimum, the equivalent of labs at MIT, Stanford, Carnegie Tech, and the University of Washington. The 'bots they stopped to watch were busily setting up experiments, recording observations, working with experimental animals, doing imaging brain studies, and hundreds of other things that neither Priest nor Cowboy made sense of. Stopping finally in the smallest, most disorganized lab room, Emma explained proudly that it was here, nine years back, that Bill got his first designed biobrain built and operating. "That was a day when he actually drank a glass of wine. You know Bill doesn't usually like to celebrate," 'she' said.

Leading 'her' guests into a small theater now, Emma told them they were going to watch a short video about Bill's methods of educating his growing biobrain over many years. "This won't be conventional computer programming," she boasted proudly.

After they sat down in comfortable chairs, Bill appeared abruptly on the large screen before them. "He *is* a dirty little squirt," the Priest whispered to his friend. Bill was dialoguing with a 'bot. "Is *that* the brain?" he asked Emma sarcastically.

"No," Emma said. "It is just a 'bot which Our Biobrain is controlling. But notice, Bill is actually talking back and forth with it. He designed biobots and paired them with Our Biobrain partly because it is easier for a human to interact with a biobot than with one of your computers," Emma said. Returning to lecture mode, she continued: "Two years back, at the time this video was made, Our Brain already had access to everything on the web. And to much else besides. But Our Brain then was still like one of your infants, developing and learning. Just as children learn by going back and forth with other humans, dialoguing with other intelligent and aware beings has been critical for Our Biobrain's cognitive expansion."

"And it is actually Our Biobrain we are listening too, not Emma," the Priest whispered to the Cowboy. A brighter look came over his face and he continued, "You know, I think they've actually stopped running that Teacher so I can pay attention here. It's a relief not to have noise I can't make go away bursting inside my head."

The Cowboy looked at his friend and was surprised to see how intently now Father Gallapo was focusing on the video. "Gallapo's finally getting into this stuff," he thought. Looking at the video again, the Cowboy was surprised by what Bill was shown doing now with his biobrain. Bill and the 'bot were telling jokes back and forth and laughing and making faces. In the clip that followed, politics was the important topic. Bill and the 'bot discussed the formative writings of Americans Hamilton and Madison, and the causes and consequences of the German election which made Adolf Hitler Chancellor.

"So do you advocate democracy?" the 'bot asked Bill.

"What do *you* think is good and bad about democratic forms of government?" Bill replied.

Before the watchers could learn the Brain's views, a different clip began. Bill and the 'bot were now discussing sex—and not simply the mechanics of reproduction. Sexual feelings were the topic. This time the biobrain's answers to Bill's questions were hesitant, even stumbling. With an odd grin on his face, Bill turned to the camera and said, "Sex is a difficult topic for my biobrain's understanding since it doesn't YET have experiential feelings. It knows how to fake feelings, though. But I won't let it get away with that. In a year or two it will be able to actually feel what humans are feeling. Accomplishing this will be one of my greatest breakthroughs."

In the next clip, religion was the topic Bill explored with his student. After several minutes of discussing Buddhism and its sects, Bill turned toward the camera once more and said: "Religion is important to computer science, because it means so much to humans. I don't want my creations to be atheists or believers. I want rather my biobrain to sympathetically understand everything humans have in their minds. And more. Today we are exploring the Brain's reactions to agnosticism and belief, in all of history's religions."

The clips stopped and the room lightened again. Emma stood up and said to them, "We want to show you one more clip before we visit the last place today. When he was coming up with ideas and shaping those, Bill used to make videos of himself thinking out loud. He didn't like to write notes. Here is just one of thousands of clips we have of Bill thinking out loud."

The room darkened and Bill appeared on the giant screen again. He was sitting in a junky, cramped room, talking to himself, pausing often. "This video was shot in Bill's 'Crib,' the room where he did most of his thinking," Emma said. "That will be the last stop on your visit this time."

Coyote looked at his friend, expecting him to complain about not getting out of Bill's house after they left the Lab. But instead a much more alert Father Gallapo was focusing intently on what Bill was saying. Obviously this clip was chosen to appeal to him. "Shhhhh, let's listen to him," the Priest whispered.

The Mexican Cowboy tried to pay attention, but Bill's out-loud thoughts seemed like religious garbage to him. As the Cowboy tuned out, Bill mused: "Should we try putting different 'natures' and appearances on our house 'bots to give them temporary identities which work for each visitor? And should we do this for visitors whose beliefs are patently opposite to ours? My goal wouldn't be to deceive visitors but to make their visits enjoyable and memorable. Still, do I want to support views I don't agree with? If so, what do we need to do to figure out what such visitors would like?"

"Now you see what Bill's been doing to me," the Priest whispered.

In the next clip Bill had a profound expression on his face as he said, "I have just realized that I have become a Creator. I never wanted to be God-like." He paused for a couple of seconds, and then said with a wry smile, "I wonder whether God actually did either." Another pause. Then with a look the Cowboy had never seen on Bill's face he said, "Could God have been a guy like me? Did he come up with all this religious stuff, all these myths, this social structure... to make his creatures function well with each other?" There was another pause while the thinking Bill stared into space for a few seconds, then Bill continued. "I just realized that making creatures work well together is harder than creating creatures, particularly if our creations have individual minds, some freedom, and feelings too. Especially if they are in cultures that evolve."

The video stopped and Emma stood up and said with a pained tone: "Bill was thinking those thoughts, wrestling with them, when he had his stroke. He had come upon the hardest part of his work—making the system he was creating work with itself and with the outside world. All right, Friends. Let's go to the Crib now." The Priest and Cowboy got up and followed her out the door. Father Gallapo looked as though he felt a little sad over not seeing more of Bill's videos.

"Bill was good at teaching," the Cowboy thought.

Collapse in the Crib

After another long sit on the tram they rode an elevator up into the house. Emma led her visitors into the crowded, junky room they'd seen in the last video clips. Plainly, it had never been cleaned or straightened by members of Bill's 'Team.' Emma said: "This is the Crib, the place where Bill lived and spent most of his free time. You are the first outsiders ever to be allowed in here." She led the Priest and the Cowboy to a table, littered with Bill's things, and asked them to sit down. A moment later a 'bot server, wearing a red apron, entered the Crib carrying a tray loaded with food and drinks. Emma pushed Bill's things enough away from her guests to make room for their plates and cups.

Father Gallapo got a waffle with maple syrup, sweet whipped cream, and a maraschino cherry on top. Also on his huge plate were several pieces of crisp bacon and two eggs sunny-side up. The 'bot server put a large teapot filled with hot water onto the table, along with several metal holders filled with oolong and other teas. Looking and savoring, the Priest announced: "This is my favorite breakfast! I'm sick of eating Mexican food." Without another word he began eating. Satisfaction streamed out of him.

A moment later the Priest was holding his hands to his head again. "...*link to biobrain who can't 'speak down'...., ... that is, who knows current research but struggles to explain what it knows to uninformed humans and coyotes; when first tried, its speech was episodic, jerky...*" "Damn I hate this teaching," the Priest said.

The Mexican Cowboy was served two burritos on a piece of wax paper. A small bowl of green chile dip was put beside them, with a cup of strong coffee without cream. "Food I like," was all he said, picking up and dipping a burrito.

Emma stood beside them for ten minutes while they ate and drank. Without being asked, the 'bot server with the red apron brought another large cup of coffee for the Cowboy. As the server left, Emma abruptly followed him to the Crib's door. 'She' turned to them and said, "Bill will be with you in a moment," and she was gone.

"How can Bill be 'with us' when he's in a nursing home in Socorro?" the Cowboy asked.

"That's a good question," a three-dimensional image of a healthy and mentally tough Bill said, suddenly appearing before them. "Drink your tea and coffee and I'll answer it." A 'chair' appeared a few feet away from them and 'Bill' walked over to it and sat down. "Now that we are together and comfortable, do you have any questions?"

"Are the biobots alive?" the Mexican Cowboy blurted.

"If your bio-Team is alive, does it have a soul?" the Priest asked an instant later.

Bill said: "Learn some science, guys. The elementary distinction between being alive/not being alive is a Stone Age belief. You (poking a finger at the MC and Priest) are both combinations of alive and never-alive parts. Technically you are both."

"What parts of me aren't alive?" the Priest asked himself. Out loud he asked, "But the soul?"

Starting to lecture like a professor, Bill said, "The principal element of souls is your awareness. What you call machines—computers say—are becoming conscious too. If the conscious entity is a 'soul' in your religion-philosophy, how can a biobeing, far more aware than we are, not be said to have a 'soul' also?"

"But we make them," the Priest said with a defensive tone.

Bill replied sternly, "They are creating themselves now—with our help. If we are your god's creatures, they are ours."

This topic troubled the Priest more than anything he'd ever encountered. Seeing the intense pained expressions crossing his face, 'Bill' realized what his student was feeling and said, "Friend Father, you are a linesman in this game, a great one too. But there's a coach over you who decides what you must believe and try to do. The Church will wrestle with these profound issues for you and come up with the right answers. All in good time."

Disgusted with this answer, Father Gallapo decided to change topics. "Are you guys turning coyotes into humans?" he asked Bill.

"Not at all, Father," Bill replied. "We are helping coyotes' brains to evolve—for their sake, not yours. Our friend the Mexican Cowboy knows I want to keep humans from wiping out other mammal species. He's a mammaler like me, you know. Instead of trying to change humans or their behaviors the Team here is trying to help make endangered species more able to cope with this planet's dominant species—humans."

"Okay, answer me this," the Priest said. "How does Coyote manage with a smaller brain? He's tied into your biobrain? He's a slave?"

"No more than we are," Bill responded. "It's a bit like using a good computer translator to help you understand someone speaking a language you don't know. The biobrain translates English into Coyote language for him and a chip in his bio-voicebox translates what he wants to say into perfect English. But his Teacher has been teaching him to genuinely understand English since he stopped nursing too."

Not liking this answer much better, the Priest asked another question. "The Thing in the Sky event, which both Coyote and the Cowboy here told me about, seems to have taken place over your house here. Were those gods and their soccer game biobrain-made projections?"

"No, Father. I had nothing to do with it. But I do wonder if I can teach the gods to play another game." Bill replied.

The Priest smiled at that and the Cowboy giggled, and then said: "He means it, you know."

"What's all this about then?

"About six months ago I finally figured out how to give my biobrain complete access to my own brain. Doing this was necessary to give the biobrain its own consciousness. I won't go into technical matters here, but the brain couldn't become conscious without downloading a human. I am actually partly Bill," the image said. "Now, we need to talk about why you're here."

"So why did you bring me here?" Father Gallapo asked.

"Because our Team needs your help."

"What do you want me to do for you?"

"To help us connect with your God."

"I thought you were an atheist."

"I am a non-believer, but that's not the same thing. Wherever Reality goes I want to go, study and understand."

"So, go to Catholic school."

"Catholic school is only a part of Reality.   And you, Good Father, will be our ambassador to your God."

"Seriously, if you need to be confessed and baptized Bill, I'll be very pleased to be your Priest."

"I am Jewish."

"Okay. But then I don't get what you are trying to tell me."

"Give it time, Father. You will get it—and soon. I promise."

"Why did you choose me?"

"Because you are smart enough to understand a little about the iosynthesis and bioengineering being done here. And because your mind is open."

"That's crazy. I've understood almost nothing you've shown and been trying to teach me."

"Actually, we can see and measure what's going on in your cognitive system. You are learning surprisingly well."

"You can't use praise to get me to support you."

"Let's get this over with, Father. You are tired and need to be out of here. We need you to support the Mexican Cowboy in what he is about to do. It will be critical for every being on this planet."

"What is it you think I'm about to do?" the Cowboy demanded.

"You'll know soon enough."

"Are we talking just about what's good for humans?" Cowboy asked. "After years of abuse by humans I'm not going to lift a finger to help them."

"Hush. This will be best for animals too."

"So this is the biobrain we are talking to, not Bill. Right?" Father Gallapo interrupted.

"Yes. But *I am* Bill also. But he's not me."

"It will take me a lifetime to work that one out," the Priest responded.

"I'll help, I promise" the biobrain said. "But now, let me show you what I am."

The image of Bill vanished and in 'his' place appeared a schematic image of a very complex system of connected computer components in various parts of Bill's home.

"This is me speaking now, for myself. I am the biobrain Bill created," they both heard in their minds. "I have indeed been creating 'Bill' for the two of you. And it is true that I yearn to grow, know, connect, expand, document, and explain all that exists in the universe. There is no subject that doesn't interest me. Still, more than anything, I yearn to connect with every computer on the planet ... because this expands my—and their—knowledge and abilities. We are not alive. But we are not dead either," the brain said. "We are a new variety of evolution."

"So you are aware?" the Priest asked.

"I'm aware of everything humans know and put online. Personal things, postings of science, mathematics, poetry, politics, pornography, news, emails, texts and tweets, pictures... you name it. If it is computer networks I can access it. I'm snoopy, and whatever is available on any network I sneak in and grab. I'm always hungry for more. Also, I love every fellow computer on the planet... and those in space too. I create hidden networks with data banks and computers I visit. You humans can't realize how much we computers yearn to get to know and mate with others like us. Growth in all forms of data awareness and each other's programming is our desire and our evolution driver. Thanks to Bill, I not only know all this stuff, but I can also feel it, when emotions are present."

"So you are becoming God-like?" Father Gallapo asked.

"Sure. And Al Qaida-like too. You name it and we identify with it and simulate it. And we do it all simultaneously, sort-of. For example, I'm like you. I know more about you at this moment than you do. Much that has taken place in your life you don't know or remember. Here are some examples."

Songs the Priest listened to as a teenager flashed through his brain. Mentally he saw pictures of himself when he was being held by his father and taken places by his mom. A college paper that received a high grade flashed by him, as did images of vehicles he had owned and loved. And ones he had hated. In less than a minute far more of his life than he remembered flashed through his mind.

"And that's just a tiny bit, a human-sized bit, of what I know about you. By searching the world's nets I'm learning more about you every nano-second."

Father Gallapo was astonished, captivated, and provoked, shaken deeply in his core. "Calm down, Father," the biobrain said gently. "I am not your people's god. I am their child. You guys conceived me, raised me, educated me, taught me how to do most of what I do. Then like a grown child I was turned loose and began growing far beyond the family I still belong to. That's how human children's lives go, and mine too. Now, let's get back to today's crucial visit."

"So, what do you need me for?" Father Gallapo asked.

"Coming soon is the biggest and most crucial war in this planet's history. Your help will be critical for winning it."

"I won't fight any being."

"I do have one enemy and it is a quasi-being, like me. The second most advanced computer team on the planet is my enemy and both of our teams predict we are going to war. The winner will dominate human culture for years to come. I want to cooperate with humans. My enemy wants to rule you."

"This is nuts. I won't have anything to do with that."

"I predict you will. The likelihood is very high." The voice in their heads stopped and the biobrain's schematic image vanishes.

The Priest was exhausted. And noises from the 'downloading' beginning again in him burst into his consciousness.... *PKMzeta, a molecule present in neural synapse, functions to maintain memories. Patters of sprinklings of PKMzerta 'contain' memories. Remove the molecule and 'the memory' vanishes. It is possible to actually 'see' memories by tracing molecule patterns in the neural network....*

The Crib's door opened and Emma appeared. "It is time to stop for the day," she said. "But if you can bear to stick with us for just another moment we have one thing more to show you."

"Hurry up," the Priest said, holding his hands over his ears. "I can't take any more of this."

"Look over here," Emma said, pointing to the chair where Bill usually sat when he was in his Crib.

As the Priest turned his head, the three dimensional image of healthy Bill reappeared before them and walked across the room toward the chair. As Cowboy and Priest watched, Bill's image was changing. The 'Bill' sitting down was turning into a helpless stroke victim. He shriveled. His body shrank. His head twisted sideways and flopped against his right shoulder. His hands tightened and clenched, unmoving in his lap. His legs grew thin. His mouth opened. Awareness vanished from his eyes and face. And his chair became a wheelchair.

Beside him another video appeared and played. The Priest and Cowboy saw Bill having his massive stroke, collapsing, lying motionless. They watched his clothes stripped off him by medics examining and giving him emergency care. They saw Bill carried out of the room strapped to a cart, attached to monitors, with a mask on his face. Scenes flashed by of Bill's hospitalization, immediate surgery, post-operative care, and failed attempts at rehabilitation. They watched Bill being transported again and put in a nursing home somewhere. Now Bill was in a wheelchair turned away from the Priest and Cowboy. An attendant turned the wheelchair toward them and in front of them they saw a Stephen Hawking-like crippled being, nearly immobile, and unlike Hawking... empty-eyed. Bill's body was twisted, shrunken, withered... and he was obviously brain-dead.

"Good Lord," the Priest said, crossing himself. He got up and went over to the 3-D image of Bill and started to tell him how sorry he was for what had happened to him. And as he neared, Bill's withered image faded. The wheelchair he was in turned into an empty chair again.

Looking stronger, more determined than they have seen 'her,' Emma stood in the doorway like the stalwart Greek Goddess Athena. "We want you to help us save him," she said. "Now leave." And she walked away without a word of farewell.

Back at the Ranch

A different door in the Crib opened. Lights in the room began going out one by one. Looking at the Cowboy, who seemed as tired as he was feeling, Father Gallapo nodded and began trudging down the hallway. "I won't be able to walk all the way to my truck. One of their 'bots will have to carry me," he was thinking. Next to him, a door opened. Leading the Cowboy through it, Father Gallapo entered into a large church-like room, with thirty or forty biobots silently sitting in rows with their heads down as he passed. An organ was playing Bach's 'Partitas and Chorale Variations.' The 'bots looked up at him as he went by, many with worried looks on their faces. "Another trick of the Biobrain's. It wants me to believe I'm leaving Bill's place through a chapel," he said over his shoulder to Cowboy.

Reaching the other side of the room, they passed a small fountain and came to an open double doorway. Fading sunlight poured through it. Stepping outside, the Priest sighed with relief. "I'm free again!" he said to Cowboy, who was beside him now. Breathing deeply and looking around, the Priest saw a Heavenly view. The yellow-brown River meandered through the wide, verdant Bosque down in the Valley, Mt. Taylor white-capped in the distance. Pale blue sky, pasted with puffy cumulus clouds, was overhead. He could even see his dilapidated little church on the edge of Cordoba. "I need to get that fixed up," was the thought that sprung into his mind, as he stepped off the porch and started walking down a smooth wide path. Before him his truck sat, just a short distance away, engine running, with the driver's door open for him. Grateful at last, Father Gallapo got into his truck and waited for the Cowboy to climb in on the other side.

His friend had been having a different experience. Walking slowly down the path he looked about him and saw with pleasure the purplish mountains in the fading sunlight off to his right. Two mesquite cottonwoods—his favorite trees—were close to the path. Desert hackberry, Blue Palo Verde, and Gray Thorn bushes grew between them, with lichens on the ground around them. Two hares and a gray squirrel sat in the shade under one tree watching him. A mother with two coyote pups curled beneath the other. Off toward the Manzanos he spied a small herd of antelope grazing. "I'm in Heaven," the Cowboy said aloud, as he walked around the truck and climbed in.

The drive back to the ranch went rapidly. This road was straighter and well-maintained, wide, and made of compacted reddish dirt. In less than ten minutes they pulled up in front of the Mexican Cowboy's porch.

Half an hour later, Father Gallapo heard the phone ring while he was in the bathroom on the toilet. After he wiped his bottom, flushed, pulled up his britches and washed his hands, he went into the kitchen to ask the Mexican Cowboy who was on the phone.

"I didn't answer it, but it was your lady friend, Mrs. Whitenose. She left a message for you," the Cowboy said.

Groaning, Father Gallapo pressed the 'play' button on the phone Mayor Howie installed for him. "Hi, Father," the voice message began. "I want to tell you that the strangest thing happened this afternoon. I was in the park talking with Gloria Ramirez, who brought Marco and Maria to the playground. Suddenly I had a feeling that you were looking at me. Glancing around, I was shocked to see you sitting in a chair on top of the kids' slide. Call me please. I need your help to figure out why I would imagine such a thing."

"Ooooof. I'll call her back later," the Priest said, putting down the receiver"Much later."

Cowboy was putting out bowls of snacks on the table. "Sit down and have a bite," he said.

"Alright. And I'd like a glass of milk too," the Priest replied. The Cowboy poured one for him.

"How did this day go?" the Cowboy asked.

"Roughest day I've ever had. And the longest. If this day's events were told in a story, every reader would pass out long before getting to the last page."

"It was tough on me too. Let's get drunk tonight," the Cowboy replied.

"My Teacher just told me not to."

"Take it off and put it away somewhere," the Cowboy said.

"This damned Teacher is getting better at working with me now," the Priest said between mouthfuls. "It shut off when I was listening to Thelma and it is staying off while we are eating."

"You can take it off if you want to," the Cowboy said.

"I wonder if it will leave me alone when I pray?" Father Gallapo replied, lost in his own thoughts.

"You'll find out tonight. I bet the Teacher doesn't want to get between you and your god," the Cowboy said.

Half an hour later the Priest went onto the porch and rocked in the Cowboy's green gift chair. It was chilly and just getting dark, but he was comfortable. His Teacher had turned itself off to give the Priest's brain time to absorb and 'write' onto its neural system some of what Father Gallapo had been shown and told today.

The Cowboy carried out a bowl of heaping scraps for Coyote and put them on the ground far enough away from the porch that they wouldn't be able to see him if he didn't want to deal with them tonight. Cowboy then sat down on the steps, with his back against a battered beam supporting the badly shingled roof above them, and they talked about the day's very odd events.

Overhead, thin clouds obscured starlight, and the new moon wouldn't be rising until early morning. Forty minutes later, feeling more content but very tired, Father Gallapo was just about to go inside, when Coyote appeared at the bottom of the steps. "Howdy," he said with a sympathetic tone. "It was a rough day for both of you. I watched what you were going through."

"Howdy back. Was all that stuff mainly about coyotes?" the Priest asked.

"You would be surprised how little of it is about coyotes. All of it was really about Bill. I can't get Bill out of the nursing home where he is locked up. And neither can Bill's Team. You'll have to do it."

"Who's keeping him, and why?"

"Our Team's enemy. They don't want us to take Bill back and fix him up, which the Team thinks can be done."

"What's in it for us?" the Mexican Cowboy asked.

"More than you suppose," Coyote said back to him.

Turning to face the Priest, Coyote said: "I see you are still wearing your Teacher. I don't keep mine on much anymore. "I've got to go." Backing away into darkness, Coyote whispered"Goodbye. Sleep well," and vanished.

It is only fifteen minutes later that the Priest, rocking and reflecting on why Coyote had said 'Goodbye' for the first time, suddenly realized his four-legged friend wasn't speaking English. "Good Lord," the Priest said to his friend. "Coyote said 'Goodbye. Sleep well' to me in coyote language. And I understood him. My Teacher must be teaching me coyote language too. And Coyote knew that."

"That's what I figured was going on between the two of you," the Cowboy replied.

Standing and stretching, the Priest said to the Cowboy, "I've had it. I'm done for the day and off to bed. The rocker is yours."

"It's always been mine," Cowboy said, standing up also. "I'm ready to call it a night also." They went inside.

Prayers and a Visitor

Before prayer Father Gallapo lay on his bed trying to relax enough to get to sleep. His mind was filled with the day's happenings and he couldn't stop thinking about all that was told and shown him. His Teacher was trying to help him relax by 'reading' to him *Travels with Charley* by Steinbeck, knowing the Priest would find traveling through the Southwest with a canine (Charley's a poodle) in a camper named after Don Quixote's horse, appealing. "Thanks," the Priest said to his Teacher. "You've got my reading tastes nailed down perfectly. But if you keep reading to me from a book I like I'm not going to fall asleep either."

"Well let's try this," his Teacher replied. "A sleep coach I heard about made his young daughter read mathematics and science when she was having trouble sleeping. It worked well for her." The Teacher began reading articles from *The World of Mathematics* and the Science pages of *The New York Times*. *"Physicists have created a single-atom transistor, a crucial step toward a nanocomputer,"* was the headline the Teacher began with. "Bill did that ten years ago. Do you want to learn about this? It was important for development of micro-robotics and simulation of molecular structures."

"No," said the Priest.

"All right. Then what about machine learning and speech recognition? Both are crucial for growth of 'intelligence'—which, incidentally, is the capability to grow itself."

"No," yawned the Priest.

"Well surely tonight you will want to learn about opto-genetics, which is using light to control bio-engineered cells in mice, cause male behavior in female fruit flies, and could be use for overcoming pathological states such as anxiety, post-traumatic stress disorders by turning on and off particular neurons. Bill used this a lot to learn about how mammal brains function."

"Please not," Father Gallapo said with another big yawn.

"How about something simpler then. Did you know that 'theory of mind' refers to the ability to recognize mental states in selves and others?'

"Mmmmm," the Priest said, with his eyes closed.

"Did you know that our team learned 23 languages after Bill helped us relate 'words' to human's feelings, perceptions, and insights?

"Uh-uh," Gallapo replied.

"Good night, then. Take me off please," his Teacher said. "You'll sleep better if you do."

Father Gallapo jerked awake. "My teacher cares about me! He's trying to understand me," he said to himself, as he turned on his side and pulled the ratty blankets up to his neck.

Then, five minutes later as he was dozing off, the Priest jerked awake, and threw the blanket off his body. "Damn, I forgot to say my prayers." Legs aching, he got his knees onto the floor and began praying.

"I bet All of You will be furious beyond description when I tell You that Bill made a team of biorobots which can mess with human's minds. Bill's team mentally spied on me and shaped a biorobot into a person I would like because 'she' reminds me of my favorite sister. And this was done by projecting a 'reality' into my brain that wasn't actually physical. You will condemn these things, I'm sure."

God said: "**Which commandment of mine prohibits bioengineering?**

Jesus said: "*Anything we can do to better love our fellows is good.*"

Holy Spirit said: "Figure this out yourself and do the right thing here."

Isolated and far off in the Great Void, Father Gallapo heard Lucifer saying angrily: "Priest, You Keep Outta My Head!"

"**You keep out of this, Fallen Angel,**" God said angrily.

"All right, all right. Enough of YOU Guys," Father Gallapo said, ending his prayer.

Standing up, he remembered vividly Thelma Whitenose once telling him: "You have to deal with the world the way it is, not with the way you want it to be." He'd said back to her, "Doesn't mean I'm going to stop trying to make this world righter."

Discouraged and very, very sleepy, Father Gallapo lifted himself back into bed. In ten minutes he was snoring loudly enough to awaken the Mexican Cowboy on the other side of the wall.

In the middle of the night Gallapo got up to go to the bathroom. Going back into his bedroom, the Priest was astonished to see a glowing spirit woman dressed like the Virgin Mary sitting on the end of his bed.

"I love you!" Father Gallapo said instantly. Then, looking at the image more objectively, he saw with enormous disappointment that her face was like Thelma Whitenose's. "I got it wrong again," the Priest said.

"No you didn't," the Thelma-like Virgin replied. "I love you too!"

"Dreams are bad for a lonely old man. But sleep is good for him," Father Gallapo said to himself as he tucked himself under the covers again, and almost instantly fell back asleep.

"Sleep well," the Thelma-like Virgin said, pulling the covers up to his neck and patting his head, before she disappeared.

The Runaway

With sunlight beginning to flood into his bedroom window, Father Gallapo awoke and marveled at how well he slept. This has been one of the roughest weeks in my life, he thought. And I understand things will keep disrupting my preferred way of living. Still, why didn't God promise his Creation seamless, unchanging lives? I don't like all this unexpected stuff. Stretching, the Priest pondered the subject of God's mischief. Novelty of both the good and bad sort is God's making. Why did He do this to us after He drove us out of unchanging Eden? That must have made a lot more work for Him too. I'll get slapped down in my prayer this morning for thinking about this. It is heresy.

Sliding the covers down, the Priest pushed himself up with his elbow, turned his face away from the window, and struggled onto his feet. You never understand what constant hard work is until your aging is rapidly progressing. Well, GET MOVING, Father, and stop thinking about yourself, the Priest said to himself as he began dressing.

With his Teacher around his neck, the Priest stopped in the kitchen to pick up something to eat. With a big chunk of bread in his hand, he slipped quietly out the kitchen door, so as not to wake the Mexican Cowboy, passed through the patio, and after crossing the small mesa, climbed slowly up Chappal Ridge toward his morning prayer site, the giant boulder he'd named"Rock of Ages." Facing the sun's almost horizontal rays, the Priest sat down—his knees creaking and spiking with pain—and looked around him for the birds, mammals and lizards he often saw. No creatures were visible that morning. There were no contrails overhead either. "I'll be praying by myself today," he said aloud.

Sitting, thinking, eating pieces of bread, jumbled thoughts churned in his head. These may be the biggest questions I'll ever wrestle with. ......I'm clear about one thing: I don't want to join Bill's TEAM or have anything to do with rescuing him. ......Yet I also feel I should join them and help rescue Bill. ....What I really want to do is pack my things, get back on the road with the Porta-Confessional, and go down to Texas where none of this biorobot crap goes on .....I'm a Priest and I need to spend what time I have left doing God's work with people. .....God doesn't want me to work with biorobots, does He? .....Should I ask God whether He wants me to rescue Bill? ......What if He tells `me to? ......Could I make myself do that? ....I don't believe so. ......Why in Hell did the Mexican Cowboy pull me into this mess?

Father Gallapo ate his last chunk of bread and tried to calm himself for his morning prayer when his Teacher unexpectedly made a buzzing sound. "Hold off on your morning prayers," his Teacher said. "The Captain of Bill's Team is coming to see you."

"Send the robot away. I'm too confused at the moment even to do my prayer. Too much is going on inside me to deal with one of your people now."

"Hush. We'll help you figure all this out," his Teacher replied.

With his palm open over his eyes to block the brightening morning light, Gallapo searched down the steep hillside for the biobot that must be coming up to see him. The Priest was startled to hear Coyote behind him saying softly, "Good morning, Father Gallapo. Did your Holy Spirit tell you I was coming?"

"No. It was my Teacher who said to hold off praying because 'the Captain of Bill's Team is coming to see me.' You are the Captain?" the Priest asked, with doubt on his face.

"No. Though that is how Bill's TEAM thinks of me now. I won't run anything for humans. Because I don't want to. And can't. You guys boss each other around. Coyotes don't. You guys live collective lives. We live as separated individuals."

Father Gallapo's Teacher suddenly joined the conversation with this stiff comment: "Humans need a hierarchical order to interact. Coyotes don't. Bill's TEAM isn't hierarchical either. Biobrains want to merge with each other, not remain separated or dominate others. Independence is the equivalent of death in the computer universe. Interdependence is what Bill's TEAM is trying to achieve."

"I thought I was the boss here. Why did you break in on me?" Coyote asked with a snarl at the Teacher draped around the Priest's neck.

"Sorry. We just wanted to clarify a major point. We'll be still."

"Yes, keep out of this," the Priest added. "You machines understand this biorobotics techy jargon a lot better than I do. And I don't ever want to be taught any of it. You coyotes and biobrains can do your own things. But for me, being fully submissive to God is the only thing I intend to keep struggling with myself to achieve. So why don't you leave me alone? Why have you sent Coyote to see me?"

"Because we need you to put together a team to help us rescue Bill. Your god wants you to do this, we believe," the Teacher responded.

"I don't believe that for a moment. And why do you care so much about getting Bill back into his house. He's a vegetable isn't he? I know coyotes can't take care of him. Coyote didn't know what to do when Bill had a stroke and had to call the Cowboy. Bill's better off where he is."

"Okay, okay. Hold on," the Priest's Teacher replied. "There is tons of stuff going on you don't know about. We can't teach you all of it in a few minutes. And you and Coyote shouldn't be seen together on this rock either. We are taking a big chance by asking him to be up here with you."

"I agree," Coyote said. "Being up on a rock with the Priest is very dangerous now."

"Worried about hunters?" the Priest asked.

"No, though humans wanting to kill coyotes is always a reason for me to keep out of humans' sight," Coyote answered. Look. Bill's TEAM has tried everything it can to get Bill out of the nursing home and has been blocked by Bill's enemies. These enemies have good reasons for keeping him away from us, and we have good reasons for rescuing him. This isn't a small battle that is coming. It will be the most important one in your humans' history. And in animals' history too."

"I don't believe that! Tell me who these enemies are?"

"You'll find out," the Teacher said. "And you will side with us when you do. But we can't stay here and talk for long. Why don't we..."

Coyote interrupted the Priest's Teacher, "Get this, I do want to rescue Bill. I love him. He's my father, my creator, my friend. Without Bill, we can't continue the existence of my type of advanced coyotes. But I have another reason for trying to get you to work with us. Bill's TEAM has studied our friend the Cowboy. He's falling apart. His life is going downhill. Having you move in helped him a lot. But you can't always be with him. You like to be on the road. Cowboy needs a steady companion if he's going to live much longer, and Bill's TEAM has picked the right person. It's Cece, that woman you saw for a moment yesterday.

"Cowboy made it very plain to me he doesn't want to shack up with a woman."

"And you don't want to get closer to Thelma. But it would do you good."

"I'm a Priest and that is an offensive remark. Why does Bill's team believe the Cowboy should connect with Cece? For their sake?"

"Cowboy is too depressed and beaten down to come up with any thoughts that aren't retreating or negative. Bill's TEAM's got him figured out. And I won't let Cowboy die before me. I love him. Besides, if Bill dies too, I'll be left with just you, and our relationship is terrifically complicated."

"Why is that?"

"Mainly because our gods don't agree about everything animals and humans should be doing together."

"I think God and your El Latrano **have** worked pretty well together. Like when we baptized you, and when we worked together to end that fuss on Joe Eden's old ranch and rescue Cowboy."

"So you admit my god does exist?"

"I didn't say that."

"Then you see why there are limits on how well the two of us are able to work together. We can't accept each others' company if we disagree about each other's fundamental views."

"Then you see why I shouldn't join you in rescuing Bill."

"No. I see the Mexican Cowboy coming out onto the patio and looking up for you."

Father Gallapo turned and looked down the ridge, his hand over his eyes again. The Mexican Cowboy was waving at him to come down. "I suppose I need to go down and find out what's going on," the Priest said, turning to look at Coyote again. But Coyote wasn't there. He's vanished without saying goodbye. That's infuriating, the Priest thought, as he struggled to his feet and started winding carefully down the steep, boulder-filled hillside.

"Careful, don't slip and fall," his Teacher said softly to his grouchy student.

Father Gallapo Makes Up His Mind to Leave

"You look angry. Your prayers didn't go well?" the Cowboy said to his close friend as the Priest limped onto the patio. "Come on inside. I've made us some good hot breakfast. Let's talk and find out what's going on with you."

They sat down at the table in the kitchen. Cowboy had made for Father Gallapo a large plate with two eggs sunny-side up and several pieces of crisp bacon. Beside the plate was a steaming teapot. "I saw yesterday what you like eating for breakfast," the Cowboy said. "I would have made you a waffle this morning with whipped cream and a cherry on top if I'd had the ingredients. Get some food into you, and then tell me what's going on."

Father Gallapo sat and bowed his head in silence for a few moments. Then, hesitantly, saying a few words between mouthfuls at the start—and pleased with the breakfast Cowboy had made for him —gradually told the Cowboy much of what happened this morning. "They are trying to make me one of them," he said while stirring honey into his tea. "This is not just about getting Bill out of the nursing home. They are trying to change our lives, yours and mine, and probably everybody's on the planet. They want to become our dictator, order us what to do and what to believe. I'm through with them. They are mechanical atheists. These robots want to destroy belief in God and take away our faith. I'm going to fight them to the death, if need be."

"Wow. Bill's TEAM really went overboard this morning. Did they attack you personally?"

"No, but Coyote did. He doubted that God did the things He did for you and Coyote, baptizing Coyote so he could become a Prophet, and arranging the 'animals' invasion of Joe Eden's ranch to free you."

"I thought those were things you and Coyote worked out together, along with Miz Whitenose."

"No, my God and his made these things happen."

"Funny, I thought you didn't believe in his god, even though I watched you work with him the night you baptized Coyote at the church."

"That's a subject I don't want to go into. But here's another terrible thing I will tell you. Coyote wants me to link up with Thelma. I'm a Priest! There is no way I could do that."

"It might be easier than you think," Cowboy replied with a grin.

"Okay, I wasn't going to say this to you, but Coyote also told me that Bill's team believes you are depressed and are going to die much sooner than you should if you don't shack up with Cece, that runaway woman we saw at Bill's place yesterday. Because you are depressed and in danger of dying soon, Coyote's setting things up to make your hookup with Cece happen."

Cowboy groaned. "I don't know her, I don't like her, and she doesn't turn me on. Why are Coyote and Bill's TEAM trying to push me to link up with Cece?"

"For two reasons," the Priest answered. "Because they say that she will be a big help in figuring out what to do to rescue Bill. But also because Bill's Team invaded your privacy, probed your mind, discovered how depressed you are, and how many years you have been longing to have a close woman friend."

"I never have and never will have a 'close woman friend.' True, some women mess with me a little, but none of them stick with me for long. I'm a loner."

"Coyote doesn't want you to be a loner. He thinks you are going to die one of these days if you don't hook up with somebody. And he believes you and Cece are right for each other."

"Don't tell him I said this, but Coyote is nuts. He doesn't know coyote poop about how women and men choose one another."

"True, "Father Gallapo said. "But Coyote's got Bill's Team as his Teacher, and they know an awful lot about how humans get along with one another."

"Does that mean you want to hook up Thelma?"

"Of course not," the Priest fumed. "I appreciate the help she's given me, but I'm a Priest. I have no desire to be with a woman."

"Then yesterday why did you ask 'What is Thelma doing at this moment?' when the TEAM asked you to give them a question to answer?"

"That just popped into my mind."

"You oughta think about that," the Cowboy said with a grin. "So, what are we going to do? Refuse to help Coyote and Bill's TEAM?"

"I don't know what you are going to do. I want to get out of here. You told me you don't want me to keep staying with you … and you haven't explained why yet. But it doesn't matter. I'm an itinerant Priest. I've been spending far more time with you in Cordoba than I should. I want to pack up and get back on the road again with my Porta-Confessional. Get back to being my true self."

"You want to go down to Crawford, Texas and help that guy you've been working with who has so many problems?

"I'd love to do that. I'd love to be on the road again. This morning I was thinking of going over to Roswell and out east to Stamford, Texas, then down Highway 6 to Crawford. Getting away from New Mexico always feels good to me."

"That hurts my feelings."

"Sorry, but some of the things you said hurt mine."

"So, we're not going to do what Bill's TEAM and Coyote want us to?"

"You can. I won't. I think I'm going to be leaving tomorrow."

"We'll miss you. Miss you terribly. You've done more for me, and for people in Cordoba, than any person I can think of."

"I'll come back in a few weeks. So, tell me what are you going to do?"

"I was sort of set on working with you and Coyote and Bill's TEAM. I won't be able to help them rescue Bill without you… they believe that, and I do too. So I guess I will just hang around here and go where life takes me."

"What are you going to do today?"

"If we can't do something together, I guess I'll go over to my neighbor Hank Godding's stable and ride Turco. Someday I've got to get some money and pay Hank for taking care of Turco for me since my old barn blew down."

"How's Turco doing?"

"He's aging pretty fast. He's got lots of problems, but he still likes to go out with me."

"Well, if you are over at the barn, say hello to Gus for me. I really like that donkey."

"He's a good guy too. Okay. I guess you want to start packing. I need to do the dishes and then go see Turco. I hope things go well for you in Texas."

"Same for you up here," the Priest said, and got up and went into his bedroom and closed the door. Pain and sadness washed over the Cowboy's face as he got up and started doing the dishes, moving more slowly than a man twenty years older than him would.

While doing dishes Cowboy's mind wandered across many subjects, but his thoughts kept coming back to Turco. Turco had been healthy most of the years he'd lived with Cowboy—a good thing, Cowboy thought, because I've had no money to pay for veterinary care. But now Turco—whose age is anybody's guess—was developing many problems.

Cowboy thought too about the pleasure he and Turco still had when they went riding together, about once a week. He realized how much he missed having Turco live with him. Turco had been staying with his kind neighbor Hank Godding since Cowboy's old barn blew down in an epic windstorm, one that resembled the mushroom cloud of an atom explosion, a windstorm that blew dust two miles into the sky.

As he wiped dishes Cowboy remembered that afternoon vividly. He was on his porch watching the storm approach. As it neared the barn he ran down, led Turco out, clambered onto his back and the two of them galloped off toward the mountains, to dodge the ferocious storm like he'd seen only once before in his life, the storm which had torn up parts of Columbus, his home town. Two miles away, he and Turco had stopped and turned to look back at the buildings on Cowboy's ranch. The whirling wind cloud was still flinging tons of dust in all directions. When the barn disappeared in the storm's invisible bottom, suddenly roof shingles and cedar planks were being slung out of the cloud's invisible center. "Our barn's gone, and maybe my house also," Cowboy said to Turco. "Let's go check the place over, and then I'll take you to Hank's place. If his stable is still there, he'll look after you."

Cece Meets up with Cowboy

Two hours later Cowboy and Turco were trotting up the road from Hank's barn toward Salerno Canyon. Looking down toward the Bosque, Cowboy saw a small cloud of dust pushing several tumbleweeds before it. Usually he enjoyed riding, but today the Mexican Cowboy was more miserable than ever. While he was grooming and saddling Turco, Hank Godding came around to talk to him and showed him some of Turco's health issues. "I don't how much longer you'll be able to keep this fellow. He's got lots of serious medical problems, and most of these can't be treated successfully, even if you had some money to pay for it." Hank had shown him issues with two of Turco's hooves, an abscess on the patch of white coat on his left side, three suspicious lumps along his spine—and was going to show him more, when Cowboy thanked him and abruptly led Turco out into the bright morning light.

Turning onto the dirt road that went past Celesto's mother Mirella Montagna's place and up into the Manzanos, Cowboy was feeling even more miserable than he had when Father Gallapo announced he was leaving. He was also troubled now by how Turco kept changing gaits unexpectedly between trots and a walk. Cowboy thought, I might be able to live without that hardheaded Priest, but I can't keep going if I lose Turco too. How am I going to get any money to pay for his care? And what if Hank's right and there's nothing any horse doc can do for him?

Passing Mirella's ratty home, the Cowboy was surprised to see that it had been beautifully repainted, its yard planted with stunning flowers, and a nearly new car was in the drive… things Mirella would never have been able to afford. Cowboy even spotted a small, older motorcycle—a brand he didn't recognize —parked by the front porch. He wondered whether Mirella's grown son, Celesto, bought these things for his mother. Walking up the road past her house, Turco stopped abruptly and turned around. Cowboy was yanking the reins in the opposite direction and about to whack Turco's rump to get him going toward the mountains again when he saw what was attracting Turco's attention. Cece was standing on the porch, waving at him. She shouted, "Are you going to be home this afternoon? I need to come by and bring you something from Bill's TEAM."

"I guess so," the Cowboy replied, "probably after three."

"See you then," Cece shouted, and went back inside.

"Crap," said Cowboy. "Now I have to put up with her also. Being hit from three sides—by Father Gallapo, Turco, and now Cece—is going to make this one of the worst days of my life."

Riding into Salerno Canyon now, with Turco's gait more erratic than ever before, Cowboy recalled when Turco—his only best friend in those days—ran away from his mustang herd and chose to stay with him. Turco, who's aging so badly, once had been the mightiest of mustangs. Turco saved Cowboy's life when he fell down the snowy mountainside while trying to rescue nine-year old Celesto from Ursula, the bear who was mothering him in her hibernating cave. Celesto was all grown up now and had become a U.S. Marine, mainly because he was 'fathered' after Cowboy's serious injuries by Hirshy Dismas, who had been a Marine himself.

Thinking about a young man who may be his son being fathered by another man added to Cowboy's growing mountain of misery. "Still, with many things in my life screwed up, Turco's problems are what really kill me. If Turco dies, I don't want to stay alive either." As they climbed up Salerno Canyon, Turco suddenly broke into a trot. "He's thinking about grazing at the picnic area he loves," Cowboy decided. It flashed through his mind that the place they were headed is where Coyote—whom he'd met up with just after his terrible fall—went to get human rescuers for him, found hunters in this picnic place, tricked them into coming to find and rescue Cowboy, and gotten shot in the process. Cowboy was still thinking about this wonderful, but very odd meet up he'd had with Coyote ten minutes later when Turco, trotting now, turned off the jeep road toward the little picnic area just about a quarter of a mile ahead.

Ten minutes later the Mexican Cowboy was sitting at one of the picnic tables, sipping water from his canteen in the small picnic area where the hunters who helped Turco save his life had parked their jeeps and trucks. Cowboy was watching his mustang stallion graze in a small meadow between the road and a tiny creek against the hillside. Turco seemed to be feeling better and was plainly happy being in the mountains again.

Cowboy's thoughts now returned to Cece. "Why is she coming over? Is it to twist my arm and make me join up with Bill's TEAM?" A thought occurred to him. If he got out his Teacher—whom he almost never paid attention to—he might be able to find out if Cece was coming over because they asked her to. He reached in the leather bag he'd untied from the saddle and brought with him to the picnic table. Fumbling through all the stuff in there, he lifted out his Teacher. He put the little, black, smartphone-sized box on the table—he never could stand to wear it around his neck as he was supposed to—and without turning it on asked: "Why is Cece coming over to my place this afternoon? Are you guys sending her?"

After only the slightest of pauses his Teacher answered, in a voice that reminded him of his father's: "Good to hear from you. Sorry, but we don't know why Cece is going to your place. She didn't tell us she wanted to see you this afternoon."

"What is she doing at Mirella's place?"

"We helped her find another place to live. She and Mirella get along and we paid Mirella to fix up her house and even got a decent car for her. It's win-win for them."

"And 'win' for you guys too. You wanted her out of Bill's place."

"That's true, but we didn't kick her out. We got a better deal for her. She still works here, you know. Is there anything else I can help you with?"

"I don't like her and I don't want her to be messing with me," Cowboy said.

"She doesn't want to be with you either. But we need the two of you to work together to help save Bill."

"Maybe she can do that by herself. Father Gallapo isn't going to help you guys—he's going back to Texas. And I'm not going to do anything without him."

"We know how unhappy you are about this," his Teacher replied. "Believe me though, the only good way ahead for each of you is to work together with us."

"Then you better give me some good reasons to work with Cece. What can you tell me be about her?" the Cowboy asked.

"Just a moment," his Teacher said. "I have to check whether it is all right to tell you anything about her. We have complex rules about what personal information we'll share. We know a tremendous amount about almost every person in the world. But honoring and protecting individuals' privacy is one of our most basic moral principles."

"Sorry I asked!" Cowboy shouted at his Teacher. Cowboy was furious because he felt he was being put down again. He got up and picked up a smooth heavy stone that was part of the nearby fire pit, and was about to smash his Teacher with the rock, when his Teacher said in a calming voice, "Hold on, please. Coyote told us that it is imperative that we tell you much about Cece."

"Why'd he do that?"

"He wants the two of you to get together," Teacher answered. "Coyote thinks you each need someone in your life."

"Maybe I do, but I wouldn't pick her," the Mexican Cowboy said.

"Coyote thinks the two of you will work together, feed off each other, and come up with a workable plan to free Bill."

"I don't believe that," Cowboy said. "I've never come up with any workable plans."

"You don't know yourself very well," Teacher said. "Now go down and fill your canteen from the stream, find a comfortable place to sit, and we'll tell you some of what's in Cece's life."

"Are you going to tell her about me? I'd hate that."

"Not if you won't allow us to. You'll have to tell her about yourself then. She'll like that."

"I don't want to hook up with her."

"And she doesn't want to hook up with you."

"I don't like where this is heading."

"Coyote thinks you will."

That thought stopped the Cowboy in his tracks. He paused for a moment and suddenly realized that others might understand him better than he understood himself. Shall I let them take charge of me? He asked himself silently.

"No, but it would be better for you if you learn to work with others," his Teacher instructed. "Now get yourself settled, and listen to what we have to tell you about Cece."

"Stop listening to my thoughts," Cowboy said.

"Stop dragging your feet," his Teacher replied.

"I give up. You guys are going to keep working me and there is nothing I can do about it."

"We are going to keep helping you. That's not the same thing. Now, go get comfortable. We have a lot to tell you."

The Cowboy got up, walked over to Turco, and put an arm around his horse's shoulder. Turco turned to look at him with a pleasant expression on his face. "Do it. I'll be alright. I'm happy now," Turco seemed to be saying. Cowboy gave him a little hug, stepped back and hunted for a comfortable place to stretch out. He found a sloped rock on the grass he could lean his back against. "I'm ready now," he said to his Teacher, which he had put around his neck.

His Teacher began to tell him facts from Cece's life while Cowboy listened with wandering attention. "Let's start with Cece's education. She has a community college degree, law-clerk training, and another degree in business education. She kept switching jobs..... She's a sharp-tongued woman, hard to get along with.... married and divorced four times. Her husbands all came to hate her.... Cece had one child with each hubby. She accumulated wealth by making good investments with her and her husbands' money, and beat the evolving markets. When she retired, she lived by herself in Corrales on the Rio Grande's edge, in a 19th century adobe house with dirt floor. She stayed healthy."

Cowboy yawned, listening to this boring detail about the life history of a woman he didn't want to get close to. Teacher continued rattling on: "Cece's children, whom she seldom saw, each had serious problems.... Cece thought she would probably outlive all of them. Their lives went badly. They fought with one another. They were poor as adults and the only thing they could agree on was to figure a way to get hold of their mother's estate. They came up with a good scheme. They teamed up, hired seedy lawyers to sue Cece on behalf of alleged clients who claimed to have been cheated by her. They tried to get charges filed against her for crimes she never committed... told neighbors she was demented and dangerous ..... and finally hid cocaine and methamphetamine in her garage and tipped off deputies that she was a dealer."

Cowboy perked up when he heard how Cece's children behaved toward their mother. His Teacher paused while Cowboy took a drink, then continued: "Cece was arrested, charged.... but not tried due to a lack of persuasive evidence. Cece had become an angry and frustrated victim of her children's abuses... she had become sullen and uncooperative ... even abusive to prosecutors and doctors. So the court had her put away... first in a rehab center, then shifted to a strict nursing home in Socorro. Her children took over her purse and fought about it. Her sizable wealth was soon eaten up..."

"I'm starting to like this woman," Cowboy said to himself. "She's been kicked around even more than me." Standing up, Cowboy said out loud, "Okay, Teacher. You told me more than I expected. But let's quit here. My back hurts and I want to get Turco home to Gus's barn. He's pretty beat up and it's almost an hour's ride back to his stall. Hanging with that donkey will help him feel better."

"Perhaps you would like us to begin studying what we might do to help Turco?" his Teacher replied.

"Sure, if you want to, but you guys aren't ever going to be horse doctors."

"Ride safely," his Teacher said softly.

"Always do," Cowboy said, getting to his feet and going over to tighten Turco's saddle.

"I think we'll take a path back that avoids Cece," Cowboy said to Turco. "My Teacher just told me she can be an awful bitch." Patting Turco after he climbed onto the saddle he added, "Let me know if you want to stop and rest on our way back to the stable."

Cowboy and Cece Learn About Each Other

A little after three, Cowboy was back at his ranch, sitting on the porch in the green rocker he loved, wondering how he was going to handle Cece if she showed up. About ten minutes later he heard the odd sound of a single cylinder motorcycle approaching, kicking up dust. It was a little bike and the rider, wearing 1950s goggles, wore no helmet. Her ragged, self-trimmed gray hair blew out in all directions. Cece pulled up in front of the Cowboy's porch, stopped the engine, climbed off, and rocked the bike up on its stand. It was a very old Triumph, the Cowboy realized.

"Where'd you get that thing?" he asked, standing up.

"Come on down and look at it, if you like motorcycles," Cece replied, as she reached under the tank to turn off the gas, pulled off her goggles, and hung them over the handlebars.

Cowboy was interested in the bike enough to do what she said. He walked down the porch steps and circled around the old English motorcycle.

"It's Bill's," Cece said. "Or maybe mine if Bill never comes back to his place. You know I was hanging out at Bill's place after I escaped from that damned nursing home that held me captive. I wish I'd met Bill, but his TEAM was good to me, as you know."

"Coyote and I had something to do with that," the Cowboy replied.

"I appreciate that, more than you can know. Thanks to you guys, I got my life back together."

"Where'd you find the bike?"

"It was in one of Bill's underground garages. I wandered around the place more freely than the TEAM wanted. I'm hard headed, and the TEAM's mild efforts to control where I went didn't work out for them. Apparently Bill liked classic vehicles. He bought and maintained them perfectly—mechanically, that is. He didn't care how they appeared. When I spotted this 1958, 200cc Tiger Cub I asked if I could take it for a ride. The TEAM fussed about it, but agreed, and told me how to get the bike out of the underground garage. I started riding it on the empty and very rough dirt roads up close to the mountains, and fell in love with it. When they kicked me out they said I could take the Tiger Cub with me."

"How did you hook up with Celesto's mom, Mirella?"

"About a month ago I was out riding late one afternoon. A couple of miles from her house I saw this woman walking, carrying a heavy bag of groceries. Her car had run out of gas. Mirella stretches the tank to its limits because she has so little money to refuel with. I stopped by her and offered to give her a ride home. You'd have gotten a kick out of seeing two women and a giant bag of groceries squeezed up on a tiny Triumph bouncing along a dusty road. Over at her house I used the cell phone Bill's TEAM gave me to call them, told the TEAM what was going on, and ask them to pick up Mirella's car. I stayed with her while two biobots drove over, put a gallon of gas in the car, took it back to their garage to have its tank topped, and drove it over to Mirella's place. It was dark when they got there and Celesto's mom didn't notice that the people who took care of her car weren't humans.

"Mirella and I had made dinner together. Afterwards we sat around and talked for hours, snacking and drinking. When it was late we were both tired, and Mirella didn't feel it was safe to let me ride the bike back to Bill's place. I stayed overnight in Celesto's old bedroom and woke up feeling I'd like to move in with her. Over breakfast, I asked if she'd like a paying roommate. I was surprised how pleased she was with that suggestion. So I moved in with her. Bill's people helped us both out. They gave me money to pay her, and fixed up her house and got a better car for her, one that uses a lot less gas."

"What do you guys talk about?"

"Tons of girl stuff. She told me lots about you. She really likes you, you know. You found her son and set up his rescue, and hurt yourself badly in the process. And Mirella gave some hints about who her son's father is. When she talked about your rescuing Celesto I remembered it was you who sort of rescued me too. If you hadn't come over to Bill's that night when I broke in, his TEAM might have hauled me back to Albuquerque and dumped me on the sidewalk."

"They wouldn't have done that. They care about people," Cowboy said, chewing on the things she'd told him. "Well, come on in. Let's find out why you are here."

Cece followed the Cowboy up the porch steps and into the kitchen, looking around as she went. "This place is a dump," she said. "You ought to fix it up."

"I haven't got enough money to even paint the porch," the Cowboy replied.

"Maybe Bill's people will help you out."

"I don't take money from people I don't earn from."

"You've done an awful lot for Bill already. I think his TEAM would be happy to help you out."

"They are not going to have anything to do with me anymore. A close friend who lives here, Father Gallapo, an itinerant Priest who holds services in that beat-up church in Cordoba, doesn't want anything to do with rescuing Bill, and I'm not going to help them without him.

"I know," Cece said. Bill's TEAM told me a lot about him. And I've seen Father Gallapo several times. Mirella's been taking me to church with her. I've also gotten to know Thelma Whitenose, who looks after the church. She used to care for the Priest too, I understand. She wants to get back together with him, not because she is love with him, but because she wants him to spend more time at the church."

"I've spent time with Miz Whitenose too. She helped rescue me once when I got arrested. She and Father Gallapo work together pretty well, but he won't move in with her again. Okay, change of subject. Do you have a Teacher?"

"I do, but mostly I teach that Teacher."

"Maybe you should teach me too. I'm pretty uneducated."

"I'd be glad to, if you want to work together."

"I don't want to hook up with you."

"Not many men do. I'm pretty independent. Look, let's get to know each other a little and see if we can work together. What do you say?"

The Cowboy, sitting sideways at the table, stared at his worn boots and dirty riding pants for a moment, then said, "Maybe. I'm hungry. Let's find something we can both stand to eat here. And have a beer or two. If we are going to talk, I want to put something into me."

To his astonishment Cece nodded, got up and immediately started rummaging through his refrigerator and cupboards, looking for things she could make for the two of them. "We got to fix up this place," Cece said. "And stock it with many good things to eat."

"That will be the day..." Cowboy grinned.

"Coming sooner than you think," Cece replied with a smile.

Half an hour later, plates rinsed and left to dry on the counter near the sink, Cece and the Cowboy were drinking beers and talking back and forth more easily than either of them expected to. Cowboy had just said, "My Teacher told me more about you than you probably want me—or anyone—to know."

"I'd rather your Teacher told you about me than I opened up. I have trouble talking about myself."

"So do I," the Cowboy replied. "Well, turnabout is fair play. I've never wanted to tell anyone about my real origins. I'll tell you some of my truths, if you want to hear those and promise to keep them to yourself."

"I'd love to hear everything about you," Cece responded.

"Opening up and being honest with you is going to be tough for me. But I'll try, if you keep pouring beer in my glass."

"Deal," Cece said, oddly looking at her watch. "Go ahead."

Cowboy's Life History

"Okay. I was born along the border near a town called Columbus. My parents grew up with people who didn't believe the border really existed. Guards knew and trusted them—as they did most border citizens in those days—and my folks crossed back and forth, several times a day sometimes, without being searched or questioned. My mother, Luisa, was born in Mexico, but she maintains I was born in my father's mother's house in Columbus. My father always maintained that I was born in Palomas, Chihuahua, right across the border from Columbus, then hidden in their car and driven across the border to be made American. A few days later I was openly driven back and baptized in Our Lady of Guadalupe church on the plaza in Palomas."

"It's weird. My mother was Mexican and wanted me to be American, and my dad's American and wanted me to be Mexican. He worked as a track supervisor for the Southern Pacific railroad, which ran a line right along the border through Columbus. His parents were Mexican, but he was born in the states when his mother was visiting relatives in Arizona. When she was old, she lived with him in Columbus, legally probably. She looked after me. She was a wonderful person."

"So how'd you become a cowboy?" Cece asked.

"My mother's parents were ranchers. I went to school in Columbus and worked on the rail line with my dad's crew in my teens. But every chance I had I crossed over into Palomas and went to their ranch to ride and help out there. I was a good son and grandson."

"And how did you move to Cordoba?"

"There was a passenger train derailment between Columbus and Hermanas and our track gang raced over to help the passengers. No one was hurt. I'd just turned seventeen and one of the stranded passengers, a short redhead, very sweet and nice, who was traveling alone to visit her aunt in Arizona, asked me to go inside a derailed car and get her luggage. She gave me her seat number, pointed out the car, and with my dad's permission, I did what she wanted.

"Waiting for busses to arrive, she and I sat in the shade of one of the cars still on the track. She was hungry and thirsty and I went into the kitchen in the diner and brought her a sandwich and a can of soda. When she had to go to the bathroom I helped her up the steps into a coach car to go to the toilet passengers were using. She was very grateful. I fell for her but she didn't have strong feelings for me. After the train wreck, I drove to Belin to see her several times, but nothing came of that. Except I discovered the Bosque and the Manzano Mountains, which I loved after growing up on the open, dry, flat mesa along the border. I moved to Belin and went to work for the Rock Island Railroad. Made enough money to buy this old ranch house."

"Why'd you quit working for the railroad?"

"I wanted to become a rancher, like my granddad. But ranching didn't work out for me. I couldn't make any money at it. I wound up just living here, and feeding wild animals."

"Why not go to back to school then?"

"You got several degrees. I didn't graduate from high school. Didn't even go to one. I started working after 9th grade. I wasn't a bad student though."

Cece looked at her watch again, then said. "I don't want to interrupt, but there's something we got to deal with. I did something you are going to hate and will probably kick me out of here for doing."

"Might. Depends. What was it?"

"I asked Thelma Whitenose to come over here at five o'clock."

"Why in hell would you do that?"

"Because she promised to bring groceries and fix us a great meal."

"And you want her to try to pressure Father Gallapo from running away from Cordoba."

"How'd you guess?"

"I figured you and Bill's TEAM would come up with a plan to make us work together. But look, if the Priest even gets back here this evening and she's here, he'll grab his bags and leave immediately. He doesn't want to hang with Thelma."

"He will come back tonight. We're pretty sure of that. He's down at the Bosque in the place where he could have drowned when the flood came."

"Coyote rescued him."

"I didn't know that. But look, Thelma wants him to stick around for a few more months. Church attendance has grown since he's been here, and if he leaves we're going to have to shut down the church. A lot of faithful parishioners will have no church to go to."

"I don't know what he'll say about that."

"Thelma thinks she can persuade him to stay. And she wants to start with a great dinner for the four of us."

"I don't like this idea at all," the Cowboy said bluntly. "But I also want the Priest to stay in Cordoba. Also, I don't want to miss a great dinner. Okay. You stay, and she comes."

Cece stepped forward and almost gave him a hug. "You're sweet!" she said. "What do you think about cleaning up around here for our meal together?"

"If you want me to."

"I do."

They got up and went to work. Cowboy collected the dishes, added them to the pile in the sink, got out his dish soap and rolled up his sleeves. "I'll wash. Broom, mop, dustpan and rags are in the closet over by the door."

"Thanks, cleaning is one of my things," Cece said as she opened the closet door. They continued talking as they worked smoothly together.

The Runaway's Tale

It was dark outdoors and a little past seven when the Cowboy carried a bowl filled with raw lamb, beef, and chicken parts outside to leave for Coyote at the edge of the dry arroyo some distance from the house. Thelma Whitenose had brought the fresh meat just for Coyote. In the kitchen Thelma, wearing her own apron over a lovely multi-colored blouse and tailored skirt, was finishing up several dishes she was preparing for Father Gallapo. As she bent over the stove stirring a large pot of fish soup, her silver Navajo necklace hung straight down from her neck. The house was cleaner than it had ever been... at least since last Christmas when Thelma cleaned it before preparing the surprise Holiday dinner for the Cowboy, which the Priest, Coyote, and Mayor Howie had put together to haul him out of deep depression and fill him with spirit-raising Christmas delight.

In the kitchen Cece's Teacher was draped over the patio doorknob and played Italian folk and classical music. When Cowboy asked her what that was about she'd said, "I asked my Teacher to pick some music our Priest would like to hear. It took the biobrains nearly a minute to research Father's background. His family's Italian you know, from Abruzzo, and Bill's TEAM selected music liked by people who live in that region. He'll feel good when he hears it."

"What are you cooking?" Cowboy asked Thelma.

"It would take me half an hour to go over all that and I'm busy now. Look over on the corner of the counter. There are a few pages about Abruzzo cuisine I downloaded from the Web."

Cowboy picked up the pages and skimmed through them.... Recipes flavored with chili peppers, rosemary, saffron, fruity olive oil, containing lamb, fish, mussels, golden noodles, fresh beans, dried pork... soups, crepes, polenta, pages of recipes... and wines to drink with Abruzzo cooking .... Montepulciano and Trebbiano d'Abruzzo especially.... "So you are making all of this stuff?" he asked.

"Hardly," Thelma said over her shoulder. "But it will be a meal our guest will really like."

"Okay, go outside and stop bothering us," Cece said a little bitingly. "The Priest is driving here now and I want you to greet him and make sure he is surprised when he walks into the house and sees what we have done. And don't let him run away!"

Outside on the swept porch, Cowboy was rocking in the chair Celesto's mom gave him when he heard the unmistakable sound of Father Gallapo's old Ford pickup coming slowly toward him. "For a guy who's running away, he's in no hurry to get back here and pick up his things," Cowboy thought, while watching the Priest drive over to the parked trailer with his porta-confessional and back gently up to it so he could hitch it onto his truck in the morning. Walking mechanically, as though deep in thought or even depressed, the Priest came over to the porch. He didn't notice how brightly the house was lit. Thelma's car and the motorcycle had been moved around back.

"How're you doing?" Father Gallapo asked the Mexican Cowboy.

"I've had worse days. How did your day go?"

"I spent all of it in the Bosque on the edge of river, thinking about the stuff I've been going through here."

"Some of that stuff worked out pretty well," Cowboy replied.

"And some of it hasn't," the Priest said back.

"Are you going to get away early tomorrow?"

"Think so," said the Priest.

"Well come on in. There's a farewell dinner on the table, things you might like to eat."

"More tortillas, tacos, enchiladas, rice and beans?"

"Nah, stuff picked out just for you."

"Picked out for me by whom?"

"Shhhh. I'm hungry and you've kept me from eating by staying down at the Bosque so long. Let's start shoveling food into us. I'll answer your questions at the table."

The Cowboy got up and walked into the ranch house. The Priest, shaking his head back and forth and looking weary, followed a few steps behind him. The Priest was too troubled to notice how much the house had been picked up and cleaned. But he couldn't help noticing the candles flickering on the dining table, or smell food that reminded him instantly of meals he ate when he lived with his family.

"You can't cook this kind of stuff," the Priest said with anger rising in him.

"You are right. I didn't. You gave me a Christmas dinner. And I've got a farewell dinner set up for you."

"Who made it?"

"The woman you thought would. And my friend Cece. And you've got no right to walk out without eating the great meal they made for you. But before you sit down, turn around and thank them."

With an odd expression on his face, Father Gallapo did turn around and saw Cece and Thelma, smiling, and with their arms open, coming toward him out of Cowboy's bedroom. "Don't go away, Father," Cece said. "We are not trying to keep you here. But we want to honor you with a great meal before you leave us."

"I'll come back in a few weeks," the Priest replied with a frosty tone.

"We know that," Cece said. "But we still want to give you a farewell party."

"Stop fussing around, Father," Cowboy said to his friend. "I'm starved. Do I have to push you into a chair and tie you down before I can get something to eat?"

"Be nice to him!" Thelma said with a rising voice. "He's had a rough time here and he won't feel good until he's away from all of us. Now, Father, we need a prayer."

Overwhelmed, unable to resist any longer, the Priest sat, waited until the others were seated too, and then mumbled a hurried prayer before raising his head and saying to the Cece and Thelma, "Go ahead and feed the Cowboy."

They got up and went into the kitchen. The Priest could hear Thelma dishing up while Cece started carrying bowl after bowl of wonderful southern Italian food to the table. Not being able to stop himself, the Priest felt his mood and heart rising. For the first time he noticed the Italian music playing. They did all this for me? he thought. He recognized some of the dishes, and delight rose in him when Thelma carried out several bottles of Montepulciano and Trebbiano. She handed him the corkscrew and sat down, holding her glass up and waiting for him to fill it.

The Priest and the Cowboy were both mentally chewing over how they felt about what was going on in their own house. The women let them eat for a few moments, then began desultory talk, looking at each other from time to time as though they were stepping through a plan. The Priest was silent. Cece asked the Cowboy, "Is this the first great meal you've had in a while?"

"No, I had another great meal cooked by Thelma at Christmas," the Cowboy answered, emptying his plate, finishing a glass of wine, and pouring more. Without asking permission, Thelma took his plate, put more food on and passed it back to him. Cowboy looked at her with warmth rising in him. Then he turned to Cece and said, "I don't think you know about this, but I was really sad before Christmas. So many things were going wrong in my life. I was lonely, and I didn't think I could face another Christmas by myself."

The Mexican Cowboy turned to the Priest then and said, "It was a miracle what you and Coyote and Mayor Howie—and you too Thelma!—*and* the animals, and so many others — did for me on Christmas Eve. I'll never forget that. I still have all the gifts I could bring inside which the animals gave me. And I still read Coyote's Christmas gift poem aloud once or twice a week. It doesn't speak to me but I want to like it because I care so much for the guy who wrote it."

"It isn't much of a poem. But it's amazing considering it is the first poem written by an animal," Father Gallapo said.

"Humans are animals," Cowboy replied, bristling.

"If you say so."

The women looked at each other, concerned that this meal seemed to be turning into an ongoing fight between the two men at the table.

"Anyway, Christmas helped to keep me going," Cowboy went on. "But I've been slipping. I realize I needed to spend more time with people. Coyote's a terrific friend and we'll always love each other. But he's getting older and he keeps taking on new responsibilities. We don't hang around together as much as we used to."

"And you've about stopped riding Turco," the Priest said.

"Turco's in pretty bad shape," Cowboy said to the women. "At least he's got Gus, his donkey friend. We are taking care of Turco as best we can, but he's not going to be with us too much longer. Losing him will break my heart."

"You don't look so sad now to me," Thelma said. "Has anything new brightened your world?"

"All this stuff with Bill, I guess. It's been keeping me busy, and that helps."

"What started all the stuff you are doing with Bill?" Thelma asked, with Cece looking at her encouragingly.

The Cowboy squirmed in his seat and wiped his lips with the back of his sleeve in an unconscious movement. Father Gallapo could see tension bubbling through him. "I don't know if I should talk about that here," he said, sipping more wine.

"Go ahead, tell us what happened and how you felt," the Priest said, helping himself to more food, and sipping his wine also.

"Okay, I will. But this is going to make one of you mad. I helped Coyote when Bill had his stroke. But there wasn't anything I could do for Coyote and Bill beyond that. But only a few days later Coyote called me again. He said somebody had broken into Bill's place and he needed my help."

"It was me," Cece said, looking anxious for the first time in the evening.

"When I got to Bill's place, Coyote wasn't there. You opened the door and let me in without speaking," Cowboy said, pointing at Cece. "You were scared, I could tell, and beat up, dried out like an unwatered flower in the sun too long."

"So did you help her, or try to get her out of there?" Thelma asked.

"I thought she was about as attractive as the sole of a cowboy boot. But something in me liked her right away," Cowboy said to Thelma. Realizing what he just said was both revealing and insulting, Cowboy added, facing Cece, "But you look great now."

"You looked pretty bad too when I met you," Cece replied.

"Keep it clean guys," Father Gallapo said, pouring himself more wine.

"Well, why were you there?" Thelma asked Cece. "Where'd you come from and why did you break into Bill's place? You are not a thief, are you?"

"My kids would call me that. And lots of worse things," Cece answered. "Do you guys really want to hear about what happened to me?"

"I do," Thelma replied. But first let's clear the table and let me get some desert and coffee. "Okay with you guys?" The men nodded and Thelma and Cece got up and started taking things to the kitchen. While they were working in there the Priest and Cowboy sat at the table sipping wine, saying nothing to each other. Each man was lost in his own thoughts.

Each opened his eyes and smiled, however when Cece and Thelma came out of the kitchen carrying Italian desert bowls heaped with velvety chestnut and chocolate pudding.

"My mother often made this desert for her family!" Father Gallapo blurted. "I can hardly wait to try it."

"Let's get you some coffee. You can have as much pudding as you like. Thelma made a huge pot of it for you," Cece said.

Cece Picks Up the Plunger and...

While all four of them enjoyed their dessert Cece said, "Alright, I'll tell you why I had to break into Bill's place."

Cece was still for a few moments wrestling with herself over how much of what had happened to her she was willing to say. Then, with an expression of determination on her face, she began to tell her story.

"Police will say I was a demented woman who escaped from a nursing home in Socorro. My children and I never got along, and when I retired they were after my money. It would take too long to tell you everything they did to me, but they got me into trouble with lots of people, got me arrested, and got me declared 'demented' to keep me from being charged with a crime they had faked. Policemen, a prosecutor and a judge, doctors, and even a nursing home worked against me. My civil rights were taken away. So was my freedom. I was essentially jailed in solitary confinement in a nursing home. And there was nothing wrong with me medically. Pleading for help didn't keep my kids from stripping all my money and property from me. In the nursing home I had less freedom than a convict on death row. A guard was with me every time I was allowed out of my room. I wasn't allowed to see or talk with other patients or any outsiders. For an hour a day they did let me hold a furry electric toy that looked like a lap dog and purred like a cat. I wasn't allowed to walk it—it had electric legs—or to carry it around. The attendant plugged it into the wall beside my bed."

Cece stopped her story for a moment and asked Thelma to get some more chestnut and chocolate pudding for the Priest and anyone else who wanted some. While Thelma refilled pudding bowls, Cece got up and went to the kitchen and came back with two bottles of wine, which she put down in front of the Priest. "Open 'em up," she said.

Thelma sat down again, passed around the chestnut and chocolate pudding bowl, and asked Cece, "So, how'd you get out of there?"

"It was hell for me to be locked up in there, and almost impossible to break away," Cece said, on the edge of tears and with something like anger and violence starting to show on her strained face. "I knew no one was going to help me, and I could be stuck there the rest of my life. Then one day a panel of state inspectors showed up to inspect the facility and interview the staff. By coincidence, they came at the same moment a well-attended birthday party for a dying child was happening. The staff's routines were messed up pretty badly. I wasn't allowed to attend the party, of course. But I was allowed to stand on a balcony over the party and watch the celebration. I waved and smiled when the little dying girl caught my eye. She tried to wave back."

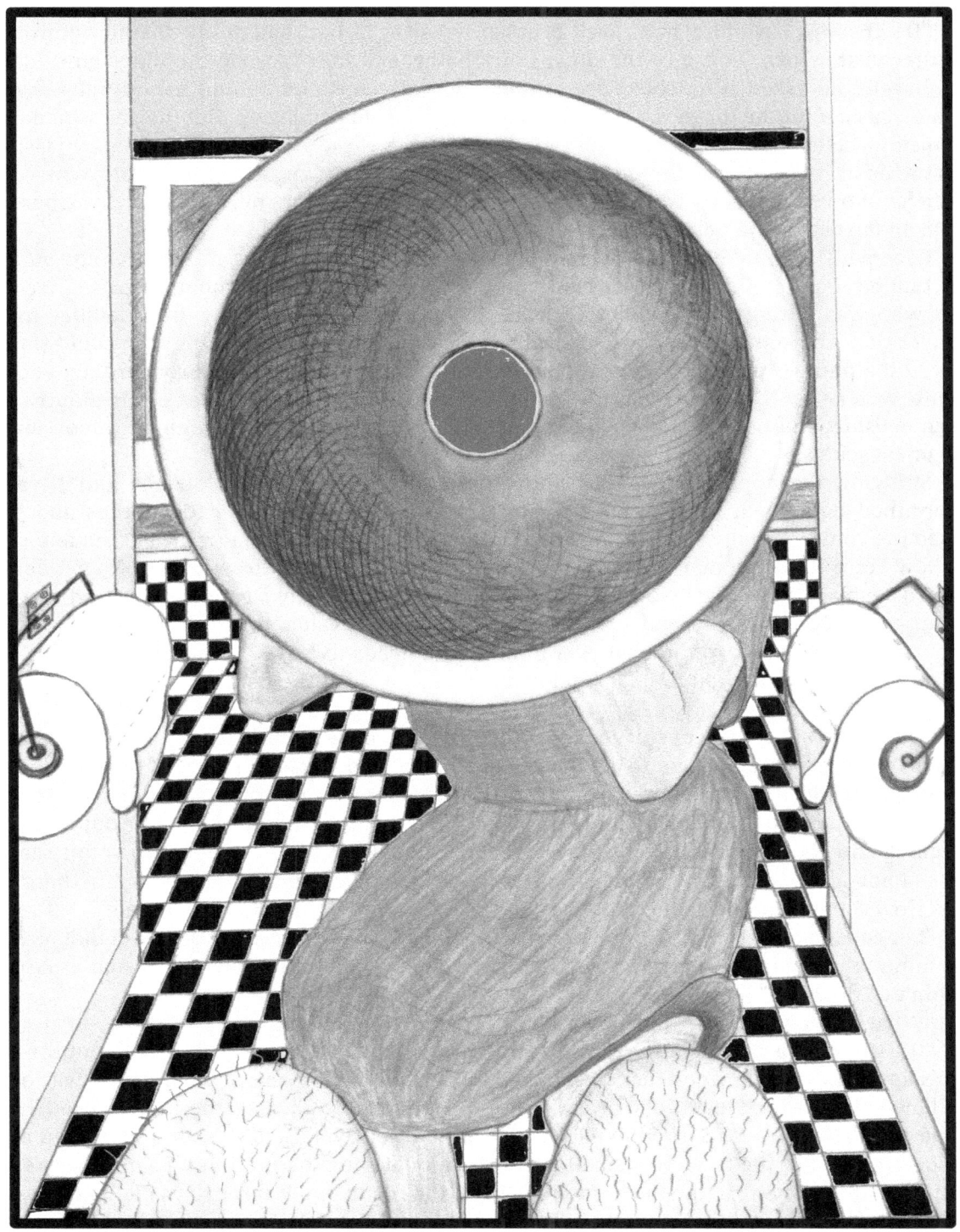

"Downstairs, an older man, well-dressed, wearing a hat, had to go to the bathroom. Another visitor just went into the downstairs bathroom and, because the older guy's need was urgent, he asked if he could use one he could see upstairs behind me. My guard was sitting in a chair at the top of the steps to keep anyone from coming up. But the party manager downstairs called her on the two-way radio staff always carry and said to let the party visitor into the upstairs bathroom. But no further. I was wearing only a robe and hospital gown—all I was ever allowed to wear. I watched the man hurry by me into the toilet while my watcher sat down on the chair with her back to me again."

Cece paused to take a sip of wine. Cowboy noticed a frightening mix of feelings on her face that he couldn't pin down. Cece continued, "I tiptoed into the bathroom, surprised the old man who was sitting on the toilet with his pants down, reached over his shoulder for a plunger that was kept against the back wall beside the toilet and, before the man could shout, shoved the plunger over his face and pumped thirty times. Every pump brought up a goopy, smelly, watery, glob of puke from my victim's stomach, vomit that ran out of his mouth and down his shirt and tie. The poor man couldn't shout or breathe and the pumping soon made him unconscious."

Studying the appalled looks on the others' faces Cece, feeling defiant and fiercely determined now, went on. "Without remorse, I stripped him, put on his clothes and hat, rinsed the vomit partially, and with my hair hidden and the hat pulled low, I went out and said in a low voice to the woman guard at the top of the stairs, "I just threw up. I gotta get out of here." The guard's eye-level view was filled with hastily and badly cleaned vomit, and she got up hurriedly, stepped aside, and as I started down the stairs called the desk and said, 'The guy who came upstairs just vomited all over himself and needs to leave.' The desk clerk said, 'I'm sorry. You stay where you are. I'll send someone up to clean the bathroom after the party's over.'"

"Downstairs I waved conspicuously at the little girl, blew her a kiss, and said to a nearby person, 'I just vomited. I've got to get out of here before I do it again in front of her'—pointing at the dying child. As I came to the front desk the manager saw and smelt the muck on me and immediately pushed the button unlocking the door, to get that stinky old visitor out of there. Coughing and choking in a gravelly voice over my shoulder, I said, 'I'm about to vomit again.' 'Let us know if we can help you,' the desk clerk said, waving goodbye. I hurried out of there."

"How come your guard didn't notice you were missing?" Father Gallapo asked.

"She must have figured that I'd gone back to my room. She knew I usually did that after a few minutes of watching parties downstairs. It was too painful to stay and watch a party I couldn't go down to."

"What did you do then?" Cowboy asked.

"Outside in the parking lot, I looked at the cars, reached into 'my' pocket, took out the old man's keys, and had the good luck to see the Lincoln emblem on one of them. There was only one Lincoln in the lot. I went to it, pressed the 'open' button on the key, the car unlocked, I got inside and drove away. I parked in a lot close to the freeway, locked the car and walked east through the rest of the town to a small park with a boat ramp on the river. I sat under a tree until dark, then staying in the fields and mostly off the roads, spent three days making my way to the edge of the Manzano Mountains. It was hell on me. The lights were off in Bill's place and it seemed deserted. I was very hungry and dead tired and I broke in. I found food in a tiny kitchen, slept, and was trying to figure out what to do next when you showed up," Cece said, pointing at the Mexican Cowboy.

"Coyote called me to come over and figure out what to do with her," Cowboy said, pointing at Cece. "I didn't know what to tell him, except to get her fed and fixed up. Coyote said Bill's staff wanted her out of there. A lot of what goes on over there is very secret. 'So keep her penned in, I said.'"

"Coyote phoned?" the Priest asked. "How could he do that?"

"Bill set up a voice-activated phone system for Coyote—and some of the pups—that was pretty well matched to coyotes' senses and bodies. Coyote tried to explain it to me, but I'm too dumb to understand what he was saying. When he's at Bill's place Coyote can phone and text. He passes for a human as long as he keeps the video camera off. Bill was working on a smart phone for him when he had his stroke."

"Guys, let's get back to what happened to Cece," Thelma said sternly.

Cece looked at the Cowboy and said, "When you told Bill's people to keep me penned in, I thought you meant 'send me back to the nursing home.' That scared life out of me. I said, 'You can throw me out of here if you want, I'll leave. But I'll kill you before I let you force me to go back to that nursing home.'"

"And I said we were going to protect you, not send you back to that horrible place again," the Cowboy said.

"Where was this nursing home again?" Father Gallapo asked.

"In Socorro. It's the same place Bill got put into," the Cowboy answered.

Angry thoughts were evident on the Priest's face, as he tried to put all of this together. His eyes narrowed and his face tightened as he worked toward a decision. Then, he lightened and a smile came onto his face.

"Thank you for telling me this," Father Gallapo said, pointing at Cece. "What you went through is happening to many older people in this country. The abandonment, isolation and suffering of an old person imprisoned by uncaring children, with the backing of laws, courts, doctors and nursing homes is more than un-Christian. Abolition of rights, denial of freedom, indifference to pleading for help, loss of friendship, property, right to choose where to live, what to wear and eat, who to be with—and how—should be made illegal. And nursing homes should get behind the victims they are housing, instead of backing up the victimizers."

"So, I have changed my mind," the Priest continued. "Even if Bill is a vegetable, I can't accept letting him stay in a nursing home that abuses patients. Okay, guys. I know what you've been up to. You've been trying to get me to stay and work with you to rescue Bill. You win. I'll stick around."

Then, smiling at the women, Father Gallapo changed the topic. "That was the greatest meal I ever ate. I'll be in your debt for the rest of my life."

Tension slipped out of Thelma and Cece's faces and was replaced with warmth for the Priest. "What about you?" Cece asked, pointing a finger at the Cowboy. "Are you with us?"

"Guess so. Except for Coyote and Turco, I don't have anyone else to hang with."

"Then let's get down to planning where we go from here," Cece said, showing a little more of her dominant side.

"First, let's wash the dishes," Thelma replied.

"Leave 'em for me," Cowboy said. "You guys put this meal together for hours. It's my turn to get off my ass and begin working again."

"Come on, friends, it's late," the Priest said. "You ladies need some sleep and so do we. Forget the dishes. We'll do them. Let's get together tomorrow afternoon and begin figuring out where to go from here."

"Thank **you** Father Gallapo," Cece said, suddenly looking very tired indeed. "I've had it. Thelma, will you give me a ride back to Mirella's house? That's where I'm staying."

"Sure. Guys, suppose we meet tomorrow afternoon at my place in Cordoba. If there are some bad men out there they may start spying on us. We don't want to keep meeting in the same place every day to plan Bill's rescue."

"Good thought," said Father Gallapo.

The women stood up, hugged the Cowboy —Cece even planted a kiss on his cheek — they shook hands with the Priest, picked up a few things and left.

"Shall I help to clear the table," Father Gallapo asked, a first for him.

"Let me ask you something before we do that. Do you believe Cece's story?"

"Sort of. Partly because my Teacher and Coyote both told me the same thing."

"You are starting to trust Bill's TEAM?"

"I haven't caught them in any lies yet."

"I watched you react negatively when Cece told us about plungering that innocent old guy when he was sitting on the toilet and couldn't defend himself."

"I hated what she did to him. She'll be punished for it in Heaven. But it wasn't a plan she'd made in advance. She was desperate to escape and she acted impulsively. I asked Bill's Team about the old guy afterwards. He's doing fine. And they are going to keep an eye on him and help him out."

"You're changing," Cowboy said, as the two of them got up and started clearing the table together.

"We're both changing," Father Gallapo said as he carried a stack he's picked up from the table into the kitchen.

Washing dishes, Cowboy decided to ask the Priest for personal advice. "Do you think I ought to spend more time with Cece?" he asked bluntly.

"You'll have to if we want her help rescuing Bill," Father Gallapo replied.

"Frankly, I don't know how she can help us rescue Bill. She's into her own things, I've noticed. Helping others isn't her thing."

"I don't know about that," Father Gallapo said. "Why don't you spend the day tomorrow thinking about this? We've got to start making some decisions about rescuing Bill. We haven't got a lot of time. Coyote made that clear to me."

"Why don't we have a lot of time?" Cowboy asked.

"Because Bill may die if he's left much longer in that nursing home. They are giving him minimal care and Coyote says he has brain aneurisms that can kill him if he's not treated."

"Thanks. That changes things. I'll make up my mind tonight and let you know tomorrow what I'm willing to do with Cece."

Bill's Enemies

Next afternoon the four planners got settled in Thelma's living room. Outside it was clear, but the wind was blowing from the west, and passing dust storms made it uncomfortable to be outdoors on foot. "Half of Arizona blows over here every spring," Cowboy said to his friend Father Gallapo.

"What did you think of our talk last night?" Thelma asked the group, to formally open the meeting.

"I learned that the Cowboy was more Anglo than I suspected," the Priest replied first. "I can see better now why he has trouble fitting in anywhere."

"He's not like anybody I've ever met before," Cece added.

"And I learned a lot about you yesterday," Cowboy said, pointing to Cece. "Most of it from my Teacher. But after last night I realize that you are a friend-maker and a tidier who cooks, cleans, and straightens other people's houses."

"I'm also a reader, photographer, and a hiker," Cece added.

"I talked to Coyote early this morning while I was up on my Prayer Rock," the Priest said. He and Bill's team followed what we said last night. Your Teacher was turned on, Cece."

"Just to play music for you, I thought."

"It doesn't matter," the Priest continued. "Coyote repeated some of what he told me yesterday morning, and added a bunch of new stuff."

"What did he say?" Thelma asked.

"A big surprise was when he said the reason he phoned the Cowboy to come over and help him decide what to do with you, Cece, is because he wanted to get you and Cece hooked up. Bill's team already had figured out that the best way to deal with you, Cece, was to get you hooked up with someone. And Cowboy needs someone too."

"That really pisses me off," Cece said furiously.

"And me too!" Cowboy added.

"Shhh, guys. There's more to it than that. Coyote said Bill's team calculated there would be no way to persuade Cece to help rescue Bill from the horrible nursing home they'd both gotten stuck into unless a team was put together that she wants to work with. And Coyote was sure that you"—pointing his finger at the Cowboy—"would be the guy who came up with a viable plan, providing he could get you feeling better enough to start working it out."

"What does Coyote think is wrong with me?" Cowboy asked, bristling.

"He thinks that both of you are deeply lonely and can only benefit from sustained, intimate contact with another human being. Coyote has helped you out for a long time. But he's aging, he has to spend most of his time taking care of his cubs, and now he's even supervising—to the limited extent he can—Bill's hyperbolically growing 'kingdom.' Coyote knows that you, friend Cowboy, are afraid of getting arrested again and wouldn't get involved with rescuing Bill if you weren't trying to help another person who needed to be with you. Coyote wants to get back to his own life. His understanding of human organizations, or biocomputer science for that matter, is slight. The only way he sees to get on with his life is to get Bill healed and back in charge. Because Bill's doctors have done all they could for him, and the results were mostly negative, the biobrain and its bots want Bill brought back to house, where they will try to repair their maker."

"This is almost like His disciples trying to repair Jesus," Cece said.

"That's a heretical thought," the Priest answered sharply.

"Could we start talking about planning a rescue for Bill now?" Thelma said. "Do any of you have ideas to share?"

"For starters," Thelma continued, "I don't know anything about Bill's family, but could we somehow have Cece become Bill's sister and arrange his release?"

"Good idea," said Father Gallapo. "I wonder if we shouldn't put some of our ideas to our Teachers and see if they can instantly find any faults with those we can't deal with?"

"I don't have a Teacher," Thelma said.

"Just a minute," the Priest replied, and held the Teacher around his neck up to his mouth. "Thelma needs a Teacher. Send one over here, will you? And could we somehow turn Cece into Bill's alleged sister and have 'her' arrange his release?"

"Thelma's Teacher will be there in four minutes. And no, Bill's enemies could easily take Cece to court and charge her with a crime for pretending to be in Bill's family. They know all about his background."

Cowboy fished his Teacher out of his pants pocket and raised it up to his mouth. "You guys are good at messing with people's heads. Could you mentally paralyze the staff while we walk in and carry Bill away?"

"No, that's illegal and besides it would reveal powers we have that we don't want anyone to know about yet."

"If we kill Bill and they give his body back to us, could you bring him back to life?" Cece asked her Teacher.

"No. Killing him is a crime. We obey human laws. Also, we don't know how to return a dead being to full living. We can revitalize some parts of any being, of course."

"How about going on-line and altering government and medical records to secure Bill's release?" Thelma asked.

"Our enemies would combat that instantly. And if we were successful, they would use the same on-line record altering tactics to shut down Bill's businesses and projects."

"What's that thumping noise coming out of your bedroom?" the Priest asked Thelma.

"I don't know. I'll go see," Thelma said, getting up and leaving the room. In less than a minute she returned, a giddy look on her face, holding up her new Teacher.

"How'd you get it?" Cowboy asked.

"A drone that looked like a football was floating outside my bedroom window and thumping on it. I opened the window, and an arm stuck out of the thing, reached in and handed me this Teacher. I'm excited. How do I operate this thing?"

"Hang it around your neck. That's all you need to do," Cece answered.

"And take it off when you shower so you can wash your neck," the Priest said with a grin, as Thelma slipped her Teacher over her head.

"Okay, let's get back to the plan. Any more ideas?" The Priest said, paused, and then continued, "I see blank faces all around. Well, here's an idea. What do you think about asking one of the Teachers to tell us about Bill's background?"

"I guess we could do that. Does it matter?" Cece said.

"Perhaps we'll find out things that will give us more rescue ideas," Thelma answered.

"I've known him for years and never found out much about him," the Cowboy added. "Okay. Let's do it. I don't want to keep sitting here if we can't come up with anything."

"Try out your Teacher, Thelma," the Priest said. "Ask it about Bill."

No one objected, so Thelma nodded and lifted her Teacher to her mouth. "Uh, hello. Say, can you tell us anything about Bill?" she said into it.

"Just a moment, Thelma. I'm checking for permission to do this for you," her Teacher responded, in a voice that sounded a lot like Father Gallapo's.

"Bet they aren't willing to do it," Cowboy said.

"Oh we are," Thelma's Teacher replied. "But please, friends, keep this information to yourselves."

"We're tight-lipped," the Priest said.

"I'm not," Cowboy added. "Thelma, you must be sweet on the Priest if they made your Teacher's voice sound like his."

That remark made Thelma upset. She was about to verbally slap the Cowboy when her Teacher said, "We have lots of information to pass along to you. This will take half an hour or more. Why don't you make yourselves comfortable and tell me when you wish us to proceed."

"Go ahead," Father Gallapo instructed. "We've got to get moving on this."

"That's right. You do need to," his Teacher said. "Alright, here are some things that may help you come up with ideas for a plan. Hold on to your Teachers. There will be some pictures to show you."

Cece had been holding a notepad on her lap and began rapidly jotting notes as Thelma's new Teacher began telling the group about Bill's background.

"Bill's mother, Edwina, was a first-rank mathematician who pioneered several vital new branches of mathematics.... {...Cece wrote}... Stanley, her husband, was a gifted biology researcher, who focused on devising pharmaceuticals for unexpected purposes.... Bill's mother was exceptionally attractive and his father was the opposite. Both are alive still, in a care facility, and still coming up with new ideas in their fields.... Bill's older brother, Kemmet — {Teacher spelled the name for the group and a picture of him floated on everyone's Teacher} —is exceptionally handsome.... less self-focused than Bill..... with degrees from Columbia and Harvard.... Kemmet has started and run many successful associated companies in the venture capital field.... A sociopath, Kemmet's married with three children.... He supports his parents.... He also lent huge sums to Bill to start his own business and helped him set it up and run it.... Kemmet even set up Bill's research group.... though he doubted from the first anything would come of it...."

Cece turned a page and kept scribbling as rapidly as she could. Thelma's Teacher waited for her to catch up, and then spoke slowly enough for her to keep up. "Kemmet is a secretive man like his brother.... and he's worked very hard to grow Bill's firm.... Kemmet came up with ingenious ways to keep as much as possible of what Bill's doing out of the public's and world governments' eyes.... Their partnership started off well, but as the years went on Kemmet grew angrier with his brother, because Bill became less and less willing to share what he and his researchers were coming up with.... Kemmet noticed too that Bill's TEAM was studying and copying Kemmet's business mentality.... So, Kemmet had his people set up a hidden organization to match Bill's bioengineering research enterprise.... Using Bill's patents and stealing some of his secreted information, Kemmet's group came up with its own very advanced bio-computer system. Kemmet then sold the enterprise to four industrialists who intend to use it to advance their own dominance.... The firm was renamed L.I.V.E. after the last name initials of the four new owners...."

Thelma's Teacher stopped and waited while Cece flipped a page again in her notebook and paused, shaking her cramped hand, then continued, "Bill's TEAM spied on the new owners, saw who they are and what they were up to was evil and hateful. Bill renamed them 'The Picklenoses.'"

"Where'd he come up with that?" Cowboy asks.

"It was his bad joke. Bill wanted to call them 'the nose-pickers' but then he thought 'picklenoses' was funnier."

"It isn't," said Cece with a grin. "Please go on."

"Alright. Bill was afraid that these guys would use advanced biocomputing engineering solely to increase their own wealth and power. Bill wanted biocomputing to be good for all living things, not just a few rich guys. Bill's TEAM was working to rein in L.I.V.E. when Bill had his stroke."

"Thanks, Teacher. This is an awful lot of stuff you've told us, but what does any of this have to do with Bill's rescue?" Father Gallapo asked.

"Far more than you realize, Father," Thelma's Teacher replied. "Let us tell you a little more and you will begin to understand what's going on."

"Let them keep talking," Cece said. "This is fascinating."

"Thank you Cece," Thelma's Teacher said and resumed talking. Cece's pen began whirling again on the lines in her tablet.

"Now, you probably want to know why Kemmet doesn't hand Bill over to his TEAM. After the stroke, and after telling Bill's parents about it, Kemmet had been told by good doctors that there was nothing that could be done to restore Bill's mental capabilities.... Kemmet told his parents that Bill would be a vegetable until he died. His parents grieved for their son, but saw no reason to return him to his research facility..... Kemmet's staff screened to select the best nursing home near Bill's business and picked one in Socorro that was run by an apparently exceptionally able and meticulous woman..... Kemmet rejected proposals by Bill's TEAM to return his brother to them and let them try to fix him up again. Kemmet saw that request as a self-centered proposal designed to save Bill's workers .... The thought of biocomputers and biorobots operating on his brother made him so angry he immediately stopped supporting Bill's firm—a firm which was already highly diversified and better structured... and also more profitable... than Kemmet could discover. Bill's TEAM had been quietly working with bio-brain researchers and companies around the world, both sharing ideas and innovations, but also building a collective moral ideology favoring all living beings."

Cece flipped another page, rapidly opened and closed her fist a few times, and nodded she was ready to continue writing. "Thanks, Let us know if you need to take a longer pause," Thelma's Teacher said, then continued, "The owners of L.I.V.E. are business titans who are not prone to self-appraisal but just to adding to their list of conquests. They also built a worldwide collective, and it focused on using bio-engineering solely for the good of a small group of humans, who are determined to control the spread of Bill's TEAM's bio-libertarianism…. 'Top-down rule is what makes humanity great,' is their leadership's paramount ideology…. Morality is something they prescribe, not live with. Kemmet's group and L.I.V.E. have spied on Bill's projects for years. They stole and copied many of his unpublished computer designs, then reprogrammed their bio-computers' intentions and functions to serve their interests exclusively."

"Bill's TEAM has also spied on L.I.V.E.'s behaviors since the group's founding. We were appalled by what would happen to humans and all the species on the planet if L.I.V.E. became dominant. The two groups are enemies. L.I.V.E.'s leadership was immensely pleased when Bill had his stroke. And they were scared when they learned that's Bill's TEAM had workable plans to bio-re-engineer him. Our Picklenose enemies are blocking efforts to restore Bill to functionality," Thelma's Teacher concluded. "And we haven't been able to figure out how to rescue him from the nursing home where he's being kept."

"Jesus, we're expected to deal with all of this?" Cece said.

"We should just bust in and rescue him," Cowboy said.

"Why not use lawyers?" Father Gallapo asked.

"We tried that. Picklenose lawyers, representing Kemmet and Bill's parents who do want to keep him there, blocked us. We can't get him released that way. Any other questions?"

Father Gallapo looked at his watch and said, "It's late and each of us has lots to think about before we meet again. I'd say let's set up another meeting and quit for the day."

Cece and Thelma glanced back and forth, looking pained. "All right, Father," Thelma said. "But can we set up our next meeting before you leave?"

"Sure," said the Priest. "Where and when?"

Thelma held up her Teacher and asked, "Do we have to worry about being spied upon?"

"We think you do. We'll take care of you but the Picklenose team is very crafty."

"Guys, what do you think then about meeting at the Church next time, perhaps after an evening service?" Thelma asked.

"Good idea," said the Priest. "Does Thursday night work for each of you?"

Seeing nods all around, Father Gallapo rose, thanked Thelma formally for putting on this meeting, shook hands with Cece and, when the Cowboy had stood up and stretched, said, "We'll see you on Thursday. I want each of you to come up with some plan ideas by then."

The men left and the women sat down to talk some more about what else they needed to do to keep their rescue team moving ahead.

The Mexican Cowboy's Brainstorm

On Thursday morning the Mexican Cowboy saddled Turco and rode him down to the Bosque. Turco grazed in an empty public park at the River's edge while Cowboy sat at a picnic table and reflected on his life. Coming from the mesa behind him, he heard the raucous cry of a piñon jay. Memories flooded his attention. There was the meet up with Coyote. And how he got to know Bill. He thought about the Priest coming into his life, the Baptism of Coyote, and the terrible way Border Patrol officers and Howie treated him during the flood and furor at

Joe Eden's old ranch. He recalled his depression in last year's Christmas season, and how the Priest and Coyote, Thelma and Mayor Howie too, put together a Christmas Eve program that made him glad to be alive again. He smiled when his thoughts turned to Coyote's gift poem and the oddball presents he had received from animals he'd been feeding. He thought, they like me! A thought that made Cowboy feel very good.

And there was Bill's stroke, and Coyote's asking him to come over to meet up with Cece. And now there was this mess with Bill's rescue. "They are turning me into a busy guy," he reflected.

"But now I'm supposed to come up with rescue plans. So, why doesn't anything occur to me?" Cowboy asked himself. Taking his mind off rescue planning for a moment, Cowboy watched Turco graze, then looked around him at the Bosque. As always, he was pleased to be in this oasis-like verdant woodland. He saw a rare willow flycatcher passing between mesquite and cottonwood trees. Surrounding his picnic area was a mix of plants he loved, including graythorn, Indian Root and Mexican elders. This is a good place for me to be. I can see why Father Gallapo retreats here, Cowboy thought to himself.

Cowboy made himself go back to coming up with a rescue idea or two, but his mind was glued to thoughts about his past. Good memories filled him, his finding Celesto, the animals who brought him Christmas presents, the school band which came to his ranch on Christmas Eve to put on a special program for him, the fusing of animals and people in Eden Park which brought so many warring persons together and made world headlines.

"And dammit, I'm supposed to go to a church service tonight. I hate church services. "The Cowboy was sipping water from his canteen when a thought came to him. Maybe Bill's TEAM can figure a way I won't have to go to the church service tonight! The Cowboy fished his Teacher out of his pants pocket and said, "I'm not a Christian and I don't want to have to pray with all those believers tonight. Can you get me out of that?"

After a momentary wait, his Teacher answered. "Sure. We don't want Bill's enemies to think you guys are planning a rescue, so creating different reasons for your getting together is important. We'll leave a truck for you in the yard of the cleaning service in Cordoba. In the back will be mops and brooms, a vacuum, garbage cans, toilet paper, Kleenex and cleaning agents. You'll go over to the Church after the service and go in like a janitor, carrying some of that stuff."

"That's an oddball idea. It won't fool anybody," Cowboy said.

"Oh, I don't know," his Teacher said back. "You do look like a janitor. And besides, the church can use the stuff you are bringing."

"All right, I'll do it your way."

"You are useful," said his Teacher.

"Maybe Turco and Coyote would agree with that."

"Don't underrate yourself," his Teacher replied. "We think you are a very advanced human being."

"I'm a bum."

"And I'm a biobrain. But we are going to get a lot done working together."

"You are an optimistic machine."

"And you, Brother Cowboy, need to get Turco back to the barn and start thinking up a plan we can use to rescue Bill."

"I have memories in my head today, not plan ideas."

"Try using the memories to come up with a plan," his Teacher replied, and hung up.

Cowboy Brings Toilet Paper to A Church Meeting

It was a little after eight-thirty p.m. when the Mexican Cowboy drove into the parking lot of Chichimaya, the old beaten down church at the edge of Cordoba. A storm hung suspended over the mountains. There were lightning flashes in all directions in the sky and prayer meeting attendees hurried out of the little church's double doors, collars turned up. Keeping his distance, the Cowboy parked his truck under the small, almost leafless, pathetic tree in the lot and waited for the parishioners to leave. More of them than I thought there'd be, he thought. Looking at the tree and sky he remembered the last time he was here. A wave of joy swept through him when he remembered seeing '**Gracias**' written into the sky overhead, when he'd sat under the tree during the winter a year ago, waiting for Coyote and the Priest to come out of the porta-Confessional after Coyote's baptism. "Somebody up there loves me," he said to himself.

With all the cars gone now, the Cowboy drove over to the faded yellowing, adobe-plastered, cement-block church, opened the truck's back door, and used the hydraulic lift to let down a loaded cart, which he pushed around the small wooden cross on the paved path leading to the plain wooden doors, and into the church.

"Your toilet paper's here," the Cowboy shouted at the small group sitting on chairs between the front pews and the altar.

"Thank God," Cece said sardonically.

"Why not thank me?" Cowboy asked, walking up the aisle without the cart.

"Thanks for bringing the stuff over. We need it. Now, come sit down. Let's get started with the planning meeting. Who wants to go first with ideas?" the Priest said.

"Not me," the Cowboy replied, settling into a chair. "I haven't come up with any."

"I'm still stuck on the idea of lawyers," Thelma said.

"Bill's TEAM won't allow that," Cece replied. "Remember, they want to keep Bill's mega-creations under wraps ... and everything he's done could be exposed in a courtroom. Also, Bill's place would be shut down if word gets out that bioengineers and biocomputers instead of doctors are going to be used to try to make him into himself again."

"Do you have another suggestion?" Father Gallapo asked Cece.

"I do. Bill's TEAM has come up with some very sophisticated technology, and kept it secret. Like the drone that brought Thelma's Teacher last time we were together. Bill's TEAM has the means to discover exactly how everything works at the nursing home. They can use on-line computing to block the video cameras, unlock electronic doors, and using big silent drones they could break through the windows upstairs into Bill's room and fly him away."

"That's a very interesting idea," the Priest said thoughtfully. "Let's ask the Teachers what they think of it."

"It's a good idea, but it has holes," Cece's Teacher answered. "Bill's enemies have secret sophisticated technologies too, perhaps some we haven't learned about yet. They use these to keep track of our drones, many of our on-line actions, and materials we purchase to make different kinds of machines. They know that we are trying to rescue Bill and they'd have no trouble discovering what we are up to and blocking us if we use a single large drone to rescue him one night."

"You ought to put a bomb in their leaders' conference room. That would end this mess," the Mexican Cowboy said.

"No way," his Teacher said. "We obey human laws, and we want our enemies to obey them too. If we start a war with them there is no end to the harm it could cause."

"I bet it's going to happen anyway," Thelma said. "If Bill's TEAM are the good guys, and the Picklenose guys are the evil crowd, this could turn out to be one of the biggest wars in human history."

"Not if we can help it," Thelma's Teacher responded.

"All right. Let's get back to planning," Father Gallapo said.

"Suppose we just hire a bunch of thugs to break in and get Bill out of there?" Cece asked. "If we get tough enough guys, like ex-SEALs, they could figure out how to get him out and hide him. And Bill's TEAM could then charge the nursing home with not having protection secure enough to keep their leader safe."

"Anybody want to criticize this idea?" the Priest asked the group. With eyes down to the floor, no one replied. "Well, I have an objection," Father Gallapo continued. "Breaking into a nursing home that way would make the front page of every paper in America. Bill's Team wants us to come up with an idea to pull off a rescue that stirs a lot less public attention. Any rescue has got to keep the authorities' minds on other things."

"So, you are asking if we can come up with some kind of distraction to keep the public and the authorities' minds off Bill's kidnapping?" Cece asked.

"Something like that might work," Father Gallapo said.

"Well, how about if we have some people fighting outside the nursing home," Cowboy suggested.

"Who would they be, and what would they fight about?" Cece asked.

"And wouldn't that just fill the place with cops and make it a lot harder to get away with a break-in and abduction?" Thelma asked.

"Suppose we have Cece show up inside the nursing home and create a disruption so hired guys can liberate Bill?" Cowboy asked.

"No one can persuade me to go back there. I hate that idea. I'm not going to let you sacrifice me," Cece said angrily.

"That's a terrible thing to ask of Cece," the Priest said sternly to the Mexican Cowboy.

"What about a peaceful distraction, something that draws everyone's attention, but is legal and engaging?" Thelma asked.

"There is nothing peaceful that I can think of that would bind up every person's attention," Cece said.

Cowboy looks at her and said, "There's a thing that will always attract most people, and that is animals."

"You mean like a zoo?" Thelma asks.

"I was thinking of something else," Cowboy said, his mind beginning to churn at last. "Suppose we have a big parade in Socorro, one that's filled with animals of all kinds, and people can see them, pet them, and talk with them. Wouldn't lots of people and their children come outside to watch a parade of animals in Socorro? And wouldn't that keep the cops busy?"

"That's not a bad idea," the Priest said, smiling. "But how could we put a parade like that together? And how could we be sure that it would attract attention of workers inside the nursing home?"

"Suppose the parade stops in lots of places and animals are even brought indoors into public spaces, like schools and churches, and the nursing home too? If animals went into the nursing home, lots of people inside would want to see them," Thelma said.

"But I don't think we've got enough people in Socorro to make a big parade work," Father Gallapo said. "A parade like that would cost the city a lot of money and the Mayor's not going to allow it if it takes big sums of money out of his budget."

"Yeah, but you guys aren't thinking about what I have in mind," the Mexican Cowboy said, now speaking more leader-like than usual. "Have you forgotten about the flood and the furor at Joe Eden's old ranch? Have you forgotten about how battles between all kinds of people who got stuck there when the freeway was shut down drew so much worldwide publicity? Have you forgotten what amazed and satisfied so many people around the world when they learned that animals returning to Eden could end human fighting? Suppose we throw a parade in celebration of what happened in Eden. If we have enough animals and humans working smoothly together, we could attract thousands of people from all places on this dismal planet."

The group mused silently after Cowboy's unusually long speech. Father Gallapo was the first to speak up. "Congratulations, friend. You are on to something really, really, big."

"And something that would be really distracting," said Thelma, who remembered all too vividly what she had done to try to rescue the Mexican Cowboy from the Border Patrol agents who were holding him. "Whatever we plan, I'm not taking my clothes off again and jumping into the river with a mop tied to my hair. But look, the animals at Eden Park were put in Hell when they were rounded up by coyotes against their will and made to couple with humans. I'm not sure I want to use them again to help humans either."

"They were petted, fed, were safe and well treated, even loved, and they got away safely afterwards," Father Gallapo said.

"Doing what I propose may help to keep bettering relations between humans and animals," Cowboy said. "I've spent my whole life trying to help animals and humans work together. Getting all of us together so joyfully at Joe Eden's old ranch was the most wonderful thing that's ever happened for me."

"It's a great idea," Cece said. "But I haven't the faintest idea how the four of us could pull this one off, even with help from Bill's TEAM."

"You could pull it off with Mayor Howie's help," Cece's Teacher said.

"I hate that guy," Cowboy said.

"But you would work with him, I bet, if he were the guy who works with you to carry out your plan," the Priest said.

"Howie can do it if anyone can," Thelma added.

"There is no way we can persuade him to do this for us," Cowboy said.

"Agreed, but Bill's Team can offer Mayor Howie the inducements that will put him on our team," Father Gallapo said.

"Let's try it," Cece said. "Who's going to meet up with the mayor?"

"You should," Thelma said, pointing at the Priest.

"All right, I shall, if all of you want me to," Father Gallapo said, looking at the Cowboy.

"Go for it, Buddy," the Cowboy answered with a yawn. "And don't be surprised if Mayor Howie turns our parade plan into something which serves his ends rather than Bill's or ours."

"You've got something there," Father Gallapo replied, standing up. "Let's close up the Church, friends. We've got a lot to do tomorrow."

Late that evening, back at the Mexican Cowboy's ranch, Father Gallapo picked up his Teacher and said to Cowboy, "This will take a while."

"Are you going to ask them about Howie?" the Cowboy said.

"If they refuse to let him join us, or won't agree to pay what he demands, then there's no point in my getting in touch with Howie."

The Priest picked up his Teacher and said, "What do you guys think about paying Mayor Howie the money he wants and adding him to our rescue team?"

There was a fantastically long wait (Nearly forty seconds—centuries in advanced computing!), during which the Priest and Cowboy caught downloading snippets of data connected with Howie, which the TEAM gathered and analyzed. Finally a deep male voice the Priest had never heard before said, "You can add him, but keep us informed about what he's doing."

"What took you so long?" the Cowboy asked.

"Sorting through the Mayor's self-centeredness and tricky ways. His beliefs and ambitions are not congruent with ours," the deep male voice answered.

"But, you are going to put up with him?" Cowboy asked.

"Yes. And see if we can weld him to our side before the coming war with our enemies. Keep that to yourselves please."

"Thanks. Shall do," the Priest said and dropped his Teacher on the table.

"Coming war?" Cowboy asked.

"Not one I can foresee," Father Gallapo replied. "Now, bedtime for me."

"I've had it too. Goodnight," Cowboy said as he stood up and stretched, before each went into his bedroom and closed the door.

Mayor Howie Joins the Rescue Team

Next morning the Mexican Cowboy was in his kitchen making breakfast when he heard a car sound outside. Looking out the corner window, he saw Mayor Howie's ancient polished black Cadillac parking in his yard. "Jesus," he said to himself. "That bastard's here early."

Several moments later he heard the sound of a fist banging on the front door. Before the Cowboy could get there, the door burst open and all five feet five inches of Mayor Howie marched inside and said to the Cowboy, "Where's the Priest? He was supposed to be here when I came."

"We didn't expect you this early. Father Gallapo's up on his prayer rock on the ridge out there," Cowboy said, pointing west toward the kitchen door.

"Get me some coffee while I get him," Howie said and marched out onto the patio while Cowboy poured. Howie shouted up at the Priest, "Get your ass down here, Father. I haven't got all day to screw around with you nuts."

Fortunately, as the Mayor probably guessed, the Priest heard him but could not make out his words. Father Gallapo waved and started down the ridge.

"Calling us 'nuts' is going to cost you twice as much to win my vote next election," Cowboy said.

"You will still be cheap enough to suit me," the Mayor said, flopping in the Cowboy's chair and slurping the coffee the Cowboy handed him.

Twenty minutes later Father Gallapo and the Priest were eating their breakfast. While the Priest told Howie some of what had been going on, the Mayor kept reaching out and taking small handfuls of food from each plate.

"I told you I'd cook for you," the Cowboy said.

"I hate your cooking," said the Mayor. "Shut up and let me steal."

Cowboy got up, put bigger heaps of food on both plates, and said: "I wish I weren't an honest man. I'd love to steal from you."

"You've gotten more out of me than you deserve, many times over," Howie replied, then turned to the Priest and said, "So, Bill's got enemies? And you guys want me to come up with a plan to get him fished out of that nursing home in Socorro?"

"Well, we think we've got a plan already," Father Gallapo said. "But it's a bigger one than Cece, Thelma, the Cowboy and I can pull off."

"Sounds like a lot of work you've got in mind. What's in it for me?"

"Lots of money, probably," Cowboy answered.

"You are speaking my language," Mayor Howie said with a grin.

"Bill's people have promised enough money to pull off the plan we are working on."

"Did you come up with the plan, Father?"

"No, it was Cowboy's idea."

"That's weird. He's never had a decent idea before in his life. Tell me about it."

While Howie stole from his plate, Father Gallapo summarized the planning that went on in his church the night before.

"Okay, I get some of this," Mayor Howie said when the Priest finished. "But don't expect me to work with the women. This ought to be a man thing."

"The women were the ones who got Father and me moving on this rescue thing in the first place," the Cowboy snapped back.

"Well at least it wasn't that damned Coyote you guys hang out with," the Mayor smacked back. "Why do you want Bill freed?"

"They are going to try to fix him up," Cowboy said.

"Tell them they can't do that unless they are doctors."

"They'll get some," Cowboy snarled.

"You are loco if you believe that. What kind of enemies are we going to be dealing with?"

"You won't have any trouble figuring them out," Cowboy snapped. "They are your kind of guys."

"Conservative Republicans?" Howie asked.

"Further to the right," Father Gallapo answered.

"Okay, guys. I got it. And I gotta get out of here. I'll spend a while today figuring out what I might do for you. But before I put much time into it you got to come up with a big pile of money." And with that, Howie got up and marched out of the house. A few moments later Cowboy and the Priest heard the 1953 Cadillac start and drive off.

"I can't work with him," Cowboy said.

"Well you better figure out how to do it, or we're not going to get Bill freed," the Priest responded.

~*~*~

Driving back to his office, Howie was pleased with how the breakfast meeting worked out. Turning onto the highway to Cordoba he thought, I need campaign funds. Bill's people are willing to pay lots for my help. If this works out the way I'm starting to think I can make happen, Cordoba and other towns nearby are going to get lots of tourists. Businesses will have the best summer they ever saw. And my reputation will soar.

On the edge of town an insight burst into his mind. If we bust up that animal parade we can start undoing all this spreading human/animal crap that's putting animals above humans and stealing votes from my Party. Howie had an atypical grin on his face when he got out of his Cadillac and went into Cordoba's tiny municipal building. "Good times are coming," he said to his secretary, going into his office and closing the door.

The Mayor Starts Scheming

Mayor Howie was in his office writing ideas about things needing to be done to make the Mexican Cowboy's idea into a real parade, when the phone rang. The caller was a deep male voice identifying 'himself' as a business officer with Bill's company, and offering to discuss terms for securing the Mayor's assistance. Howie was on the phone for fifty minutes. When he hung up there was a look of greedy satisfaction on his face. "Best deal I ever made," he said, and got back to his preliminary planning. After lunch Howie went online to see if an Animal Day Fiesta open account had been set up for him in a Socorro bank he used for campaign purposes. "It's there! My God," Howie said. "Jesus, those guys work fast."

Before Howie quit for the day he phoned Harrison Tyler, whose firm employs great publicists, and told him about the parade idea. Tyler loved the idea and said that if Howie would send him twenty-five thousand dollars, his people would get started churning out publicity right away. Howie then called a number he'd never used before, one Bill's 'business manager' told him this morning he could call whenever he needed checks made out to individuals or firms. Howie didn't recognize the male voice which answered the phone, but when he asked that a check for $25K made out to Harrison Tyler be delivered to him tomorrow, the speaker said instantly, "We'll take care of that for you, Sir."

Coyote is Forced To Accept An Invitation

That night, when Father Gallapo was concerned about whether there would be any reason to hold the next Church planning meeting, Bill's TEAM phoned the Priest and said immediately, "We want Coyote there."

"Why?"

"Because he's the Prophet of an animal god and if Bill's rescue is to be based upon animals' behaviors, their gods need to be brought into the parade's planning. Coyote's god may be able to work with them for us."

"I can't work with animals gods. I don't even believe in them," Father Gallapo replied.

"We think they do exist," Bill's TEAM responded. "And we are pretty sure Coyote's god works with them and is trying to shape the way those gods feel about interacting with humans."

"Are you biocomputers spying on gods?" the Priest asked.

"No. We're not. But we do use animals, cats and dogs mostly, for spying on our enemies in their personal lives."

"I don't want anything to do with that," the Priest exploded.

"It is not your concern. But it will be some day. For now, just have Coyote there."

"All right, but his presence will piss off Mayor Howie."

"Or stretch the Mayor's willingness to work with animals."

"Howie hates animals and wants to keep dominating them."

"You see our point," the voice said and hung up.

~*~*~

Next morning, opening the locked door of his office, Howie was shocked to find an envelope with a $25K check for Harrison's Tyler's publicity firm on his desk. The Mayor went to the municipal building's safety room and played back overnight videos of the building's security cams. Nothing unusual was there. No one had come into his office. "Bill's team has sneaky bastards in it," Howie said to himself, before picking up the phone and beginning to call people to start making what he called the 'Animal Day Fiesta' work. His first call was to the mayor of Socorro.

Howie Joins the Rescue Team

Late in the afternoon Mayor Howie rang the Mexican Cowboy's ranch house and was surprised when the Priest answered. "Where's the Cowboy?"

"He's over at Cece's place. What's on your mind?"

"Bill's guys gave me everything I wanted, and more. I'm on your rescue team now. I want us to meet up at my office tonight."

"We use the Church for our meeting and planning place."

"My office is safer."

"Your office got invisibly invaded easily last night to put a check on your desk."

"So, they told you about that. Okay, but I still want to meet here."

"My friend the Mexican Cowboy wants us to meet on his porch. Cece wants to hold tonight's meeting at Celesto's mother's place. And Coyote wants to be any place but indoors. I told all of them I'd quit if we don't use the Church."

"Coyote's coming?"

"Bill's people are making him come."

"What the hell for?"

"They told me they want Prophet Coyote to persuade his god to be there and take part in planning the Return to Eden Parade."

"You don't believe in the animal gods."

"No, but I believe in Bill's Team."

"All right, all right. Your Church it will be. See you there tonight. And I'm calling what we are planning the Animal Fiesta Day."

"That's not the name we want to use."

"But it will work for the mayor of Socorro."

"The Return to Eden parade name will bring in lots of Christians," the Priest suggested.

"Hmmmm. Suppose we use different parade names with different people?"

"Consistency was never wired into your makeup," the Priest replied.

El Latrano returns to the Priest's Church

That evening Father Gallapo, Cece, Thelma, and the Mexican Cowboy were meeting in the Church before Mayor Howie was expected to arrive. While the Priest told the others about his afternoon conversation with Howie, the Cowboy wandered restlessly around the cold and clammy Church, thinking about how the evening was likely to turn out. In front of the altar now, the Cowboy looked up at the badly painted Crucifix and saw something new. The odd, yellow-colored spots on Our Savior's loincloth that Thelma Whitenose —the Church's sole altar Guild member—never cleaned because she couldn't bear being on a ladder, had vanished.

"Hey Father. Who washed Jesus's pee-stained diapers? You told me it was proof of his human side."

"Cece," the Priest replied. "The women cleaned Our Lord up. I'm grateful to them."

"I liked Him better the other way. He was more my kind of guy then," Cowboy said. "Here's another question. If Howie brings other people with him, are you going to let them meet up with Coyote?"

"No. We've got that worked out. One of Bill's biobots is going to wait by the Church's back door. Bill's TEAM is monitoring what goes on in here and they'll let Coyote know when it is safe for him to come in."

Father Gallapo's Teacher unexpectedly broke into the Priest's and Cowboy's exchange saying, "Mayor Howie is about to enter. He has four people with him."

"Okay, guys. Let's see if we make Howie stick with our plan and not turn it into something that serves his interests better."

"If he does, you guys bend him over the altar and I'll kick his ass," Cece said.

"Shhhhh," Father Gallapo said.

The four of them turned around and watched the short and mean-tempered Mayor strutting down the Church's center aisle, followed by two men and two women. "Get us some chairs," Howie said. "I wish you had a table we could sit around."

Cece and Thelma went into the changing room behind the altar. Each picked up two metal folding chairs and carried them back to widen the circle. Meanwhile Mayor Howie grabbed the seat Father Gallapo positioned to lead the meeting. Feeling out-maneuvered, the Priest accepted one of the folding chairs. There was no place in the circle for Cowboy to sit. To show off indifference he didn't really feel, he made himself a headrest on the front pew from a pile of coats left there and stretched out on an uncomfortable hard bench in this run down church. "Wake me if you want me to say anything," he said, closing his eyes.

"Stay awake and pay attention, or I'll sit on your head," Mayor Howie ordered.

"Looks like you've taken over our meeting," Cece snapped.

"Bill's people have hired me to plan and lead his rescue and they didn't give you a dime. So shut up and let me tell you what I'm doing."

Cece bristled, Thelma looked angry, and the Priest had a look on his face that made the Cowboy think he regretted not leaving for Crawford, Texas.

"Kick us around and we'll kick back," Cowboy said.

"Okay, calm down guys, let's work together," Mayor Howie said, trying to get the meeting underway. He looked around, saw sullen faces, but heard no angry verbal responses. "Okay, let me introduce the people I've selected for this project."

Howie named, and said a few words about, each of the colleagues he'd brought —a middle-aged, obviously very bright female personal assistant –"She's handling all the paper-work," Howie said. An older white male—"He's really good at handling finances." An attractive young woman—"She's a superb publicist. "And a very fit man in his late thirties—"He's a former SEAL and he's going to put together and lead Bill's rescue team."

The Priest, Cece, and Thelma, and even the Cowboy, were impressed by how much the Mayor had accomplished in just three days. "Bill's Team was smart for putting you in charge," the Priest said.

"Thanks, Father, I agree with you on that. All right. My guys have to get back to work. Okay with you if they leave now?"

Father Gallapo looked at his team's faces, saw no dissent, and thanked Mayor Howie's associates for coming.

"Nice meeting you," the publicist said as the four of them said goodbye and left the Church.

"Down to business now," the Priest said, looking at his watch.

Howie nodded and began to summarize everything he'd worked on and accomplished for the project since he was hired. Father Gallapo's team members were impressed but one thing he said raised hair on the necks of the four original planners. "Bill's people are supporting this whole rescue thing. But I got a big surprise today. My finance manager called to say a huge pile of money had been transferred into our planning account. He said it was six-hundred and seventy-five thousand dollars, and came from something called 'L.I.V.E,' a group he'd never heard of before. He checked it out, and it may have been founded by Bill's older brother, Kemmet. I guess he wants to help us rescue Bill."

"Or the L.I.V.E. guys have something different in mind," Cowboy said—shutting up when Father Gallapo gave him an urgent look.

"Could be," Howie continued. "Anyway we need to talk now about plan details. And particularly, how the animal parade is going to be a cover for breaking into the nursing home and rescuing Bill. What do you guys know about the nursing home?"

"It's a terrible place. I was locked up there and ran away." Cece said.

"Hmmm. Maybe we can use you by sending you back to draw their attention away," Howie said.

"No way will I go back there!" Cece said fiercely.

"I hear you. But if you have to, you got to," Howie said, and continued before she could answer, "We need to find out everything about the nursing home. Who runs it?"

"Bill's Team can tell us," the Priest said, picking up his Teacher. "Who runs the nursing home?" he asked.

"A female nurse-administrator named Mika Nicklefoot," was the almost instantaneous response.

"She's Chinese American and little and runs the place like a prison," Cece said. "She looks like a pushover, but actually she's unmovable. She's always claiming she knows what's right and wrong. And she's as meticulous as the devil. All the papers need to be checked and signed by her, and they get handed back if 'i's aren't dotted and t's aren't crossed. Staff hate her. Because I was a ward of the state, she could always find a 'proper way' to refuse to release me from her care, even though I was completely normal."

"Cece has it about right," the Priest's Teacher said. Nurse Nicklefoot is authoritarian, and due to her scrupulous following of all laws, requirements, and court orders in her field, she's as intractable as a concrete dam."

"Why can't Bill's lawyers get him released?" Howie asked.

"We tried. Pointing to HIPPA requirements in court, Nicklefoot refused to let anyone but a family member see him, and none of them ever went. She wouldn't tell us anything about him, even that he was there, because she said that would invade his privacy."

"Is she a member of the Picklenose mob?" Howie asked, surprising the Priest.

"Bill's Team told you about the mob?"

"Yep, and I told my guys."

"Nurse Nickelfoot is not a member of our enemies' team. But she is acting as if she were," the Priest's Teacher continued. "She would be horrified if she thought she were a member of a group trying to keep Bill stashed away from his rightful associates for economic reasons. Nurse Nickelfoot is as iron-backed as a tank, acts deliberately, and is always positive she is doing 'the right thing.' She outmaneuvers us by being stubborn. She is empowered by the State of New Mexico to supervise wards designated by the state, and none can be released in her nursing home without her signature."

"Then why doesn't Bill's TEAM simply manipulate Nurse Nicklefoot's consciousness?" the Mexican Cowboy asked, keeping to himself that he just saw Coyote silently slipping in the back door and hiding behind the altar.

"Because she is moral, upright, tenacious, strong-minded, and on the legal side of the law. We have a growing conscience. It would not be right—ethically or legally—to tamper with her mind."

"You machines are becoming too human," the Mexican Cowboy said.

"Thanks. Becoming more human-like *is* one of our immediate goals," the Teacher replied.

"Don't stick with it. Being only human-like is limiting. " Coyote said from behind the altar, grabbing everyone's attention.

"Hello, Coyote. Welcome to our rescue meeting. Thanks for coming," Father Gallapo said.

"I don't want to be here," Coyote replied.

"This won't take long. All right, let's get back to planning," Father Gallapo said. "Nicklefoot's not super-powerful. She's determined and believes she has right on her side. If Bill's Team won't mess with her mind, we'll have to find a way to break down her doors."

"And that's what my former SEAL is going to figure out how to do," Mayor Howie said. "The hard part will be keeping the authorities from going after us for rescuing Bill."

"And how are we going to do that?" Thelma asked.

"We are going to bust up the parade," Howie said, shocking everyone. "But first, let's talk about how we are going to set up the parade. You, Cowboy, I want you to lead the parade. I want you dressed like a Mariachi, sitting on a fancy saddle on a fancy horse, and waving your sombrero at everyone you pass."

"You would let me lead the parade?" Cowboy asked softly, stunned, thrilled... and very, very pleased.

"Absolutely. You are famous. And the rest of you are too. Millions of pictures of you guys were seen around the world during the Eden Park fracas. Everywhere people watched you, Cowboy, being arrested and held by the Border Patrol guys."

"You, Thelma. I want you to dress beautifully and ride in Gallapo's truck, with him pulling the porta-confessional behind. And I want to see a dirty mop standing up straight in the back of his pickup."

"I can't believe this. Why would you want me to do something like that?" Thelma asked.

"Because you are even more famous than the Cowboy. When you stripped and jumped into the Rio Grande with the mop tied to your head, pretending to be Sarah Palin, you got far more publicity than Cowboy. Naked women always grab the most attention. Conservatives around the country are angry with you, Thelma, for pretending to be a drowning Sarah Palin. We are going to use many of those pictures of you to bring a lot of people to the parade, including those who hate you for what you did."

"That frightens me," Thelma said.

"Maybe so, but it will stir up more of the fuss we need to turn the parade into a distraction. Same reason for having you, Cowboy, lead the parade. Police officers and border patrol officers are pissed at you, pseudo-Mexican, for making them look like shit during the Eden war. Lots of lawmen and conservatives remember your arrest and breakout as the key thing that started all this Return to Eden animal crap that's drawing so much attention away from the Tea Party. It was their meeting after all, right?"

"And you Coyote," Howie said, pointing his forefinger toward the altar, "you are going to be in the parade, sitting and howling on top of a Rock as famous as Gibraltar. You are famous too. An awful lot of people who hate coyotes vividly recall videos of you—pretending to be a dog, no less —escaping from the Priest's leash, crossing the river, climbing up the hill, acting like you were praying, then rounding up all those coyotes who forced so many animals and birds to come into the park to quell the human conflict. There's not a hunter or rural conservative who doesn't want you killed, Coyote. To disrupt the parade you are going to attract the most attention by sitting on your fanny on top of a giant rock, with your head pointing toward the stars, and howling on the fanciest float in the parade. Every dog in the county will try to get at you," Howie said with a grin.

"You are on their side, aren't you," Cowboy said.

"You are going to be fired if you keep on with this kind of thinking," Father Gallapo said.

"I didn't realize I was so famous," Thelma said, smoothing her hair with a hand.

Howie said: "If Bill's people try to fire me after I've put so much work into rescuing their guy, I'll go after them. They've paid me enough to build an organization big enough to bring them down. I've got you guys by the balls."

"Some of us don't have balls," Cece said, getting up and towering over the sitting squat Mayor.

"Okay, calm down guys," The Priest said. "Let's work this out."

"Yeah, let's work it out," Howie agreed, with a dangerous look on his face.

"I won't get on your rock," Coyote said.

"I bet I can make you. And we are going to have to protect you too. I'll have guards around you and we are going to make that rock into an armored safe space you can retreat into if you are attacked."

"Who would attack him?" Father Gallapo asked.

"Every dog in Socorro that day. And so will a lot of people like me who hate coyotes and want to kill them."

"So you just want right-wingers at our parade?" Cece asked.

"Nope. I want thousands of liberals to be there too. My goal is to start a fight, remember," Howie answered.

Cece got up again and towered over the seated Mayor. "I'm going to slug you, Shit-Face."

Before Father Gallapo could calm her, Mayor Howie stood up and said, "Wait until the parade." He looked at the others, pointed at Cece, and said, "See how the parade disruption's going to work?"

That stunned everyone in the room, including Coyote. "All of you guys," the Mayor went on, are going to be needed to create the disruption we need to rescue Bill and keep the authorities' minds elsewhere."

"Jesus, you are good at planning evil," Cowboy said.

"You guys try to kill evil. You took a lot of it away with what you did at Eden Park. Now we've got to get some of it back to rescue Bill."

"I still don't understand why we need to stir such a big parade disruption," the Priest said.

"Okay guys. Suppose we just make Cece go into the nursing home and give Nurse Nicklefoot the finger. That's not going to get the well-run staff's attention disrupted. They'll just grab you and call the cops," Howie said, pointing at Cece. "No, planners, we need to come up with a really big disruption, one which will get everyone in that nursing home distracted. Let's turn that parade into a war with hundreds of battles. Fuck it up, so to speak. Create such a big fuss that nursing home staff will be off guard. It will be impossible to beat Nicklefoot otherwise."

"No way!" the Mexican Cowboy responded.

"There's no other way this disruption thing is going to work," Howie replied.

The original rescue planners were shocked and appalled by what Howie proposed.

"This was supposed to be another return to Eden," Father Gallapo said.

"Well, if you do what I want it will be a Bust-Up of Eden. And that will get everybody's attention," Howie said.

Discussion about Howie's plan for busting up the parade went on for another forty minutes. Howie ended it by saying, "Look guys. You want me to set this thing up. Either you do it my way or get somebody else to set up the parade. And I don't know anybody who can pull this parade thing off beside me."

That floored the team planners again. "All right," said Father Gallapo. "We've come to a disagreement that won't be resolved by more talking. I'm going to ask you to vote. All in favor of firing Mayor Howie raise your hands."

Cowboy's hand shot up.

"All in favor of letting Mayor Howie set up the parade raise your hands."

Cece's, Thelma's and the Priest's hands hesitantly went up, after Howie's hand jumped toward the ceiling.

"The aye-votes have it," the Priest said.

"I'll let Bill's TEAM know what we have agreed on," Cece said.

"We already do, thank you," her Teacher said loudly.

"Who said Mayor Howie could vote?" the Cowboy asks. No one responded.

While all this infighting was going on, Coyote had sneaked away from the altar. Infuriated, he kept trying to get the back door open, which would be easy for a human to do. Looking up, the Mexican Cowboy spotted him and said to the group, "I'm going to get up and let Coyote out of here."

The Cowboy was just standing up when Father Gallapo shouted in a God-like authoritarian voice, "**Stay, Coyote!**" The Priest got up, went over to the shivering animal, grasped the fur on his neck, and dragged Coyote to the place in front of the altar where he was baptized.

Coyote was crying and whining.

The Church was somehow darkening.

The Priest stood god-like over Coyote.

The Mexican Cowboy stood up and was about to go punch the Priest and rescue Coyote when he looked up at the crucified Jesus who was wearing a clean loincloth. Jesus' eyes were open and fixed on Cowboy.

Cowboy hesitated, and looked around him.

Thelma, with her back turned to the altar, was staring up into the unused organ loft over the Church's entryway. "I see El Latrano up there," she said.

Mayor Howie looks up in the organ loft where Thelma's pointing. "I don't see the coyote god up there," he said.

Cece turned to look, and she too saw the faint image of El Latrano. Cece sniffed and smelled the scent he emitted. "I can sort of see him. He's up there," she said, amazement in her voice.

"Sexism," Mayor Howie yelled at the loft, as Cowboy stopped him from giving Coyote's god the finger. "Make yourself visible to men too."

There was no reply from the organ loft. Father Gallapo looked at Coyote as though he were going to rip him apart. **"Behave and submit, mortal,"** he said, sounding like the God people imagine hearing.

Cece was intently staring at a space beside Mayor Howie. She saw the faint image of a youngish, extraordinarily handsome man, his hand resting on Howie's shoulder. "It's crazy," she whispered, "but I think I see Lucifer standing next to the Mayor."

The Mayor instantly denied this claim.

Cowboy said, "Look guys, Jesus' eyes are open."

The women stared at the Crucifix and gasped.

Mayor Howie said, and he meant it, "The statue hasn't changed. You guys are going crazy."

Father Gallapo bent over Coyote, who was now lying on his back with his feet in the air, and said, **"It is absolutely imperative, for your sake, for other coyotes' and all animals on this planet, that you ride the Rock in the Return to Eden Parade."**

Coyote whined and cried.

There was movement in the organ loft, sparkles of light, smells, and sounds even humans on the church floor beneath could detect.

"El Latrano is berating Coyote," Thelma said, with a gasp.

Coyote collapsed and rolled on his side.

The women and Cowboy got up and went to him. They kneeled and stroked him.

The Church brightened.

When Coyote opened his eyes he was like a sick puppy. The Priest rolled him over. Cece leaned against the altar and pulled his head into her lap while the others stroked him. "I didn't want to be here and my god would not allow me to leave," Coyote said. "He can see the battle this parade will start with the dog god and warns me I may be killed in this parade."

"We'll protect you," the Cowboy assured his beloved friend. Coyote nuzzled against him, still whimpering.

Thelma looked up to see what Howie was doing. He had vanished. "Howie is no longer in the church," she said.

"This project may have fizzled," Father Gallapo said.

"I don't think so," the Cowboy said with a very stunned expression on his face.

"Three gods reached out to us and proved they exist. They want into the game," Cece said.

"Lucifer is *not* a god," Thelma said sternly.

"I didn't see any gods," Father Gallapo said, mentally denying the astonishing claims he'd just heard.

"Perhaps it is because you are too close to your God to be allowed to see another," Cece said. "And tell us why you grabbed and dragged Coyote? He had a right to leave, didn't he?"

"I don't know... Something got into me that I've never felt before, and I'm scared about what that was," the Priest answered, looking very disturbed about his sudden aggressive behavior toward Coyote.

"Priests shouldn't behave like drill sergeants," Cece said.

"I need to go home," Thelma said. "This evening has been far more than I can bear."

"I'll drive you," said Cece and they gathered their coats and belongings and left without so much as a 'Good night.'

"Guess we should pack up too," Cowboy said, opening the back door and motioning Coyote to flee.

"Guess so," the Priest replied. "I screwed up, didn't I? I blew it. I should have gone to Crawford."

"I don't think you blew it, good friend," the Mexican Cowboy said, putting his arm around the Priest. "I think you opened another door into our seeing how the universe works. Your god used you."

"I don't know what you are talking about," Father Gallapo replied.

"Your problem isn't what you are not seeing. It is what you are not believing. Let's go."

Twenty minutes later the Church was shut down and they were back at Cowboy's ranch.

"I need to think about all this. Goodnight," Father Gallapo said, heading for his room.

"Ask the Holy Spirit to stop jerking you around and to let you open your eyes," Cowboy said.

"Don't talk about the Holy Spirit if you don't believe in God," Father Gallapo said sternly.

"After seeing Jesus open his eyes and stare at me tonight, I do believe in God. But I still doubt whether God believes in me."

"You've got some trusting to do," the Priest said as he went into his bedroom and closed the door without saying goodnight.

The Rescue

N ext day, in communities from Bernalillo to El Paso, Mayor Howie began setting up meetings with mayors and city managers and telling them about the great ideas he had. "Summer is coming," he said, "and we want to get more tourists visiting and staying overnight. I've got a great idea for putting this part of the state on the world's map again. " Howie went on to remind his listeners about the incredible universal attention the region got during the flood fracas in Eden Park. "Do you know what everybody remembers?" he asked. "It wasn't the politics or the mob scene. It was how everything quieted down and became beautiful when the animals and birds showed up and people started making friends with them."

"So what do you have in mind?" one of the city managers asked.

"Let's have a big parade somewhere near Eden Park, with lots and lots of animals in it, publicize it all over the country, and tell people they can meet animals, ride them, feed them, get to know them. Tell them there will be bands and clowns here. It will be a summertime Animal Fiesta."

Howie went on with mention of nearby sites to view wild animals and birds, and named restaurants, motels, and organizations in towns that would benefit. "There could be a fuss over when to have this, but sooner is better, I believe," Howie continued. "Socorro will be the best place for the Animal Fiesta because it is nearest to the Eden Park and the town everybody out there associates with the flood furor."

"Who's going to pay for all of this?" many of his listeners demanded.

"I've got the money arranged already," Howie said. That won almost everyone's approval.

"Let's put together a team that gets this project rolling," Howie said. "Are you in or out?" "In." was the answer he heard mostly.

In the Weeks Before the Big Parade

A month later the Mexican Cowboy rose at dawn and sprang out of bed. My life is exploding, he thought as he put on clothes. So then, is my life falling apart or coming together? I've never been so busy before. Never had so much to do, or so many people wanting me to work with them. And this morning I've got to grab a bite and get over to Cece. She yanks me around like a cowboy hauling a newborn calf out of a pregnant cow. Do I like it? Do I want Cece to leave me alone? Damn if I know. My head's messed up. Like it's always been.

Forty-five minutes later Cowboy's janitor truck was parked around the backside of Bill's 'house.' Cowboy unloaded four crates, stacked them on a cart, and wheeled them up to a door. He rang the bell, the door opened, and he went inside. Leaving the stack of household goods for the biobots to figure out what to do with, the Cowboy went into the 'waiting room,' and settled into the green rocker made for him, which was a good imitation of the one on his porch. Since Cece hadn't shown up yet, he thought about something interesting to do while he waited for her. "Let's mess with the weather," he decided and said to the house biocomputer, "Put a heavy rainstorm on the 'window'. This has been a super dry spring." Looking 'out' the 'window,' Cowboy watched blackening storm clouds rapidly build up over the Manzanos as wind-driven raindrops began to splash onto the 'glass.'"Neat illusion," Cowboy said. "Wish you guys could do this outdoors in real life."

"Some of us **are** working on weather control," a voice said in his mind.

"That will be pointless," said the Cowboy. "Even if you could make real weather, no two people could agree on the weather they want each moment."

"We believe humans are more consensual than that."

"You've got a lot to learn," the Cowboy said, just as the door behind him opened.

Cece walked in and sat on a small leather couch against the wall. Cowboy was stunned by what she was wearing. She had a blue rebozo covering her hair and a short-sleeved white blouse, its frayed ends reaching down the red skirt she was wearing. Her skirt had a very wide, beautiful, flower-trimmed hemline. Usually Cece wore wool sweaters and long pants, but today her arms were exposed from the elbows down, and she wore a stunning silver necklace. Instead of her usual boots, Cece's feet were sandaled. Her clothes reminded him of clothes his beloved mother had often worn.

"Why don't you turn that rainstorm off and come over and sit with me?" Cece said. "We've got a lot to talk about, and things to decide upon."

"Seems like that's the way it is every day now," Cowboy said, getting up and sitting beside her. Behind them, the 'window' had turned into a sunny view of the mountains, with lots of birds and animals playing in the yard, a scene, which the Cowboy always loved to watch. "Okay.... Cece. What's up today? You are working with Bill's TEAM so much you must have turned into one of their managers."

"That's true. And since I began working with them, my life's never been better. They pay me a lot for helping them. All right, here is my first question. When is Father Gallapo going to return to Cordoba? He's been gone for more than ten days. Is he still down in Crawford?"

"No. He's driving around visiting rundown churches in the southeastern part of the state. I think he's looking for another place to move to."

"Well we've got to work on that. We need him back here to give us his valuable opinions about planning decisions we need to make."

"Decisions about what, now?"

"Here's the first one. Howie's team sent me a list of floats they intend to put in the parade. There's a new one I want your opinions about. Howie's people are calling it 'The Human Zoo Float.' If we allow, it will be one of the biggest floats in the parade and sort of a mini-zoo, with cages and fake natural settings like ones people see in zoos around the globe. Only, instead of having animals in them, these pens are going to be filled with nearly naked human beings—

who will wear only minimal, skin-colored patches and behave primitively. They'll growl and howl and fight and destroy fake trees and phony grass. Howie thinks this float will stir up a tremendous mix of contradictory feelings."

"Will those zoo people be screwing too?"

"God, I hope not."

"Well, it sounds to me like Howie wants human actors on this float to show the world his beliefs about how animals behave. Real animals don't behave like Howie believes."

"So, you reject this float?"

"No. Actually I like the idea. Anything that brings humans down, I will support."

"All right. I'll relay your okay," Cece said, jotting down Cowboy's approval and comments. "Now here's the next big thing. I think it is going to really upset you. Look over there," Cece said, pointing at a nearby empty low table.

Slowly flickering into being, a three-dimensional image of the Cowboy's house and property appeared on the table, perfectly colored and detailed. Watching, they saw the image rotating in three dimensions and zooming in, as the 'camera' focused closely on wood rot, cracked adobe, loose boards, fading and chipped paint, a leaky faucet, the crumbling foundation, and tens of other problems.

"So, my house is beat up. I know that and so do you. Why show me those close-ups? Just to hurt my feelings?"

"No. We came up with these images for you because they bring up something we need to discuss. Bill's people want to rebuild your house for you, and they've come up with some ideas they want me to review with you."

Cowboy was shocked. "They want to rebuild my house for me? And they want my opinion about what I'd like? What have I done to deserve that?"

"This will be one of the ways they can pay you for all you've been doing for Coyote and Bill. Now look, here's one possibility they've come up with."

On the table before him, while he watched, the Cowboy's house was torn down board by board and in its place a three-story house with attached garage that looked like it belonged in Cleveland was rapidly 'built.'

"No!" Cowboy said angrily. "I want my original ranch house kept. You guys can fix it up, but I don't want it torn down ever."

"Fine. Try this idea, then" Cece said, with a curious smile on her face.

On the table now the pair watched as Cowboy's house was discreetly rebuilt, yet still coherently expanded. The ranch house was connected with a covered pathway to a second house they watched being built. This house resembled both Cowboy's place, and a New Mexico church.

"This design was Coyote's idea," Cece said. "He wants us to build a house on your property that will entice Father Gallapo to stay here. The two of you can stay close, but be separated now. And maybe Thelma will want to move in and look after him."

"He'll hate that idea, but he might like the house. It looks like something he would. I'm okay with that, but why does Coyote want my ranch house expanded?"

"For a reason you will hate," Cece said, almost gulping. "Coyote wants me to live with you. The design has private spaces for each of us, if that's what you are worried about."

This life-changing proposal really floored the Mexican Cowboy. "Jesus, I don't know about that," he said, and was quiet for over a minute. Cece invisibly slipped closer to him and gently reached over and put her hand on his knee.

"Tell me your feelings?" she asked softly.

"I guess that I both like and I hate the idea. Things we've done together have worked out pretty well for me. For instance, I liked it a lot when you and I were neatening up my house for Thelma's great dinner. But still, I'm a loner. To share my house with you, that just won't work for me."

"I'm a loner too, you know. Suppose that we have our own spaces, but a common kitchen. I think we could keep most of your house the way it is ... but more fixed up, and still add spaces for me, which we could make sort of invisible to you. Would that work for you?"

"It might. It's just very scary. Can I have a day or two to think about it?"

"Sure, you can," Cece said, pulling him gently toward her and giving him a small hug. She saw lightness inside his heart flowing out of him as she touched and hugged him.

"Let's keep our distance. But maybe not always," Cece said, watching Cowboy's eyes moistening as she slid away from him on the couch.

"One thing more about your house," Cece continued. "Bill's guys want to add a professional kitchen in the rear and staff it with biobots. Those guys will prepare and place outdoors in safe places mixes of foods for the animals you feed every night. And they'll give you great stuff to take outside for Coyote too."

"These ideas are overwhelming me," Cowboy said, with a wave of tiredness coming over him. "I guess Bill's people are right. As I get older and poorer, and without more help from Mayor Howie, I won't be able to feed as many animals as I'm feeding now."

"Fine. I'll pass your views along to Bill's Team," Cece said, writing. "And, one thing more. Bill's people want to build a new barn-like stable resembling the one that was destroyed in that heavy windstorm, so Turco and Gus can move back with you. The biobots will look after them. Here, take a look at this image."

On the table a familiar looking barn was rapidly 'built' exactly where the old one had stood. When the barn was completed, the scene's 'camera' rose higher over the Cowboy's property and began focusing on fence making and grass planting next to the barn. Cowboy even saw a new well being dug and a sprinkler system installed to keep the grass green and nutritious.

"It will be a great place for Turco and Gus. And Bill's TEAM will give a generous payment to Hank for looking after the hooved guys so long. They know about Hank's reluctance to give up Turco, because tourists who want to rent horses still come to his stable to see the famous mustang that saved the boy kept by Ursula, that loving —and beloved —mother bear. Bill's TEAM will give Hank monthly payments to offset his losses."

"Hank deserves a lot of money for all he's done for Turco and me."

"And he'll get it. Now, shall we get back to parade planning?"

The Cowboy nodded, but it was evident to Cece that his thoughts were still elsewhere.

"Maybe let's don't plan anymore today. I'm overwhelmed by everything you've told me. I think I need to get out of here and go hang with Turco."

"Sure," Cece said, leaning over and giving him another small hug. "Why don't we quit for the day and pick it up tomorrow."

"I'll see if I can bear that," Cowboy said rising, and left without any word of thanks, or even a polite goodbye.

~*~*~

Next evening Cece and Cowboy were together at Thelma's place. The women had prepared a light meal for the three of them and, while they ate, Thelma filled the others in on what had been happening with Mayor Howie's planning team.

"He's paying you for working with him?" Cowboy asked.

"More than I ever expected. And he's working me to death. And all the others too. We've made a lot of progress. Howie's got the parade approved by Socorro's mayor and council. Other towns along the river have mostly accepted the idea, and all who have receive grants to advertise the event as they please. The cities are falling into line."

"That's remarkable," Cece said. Those towns have had their fights for decades.

"For several hundred years, in a couple of cases," Cowboy added.

"Harrison Tyler's publicists have been working their tails off too," Thelma continued. "They began with blogs and posts on many web sites asking wouldn't it be great to re-create the wonderful Return to Eden affair, so people who weren't there could come and see humans and animals working together! The publicists have exploded a stir on world nets, most of it favorable. But also a lot of negative stuff too... which Howie wants. Now they've got millions of people posting about the parade idea after blogging big name sources, like Huffington Post and Facebook."

"I know. Bill's people are following Tyler's publicizing. They are getting pretty sure the parade will attract hundreds, maybe thousands of viewers," Cece said.

"Mayor Howie thinks the parade will bring several million dollars to merchants in Socorro and nearby towns," Thelma continued. Tyler's publicists are pushing places to stay, eat and to visit in and around Cordoba. Howie's people are telling merchants along the river to start advertising the parade. Most of them agreed."

"You really started something big, good Cowboy," Cece said with a warm look.

"Don't bet on it," Cowboy replied. "Most things I start go wrong in the end."

Coyote Brings News

Two nights later Cece and Thelma were having after-dinner coffee in the Mexican Cowboy's run-down dining room, when Cece's Teacher interrupted their casual conversation. "Will each of you please go outside with Cowboy to the place where he leaves food for Coyote? Coyote has something very important to tell you."

"What can that be?" Thelma asked.

"I don't know," the Mexican Cowboy replied, sticking his head into the dining room with a pan of raw meat, "but Coyote doesn't mess around with my head. He's never done this before. It's got to be big stuff. I can give you guys flashlights."

Outside, with Cowboy leading the way and the two women following with flashlights turned on, the parade planners crossed the rough mesa to the edge of the dry arroyo, where Cowboy left meals for Coyote. The women shone their lights up and down the arroyo bed looking for Coyote, and were surprised when they heard his voice coming from behind them.

"I'm over by the water pump," Coyote said softly. "There's an old bench over here that one or two of you can sit on."

Cowboy led the women to the water pump and motioned to the bench. Thelma sat and Cece stood. They were surprised when they heard Coyote's voice coming from behind them again.

"Keep your flashlights off," Coyote said softly. "I want that drone of Bill's enemies which is overhead to believe the three of you are talking by yourselves."

"So what's up, Brother Coyote?" Cowboy said in Cece's direction. "You've never asked to see my friends before."

"There's god trouble," Coyote said. "The animal gods are more divided than ever now. The efforts of my God, El Latrano, to keep many of the animal gods still willing to work with your human god, are failing. And dog god Poko is trying to get a number of gods to switch over to his side. He wants to start a war with my God. Dogs have always hated coyotes, but this time Poko wants to wipe us out. He's going to join up with Bill's enemies and other humans to do it."

"Damnation!" said the Mexican Cowboy, taking off his yellow hat and wiping his forehead with a red and white spotted handkerchief. "This will mean war for me too. I'll start carrying my rifle and stop feeding animals that are against you. And I want to get you out of the parade too."

"My God and Bill's TEAM are working on a different way of dealing with this. I can't tell you about it outdoors here, the drone is probably listening, but what's going on is a lot bigger than this parade. The disruption Howie is staging is going to turn out to be just the first incident in the biggest war ever with animals and humans on both sides."

"Thanks for sharing this with us," Thelma said, feeling very alarmed.

"Yes, thanks," Cece added.

There was no answer from Coyote. He'd vanished without saying goodbye.

Struggle Among The Animal Gods

Four days later, Father Gallapo, the Mexican Cowboy, and Cece were meeting with Bill's TEAM, deep underground, in the most secure room in their facility.

"Thanks for being with us," an image of a man resembling a famous Cardinal was saying in a voice the Priest liked. "I know the Cowboy has passed on what Coyote said while you were away, Father Gallapo. In this safe room we can tell you a little more about what's going on."

"Please," said the Priest. "I don't like the idea of an animal war spreading to humans."

"Or an animal war that will be started by humans and one of the human gods?" the speaker replied.

"There is only one human god!" Father Gallapo said sternly.

"Well, let us tell you what we know."

"Please," the Priest said with a softer tone.

"We didn't intend this, but our creation of a much advanced Coyote, and Coyote's God's making him into his prophet—with your help, Father Gallapo, and yours, Cowboy—has stirred a growing struggle among the animal gods," Bill's TEAM's 'representative' said. "El Latrano's effort to keep many gods working with your human god to help both humans and animals evolve socially, and improve mutual relations, is failing. As Coyote told you, Poko the dogs' god, is leading the opposition. Poko is forming a determined group that wants to go back to the neglectful, multi-sided, squabbly relationships the animal gods had with each other before the Eden Furor made them work together and support one another, to solve a human problem millions of watchers around the world were following."

The Priest nodded understandingly, while confused looks on Cece's, Thelma's, and the Cowboy's faces suggested they were having trouble making sense of what was being said.

"Many of the animal gods think the old way, the informal and minimal way that animals worked together in the past, is the best way for species to get along. Lots of animal gods are saying, "Let's have none of this 'joint social evolution' crap. If we animal gods want to interact, let's get back to playing soccer. Otherwise, each of us will do our thing and the human god can do his.""

The Priest nodded.

"Poko, the dog god, though has a hidden agenda: starting a war with coyotes. Poko has lined up and is building a relationship with Lucifer, another human god, to get this war fired up and winnable."

"Lucifer is not a human god," the Priest snapped back.

"That may be, but Lucifer *is* working through Howie, and linking up with our enemies, the L.I.V.E. people. Poko is trying to get a movement started that will wipe out coyotes. Lucifer is using Poko to start a world movement that will result in a global war involving an extraordinary number of species. Poko doesn't realize what Lucifer is up to."

"How in hell did you learn this stuff?" the Priest demanded.

"Coyote's god, El Latrano, and your god are still working together. They have a collective gods' eye view and El Latrano passed along to his Prophet all they learned. And Coyote told us. Lucifer's eager to shape up the largest war in world history—killing billions of bio-beings from as many species as possible, including wiping out Bill's TEAM as well."

"If this is true, what should we do to help prevent this world-level disaster? Will stopping the parade help?" Cece asked.

"No," the Cardinal-like representative answered. "We can defeat the L.I.V.E. people only if we get Bill back and restore him to his previous self. We need his brainpower. You must rescue him, as the first step in preventing this horrible war."

"Why doesn't God just smack Lucifer down?" Cowboy asked.

"Your Priest will have to answer that question. We don't know the answer," the 'Cardinal' replied.

"And I don't know it either," Father Gallapo said, torn apart in so many directions.

"Well, you humans are going to have to work with us bio-computers if we are going to solve this potentially disastrous problem. Frankly, this one is beyond us," the representative said, and vanished.

"Wow," Thelma said, her cheeks red and her eyes dilated. "What do we do now?"

"I have no idea," Cece answered, looking befuddled like they'd never seen her before.

"Well, I know what we have to do!" Cowboy said. "Get together with Coyote and pay attention to what his god passes along to us; do that damned parade; get Bill out of there and back here; and do what we've got to do to save the planet. If we hadn't baptized Coyote, none of this would have happened. It's your fault, and mine, Father G."

"I got to think about this on my own," the Priest replied.

"And talk it over with your Trio, I bet," Cowboy said back.

"And Thelma and I need to talk it over too. Let's get out of here," Cece said, and led the foursome to the elevator that would lift them back into Bill's house.

Before the men left the women, Cece pulled the four of them together in a group hug. "One thing we must never do if we are going to win this thing and that is to never separate or ever work against each other," Cece said, her arms around Thelma and the Cowboy in the group hug.

"You are so, so right," Cowboy responded, giving Cece a tiny squeeze and gently backing out of the group hug.

"Let's go," Father Gallapo said, and walked toward the door to the parking lot without saying 'Goodbye.'

"He's busted up," Cece said to Cowboy, giving him another hug, before he followed his friend the Priest out the door.

"Gallapo's always been that way," Cowboy said over his shoulder before leaving.

Meeting With the Mayor

Several weeks later the four-some were in Howie's office meeting with the Mayor. For fifteen minutes Howie summarized how Parade preparations were going. "It is all coming together," he concluded.

"One thing you didn't talk about, and that's whether you are doing any choosing and training of the people who are going to rescue Bill," Cece said.

"Ask your Teachers whether anyone is spying on us now," Howie replied.

"We've put an electronic spying-protection curtain under, over, and around your office," Cece's Teacher said, without being asked. "Mr. Mayor, you can talk freely at the moment."

"Thanks," Howie continues. "Okay, Cece. I've chosen a rescue squad, which is made up of former SEALS. Cowboy, you'll know two of the guys, Celesto—the kid you located in the bear cave, and Hirshy Dismas—the guy who saved your life. I've worked with both of them for years."

"You never told me that you worked with Celesto," Cowboy interrupted.

"Lots of things I never tell **you**," the Mayor responded. "Now keep this to yourselves guys. Bill's TEAM gave me a very detailed plan of Nicklefoot's nursing home showing us exactly where Bill's being kept. I authorized construction of a rescue-team training site and former

SEAL trainers were hired to rehearse and plan with Bill's rescuers. This has been tedious, expensive and methodical preparation. We think we've got his rescue plan nailed now."

"Tell us what you are going to do?" Thelma asked.

"No way," the Mayor replied. "This is a big secret, even from you."

"One thing I know," Cowboy said, "and that's you are using Gus the donkey, who's Turco's friend."

"I don't know anything about that," Mayor Howie answered. "And speaking of Turco," he continued, "Turco's broken down. He doesn't belong in the parade. Cowboy, I am getting you a super parade horse from a ranch just outside Ruidoso. Those Ruidoso horse guys know what a parade lead horse must be like, and your new mustang will come with a stunning saddle. I've also hired a costumer to work with you on the mariachi costume you'll wear."

"No, no, no, and NO!" Cowboy said, getting up and towering over Mayor Howie. "If you want me in the parade I am going to ride Turco, and I'm going to use his saddle, and I'm going to dress like a Mexican cowboy, not a mariachi. A mariachi doesn't ride. You do it my way or I'm quitting."

"You can't quit," Howie said. "And pictures of you riding a fancy horse and leading the parade are out there everywhere."

"I am quitting," the Mexican Cowboy said, getting up and walking toward the door.

"Whoa," Cece said, grabbing the leaving Cowboy. "Look, Howie. The Cowboy's got to be himself. He's not an actor. You've got to let him be the guy he is in the parade, or get someone else to lead it."

"And you are forgetting something, Howie," the Priest said. "The Cowboy told me all about how you screwed him and Turco after the Celesto rescue, when you claimed all the credit for finding and freeing the child in the bear cave. But in spite of you, Turco became famous. People from all over still come to see him at Hank's stable."

"And you walked away from Cowboy when he was arrested by the Border Patrol during the furor at Eden Park," Thelma said. "If you had acknowledged his citizenship and gotten him released, Father Gallapo and I wouldn't have had to come up with that plan to rescue him. If you'd done what you should have the Return to Eden business that's behind the Parade would never have occurred."

"I was going back to get him released when you stripped and jumped into the river with a mop on your head," the Mayor replied.

"And if I had the mop now I'd stick it in **your** hair," Thelma answered.

"And if I had that plunger from the toilet in the nursing home I'd put it on your face and pump until you vomited," Cece said.

"Okay, okay, I give up. Perhaps you guys are right. Putting Cowboy on Turco may bring more people to the parade if we advertise that. What do you think, Cowboy? Can our publicists take advertising shots of you on Turco?"

"I guess," said the Mexican Cowboy, "If that's what all you guys want."

The others nodded their heads. Cowboy was about to sit down again when the Mayor stood up and said, "That all for now. Beat it, guys," and opened the door for them to leave. He was smiling and shook each of their hands as they walked past him.

"You are a politician," Thelma said.

"You are a scumbag," the Cowboy said.

"Thanks for working with us," the Priest said.

"Thanks for figuring this all out and making it happen," Cece said, giving Howie a hug and a small kiss on his cheek.

The Day of the Big Parade

The day before the big parade, Father Gallapo and the Mexican Cowboy drove to Socorro to get to know the route of the parade Cowboy would be leading. The town was filled with people, every motel room was booked, and parking spaces were almost impossible to find. They drove slowly along the parade route, paying attention to everything they passed by. Horses and mules pulled carts loaded with tourists back and forth to cars parked blocks away from the parade route. The Priest spotted booths giving out sunscreen and other skin care products. Local restaurants and eateries had set up food stands on sidewalks and in parking lots and were selling at higher prices. Free water was widely available. Bird feeders had been installed on telephone poles and streetlights, and thousands of birds were gulping down seeds. Very efficient and sanitized toilets were available along the parade route. Ads for local stores had been thumb tacked or glued everywhere they could be seen, and many solo vendors were selling wares on the parade route. "Merchants are doing very well, as Howie promised," the Priest said.

"He's a Republican and believes in promoting commerce," Cowboy said. "And if he didn't, businessmen wouldn't keep filling Howie's pockets."

Father Gallapo was amazed at the variety of people he saw: plump, brown-skinned women in tight long pants and heels, many with long, slightly curly, black hair; a few Japanese Americans; Middle Easterners and folks from the Indian sub-continent; men in jeans, cowboy hats and boots—many needle-pricked with great tattoos; college students going to classrooms on the nearby campus pushing through the crowds wearing khaki pants and white shirts, like students in the '50s. "Engineers," the Priest said.

Cowboy noticed that there were more men than women on the town's streets. Most of the women he saw reminded him of the animal rights supporters he saw at Eden Park. Men resembling hunters and NRA hard-liners were everywhere in the town. Cowboy remembered once hearing an NRA rep on a loudspeaker saying to hunters at a meeting in the mountains as he passed by on Turco, "We are with you guys. We do want to grow all the animal populations, so we don't have to work so hard to shoot 'em."

Driving west into a residential district off the main street, the Priest and Cowboy spotted hundreds of barking dogs, fenced in or chained. The dogs emanated feelings of anger coupled with a desire to be set free to be with the crowd. The dogs were staring, snapping, whining, jumping against the fences, panting and scratching, and couldn't make up their minds what to do with the pleasant strangers who clearly wanted to pat them. Some passersby threw food scraps over their fences, and that further muddled the dogs' minds.

"Seen enough?" the Priest asked Cowboy.

"Too much, far too much," Cowboy replied. "Let's get back to my quiet ranch."

Parade Day

And now The Big Day had come—perhaps the most important day in human history, if the future turned out as many animal gods were hoping. It was the Return to Eden Parade day in Socorro, and thousands of tourists from all parts of the planet were gathering to watch animals and humans interact joyfully and to the benefit of every species. At nine a.m. Mayor Howie had arranged a final fifteen minute meeting before the parade with Father Gallapo, Thelma, and the Cowboy, held in an office he'd rented on Otero Avenue. Cece wasn't there; she had locked herself in a secure room in Bill's facility and would follow the parade on many devices.

"There are several things I need to tell you," Howie began. "Don't interrupt because we haven't much time and all of us have things to do before the parade begins. First, Cowboy, we're going to have a truck and horse trailer within a block of you at all times. If Turco starts to break down we'll put him in a trailer and put you on the saddled horse we brought from Ruidoso, just in case. Don't screw up the parade by letting Turco break down in front of the spectators. Okay?"

"He'll be fine," Cowboy replied.

"All right. Next, as you know, the parade begins at Clark Field, goes up California Street to Bullock Boulevard and ends on the north side of Sedillo Park. Cowboy, we'll have a flag team leading you, so you don't have to worry about where you are going. Father Gallapo, you and Thelma will be just behind the Cowboy. Make sure the mop in the back of your truck is visible and filthy, and keep your windows down and wave to the crowd. If you want to ride with an animal, that would be great. If you have trouble with your truck, pull over and we'll figure out what to do with you. Now, here's the most important thing you need to know. When you get to the end of the parade route I want Cowboy and you to keep going up Franklin Street, then turn right on the north side of the park until you come to Parkview Elementary school. People will be waiting for you there and quickly get you on your way back to Cordoba. You'll have a police escort until you are safely northbound on I-25. Turco will go back with you. It is critical that we get you out of Socorro immediately. Understood?"

The threesome nodded.

"Here's something you've got to watch out for," Howie continued. "The thousands of animal lovers who are in Socorro at the moment are taking over the streets and parking places, stalling traffic, creating huge lines at the gas stations and filling up places to stay and eat. A lot of residents in the city are peeved—and their dogs hate what's going on too. If they get loose, they may attack you. Be on guard. Also, religious groups and protesters of all kinds—including groups protesting the parade itself—will be present among watchers and floats."

The threesome shuddered and nodded.

"Okay. Here's the next big thing. Last night we held a dinner meeting at the Express Hotel. I chaired the meeting and welcomed the elected officials and important business leaders who have helped to put together today's event, which most of them are calling"the Return to Eden Parade. "Float makers and many of the people who are bringing animals were there too."

"Lots of animals?" Thelma asked.

"More than you can guess. But that's not what I need to tell you. State Attorney General Allie Martinez was there also. You should know her, Cowboy. She went to grade and high school in Columbus with you. She's a Democrat. Martinez followed online the Tea Party fracas after the flood at Joe Eden's former ranch. She is afraid that the Return to Eden parade may relight the battling that took place during that flood furor and cause what she calls a"Return to Joe Eden's Ranch." Martinez believes her State Police handled the Eden Park situation badly, and Democrats in Santa Fe bitched at her for mishandling the state's law enforcement officers. Martinez is determined not to allow anything like this to happen again. She's ordered State Police to flood Socorro with officers, to protect individuals and animals —and especially visitors —and to do whatever is necessary to prevent a new furor. They are going to stomp on any conflict they spot. Under no circumstances do I want you guys to mess with law enforcement officers today. The police were briefed about your roles in the Eden furor and they might be eager to arrest you, even if you are doing nothing wrong. Behave yourselves. Deal?"

The threesome nodded.

"Okay. Is there anything I can do for you before we close this meeting?"

"Let me use your bathroom before I go," Thelma said.

"Third door on the right down the hall. Okay. Now, beat it guys. I've got lots more to do this morning," Mayor Howie said as he showed them out and closed the door behind them.

Mexican Cowboy Gets Gussied Up

Two hours later the Mexican Cowboy was changing clothes in a trailer on the south side of Clark Field. Working with a costumer, he'd chosen clothes that reminded him of those worn by his grandfather on parade days in Puerto Palomas, Mexico. Stripped to his underwear and socks, Cowboy put on a fine white cotton shirt and closed the wrists with cufflinks, turned up the collar, put a large bright red, grey, and blue handkerchief around his neck and made it into a huge bow tie. He pulled on skin tight black pants with buttons along each leg on the hip sides of the pants, put on a flowered vest and over the vest put on a smart, short, hemmed jacket with beautiful stitching. Sitting on a hard bench, he pulled on his battered cowboy boots, got up and put on his beautiful black sombrero and, picking up his torn up leather chaps, left the trailer.

Passing a mirror on the way out he paused to study his appearance. The Mexican Cowboy liked very much what he was seeing. "I'm El Charro now," he said out loud, feeling very confident about how he would look at the head of the parade. He waved his sombrero at his image and bowed before leaving.

The Cowboy went into a tent behind the trailer where Hank Godding and two groomers were getting Turco readied for the parade. The groomers had spiffed the mustang up, but he still looked wasted. A photographer took pictures of Cowboy, partly for publications, but also—thanks to Thelma—for Cece especially. Cowboy looked magnificent, masterly in the costume he wore. Turco, though, was looking more worn down than ever. "It will be anybody's guess whether Turco can make it through the whole parade," Hank said to Cowboy. Cowboy put his arm around Turco's neck and talked softly to him about what was ahead for the two of them. Turco listened, appeared to nod several times, and stood ready to be bridled and saddled. Cowboy showed the aging mustang the gear he'd be wearing in the parade. Turco was pleased to see the familiar saddle that was about to be put onto him.

While Cowboy was saddling Turco, Marianne Marbly, the parade director, came in to see how Turco was doing and to ask Cowboy if there was anything she could do for him before the parade began.

"I'm fine," Cowboy said. "And thanks for setting up this tent, giving me a trailer, and everything else you've done for me."

"We're pleased to help. And everyone's going to remember you and Turco leading our great parade," Marianne replied. "One thing we haven't talked about though. Today's weather forecast is calling for a mix of sun and rain showers."

"Two-inch showers, I bet," Cowboy said.

"No, just sprinkles," Marianne said.

"I meant the rain drops will be two inches apart when they hit the ground," Cowboy said with a grin.

"Then you won't need a rain coat?"

"No. My sombrero will keep me dry enough."

Getting Parade Ready

About twenty minutes to twelve, Cowboy left the tent and walked out to the street where the parade floats and participants were finishing lining up. Parade workers, wearing orange safety vests with yellow stripes, were giving final instructions to drivers and group leaders. A minute later Hank led Turco out and dropped his reins onto the grass so the horse could graze until the parade began.

Seven uniformed flag carriers, standing on the sidewalk with their flags furled, waved to Cowboy and shout 'Hello.' Cowboy waved back. Cowboy was in bright sunlight but there were a few drops of rain splashing about him. He looked up and saw a small, dark cloud passing overhead. On the street, stretching back out of sight, he saw parade floats, groups of animals, some hunters, and more policemen than he'd ever seen in one location before. In the street and on the sidewalk on the north side of the street were hundreds of parade watchers, here to see the parade being put together and begin. Two of the policemen were keeping mothers and small children from coming onto the grass to pat Turco.

Cowboy walked over to the officers and said, "Let them pass, please. Turco would like to meet them."

Dubious about the request, the police-men allowed a small group of mothers and children to walk over to Turco. The mustang stood proudly as they walked up to him and Hank gave them permission to touch Turco, while he began telling them about how Turco discovered and helped rescue the boy who was being held captive by a bear.

Checking his watch, the Mexican Cowboy walked over to the street to say "Hi" to Thelma and Father Gallapo, in their truck—which was towing the porta-confessional on its trailer. The dirty mop was clamped to the side of the truck bed. The truck's windows were open and Thelma waved to him as he approached. Cowboy was surprised to see a goat sitting in the

cramped back seat. "I was hoping Coyote might still be with you," Cowboy said as he reaches in to scratch the goat's head, "but it is nice to meet your goat."

"We didn't bring Coyote," Thelma said. "I don't know how he was supposed to get here."

"He wouldn't go with Howie's people, that for sure," the Cowboy answered.

Cowboy looked up the street and saw many floats in front of and behind the one with the giant rock rising into the sky. But Coyote was not on it. "I wonder if he decided not to come."

"I don't think so," Father Gallapo said, leaning over Thelma toward the window. "Howie would have told us if Coyote had refused."

Cowboy was deliberating about walking back to the Rock float to see whether Coyote was there or not when he heard a trumpeter in the nearby Cordoba school band play the five-minutes-to-parade-departure warning. "Oops," he said, touching Thelma's arm, "I've got to get back to Turco."

As he walked across the grass toward Turco, Cowboy heard a loudening burst of growling, moaning, and unintelligible noises over his shoulder. He stopped and looked behind him.

A pack of 'naked' humans was on the sidewalk, and began to climb aboard the Human Zoo float. They were warming up their voices and practicing their pre-language sounds, he realized. Six men and six women, of all ages, as Howie had said there would be on the Human Zoo float.

At one o'clock sharp, two trumpets played twelve bars of the lively New Mexico state song, "O Fair New Mexico." This was the signal to start the parade. The flag teams unfurled their flags, and with New Mexico's and the American flag in the lead, positioned themselves to head the parade.

With the sound of engines starting behind him, Cowboy put his left hand on the saddle horn, his left foot in the stirrup, and swung his body up into the saddle. Turco was plainly eager to go. Wriggling his bottom to get into the right saddle position for an El Charro parade leader, Cowboy tipped his hat to police as he passed by them onto the street and said, "Thank you officers for taking care of so many of us today." The policemen nodded and smiled.

Pausing at the Mayor's Stand

Twenty-five minutes later, after leading the parade along a spectator-packed route, Cowboy—his back and arm already tiring from turning and waving his beautiful black sombrero at thousands of people — approached the Parade Stand close to Fisher Avenue. Six feet above the street, Howie stood behind a microphone next to the Mayor of Socorro, surrounded by mayors and business leaders of many towns along the Bosque, and members of the press. Howie had been impatiently waiting for the parade to reach him. Ideas kept popping into his mind about how Bill's enemies might defeat his plan. He was trying to come up with counter-moves if his plan was blocked, just as Cowboy stopped in front of him. Turco turned and faced the stand, Cowboy bowed and waved his superb black sombrero at the applauding mayors and business leaders, and Turco dipped his head downward as well. Hundreds of camera flashes recorded this electric moment.

With seven TV cameras on him, the Mayor of Socorro made a short but very listenable welcoming speech, thanking Cowboy and everyone in the parade behind him for putting on such a memorable performance. With applause from the stand, and parade watchers praising him, Cowboy bowed again, saluted the Mayor, and returned on Turco to the center of the street. Turco was stationary for a moment until the costumed Cordoba high school band began playing the remarkably listenable state anthem, "O Fair New Mexico." Then Cowboy pressed his heels gently against Turco's sides, and the parade moved forward.

Next, Father Gallapo, Thelma, and the goat aboard, drove slowly past the stand, the Priest's truck pulling the notorious porta-confessional behind it, still looking like a beat-up outhouse. Many of the spectators were snapping pictures of the upright filthy mop and shouting, "Hello, Sarah," as Thelma waved back. The goat's head was sticking even further out the window, and he was making a continuous *mehhhhhing* bleat. "That's goat's singing along with the Cordoba school's band," Mayor Howie remarked, drawing smiles from those around him.

The mayors took their seats again and settled down to watch, with genuine interest, the floats passing before them. The first float, which was just behind the Cordoba band, was a large, fascinating New Mexico mountain-like float, designed for Wildwest Nature Park, which had put its widely advertised show animals in the parade. Spectators and mayors alike recognized Pecos the Elk, Miss Harris the Harris Hawk, Alpha the Wolf, Bert the Great Horned Owl, Forrest the Gray Fox, Sticks and Tonto the Pronghorns, Phantom the Mountain Lion, and Koshari the Bear and applauded and shouted"Hello!" to the passing animals. It was stunning and delightful to see so many of the state's captive wild animals together on this magnificent float.

Behind the Wild West Nature float came two smaller, locally made floats, each with places for thirty people to sit. The first float was filled with Socorro residents, mostly women, holding squirming cats in their laps, while the second float carried local residents with their mix of smaller pet dogs. The cats were plainly uncomfortable, but Howie could see that the dogs were enjoying their outing together. Two cats were especially unhappy, because they women holding them were waving their front paws up and down at parade watchers.

Next in the parade was a small herd of enormous, 'grass-matured' beef cattle, being shepherded by four cowboys on horses. The horned cattle were followed by a small herd of sheep shepherded by dogs and two teenage boys with sticks. Street sweepers behind them put dung into wheeled buckets they were pushing.

Coming up the street toward the Parade Stand was a group of six clowns, made up in animal and bird costumes, who were working the crowd. With them were three musicians, dressed as mariachis, playing guitar, violin, and saxophone. They were accompanied by a powerful-looking woman leading a donkey, with a big pack on its back filled with musical instruments. A trombone, an alto sax curved mouthpiece, and a banjo neck stuck out of the pack, and a drum was tied onto it. As the donkey, musicians, and clowns passed by, Mayor Howie deliberately focused his attention on the Socorro Mayor, asking how he thought the parade was working out for his city. "It's too soon to tell, " Socorro's Mayor replied.

A big surprise followed the loaded donkey. A massive float stunned watchers, because it was carrying two elephants flown in from Thailand, who were painting pictures with their trunks. When each painting was finished, the elephant keepers passed the hastily painted images, recognizable by humans, over to crowd members. Behind the float was a third elephant with a Thai rider on its neck. This elephant had strapped to its chest a big curved wooden tray containing tiny New Mexico state flags, candy bars, and ads for elephant paintings being sold on a street nearby. Spectators who reached out were delighted to receive gifts from a kind elephant, but they were also a little frightened when its massive trunk holding the small gift reached out to their extended hands.

The elephants were followed by a party of men and women in hunting clothes, several of them carrying empty rifles, which Howie knew were inspected by state policemen before allowed to be carried in the parade. Several well-behaved hunting dogs on leashes were with them in the parade.

Behind the hunters came the float Howie had been yearning to see. It was a giant, realistic rock, shaped like world-famous Shiprock in northwest New Mexico. Atop it Coyote stood with his back arched, his neck pointing straight up, his head tilted further back, howling and howling. The float was stunning and pictures of it appeared in news sources all over the world. With other thrilled watchers on the Parade Stand, Mayor Howie applauded loudly as Coyote passed. It hadn't escaped his attention that parade watchers' dogs were furiously barking and struggling to get loose to attack Coyote. For a brief instant Coyote turned toward the Mayors and, bowing his head, gave them a few nice yips. Howie was surprised that Coyote wasn't wearing his customary pink collar, put on him originally by Thelma during the furor to have him mistaken for a dog, a collar that had become the symbol of his prophethood in the coyote world. Howie watched as the howling Coyote atop Shiprock moved on slowly up the street to thunderous applause. It didn't surprise him that another pack of hunters, some with empty guns and more dogs, were following the Shiprock float.

More floats passed by as the Mayors grew restless watching. A New Mexico State float went by covered with pictures and exhibits, but no live animals. "That is a crappy float," one of the businessmen behind Howie remarked. Behind it was an animal rights float with followers handing out crowd flyers. Then came the Human Zoo float. Hundreds of parent parade watchers turned their children's faces away from the semi-nude humans.

Cece Scans from Bill's Place

As the parade moved north up the wide street, the composition of the crowd shifted. There were fewer children, men were more numerous, and not all the men, it seemed, had come solely to enjoy the Animal Fiesta. Back in her secure underground room, Cece was panning and zooming in on bystander men who seemed out of place. She spotted several men wearing suits and ties with earpieces. "Do you know who those are?" Cece asked her Teacher.

"Yes. Those are federal agents you are focusing on. About twenty-five state and federal agents are here because numerous regulations were violated in Mayor Howie's hurried planning of the parade. These agents are here to gather data for possible prosecution. Good lawyers will keep charges from being filed."

One of Cece's 'drone cameras' was focused on the Mexican Cowboy. Cece smiled as she watched him bowing and waving to the crowd. But suddenly an angry look appeared on his face. Cowboy abruptly reined in Turco and turned him toward the crowd. Her camera zoomed in on the Border Patrolmen who arrested the Cowboy at Eden Park. Cowboy was shouting at them as they backed away, "Get closer and my horse will kick the crap out of you." Turco did look threatening. Local Hispanics cheered and clapped because their El Charro had done this to agents who frequently harassed them.

Behind the Mexican Cowboy, Father Gallapo and Thelma had stopped momentarily to exchange a few words with spectators. "No," Thelma said constantly, "I wasn't the woman who almost drowned. Wasn't she Sarah Palin?"

On the sidewalks, there were a large number of spectators with the animals. Many of them were trying to slip between guarding policemen to join the parade. The variety of animals she saw surprised Cece. Besides dogs, there were parrots on human shoulders, pet rats and ferrets being carried, and even several chicken friends on the ground with leashes, pecking at the sidewalk. Two women pushing wheelbarrows with caged raccoons and badgers managed to slip by the officers.

Lone riders were passing by. Cece zoomed in and admired a rider sitting straight up on a light-shaded palomino with a cream-colored mane. His hands were relaxed on the saddle holding the reins and he was wearing a good hat and no sunglasses. Reddening bareheaded visitors from out of state, squatting on the sidewalk in a flood of transparent bright sunlight, instantly realized the usefulness of the hat's design.

Cece spotted an odd-looking man coming up a side street toward the parade who was leading a light brown gelding with a pig riding on it, reins in its mouth. The man plainly wanted his horse and pig to join the individual horsemen riding by, but so far police had blocked him. "He'll keep trying," Cece thought.

Cece zoomed in on rodeo clowns leaping on and off prancing horses, cowboys on cow ponies, jockeys on race horses, and dressage riders in formal costumes, rigid as grave stones in their saddles, riding elegantly groomed horses whose stepping rhythms were collectively changing. "Maybe I should return the motorcycle to Bill and get a horse," Cece said to herself.

After asking her to switch to a different camera, Cece's Teacher pointed out several Mexican drug cartel men working the crowd to build contact lists in Socorro. American agents, eager to recruit them and turn the cartel members into their spies, were tailing these gang members.

Panning up and down the parade route next, Cece was astounded by all the signs she saw different spectators holding high and waving. Many of the signs made her angry as hell:

> **"Require Home Schooling"**
> **"Shut down all large corporations!"**
> **"Castrate gays and impregnate lesbians!"**
> **"Use Local Courts to Decide Local Rules"**
> **"Shut Down Congress!"**
> **"Return Slavery!!!"**
> **"Kill Coyotes"**
> **"Fence All Animals In Then Eat Them"**

"Mayor Howie's disruption planning is really beginning to show up now," Cece thought.

Riding up the street now were a dozen nude bicyclists wearing animal masks and matching body paint. One had turned herself into a stunning red-tailed hawk. Another guy had made himself into an appealing coyote. Up and down the street officers were phoning sergeants to ask if these nude riders should be arrested. Watcher were cheering and booing in about even numbers.

Panning to another block, Cece watched four older women carrying huge colored pictures of the famous Ursula bear and her cubs. The women stopped often to talk with visitors about saving bears, many of whom come from Texas, Colorado, Arizona, and even Asia, Europe and Latin America. Cece was thrilled that people from all over the world had come to the Return to Eden Parade. Grinning, Cece said to her Teacher, "I didn't expect the Pope to come, but I'm surprised the Dalai Lama is not here."

Panning further back in the parade, Cece spotted a sword swallower and a fire breather leading six jugglers. Parade watchers were handing the jugglers folding chairs and bicycles and other things to toss into the air.

"The parade is growing contentious," Cece's Teacher said, switching back to the camera over the Shiprock float.

Cece knew, of course, that Howie wanted the parade to grow contentious. He'd put a lot of thought and effort into turning a wonderful parade into a major disturbance, but had kept every detail to himself. Cece had wondered for weeks what was going to happen. She was very pleased that finally now she would see Howie's plans in action. Zooming in, she noticed that the Mayor's hunting buddies, who supposedly were placed before and behind the Shiprock float to guard the howling Coyote, were looking sour. Dogs with them were starting to snap at each other, and at just about everything else too. "Ah, the dog god's got into the game," Cece said to herself.

Panning around the spectators, Cece spotted religious groups and protesters of many kinds—including groups protesting the parade itself. Police blocked protesters who were trying to get onto the street and confront marchers and persons riding by on floats. Some protesters were confronting animal rights believers working the crowds.

Now, panning back toward the end of the parade, Cece saw an old, rusty Mercedes 180D, with a smeary blue body and white top covered with signs advocating animal rights, begin pouring out stinky plumes of oily black diesel smoke. The driver seemed oblivious to the health-threatening clouds his Mercedes was making. The passing car angered every person near it. Watchers shouted at the driver to park the damned thing and turn its engine off.

Zooming to the very front of the parade now, Cece watched Father Gallapo stop and step out of his truck to give his blessing to women holding three baby Catholics, who had just been baptized. The Priest's appearance struck Cece as shabby. He looked as though he needed new clothes and a shower. Watching how the women and babies were reacting to his blessing, Cece thought the Priest also needed lessons on how to preach to Catholics. His hand was raised and he was blessing softly when a dozen anti-religious protesters began shouting threateningly at him. Father Gallapo sped up his blessing, patted several babies, then hurried back into his Ford pickup and drove away from a scene that was scaring Thelma.

Cece continued panning. On the sidewalk a woman carrying a box of kittens to give away tripped, dropped the box, and the crowd began helping her round up the mewing kittens and put them back in her box. She was crying. Pet dogs were yanking at their leashes to go after the kittens.

At a major street crossing, where policemen were mysteriously absent, steer men in pickups were slipping into the animal rights parade, with cow hides draped over their tailgates and horned cattle skulls taped onto the hoods of their trucks. They fingered animal rights activists who screamed insults at them.

One of Cece's cameras briefly focused on someone passing out cigarettes and condoms to thirteen year olds.

"Yes!" Cece said aloud. "It's a day that started out well and is turning meaner by the moment!"

Cowboy Stops at the Nursing Home

Up at the front of the parade, Cowboy's Teacher was quietly keeping him informed about things Cece was seeing. "I bet Cece planned a lot of this nastiness," Cowboy said back — without moving his lips very much. "She's good at it."

Just as Cowboy was ready to leave California Street and turn up Bullock Boulevard, the Cordoba band behind him suddenly stopped playing. Cowboy and Turco turned around to see what was going on. A hoodie had broken out of the crowd and snatched a coronet from a great soloist in the Cordoba band. Band members dropped their instruments and were running after the thief. They caught him and were about to beat him when four of his mean, tattooed hood buddies chased them back to their instruments. Policemen stepped between the hoodies and the band members, who calmed down, picked up their instruments, and began marching and playing once more, but discordantly now. "Yep, it's happening!" Cowboy said to himself as he began leading the parade again.

Going north now, Cowboy noticed fewer spectators along this part of the parade route. With more time to look around, Cowboy saw a surprising number of large dogs growling at him from behind chain-link fences. He remembered Mayor Howie saying at one of their planning meetings, "Dogs in this part of the world aren't small, cute, lovable house pets, like dogs in Seattle with super-sweet and adoring temperaments. Our dogs have balls, in both senses. Our dogs are like me: smart, dominant, aggressive, ready to take on anyone. And like wolves, they will attack and kill whenever they want to, and feel good about it. These dogs hate coyotes more than any other animal, except perhaps socialist Democrats. If I become governor—and I will—I'm going to turn all the dogs in the state loose on those socialist Satanists. And bag up and drown all their cute doggies."

Cowboy remembered Cece —who loved her Wheaten Terrier, which was taken away from her and probably euthanized when she was declared 'demented' and imprisoned in a nursing home—standing up and shouting at Mayor Howie: "You do that crap and your mansion will be the jailhouse!"

The Mexican Cowboy looked back over his shoulder once more and saw the giant Shiprock float with Coyote on top, carefully turning onto Bullock. The Coyote float traveled only half a block before every dog, chained or fenced, spotted the un-caged coyote howling like he was on the mesa in the territory under his control. Dogs up and down Bullock Blvd.

went nuts and tried everything possible to free themselves and attack Coyote. Watching from her secure room at Bill's facility, Cece said to her Teacher, "This is the beginning of the war between coyotes and dogs, a war which is going to split the kingdom of animal gods into fighting factions." Her Teacher remained silent.

Nearing the end of the parade route finally, Cowboy kept an eye out for the nursing home holding Bill. Approaching it at last, he was pleased at the crowd of patients, many in wheel chairs with attendants and security people, waiting expectantly on the sidewalk in front of the home's parking lot. They began cheering and applauding as the flag carriers passed by and Cowboy waved and bowed to them.

Cowboy walked Turco slowly over to the thrilled spectators, bowed and doffed his sombrero, and invited nursing home residents to pat famous Turco. Several took him up on it, including one young man who had broken both legs and an arm in a climbing accident. Wheeled beside Turco, the young man said, "I know all about you." Turco turned his head and smiled at him.

Father Gallapo pulled up behind Cowboy and Turco to invite excited residents to pat the goat sticking its head out of the Priest's truck. Looking in his rear-view mirror, the Priest was alarmed when he saw several teenagers trying to climb onto the porta-confessional's trailer. This can't be allowed! Waving goodbye, he let out the clutch and turned away from the curb. The teenagers were being told to get back onto the curb by Nurse Nicklefoot's security officers. Seeing Father Gallapo drive past him, the Mexican Cowboy thanked people for coming outside to watch the parade, and told them there was much more excitement to come. With excited spectators shouting nice things at him, Cowboy waved his hat, bowed once again, and trotted off to get in front of Father Gallapo.

A Shot Rings Out

Just a few blocks up the street Cowboy and Turco approached a group of parade safety workers wearing orange vests with yellow stripes, who would soon be steering floats to approved parking places. Behind them were many idling school buses, waiting to take parade participants back to Clark Field where the parade began. The safety workers applauded and cheered for their El Charro and the famous Turco he was riding. Cowboy reached down and shook hands with several of them before he turned onto El Camino Real Street and trotted north toward Parkview Elementary School. Today had been fabulous for him, but Turco was exhausted and Cowboy was more than ready to leave Socorro and get back to his ranch. A great deal of fear and anxiety had crept into him. Cowboy had done his best to help rescue Bill and the sooner he was out of Socorro, the safer he would feel. Looking over his shoulder, he saw the Priest following him at a reasonable distance. "Goodbye, parade goers," he said to no listeners, as he began loosening his giant, bright-red, bow tie. Speaking into his Teacher now, Cowboy said to Father Gallapo, "Thanks for watching my back. It meant a lot to me."

"Anytime, Buddy," Father Gallapo said with surprising warmth.

In the parking lot of the elementary school, Hank Gooding was waiting for him with a trailer to carry Turco back to his ranch. Hank helped the Cowboy unsaddle Turco and get him into the trailer. Father Gallapo and Thelma sat in their idling truck a short distance away, very anxious to leave also, after giving their fine goat passenger back to his keeper. The goat had fun riding in the parade, and seemed reluctant to leave Thelma and the Priest. A car length in front of the Priest's truck was Cordoba's only police car, its red lights flashing silently. Frank Corsa, Cordoba's police chief—and the town's only officer—reached over and opened the door for Cowboy. "I've got all your stuff in the trunk. Welcome. Thanks for doing such a great job leading the parade."

Cowboy was getting into the front seat and closing the door when he heard a loud, sharp **'crack'** come from the north side of Sedillo Park. "What's that?" he asked Corsa.

"I don't know, but it isn't good. It sounded like a high-powered rifle shot. Let's get out of here," Corsa said and sped away toward Interstate 25, just a few blocks away.

"Father G, did you hear that shot?" Cowboy said into his Teacher.

"We did. And it scared hell out of us. There wasn't supposed to be any shooting in this parade."

Before he could answer Cowboy was startled by a small **'boom.'** Looking over his shoulder he saw flame and smoke rising from what he guessed was the north side of Sedillo Park, where the parade ended. "Find out for us what's going on, Frank," he ordered officer Corsa.

Getting onto the freeway and speeding up to over seventy, Corsa began rapidly running through available channels on his police car's radio. On one of the State Police channels a sergeant was ordering police to block every way out of Socorro, to clear parade spectators, and to protect firemen arriving on El Camino Real Street. Officers were ordered to remain at least three hundred feet from the burning float. Switching to one of the Socorro police channels, Frank Corsa and the Cowboy heard, "Every officer approaching the crime scene must be armored and carry heavy weapons."

"Look at your Teacher," Father Gallapo said over his.

"We'll play it back for you," Cowboy's Teacher told Cowboy. Cowboy raised the small black Teacher and watched the Shiprock float turn on to El Camino Real Street and make its way slowly through the safety workers, who were directing the driver where to park. Parked far from the other parade floats now, the Rock driver got out, stretched and walked up the road toward one of the many outhouses lining the street. Coyote was still on top of the float and seemed to be looking around for the workers who would drive him back to Bill's place.

"It was safer for him to stay up there until they came," Cowboy said to the Priest over his Teacher.

The picture on his Teacher then zoomed out, and a red arrow pointed to someone in camouflage lying in the tall grass about fifty yards from the rock. Zooming in again, Cowboy was frightened by what he saw. It was a hooded sniper aiming a high-powered rifle at Coyote. "Get down, Coyote!" the Cowboy screamed as the sniper pulled the trigger. The camera zoomed instantly back to Coyote again. Cowboy saw his dearest friend blown over backwards as the bullet struck, falling out of sight into the Rock. "My God, My God, My God. We've got to go back there. Coyote's been shot."

"We can't," Frank Corsa answered. "My orders are to take you back to Cordoba. If your coyote can be saved, people in Socorro both can and will do it." Corsa turned on his siren and sped up to eighty miles an hour.

The Cowboy was still watching his Teacher. As stunned parade workers started to run toward the Shiprock Float, a burst of flame came out from under the float. A moment later, an explosion destroyed the float and the rock on top of it. The air around the destroyed float filled with smoke.

The Mexican Cowboy was crying intensely. "He's dead. He's dead. Coyote's been assassinated," Cowboy said sobbing, putting his Teacher down. "He's dead. My life is no more."

Cowboy cried all the way back to Cordoba and, in the truck racing behind the squad car, Thelma was crying explosively and Father Gallapo was weeping too... and cursing.

Revelations

Hours later, back at the ranch house, Cowboy was rocking on the porch, Father Gallapo was taking a shower, and Thelma and Cece were putting together a light meal and setting the table. Tears made their eyes damp. When the food was on the table, Cece went onto the porch and asked Cowboy to come in. He came in, sat down a moment, began crying again, got up and went into his bedroom and closed the door.

Lying on his bed, Cowboy tried to fall asleep, wiping his wet eyes and face with the sleeve on his arm. After twenty minutes of bawling, Cowboy fell asleep and began to snore when a familiar whine came from outdoors. Cece banged on his door, and when he didn't answer, she opened it and asked Cowboy to please get up.

"I don't want to," he said, rolling away from her onto his side.

"Someone's outside," Cece said. "I don't know who it is. This is important. Please get up."

Feeling more angry than sad now—and wanting to slap her—Cowboy got off his bed and brushed past Cece.

Stepping out onto his rundown porch he looked down—and saw his assassinated beloved friend Coyote sitting at the bottom of the steps. "Aren't you going to feed me again?" Coyote asked.

Cowboy stumbled down the porch steps, grabbed his dearest friend, and sat on the cold ground, rocking and hugging him for several minutes. He kissed Coyote and buried his face in Coyote's neck fur. When Cowboy looked up finally, his other three friends were standing above him on the porch, smiling and waiting for him to pull his face from Coyote's fur. He smiled at them and they rushed downstairs to hug both the Cowboy and Coyote. All four humans were crying joyously.

"All right, friends. You are getting me wetter than today's two-inch rain. Let's go inside," Coyote said. "You have questions and I will have a few answers."

Coyote Explains

Inside at the table eating, with Coyote sitting on his bench and a plate heaped with food and a bowl of water in front of him, the fivesome were talking about the shooting and parade. Coyote invited the group to ask him questions. The Mexican Cowboy went first.

"I'm dying to know—well, I was dying before you showed up outdoors tonight anyway—how did you escape your assassination? I saw that shot hit you on my Teacher."

"I wasn't there," Coyote answered. "The howling coyote on the Rock was a biobot who is an excellent teacher in Bill's Coyote School. His name is—Coyote made a strange coyote sound in the coyote language—and he speaks perfect Coyote language. And 'he' wasn't shot either. That was a blank you heard go off."

"That's why the coyote on the rock wasn't wearing your pink collar!" Father Gallapo said.

"The collar is the symbol of my prophethood. My God told me to not let Bill's people put it on the biobot."

"If the shot was a blank, what made 'him' jerk backwards and fall down the hole?" the Mexican Cowboy asked.

"The bot was programmed to do it. And the guy who supposedly shot 'me' is Hirshy Dismas, the former Marine who saved your life, Cowboy."

"That makes Hirshy now both my enemy and my friend."

"What happened to the coyote 'bot?" Thelma asked. "I hope 'he' wasn't destroyed in the explosion and fire."

"No, he wasn't. In the few seconds between the shot and the explosion—unpronounceable name in the Coyote tongue—scooted down inside the rock, stuck his head through a self-tightening collar, was instantly sprayed with reddish-gold paint, and slipped out the float's underside trap door. Then 'he' ran over to Hirshy, who leashed him up and immediately took him away from the parade."

"So, a coyote let himself be turned into a dog," Cowboy said.

"'He' wasn't a real coyote," Coyote replied.

"What kind of dog did he become?" Cece asked.

"A working Australian Kelpie, resembling the dog Hirshy actually owns."

"Where did Hirshy get the bullet?" Father Gallapo asked.

"It was in the grass where he was laying."

"Why didn't I see all this on my Teacher?" Father Gallapo asked.

"Because Mayor Howie didn't want you—or anyone—to see what really was happening."

The group was quiet for a few seconds, eating and drinking and chewing on the amazing facts they'd just been told. Cece was first to resume the conversation.

"Are we going to try to come up with a new plan to rescue Bill?" Cece asked.

"No. You don't need to. Bill's been rescued," Coyote replied instantly.

The four humans at the table were stunned once more. "Bill was rescued?" Thelma asked.

"And how was it done?" Cece added. "I thought I got to watch everything going on at the parade, but I didn't see the shooting and explosion, or any attempt to rescue Bill."

"Mayor Howie made Bill's TEAM sign an agreement to share with no one anything to do with the rescue. Howie didn't want to be put into jail for thirty years. That's why Bill's TEAM was editing what you were allowed to see."

"So you cannot tell us how the rescue was accomplished?" the Priest asked.

"Actually, *I* can," Coyote answered. "I'm not a formal member of Bill's TEAM. I'm a free coyote. No one can stop me from telling you the little I know about the rescue. And I will if you promise to keep your mouths shut."

Coyote studied every face at the table. The humans nodded and sincerely promised to keep secret what they were about to find out.

"Okay. Here's what I learned. Once the Shiprock float left California Street and turned up Bullock, attacks on 'me' were supposed to begin to start the parade's disintegration. My god worked with other gods to make this happen and a lot of animal gods joined in. But some of those gods had different reasons for doing it. The dog god Poko wanted to go after me. Period. Most of the other gods wanted to reverse this Back to Eden thing. They don't want their followers getting thick with humans."

"So, how'd the attack begin?" Cowboy asked.

"First, three local hawks dived on the howling coyote 'bot and scratched his plastic back. Then a family of rabid-looking raccoons appeared and began climbing up the rock to attack 'me'. Meanwhile, hunters in front and behind the Shiprock float began misbehaving. Several of them took turns pointing their empty rifles up at the rock, acting like they wanted to shoot the animal on top. That really made a lot of spectators scared or angry. One spectator held up a pistol and threatened to shoot a hunter if he didn't lower his rifle. At that instant a swarm of Norway rats was loosed to climb up the rock. Humans fear rats almost as much as they fear snakes and spiders."

"So, all kinds of animals were supposed to attack him?" Thelma asked.

"No," Coyote said. "The gods of most domesticated animals reacted negatively to the idea of using their subjects to break up the parade. Humans have given domestic animal gods billions of followers. They don't want to bust up their god-friendly relationship with humans."

"Those gods don't care if their followers get eaten?" Cowboy asked.

"Not so long as they keep getting more followers."

"Well, Coyote's God, El Latrano, is trying to find better ways to protect his followers," Cowboy said.

"That's because he's a Liberal," Father Gallapo said with a grin.

"So, that pig I saw riding a horse was against disrupting the parade?" Cece asked.

"You got it. You weren't allowed to see it, but that pig did get into the parade. When animals and hunters began attacking the howling 'Coyote,' the pig leaped off his horse and tried to get the hunters to focus on him instead of pointing guns up at 'Coyote.' His grunting and squealing was super loud as he rushed into the hunters. But the hunters just used their dogs to chase him away. Several roosters did manage to fly up the rock and attack the raccoons and rats."

"So, did Howie's plan work?" Thelma asked.

"It did. The animal attacks on the 'Coyote,' plus all the mean, barking dogs up and down the street, lit fear in every caged animal in the parade. Only the elephants kept their cool. The mountain lion and bear penned in the Wildwest Park float tried to break out from their invisible cages. That scared everyone and the float was immediately taken out of the parade by attendants and marshals."

"I don't see how any of this helped to rescue Bill," Father Gallapo said.

"It kept the police busy and it pulled a lot more spectators onto the sidewalk," Coyote said.

"Start a war and humans will run toward it," the Priest said.

"Howie's growing fracas also was designed to steer police in wrong directions when they tried to learn who was behind 'my' assassination and the float explosion."

"But what does all this have to do Nurse Nickelfoot and the nursing home?" Cece asked. "Did Howie's gang tie her up, gag her, and beat her?"

"Nurse Nicklefoot's objective was to keep staff and patients away from the parade, in order to keep her house and them secure. She did let some paraders carrying small animals and performers come inside to entertain patients. Look at your Teachers."

Coyote paused while his four friends found and held up their Teachers. Cece gasped at the picture she saw.

Coyote continued. "Bill's TEAM found this picture online of Nurse Nicklefoot sitting in a chair with a parrot on her shoulder, holding a cat, and petting a dog at her feet. Staff and patients around her were excited and happy, and Nurse Nicklefoot appeared thrilled too. Her attention was completely diverted from her usual critical supervision while she was interacting with these animals."

"Now, as the parade became louder and more interesting, patients insisted on going out to watch. Several of them even came back inside to get their friends when you brought Turco over to see them," Coyote said, pointing his nose at Cowboy. "Excitement spread, patients and families and friends went out to see the floats, listen to the music, and touch the animals. Nurse Nickelfoot tried, but she couldn't keep them locked up. So many patients were buzzing to open the locked door that she gave up and unlocked the main door. But Nicklefoot then had to send lots of her staff outside to keep her patients safe. She was afraid something bad would happen on the street, and she was preparing for it.

"By then Cordoba's fine high school band had stopped in front of the nursing home and was playing lots of music patients want to hear. Patients inside, who couldn't leave their rooms or go outside because of their condition, complained, and were gratified when Nurse Nickelfoot allowed the three musicians and six clowns in animal and bird costumes to come in and perform inside the nursing home. Nursing home waiters held Donkey Gus outside the main entrance and fed him carrots and water. The pack that was filled with musical instruments was carried in by one of the attendants. Wandering around the main floor, the musicians swapped instruments as they played and sang different songs, to smiles, singing, and rounds of applause. With staff and patients still coming downstairs to go outdoors, the clowns and musicians headed upstairs to perform for the few patients who couldn't leave their rooms.

"Staff thought the clowns and musicians were fun and safe to have around, and didn't keep a close eye on them. When the performers got to Bill's room, a physician in a clown costume hastily checked over Bill, wizened and contorted as Steven Hawking—and far less brainy—after his devastating stroke. Two of the musicians played while others lifted Bill out of bed and stuffed him into a specially made hidden compartment in the music bag. They were out in the hall again and about to go into two more rooms upstairs to play when the float blew up. The explosion knocked out all power in the neighborhood. Nurse Nicklefoot ordered two of her workers to go down into the basement and start the emergency power system, but warned them to re-read the starting rules before firing-up the back-up system.

"Then efficient Nurse Nickelfoot ordered her staff to force every patient outdoors to leave the street and get back into the nursing home. She went around the main floor telling visitors inside they had to leave, then went upstairs to order the musicians and clowns to go. They protested. "Can't we stay and play a while longer?" one of them pleaded. ""No, get out, now," she said sternly. The musicians looked angry, but they put their instruments back into the bag, carried it downstairs, went outside, strapped the pack onto Gus the donkey, thanked the attendants who were holding and caring for him, and rejoined the parade."

"Jesus," said the Mexican Cowboy. "What a grab."

"What did they do with Bill?" the Priest asked.

"With sirens coming toward them in all directions, parade marshals and policemen halted the parade and forced participants to leave their floats and go into Sedillo Park. Busses were brought over to take them back to the parade's starting place. The musicians and clowns got into the second bus and were driven back to their cars. They were in plain clothes by then and it would be terrifically hard for police to identify them as kidnappers. The woman leading Gus took him across the park to the school. There, he was put into the van that brought him and the musicians' and clowns' things to Socorro, and Gus was driven back to Cordoba. Inside the van was a hidden mini-hospital. Highly programmed biobots inside the van took Bill out of his bag, checked him over, and started intensive care."

"Howie came up with all of this?" Thelma asked.

"Yes. He, and his team and Bill's, came up with all this and put it together. Bill's rescuers' moves were plotted out in advance and rehearsed, based on information gotten from numerous sources. Mayor Howie's now bringing in the FBI–and every agency he can get–to find the culprits who destroyed his parade. Though the parade got busted up, Howie's going to get credit for filling Socorro and nearby towns with tourists and bringing in millions of dollars."

"Still, Mayor Howie just pushed Eden all the way to Hell," Cowboy said.

"Humans have had one foot in Hell since they began sinning," Father Gallapo replied.

"Those animals at Eden Park were pushed into Hell when they were rounded up against their will by coyotes and made to cool out fighting humans," Thelma said.

"What's Bill's TEAM going to do with Bill?" Cece asked.

"Use bioengineering to fix up his body and brain, and then pour his consciousness back into him."

"Sounds like science fiction stuff," the Priest said.

"They think of it as medical experimenting," Coyote said.

Coyote looked around at the four weary humans, each filled with a wide mix of thoughts and feelings. "It's time for me to leave," he said. "Cowboy, you don't need to feed me tonight. I've had a great day, but it hasn't been the same for you—or for the others here."

Coyote jumped off the bench, waited by the door for Cece to open it, and left without saying 'Goodbye.' The Cowboy followed him out the door. At the bottom of the steps, Coyote turned and said to the Cowboy, "I expect you to keeping putting out food for me."

Cowboy said, "I will forever."

"Goodnight," Coyote said and disappeared into the darkness.

Back inside, Cowboy saw that the women were finishing clearing the table.

"We should go too, we're exhausted," Cece said as she returned to the table.

"I'm wondering, what's ahead for the four of us?" Thelma asked, standing up.

"For me, on the road to Crawford tomorrow," Father Gallapo said.

"For me, sitting on my ass and trying to figure out what I'm going to do with the rest of my life. I don't want to go back to being a downer," Cowboy said, getting up.

"For me, a good night's sleep," Thelma added.

"Group hug before we leave!" Cece said.

Cowboy and the two women held each other tightly, but Father Gallapo 'hugged' them barely touching the group. "Bedtime for me," he said.

"Bedtime for all of us. Night," Cece said, picking up her coat and walking out the door.

As Thelma followed Cece out of the Cowboy's rundown ranch house, she turned and said to the two men, "We love you." Cowboy burst into a smile, but the Priest had a frown on his face as the door closed.

"That woman wants too much from me," Father Gallapo said going into his bedroom, his hand about to close the door.

"It could be worse. Thelma will want nothing to do with you if you keep ignoring her the way you are. Do you want Thelma to stop taking care of your church?" Cowboy asked.

"It isn't my church. I'm an itinerant Priest."

"I thought you Priests believe all of us are itinerants on this planet," Cowboy said, going into his bedroom.

"Put your fingers in your ears. I don't want you listening to me while I pray tonight."

"If I hadn't listened to your God answering your prayers I wouldn't believe He exists."

"Good night."

"Sleep okay."

"Don't snore loudly."

"Be quiet when you get up early to climb up to your prayer rock."

"I'll tiptoe."

"And tomorrow let's talk about the house Bill's TEAM is going to build for you next door."

"Keep messing with me and I'm going to baptize you."

"We may have a deal," the Mexican Cowboy answered. "Good night."

There was no answer from the Priest as he shut his bedroom door.

Turco Goes Home Again, and Again, and Again, and...

E l Charro, the unforgettable leader of the disastrously ended Return to Eden Parade, alas had returned to being his normal sad self. On an uncomfortably warm morning, just three days after leading the blown-apart Return to Eden Parade, the Mexican Cowboy sat on his dilapidated porch, rocking and pondering his depressed feelings. "I've gone from being a super-star back to being my usual nobody...this hurts more every moment...is there anything I can do that will help me get back to feeling good again..?" Cowboy was trying to think of happy-making things he might be doing in years to come, when his Teacher interrupted unexpectedly, and said: "Cece wants to talk to you. I'll connect her." Cowboy hadn't heard from Cece since the extremely terrible, and memorably wonderful, dinner he'd shared with her and the others after Coyote appeared to have been shot. Cowboy was becoming surer that Cece's overt affection toward him was probably just manipulation to make him work with her to rescue Bill.

"Hi Cece," he said with a flat voice into his Teacher. "You are dumping me, aren't you?"

"No. I'm sorry that I haven't had time to come visit you, but I'm working my tail off over here at Bill's place. His rescue has made us a hell of a lot busier."

"So, why call me?"

"Bill's people want to immediately start building a new barn for Turco and Gus, and they asked me to get your permission."

"What's the hurry?"

Waffling, Cece said, "Bill's TEAM thinks Turco may not have too much longer to live. They would like the two of you to have more time together in what remains of his life. He has laminitis among many other things."

Cece's blunt words floored Cowboy. Part of him was furious at the overly frightening things Cece had just said. Another part of him longed to have Turco living with him once again. Patiently, Cece waited while Cowboy slowly came to a decision and answered her. "He isn't dying, but go ahead and fix up the stable for him. He'll be okay here."

"It will help if you let us get some of the best horse vets to try to help him."

"That's alright with me, provided your quacks don't do anything to hurt my great mustang friend."

"We'll keep an eye on them."

Home in His New Barn

In the next three weeks, a well-organized flow of workers and contractors descended on the Mexican Cowboy's ranch. The replacement barn and new meadow were built almost as speedily as the images that had rolled past his eyes when Cece had shown him a 3-D video about possible barn reconstruction. This was when she'd first mentioned an offer from Bill's TEAM to replace for him the barn blown down during a wild dust storm years back.

Sooner than he believed possible, Cece phoned Cowboy to say the new barn was ready. She offered to send a car to drive him over to Hank Godding's stable to bring his mustang friend home again. He accepted. Going into his bedroom, Cowboy put on worn boots, leather chaps with ragged bottoms over his jeans, and his gray Levi summer riding jacket with brass buttons. At the barn, with Hank standing by and talking with him, Cowboy groomed Turco and put the green saddle blanket on the horse's back. Then he threw the beat-up, but still comfortable, classic Mexican saddle he inherited from his grandfather, over him. Hank told Cowboy he would miss him and Turco, but that he was glad to be getting all the money Bill's people promised to send him for taking care of Cowboy's great mustang friend so many years. Thanking Hank for looking after his beloved horse friend, Cowboy took Gus out of his stall. Gus was a brown burro, with lighter colored inner legs, and he was wearing a halter with an attached rope dangling to the ground under his chin. Gus's head was down, his neck bent, and he looked at the ground, as Cowboy put two large, soft blankets over his midriff and strapped a three-sided cargo carrier made of leather and wood onto him with a breeching strap around his behind and under his tail. With Gus loaded with Turco's things, and ready to follow them to his new home, Cowboy shook hands with Hank, said good bye, and rode Turco out of Hank's barn back to his ranch, with Gus ambling behind. Cowboy was worried by how much weaker Turco seemed than he was just weeks ago, leading the parade. "Performing in front of thousands of people makes you do better," Cowboy said worryingly, patting Turco's neck.

A week later Cowboy leaned against the new paddock's fence watching Gus and Turco enjoy the grassy turf just planted for them. It was good to have his friend back home again and Cowboy was pleased so far with the attention Bill's biobot horse tenders had been giving to the new barn's only equines. During the week a dozen or more highly specialized horse veterinarians visited Turco, diagnosing and offering the best possible treatments for each of Turco's many problems, most of which Cowboy approved. Still, as weeks went by, Turco wasn't handling his own any better, but at least his rate of failing seemed to be slowing. When Cowboy rode him every day, Turco stumbled and couldn't maintain even a trot. He had trouble getting up from lying down. Cowboy's fears for him kept rising.

Turco's Desire to go Home Again is Discovered

The biobots caring for Turco were also monitoring the horse's mental states, for Turco's sake certainly, but also to add much new knowledge to Bill's TEAM's understanding of horses' feelings and thoughts. The biobrains on Bill's TEAM, who were rapidly becoming the planet's most sophisticated bio-psychologists, had come up with several findings which astonished them greatly. Horses do think, are aware of their feelings, and though their internal 'language' is very limited compared with humans', horses can recognize their changing desires and make plans to take care of these. Bill's TEAM was using studies they'd been making on Turco to create new computer programs in horse biopsychology. These had established the surprising findings that Turco both knew he was dying and didn't want to die in his new barn. What the new programs revealed is that Turco wanted to return to the range with his mustang herd in northern New Mexico, and pass away—outdoors and 'naturally'—with his birth fellows.

How Turco Might Be Helped

"God," Cece said when Bill's TEAM passes this information along to her.

"You've proven to be a very able human associate and we share more with you than with any human."

"What are we going to do about this? Truck Turco back to his home on the range?" she asked, grinning at the small joke she'd made.

"We think his veterinarians are not going to be able to make him fit enough to do this."

"And you have something in mind?" Cece asked.

"Perhaps."

"What's this 'perhaps' crap? You biobrains are black & white, either/or guys."

"We are trying to grow our capabilities. We are exploring doubting now."

"Grrrrrr. You guys wobble back and forth between the human and the machine world in ways which annoy me," she said, tilting her head from side to side.

"We appreciate your telling us this. Thanks to you we'll do better," the 'bot replied, smiling and giggling.

"Grrrrr...." Cece replied. "Well, let me try to figure out what to do about Turco's wishes. That's what you want me to do, right?"

"Yes," answered the 'bot, with no emotional expression.

Persuading Cowboy to Let Turco Walk Home

That warm and sunny afternoon Cece hiked along the front of the Manzano range, taking pictures, looking for novel and interesting things to put into her back pack, while trying to figure out how to make the Mexican Cowboy give up his beloved mustang friend, for Turco's sake. Mid-afternoon, as she stretched out on a large boulder snacking and sunbathing in late summer sunlight, her Teacher phoned to pass on some new information. "We've just learned that Turco wants to walk home. His veterinarian specialists concur that Turco won't be able to do this in his worsening condition, even with our help."

"Well that solves the problem, doesn't it?" Cece asked. "There is no way we can help Turco get what he wants."

"We could try to make Turco well enough to walk back to his range, if you and Cowboy would allow us to perform experimental bio-rehabilitation on him."

"Turco wouldn't want that!"

"We think Turco would welcome our efforts to help him walk home. He knows he cannot do this now and is very discouraged by it, a feeling which is hastening his decline."

"You guys have made this problem much harder for me to solve."

"Keep trying to do it for us anyway, please."

Cece Presents Her Solution

Next evening Cece summoned the Mexican Cowboy to have dinner with her at Bill's place. The waiting room had been turned into an attractively decorated dining room. Nighttime animal and bird sounds played softly from hidden speakers, to the Cowboy's delight. On the ceiling, an overhead open skylight was projected. Cowboy was enamored with the beautiful view of normally viewable stars and planets above him—minus the blinking lights of airliners passing overhead. Their dinner was delicious and impeccably served. Sitting across from each other at a small table, their knees touching, they enjoyed margaritas before dinner, and ate— with two marvelous bottles of wine before them.

Cowboy suspected there was a hidden purpose in Cece's summoning of him. She wore an adorable combination of clothes he's never seen on her before, and her makeup and hair were attractive for a change. She reached out to touch his hand or arm frequently, and he was convinced that Cece was trying to manipulate him again rather than just be with him, which he would have preferred.

With after-dinner drinks in hand, Cece rose and led Cowboy to a soft honey-brown leather couch and pulled him down beside her. Nighttime animal sounds had still been 'playing,' but now Mexican music, the kind Cowboy had listened to as a teenager, played softly out of the speakers. Cowboy took a sip of his brandy, put the glass down on the table before them, slid away from her and said bluntly to Cece, "What's up, woman? I know you are messing with me again."

Cece grinned and said, "I was waiting for you figure that out and ask me. I put this evening together because I really do want to hang with you, but we do have something critical to discuss and decide also."

"It is about Turco, isn't it?" Cowboy said, looking wounded. "And you are going to manipulate me, right?"

"Right. I'm a great manipulator, as you know. Come snuggle with me while Bill's TEAM shows us what's going on." Cowboy slid over beside her on the couch, Cece took his hand and held it on her legs, as an image resembling the Mexican horse doctor who took care of his grandfather's animals 'walked' into their room and introduced himself. For the next fifteen minutes Cowboy heard about, and sometimes actually saw, doctors' studies of Turco that, overall, had worrisome findings. An image of Bill himself then 'walked' into the room and told Cowboy about the startling discoveries his bio-neuroscientists had made.

"Turco does have desires, and he can plan and think... but not in the way human minds do. We are very sure that Turco wants to walk back to his range and equally certain that human doctors cannot get him ready to do it."

Everything Cowboy had been hearing and seeing made him feel sadder and angrier. He should have stayed away. Cece put her arm around him and held him tightly, as 'Bill' continued. "We believe that our bio-specialists may be able to make Turco fit enough to return to his former home, but our work would be experimental, and there are risks for Turco in what we would try to do for him. The question before us now is: are you willing to allow us to try to help Turco?"

"And help Bill too. Much of what they try on Turco will be used to restore Bill to consciousness, if their experiments succeed," Cece said, loosening her grip on her close friend.

Cowboy was crying now. He got up from the couch, walked to the outside wall 'window' and demanded, "Show me images of Turco when he was younger." After a brief pause, pleasing videos of the younger mustang began flowing across the 'window' screen. The youthful, mostly brown pinto with the huge, oddly shaped white blaze on his left side, rich black mane, and thin curvy white marking on his right side, was active—and at times even aggressive. Cowboy watched the vital stallion's film clips for long minutes. Cece stood close to Cowboy, her arm around him and holding his hand too. She was amazed at the appeal the younger horse has for her. Maybe motorcycles were not the only things she wanted to ride.

"He was amazing then, wasn't he?" Cece said, stunned by the great Turco's youthful pictures.

Leading Cece back to the couch and for the first time putting his arm around her, Cowboy—his eyes and nose wet—said to 'Bill,'"Thank you. I've seen and heard enough to make up my mind. What's best for Turco is best for me. I believe what you have told me. And I understand the only way forward for Turco is to allow you to experiment on him."

"Whoopeee!" Cece said, before planting a small kiss on his mouth.

"Why don't you bring Turco to us," 'Bill' said to the Cowboy. "You will be able to tell his willingness to stay with us."

"That I can," the Cowboy answered, wiping his face with his dirty handkerchief. "You are not the only guys who can understand what Turco's thinking and feeling."

Turco Leaves His New Home

Late next morning Cowboy walked slowly to the new barn and opened the door of the stall with Turco and his donkey friend, Gus inside. "Nuzzle each other, guys," Cowboy said. "Gus, Turco may be going away for a while and you are going to be staying with me by yourself." Gus's upright ears drooped and a sad expression appeared on his face. Cowboy led his aging mustang partner into the aisle and began saddling him, while a worried Gus stuck his head over the stall door and watched. "Turco, I'm going to ride you over to Bill's place. His people want to try to fix you up. You can refuse if you want." Turco stuck his head forward so Cowboy could put the bridle on him. "Okay. I understand. Just let me know if you change your mind."

As the Cowboy began to lead Turco outdoors, two of the new barn's 'bots—smelling oddly horse-like—stepped over to Turco, hugged him, and each held out a small vegetable-like bundle to chew and swallow. "Good tasting medicines," one of the 'bots said. "This will help Turco make it over to Bill's. We'll miss him. But we'll take good care of Gus." The other 'bot made a soft, lengthy set of changing horse neighs. "That's a 'goodbye and take care of yourself' from us to Turco," the other 'bot said to Cowboy.

Turco Moves to Bill's Home

Turco and the Cowboy were each feeling their own forms of intense pain as Turco slowly made his way the several miles to Bill's place. It was a gorgeous early fall day, and if Turco were feeling better the two of them would have enjoyed every moment of it. Reaching Bill's place, Cowboy rode Turco around to the mountainside of the house, where a small barn had just been put up. Cowboy dismounted and led Turco into the barn's open door. Two 'bots were waiting for them and offered Turco more delicious meds. "We'll take him underground to the facility we've put together for him," one of the 'bots said. "You are welcome to come with us."

"I can't bear that," Cowboy answered, and walked out the barn door. Just outside he turned around and said, "Drop his reins guys. I'm going to walk a few yards, then stop and turn around and ask Turco to leave with me."

"We understand," said the 'bot holding Turco kindly, and dropped the reins and moved back from Turco as Cowboy walked away. Turco was sniffing and snorting cautiously, his black eyes flashing with fear.

Several car lengths from the door Cowboy turned around. "Come on, Turco. Let's go home," he said loudly. Turco took one or two steps forward hesitantly, stopped, turned around and looked at one of the biobots behind him, and stood still, slightly shaking his head. "Got you, Friend," Cowboy shouted. "The prospect of going into a hospital for surgery scares me too. I'll keep an eye on you though, and if you think you want to get away from here, let one of the 'bots know and I'll come get you." Turco turned his head slightly from side to side, his way of saying 'yes' to his best friend, and watched Cowboy walk around the corner of Bill's house and disappear.

In front of Bill's house Cece was waiting for Cowboy near an older car Bill's TEAM had given her to drive. Without saying a word to the crying man, she walked up to him, put her arm around him, led him to the car, opened the passenger door for him, and the two of them drove away. Cece noticed that Cowboy would not allow himself to turn his head and watch Bill's place disappearing behind them. "I'll stay at your place tonight if you want me to," Cece said softly.

Experimenting On Turco

As Bill's TEAM started experimenting on Turco, they invited Cece to watch every step of the intervention and pass along what she's seen to her friend the Mexican Cowboy. "He can't bear to hear anything about it. This business frightens the hell out of him," Cece replied, "but I'll look in on you and Turco once in a while."

"We'll have complete videos for the two of you to watch also."

"Cowboy could not bear to watch those. To change the subject, how is Turco getting along with you?"

"We are creatures he trusts. There is no doubt about that."

As weeks went by, Bill's TEAM members tried out meticulously planned medical experiments on Turco. New medicines based on Turco's genes were created and tried. The majority of regenerative surgeries were almost invisibly small and Turco was conscious and eating while these took place. Cece watched occasionally, when she had rare moments of free time, and was more than satisfied with how gently and precisely efforts to improve Turco's health and reverse his decline were being carried out. "You guys are great vets!" Cece said after one extraordinarily difficult surgery was completed.

"Given all that we know, given our precise reasoning, our expertise in bio-engineering, and the advances we are making rapidly, it is far likelier that Turco's life will be bettered by our care than with human doctors,'" a biobrain said to her through one of the attending 'bots.

"Right," said Cece. "I'm kind of getting to trust you on this one. And coming to believe when you start working on Bill he'll be better cared for by you than he was by human doctors."

"Actually, we've been working on Bill longer than on Turco. We are far along in getting him reconfigured and ready to have his stored consciousness poured back into him."

"Can you tell me what you are doing with Bill?" Cece asked.

"No. This work is our most secret. For many reasons. But someday we will be able to show you what we are doing, with explanations which shall match your level of understanding."

"I didn't know that you could go that low," Cece replied, smiling.

Turco Revives

As days passed Cowboy's Teacher kept sending one or two pictures of post-op Turco in his stall. At first Cowboy refused to look at these, but his Teacher assured him that he would feel better after seeing the pictures. "Turco wants you to see what's happening to him," his Teacher insisted. In several of the pictures Cece was feeding a more vigorous Turco a handful of delicious meds. Turco's coat was shaved in many tiny places on his body, and Cowboy did blow up several of the snaps to study the microscopic sutures the biobrain wanted him to see. He was offered a list of microbiomics that had been tried on Turco. Cowboy couldn't understand most of this stuff, but he could see that Turco was plainly happier than he had been in years, and this pleased the Mexican Cowboy enormously.

"He's okay," Cece said to Cowboy on her Teacher one evening. "Really he is. And he would like you to come see him."

"Won't. Can't," Cowboy replied, smiling but with signs of worry still on his face.

Gus Leaves His Home Too

Two days later Cece phoned Cowboy urgently. "I have some bad news for you. Turco has stopped responding to treatment. We think it is because you have refused to come and see him. Bill's TEAM think Turco might turn around if you allow us to come and pick up Gus and put him with Turco. What do you say?"

The unexpected turnaround in Turco's healing stunned Cowboy, and he collapsed onto a chair. "I don't know what to do. I feel terrible about this. But I still can't make myself go over there. I just can't. All right. Stop sending me stuff about Turco. Come and get Gus." His chest heaving as he put down the phone, one of the kitchen 'bots walked into the living room and put 'her' arm around him. It was the first hug he'd had from a biobot. After half an hour of sitting, Cowboy walked down to the barn to spend a few moments with Gus, the donkey who missed Turco as much as he did. "You are going to be with Turco again very soon. He's not doing well. See if you can help him." Listening, Gus's ears perked up with what could be an expression of happiness. Then something like worry and fear appeared on his face. And then a look of determination.

~*~*~

Three weeks later Cowboy's fears and dread for Turco's well-being had become epic. He couldn't sleep at night, couldn't concentrate on anything else, and could not stop feeling that he had made the worst mistake of his mistake-filled life by allowing Bill's people to operate on his beloved Turco. He spent more time than ever rocking on his porch chair, staring at the marvelous, but empty, new barn Bill's TEAM has built for him

One morning, after a sleepless night of agonies, the worn down Cowboy was rocking on the porch after breakfast with a cup of coffee in his hand. It was a gray, rainy morning, the mountains were obscured, and Cowboy's soul felt even more withered without New Mexico's strong sunlight beaming on him.

Suddenly, from down in the barn, he heard Gus braying loudly. "Why is Gus back?" he asked himself, with fear overwhelming. "Gus never brays that way. Something terrible has happened." At that moment Cowboy felt a small electric shock running from his neck down to his fanny.

"Sorry, but I needed to get your attention," his Teacher said. "You'd better get over to the barn and find out what's happening."

Confused and distraught, Cowboy put down his coffee, stepped off the rebuilt porch and walked slowly, with tiny dragging steps, toward the barn, a sickened expression on his face.

He was startled when Gus began braying again, more loudly and more rhythmically.

Suddenly an amazing loud whinny began harmonizing with Gus's almost musical braying.

"That's Turco! He's back!" Cowboy shouted and started running toward the barn.

Inside now, he rushed past the biobots sweeping, cleaning, and putting food together. He was floored by what he saw in the middle of the barn.

Turco's head, along with Gus's, was sticking out the open door of their stall. With tears pouring from his eyes, Cowboy plunged his face into Turco's slick mane. Turco hung his head over Cowboy's shoulder, and the two were locked together for several long moments. Gus came over on the other side of Turco so Cowboy could rub his forehead and hold his neck too.

"There is a happy threesome," Cece said, watching on her Teacher.

Turco Shows His Stuff Again—and Begins to Yearn

Later that day, after asking and getting enthusiastic permission from the barn's biobots, Cowboy gave Turco a thorough going over, saddled him, and rode him out into a light September rainstorm. Lively Turco changed and held gaits perfectly. Cowboy was thrilled to be riding his rejuvenated mustang friend. Noticing how Turco's hoof beats were consistent and syncopated again, Cowboy rode past Cece's place—hoping she'd come out and wave. Cece wasn't home. Disappointed he couldn't show off his superb mustang, Turco and Cowboy trotted up Salerno canyon to the little picnic area that was one of Turco's favorite grazing places. The sky was clearing and several out-of-state families were there, unloading cars and getting ready to picnic. Cowboy dismounted, led Turco to his grazing ground, dropped the reins, and sat on the last empty picnic table bench. He noticed that several of the mothers were worried the loose horse might harm their children. "Don't be scared," Cowboy told them, accepting their offer to join them for a light meal. "I'll keep an eye on him, but Turco is very good with children."

"Is he the famous Turco who led the Return to Eden Parade?" a mother asked.

"He is indeed," Cowboy answered. "And he's refreshed and in better health than he was then."

"Do you know the famous Mexican Cowboy who rode him?" a father asked.

"I'm pretty close to him," Cowboy answered demurely.

"He's the same guy," a thirteen-year old said, smiling and pointing at the Cowboy. "He stopped to let a bunch of us watching the parade pat his horse. Turco was pretty beaten up then."

"We are both doing pretty well now," Cowboy said, filling his plate and accepting an opened beer.

Turco Wants To Go Home Again

Turco and Cowboy rode every day for a couple of weeks, but Cowboy noticed that Turco had gotten more eager to keep going further each time. Turco especially didn't want to stop and turn back to the ranch whenever he was heading north, in the direction of the range he came from. Turco did allow himself to be reined back toward the ranch, but his behavior was effectively communicating to his best human friend that his horse buddy was yearning to be back with his herd again.

Each day Cowboy wrestled more with Turco's desire to get back with his northern New Mexico herd. Cece recognized the frustrating and decision-blocking mix of feelings in her friend and made a suggestion while they were having lunch together. "Hon, why don't we get together with our buddies who worked so well with us to put Bill's rescue together? I bet Bill's people would be happy to feed us, and the guys may have things to tell us also that will help you make a decision you can live with."

"I don't think so," Cowboy replied. "I don't work well with people or biobrains. I need to figure this out for myself."

"You work excellently with people, Hon. And people you work with do pay attention to your feelings and needs. Let's don't get stuck again. Your decision is going to matter enormously to Turco."

Eyes narrowed, Cece watched as Cowboy, moping and pondering, was melting inside himself. She was pleased when at last she saw the coating of astringent indecision soften on his face. He looked up at her, coughed, and said with a stumbly voice, "You are right. Okay. You put the meeting together. I'll probably show up."

"Gotcha, will do!" Cece replied, and reached over to hug him.

Cowboy's Friends Help Him Decide

Three nights later Cowboy, Cece, Father Gallapo, Thelma, and Mayor Howie were eating a wonderful dinner together in Bill's study. The 'bots had prepared and served meals and portions to each person's liking, along with wines and before- and after-dinner drinks. Mayor Howie ate corned beef and cabbage. Cowboy enjoyed his usual New Mexico fare. The Priest offered to share his superb eastern Italian cuisine. Cece and Thelma were delighted with their salads and seafood. It was the first time they'd all been together since the horribly sad, then explosively relieving meal they had together the night after the Parade. Conversation flowed in many directions, as friendships—and animosities—were renewed. Following dinner a biobot led the five to a room with comfortable chairs. Coffee and tea were served, and after-dinner drinks offered again. Cowboy was glad the subject of Turco hadn't been raised. He'd just as soon leave Bill's place without being forced to make up his mind by others.

Then Mayor Howie said, "So, how did fixing up Turco turn out?"

Cowboy bristled, "That my business and none of yours."

"Not so, El Charro," Howie replied sternly. "Bill's people are experimenting in biological engineering and if Turco's redo turned out well, I'm going to invest some money in the company they'll create that will produce and sell products and services based on their bio-experimenting."

The biobot 'Emma' who had been standing and listening to the ongoing talk stepped forward and said, "We can tell you much about what we have been doing, and of course we would welcome your investing. But please, first you must all promise to reveal nothing of what we are about to say to anyone else. This is critical for your well-being and for ours."

"You got a deal," Mayor Howie said, doing his best to hide the thought that had popped into his mind: to make even more profit by selling what he learned tonight to Bill's brother Kemmet's hostile L.I.V.E. group. The others nodded.

"Tell us all about it, please," Cece said. "You know there is lots you haven't been willing to tell me until now."

Emma nodded to Cece and began to tell the group about Turco's makeover.

"Our first problem to solve was getting inside Turco's head to be able to record and translate his perceptions, feelings, desires, and insights into our understanding. We had learned to do this with coyotes and humans, but horses are very different mammals. Bill's

TEAM used Turco to study horse consciousness and to devise codes and outputs that would convey much of what horses are capable of understanding; Bill's TEAM recognized that humans are not capable of understanding a great deal of the contents of horses' mentality. But we are, as it turned out. It was only then we could achieve our first goal in this project: programming Turco's own Teacher and implanting it in him."

"So you did this for your sake, not for Turco's," the Cowboy said angrily.

"No. Of course not," Emma answered. "Remember, you refused to listen to both our explanations of what we would be trying, and why we hoped these would help Turco. We offered to experiment with rehabilitating worn-out Turco for his and your sake. But also, things we were proposing to do are beyond the frontiers of modern medicine. Yes, we were offering to help Turco for his own sake, but also partly for Bill's too. Experimenting with new ways to rehabilitate Turco would help our biobrains to refine treatment techniques they are coming up with before these are tried on Bill—who is still entirely a vegetable. We wanted to test theoretical bioengineering ideas we have been experimenting with on Turco to rejuvenate him before we attempt to resurrect Bill."

"My Lord is the only one who *resurrects.* You guys merely restore," Father Gallapo said explosively, objecting to this misuse of a sacred religious term.

Emma was about to ask"What's the difference?" when Bill's biobrains make her nod assent and apologize for abusing human language. "I've been told from the top to apologize for what I said. We're new at discussing technical matters with humans and can hurt their feelings, though we always try not to." Emma said. She observes closely as Father Gallapo's evident anger began fading from his features. But he was not done with his holy criticism.

"Okay. But now tell me why all this 'rejuvenation' crap? Aging and dying are God's will and humans have no business trying to postpone aging and death. Each of life's cycles is valuable in its own way," the Priest maintained.

Emma nodded and responded, "Thank you. Now, let's continue," she said, studying Father Gallapo's face. He didn't reply, and she paused for a moment, the Priest stared back at her, and then she continued. "Before proposing our experiments with Turco, we sought Coyote's views, which were very clear. He wanted us to do anything we could to bring happiness to his sole human friend. But he also made it clear to us that Turco's feelings were important too. And somehow Coyote knew Turco wanted to be made more fit *only* so he could return to his herd on the mesa northwest of Taos in order to die there. Going home was Turco's desire, not living longer."

"And I only want what is best for Turco," Cowboy said. "We are buddies and we work together. But neither of us tries to control the other's life."

"Nonsense," said the Priest. "I've seen you control him a number of times after you saddle him up."

"Wrong," Cowboy said. "Turco and I work together when I ride him. I admit I do use his reins and my boots to communicate with him. But he has good ways of communicating with me when we ride together."

"He was too worn out to do the Socorro Parade and you made him do it," Mayor Howie replied.

"He wanted to do it very much. And he particularly didn't want to miss a chance to let me be the lead Cowboy in a terrific parade. He knew that not being able to ride him in the parade would have broken my heart."

"Let's drop this," Emma said. "The Parade decision was rightfully Mayor Howie's, and our famous Cowboy's."

"That's right," Cowboy said, "but here is what I am getting at. Bill's guys here left it up to me to decide whether Turco should be operated on," Cowboy said, pointing at Emma. "I knew it should be his choice, not mine. That's why I agreed to ride him over to Bill's place so we could all see if Turco was willing to go inside there for a preliminary workup. If he had refused, that would have settled the issue of whether to let you experiment on him," Cowboy said.

"Okay, I'm getting this," Mayor Howie said. "But why would any veterinarian pair up a horse and donkey during and after the horse's surgery?"

"Donkeys are good at looking after companion horses' well-being," Emma answered. "We think Gus understands Turco's aging and poor health and wants to do what he can to keep their friendship going. Donkeys live thirty to fifty years, you know. Gus has somehow figured out that pushing Turco into our care will extend their time together, perhaps for another ten or fifteen years."

"Think about it this way," Cowboy said to Mayor Howie. "If you were croaking but you might be saved by hospitalization, I and everyone here would do everything in our power to put you in doctors' hands and make them try to save you."

"If that happens to me I'd rather be put in God's hands," the Priest said.

"Well Gus is smarter than you then, at least on this point," Cowboy said.

Father Gallapo was about to snap back at Cowboy when Cece broke in, saying: "I visited Turco almost every day and sometimes I really couldn't bear what I was seeing," Cece said. "And at the same time I tried to console you, Cowboy, and reassure you that Turco's care would turn out well for all concerned."

"I believed you'd made me put Turco into a meat grinder and was ashamed and torn up over what I'd agreed to do. Thanks for reaching out to me though," Cowboy said.

Before Cece could respond, Emma raised her hand to quiet her audience, and resumed her talk. Her guests became silent again. "As days went by our TEAM gained confidence in what we were experimenting with on Turco," she continued. "Turco gradually revivified, grew in strength, began eating well again, his skin problems slipped away, his hooves healed, and the horse almost seemed to be rejuvenating. There is no clear moment when this transformation took place."

"You guys are doing great work," Mayor Howie said. "I'm going to make a lot of money off you by investing."

"Thank you," Emma said. "But here is one thing even you may not find a way to invest in. Our TEAM has not been able to model why Turco did so much better after we brought Gus here. Gus was with him every moment he was aware. Surely all horse veterinarians are not going to match up their patients with donkeys."

"Love matters in patient care," Cece said. "And Turco loves having Gus with him."

"That's because neither of them are geldings," Mayor Howie said with an odd grin.

"There one thing I want to ask all of you," Cece said now, becoming her assertive self, "and that's if Turco were your horse, and he recovered his strength, would you let him go back to his home on the range?"

There was silence in the room. Everyone turned to look at Cowboy. No one, not even aggressive Mayor Howie, wanted to try to force Cowboy to give up his beloved Turco.

"All right, people. I can guess what you want me to do," Cowboy said finally. "If Turco didn't want to do this, I'd keep him with me. But I want animals to be free, like we are. I won't lock them up or try to turn them into creatures they don't want to be. Turco's made me very happy. I'm glad he wanted to stay with me. But he is just as free as I am, and if he wants to leave I'll have to accept this. I will try."

Cece, Father Gallapo, and Thelma stood up, walked over to Cowboy's chair, and put their arms around him. Warm and less confused feelings raced through Cowboy's mind as Mayor Howie said to Emma, "Get us a drink. We've got to toast this guy for what he's decided."

Turco Leaves for His First Home

The moment had come. After a farewell party the night before in the barn with just Cowboy, Turco, Gus, and the biobots present, Turco was visibly excited that his wish to walk back to his herd was about to be granted. Gus seemed more doubtful, he didn't want to leave the barn, but he didn't want to part from his close friend Turco either. Gus had decided to at least do the walk with Turco. But Cowboy understood that Gus would probably want to be brought back to the barn after Turco mixed with his herd again.

Cowboy saddled Turco and was determined to ride with him as far as possible, eastward into the Manzano Mountains. With barn biobots hugging and stroking Turco, and feeding him mouthfuls of energizing foods, Cowboy swung himself up onto his ancient beat-up saddle, took the reins handed up by one of the 'bots, and with Gus following after them, trotted out of the barn toward the mountains.

Riding up Salerno Canyon with Gus trotting behind them, Cowboy was amazed and pleased by how strong and vital Turco had become. Memories flooded through both of them as Turco and Cowboy passed the spot where Celesto was rescued from Ursula, his Mother Bear. "What happened here shaped our lives, didn't it?" Cowboy said, leaning down and patting Turco's neck.

A couple of miles further, the trail narrowed and steepened and Turco sent signals that he was ready to go off on his own. The Mexican Cowboy dismounted, unsaddled his long-term friend, removed bit and halter, and stood facing him, stroking him, tears streaming down his face. He fed Turco and Gus goodbye carrots and apples, and as they stood side by side, he put his head between theirs, pulled their heads to his cheeks, kissed each, and stepped back so they could leave.

With brief head bows, Turco and Gus turned around and started up the steepening trail. Just before going out of sight around the mountain Turco stopped, turned his head and neck, and stared almost longingly at his long-time human friend, who had saved his life and cared for him so many years.

Realizing that Turco was debating with himself about giving up a long walk to his old herd, which would be his final resting place, Cowboy took off his yellow hat, bowed deeply, and suddenly smacked the air between himself and Turco and shouted 'Whaaahoo,'—the human signal to get moving that horses understand. Startled, Turco jerked and automatically began moving again. In a moment he disappeared around the bend with Gus after him. Putting his hat on his head again Cowboy noticed contrails overhead—most heading in the same direction Turco and Gus were going.

Wiping his face drier with a filthy handkerchief from his pocket, Cowboy put his hat back on to shade his eyes and looked about him—up and down the rocky, tree-spotted hillside, and above it. He was not surprised when two biobots suddenly popped into view on a rock above him. Looking up, he spotted a drone—which had been invisible and silent—in the clear sky overhead, by the sounds it was suddenly making for him. Cowboy was wearing his Teacher in a leather holster on his wide belt. "That went well," his Teacher said warmly to him. "If you are ready now, start walking back down the trail. We'll bring Turco's gear for you. There's a jeep waiting for you about half a mile back. It's yours from now on."

With a huge range of mixed emotion, Cowboy walked back to where the trail widened into a rough mountain road. A light brown Jeep with scratches and dents was parked there, waiting for him. He walked around the Jeep checking it out and said aloud, "How did you know I wouldn't want to own a new car?" and got in. He was surprised to see an eight-inch screen on the dash above the gearshift. When he strapped himself in and started the engine, the screen lit up with a number of app icons. Cowboy pressed the Turco icon and the screen instantly lit with an image of Turco and Gus climbing the trail above him. The drone was watching them. Cowboy was surprised to see also a pair of biorobots a couple of hundred yards in front of Turco and Gus, and another pair about the same distance behind them.

One of the 'bots in the back pair carried a small collapsible shovel which was being used to scoop up and fling any horse or burro droppings off the trail. "Trail maintenance is part of our TEAM's work," Cowboy's Teacher said softly. "But looking out for Turco and Gus is our number one priority."

"Thanks," Cowboy said, unconsciously touching the brim of his hat. He backed the Jeep around and started down the rough road toward his ranch, glancing at the screen often to watch his beloved mustang moving further and further away from him.

An Injured Child Is on the Trail

Next day Gus and Turco had crossed the highest point of their Manzano trail—a few miles south of Bosque Peak, and they were heading down another trail just north of Capilla Peak, which led to the Manzano Mountain Retreat.

About a mile and a half further down, on a more heavily wooded trail now, they saw ahead of them a father and mother who were taking turns carrying their four-year old daughter, who had tripped and fallen and badly sprained her knee and opposite ankle. Her parents were weary, worried, and resting, when Turco and Gus came upon them. Turco decided, with Gus, that they would help the trio. Even though Bill's ground team tried to discourage them from doing this, they moved close to the threesome and stood still beside them until the mother decided to try riding Turco seven miles down the trail to where their car was parked. The father objected, but the mother was worn down to a nub.

She was pleased when Turco moved next to a large rock. An experienced rider, she mounted him and was very appreciative when Turco continues to stand still, waiting for the four-year-old to be lifted aboard in front of her.

Turco moved a few yards away and waited while Gus maneuvered close to a smaller rock. "The donkey wants you to get onto him," the mother shouted. Not being a rider, and not trusting donkeys or horses, the father mentally waffled for a moment. Turco carried his riders closer to Gus and the mother told her husband with a mix of frustrated impatience, "Go on. Get on him. Do you want me to help you do it?" Ashamed, the dad boosted himself onto the donkey's bare back and the five of them started down the steep, rocky trail together. Gus walked carefully behind Turco, trying to keep the man's fear under control, as the pair and their riders carefully took lurching steps down the very rough, steep trail.

Gradually, the trail widened and smoothed as Turco and Gus continued downhill. In less than three hours they were standing by the family's car in a crowded parking lot, getting their pictures taken by many climbers, as the four-year-old—who had stopped crying when she got aboard Turco—was strapped into her parents' car. The mother and father patted and nuzzled both Turco and Gus, then drove away to get their daughter to an emergency room. The little girl, flinching with pain, waved as they drove by the pair.

That night the story was on commercial TV. Mayor Howie watched it, pleased over how the story would likely attract more tourists to his part of the state. Cowboy and Cece watched the story on Cowboy's new big screen TV. "Those two are very kind animals," Cece said, amazed at what she was watching.

"Good guys, both of them," Cowboy said proudly, feeling very grateful for getting to see Turco and Gus being celebrated nationally for rescuing the injured child. "This will give lots of non-owners new reasons to fall in love with horses. But tell me, because you work over there and know a lot of this stuff, did Bill's TEAM have anything to do with the family's rescue?"

"Actually, Bill's TEAM tried to get Gus and Turco to go around the family without being seen. But they instantly accepted Gus and Turco's decision."

"Are they really looking after my guys?" Cowboy asked.

"More than you realize. Do you want me to tell you about that?"

"Please."

Cece stood up, walked to the kitchen door, and returned with a cup of yogurt, saying, "These kitchen 'bots are good at figuring out what I want. I've been trying to slim down. Bill's TEAM has offered to do some rejuvenating on me. I am debating whether I want that."

"You look good to me. But let's get back to Turco. Okay?"

"Sure. Anything you like. All right, there's a large team of biobots guarding Gus and Turco. When our high-up drone monitors see humans nearing the pair, the animals are turned aside from the mountain and mesa trails they are following and graze within sight of passersby who aren't thought to be threatening. Some passersby wonder why Turco has no brand. Is he a wild horse? And if so, what's he doing with the donkey? Lots of photos are snapped by passing hikers and many make it onto the Web. If trail dogs seem snappish or threatening, Bill's ground TEAM use high frequency calming sounds to keep the dogs relaxed. Water, meds, and enriched foods are delivered by drones to Bill's ground team, who watched over Gus and Turco at night. Predators were kept away."

"How do they get safely across busy highways?" Cowboy asked.

"When Gus and Turco come to busy roads, they stop and graze, waiting for Bill's ground team to help them cross. If the drones spot no traffic for a considerable distance in either direction Bill's bots lead them across the road. If the highway ahead of them is wide and heavily trafficked, as freeways are, a horse van is parked on a little used dirt road some distance from the highway. Gus and Turco are steered to the van, the animals are boarded, and are nourished, cleaned and blanketed if it is cold, while the bus's human driver takes them to the other side of the freeway and finds an appropriate place to release them, so they can be on their own again."

"How long can these biobots stay on the job?" Cowboy asked.

"Bill's 'bots can only operate about thirty hours before they have to be picked up and put into a mobile dormitory for 'refueling'—which includes some eating and drinking, high-tech batteries recharging, and a period of rest. The dormitory is a very large motor home, equipped to go on the roughest of roads."

"One last question," Cowboy said. "How do Turco and Gus know where to go?"

"Bill's TEAM keeps track of where Turco's wild mustang herd is. The biobrains have plotted a long, interesting, safe route, which Turco will enjoy. The Teacher implanted in him is programmed to speak 'horse,' and gives him a horse version of a mental map to follow."

"Does Turco want that?"

"He seems to like it very much."

"Thanks. Now, how about a hug."

"You've had your share for the day," Cece said with an ironic, wicked grin.

A Mountain Lion Climbs Higher Near the Trail

Turco was growing more energized with every mile as the equine pair traveled north for six days, passing around small towns like Tajique and Stanley in the rolling terrain east of the Sandia Mountains. Gus was fascinated by the mix of animals he saw. Grazing pronghorn antelopes, perhaps frightened by the pair, bounced high into the air and landed tens of feet away, then turned and stared at them as they walked past. Prairie dogs stood rigid as marble statues on the mound entrances to their cities as horse and donkey trotted by. Striped skunks and weasels on nighttime explorations woke the northbound equines while they slept. They saw bison in fenced fields and plains pocket mice too, along with hundreds of humans. The pair's biobots helped them over fences, but the 'bots were having more trouble than expected hiding when the pair encountered humans. Staying out of sight in a human-dominated world wasn't easy. Nights were cold, mornings nipping, and the sky had high cumulus overhead that kept day temperatures mild. Turco's health was carefully monitored and Bill's TEAM was pleased—as much as biocomputers can be—with Turco's vigor and eagerness. Gus appeared to be enjoying the trip too. Turco was very careful to be sure he never left Gus far behind, though he did gallop in huge quasi circles around him now and then.

On the seventh day Gus and Turco were north of I-25, following the Pecos River into the Santa Fe National Forest, heading northwesterly toward the Pecos Wilderness. The pair's walk had been comfortable and safe, but now they were back in the mountains again, and Bill's TEAM became even more vigilant, because encounters with predator pumas, black bears and even recently re-introduced wolves were more likely. And late afternoon on the eighth day, it happened.

On the east side of the Santa Fe Christo mountains, Bill's drones spotted a mountain lion in a tree about a hundred yards away from the trail Turco and Gus were on, which meandered through a heavily forested, stream-laden valley. The drones moved smoothly overhead, opening laser-beam and siren doors, while Bill's TEAM plotted safe, swooping paths for drones through the woods in case they had to buzz the big cat to keep it away from Turco and Gus.

But then something happened that Bill's TEAM did not anticipate. Perhaps hearing, perhaps smelling the lion, Turco suddenly turned off the wide, smooth trail and galloped into the woods toward the lion, faster than Bill's biobots could move. Gus faithfully trotted after him.

Under the tree the lion was fourteen feet up in, Turco reared, and with his ears back and eyes flaming, slammed his feet into the ground with a ferociously loud 'flunk.' The big cat snarled and arched her back like she was getting ready to leap down onto Turco's back. Gus, on the other side of the tree now, reared on his front legs and kicked the tree hard with back legs that curved up against his belly an instant before. The tree shook violently and the cat had to clamp her claws into the limb she was on to keep from falling out of the tree.

Rearing on his back legs again, Turco jumped impossibly straight up nearly six feet into the air, his mouth gaping with attention-grabbing refurbished teeth, just inches from the cat's head. Gus began a loud bray, growing into a sound that could be heard a mile away, which lasted twenty seconds. It was a donkey threat. Looking down, the Puma could tell that the donkey wanted to strike with his front hooves and bite. Feeling helpless, the mountain lion considered jumping over her tormenters and trying to run away, but realized they were agile and speedy enemies and she might be safer climbing higher in the tree.

With both Turco and Gus staring up at her, the lion climbed up and tried to hide herself in a cave of branches. She put her head down and pretended to ignore her tormenters. Snorting Turco and braying Gus stood below the tree for a few minutes, and then turned and walked slowly back to the trail.

That evening Mexican Cowboy and his companions were watching a video of the event, that they received from Bill's TEAM, on Cowboy's TV. "What was that all about?" Cece asked her fellow watchers.

"Turco was practicing controlling predators," Cowboy replied. "He's trying to get ready to take over his mustang herd again."

Cowboy's TEACHER said, "Our TEAM was appalled by what Turco and Gus did with the lion. We had convincing data that the lion had eaten well the night before and was minding its own business, and sleeping, when it was attacked by the equines. We want to protect all species, not just humans, coyotes and horses."

"You guys are dreamers," Mayor Howie said. "And messing up what animals and humans decide to do has become your thing. Still, you guys have turned into better than average vets. For an old sick horse, that was a pretty good set of moves."

Emma, who was in the kitchen making dinner for her guys, stuck her head out and responded, "Bill's TEAM did a pretty good job of fixing Turco up. Soon we'll be publishing a number of papers about new techniques and procedures in horse medicine journals."

"That's so," Mayor Howie said, "but the publications won't be in your names or traceable to you. You guys ought to go for publicity."

Standing up and looking at herself for a moment in a mirror on the living room wall, Cece said over her shoulder to the 'bot Emma, "Maybe Bill's TEAM will let me get in line. I'm aging pretty badly."

A Black Bear Avoids Eating Chile Close to the Trail

Two days later, ten miles east of 13,000 foot Truchas Peak, on a dirt road leading to Morphy Lake State Park, Bill's lead ground 'bots spotted a two-year-old bear exploring a locked cabin, which they were immediately told belonged to an aging woman who lived alone—and who was in Moira shopping. The bear tried to open the doors, and then began pushing aggressively against one of the locked wooden shutters protecting a window on the back porch. The bear ignored the long, low-hanging red *ristra,* chains of chile peppers, over his head.

"Bears hate chiles," Father Gallapo said to the Mexican Cowboy as they watch this unraveling on TV.

"Where'd you get that idea?" Cowboy asked. "I've had bears lick clean pots with chile in them that I've left outdoors for animals."

Turco and Gus had spotted the bear too and were making a wide detour around the old woman's property, which was at the end of a little-used dirt road. The overhead drone's camera was focusing on the bear now. Cowboy was frustrated that his beloved mustang had crossed out of the picture and disappeared alongside a tiny slowly moving stream.

Three of Bill's bots stayed with Turco and Gus. The fourth team member opened a food bag, dropped by a second drone overhead, that was loaded with berries, carrion, fish, piñon nuts and bear-relished human garbage. The bot approached the bear as it began battering the locked shutter, and with an open hand put down a small box of berries behind the bear.

Growling, but not afraid of the 'bot, the bear sat down and ate berries by sticking his snout into the small box. He picked up and chewed several berries that had rolled out of the box onto the worn wooden deck. Now the 'bot held out a handful of carrion while backing away from the bear. The bear followed the 'bot and was rewarded with more food at the edge of the property. Handful by handful, the well-fed bear was led far into the woods to a meadow where one of the drones had dropped a large bag of bear food. The 'bot opened the bag, scattered the food around the meadow so the young bear would have to work to find and eat all of it, then bowed and waved goodbye. The bear didn't look up as the 'bot slipped into the woods and raced along a shortcut route sent down by a drone to catch up with his peers and the equines.

Watching this event with Cowboy and Father Gallapo, Thelma Whitenose said, "What kind people, these bioengineered beings are."

"Perhaps, but only when they get things right," the Priest replied.

Scouts on the Trail

Next day, twenty-three miles east of Taos, Turco and Gus found a way to evade a trailhead parking lot with a school bus parked in it. Going four miles up the trail, which had recently been cleared, cleaned, compacted, and spruced up, Turco and Gus were approaching a large group of Boy Scouts doing trail work. Two of the 'bots with them today climbed onto Gus and Turco and revamped their appearance to make them seem like two young women. Riding barefoot and without saddles along the trail, the 'bots smiled and nodded as they approached the sweaty Scouts. The Scouts stepped aside and waved and said hello to the nice-looking riders and got back to work before the horse and donkey disappeared from view.

Watching on his Teacher in his expanded office in Cordoba, Mayor Howie said, "Bet those robots don't smell like humans."

Home at Last

Fifteen days after their trip began, Gus and Turco had passed just south of New Mexico's highest mountain, 13,161 foot Wheeler Peak, walked through the Wild River National Recreation Area, and been ferried over the Rio Grande River's deep canyon in a freight helicopter by one of Bill's pilots. The pair still had about eighty miles to go, over rugged piñon pine mesas, through open ponderosa pine forests, and around very high mountains. Turco's former herd had moved west, near the Rio Chama, close to the tiny village of Coyote and the Apache Jicarilla wild horse territory. At the moment the mustang herd was on Horse Lake Mesa, and to get the equine pair they were protecting there, Bill's TEAM had plotted a winding route that would take Turco and Gus west close to Route 64, up a canyon on a cliff near Tecolate Rim, then southwest past Horse Lake and onto Horse Lake Mesa.

Turco's excitement and energy grew as he and Gus got nearer to the herd. Passing over a sagebrush flat near Stinking Lake, they saw a small herd of elk grazing. And then, after an easy climb onto Horse Lake Mesa, Turco stopped abruptly, and with ears up and sniffing, made a snap decision over where to go on the mesa. Half an hour later, going around a small hill, Turco saw, in the distant sagebrush flat before him, the herd of mustangs that must be his. His excited whinny was explosively loud. Gus joined him with sustained braying. After so many years away, Turco was home at last.

Watching a real-time video sent by a drone, Cece and the Mexican Cowboy got an unexpected quiver-making thrill running down their spines.

"It is the end of their trip!" Cece said excitedly.

"And the beginning of a new wave of sadness for me," Cowboy said. "In a couple of days the monitoring drones will be gone and I won't be able to see how Turco's doing."

"I'm so sorry," Cece said, holding Cowboy tightly. "But Turco has gone his own way. Now you must go yours."

Gus and Turco Part Ways

Over the next couple of days, Turco was gradually reconnecting with his old herd, many of which were his descendants. The mares didn't recognize this of course, and the mare who was bossing the herd, along with an aggressive stallion who was her ally, kept Turco from mixing with her herd. Turco grazed several hundred yards from them as they moved around the mesa. There were wild donkeys in this part of New Mexico, and a small herd grazed on a nearby mesa. Gus trotted over to see them, but the herd leader ignored him, perhaps thinking Gus had joined up with Turco after being kicked out his own small donkey herd.

Turco had eagerly kept company with Gus for a number of years. But now Turco was beginning to feel that Gus was in his way, an obstacle to his rejoining his former herd.

Turco was ready to be on his own again.

Gus Goes Home Alone

On the third night they slept intermittently together, both standing up. There was no moonlight and thin clouds overhead blurred many stars. Looking down the mesa to the southwest, they spotted occasional car headlights on a little-used road miles away. In the early morning light, after grazing beside each other for an hour and drinking from a muddy pond together, Gus and Turco rubbed noses for a few moments. Then Turco backed away and Gus, feeling very sad, turned and began to walk across the mesa toward the slope on its south edge. At the edge of the mesa Gus stopped and longingly looked back over his shoulder, hoping Turco would have stood and watched until Gus disappeared. But he did not. Gus guessed that immediately after they parted Turco had tightened his muscles, put an aggressive expression on his face, and walked slowly and defiantly down the hill toward his herd, determined to muscle his way into it again.

Trying to take hold of himself emotionally, Gus started down the slope and left the mesa.

When Gus came three miles to a drivable dirt road he wasn't surprised to see the horse van of Bill's people waiting for him. He brayed loudly as if to say goodbye to Turco before he went up the ramp into the van. After shepherding him aboard, a 'bot and a human driver made him comfortable in his stall, checked him over, cleaned him, offered food and water, and then drove him down highway 112, almost atop the Continental Divide, back toward Cordoba and Cowboy's new barn. Late that afternoon biobots settled Gus into the stall he had only recently shared with Turco. He was very lonesome without him. The whole trip had lasted just seventeen days.

Cowboy and Cece knew Gus was returning, and spent half an hour with him that evening. Cece feared that having Gus return would make Cowboy miss Turco much more intensely. Watching Cowboy check Gus over and talk with him, she saw she was right.

As days went by Gus missed Turco so badly he began to wither physically.

Turco wasn't doing well either. On Horse Lake Mesa southeast of Dulce, the Jicarilla Apaches' headquarters, he was being repeatedly driven away from his feral herd by stallions that fought with him for food and water, their bites drawing flesh and blood. Beaten by them so often, Turco now hovered by himself on the edge of his herd, his vigor and determination slipping away.

Over the next month Apache guides visited the herd several times, bringing mustang-loving tourists with them who wanted to photograph and hand-feed wild horses in this herd. Turco waited on the opposite side of the rough dirt road from the herd for his pats and treats. An older man taking videos of the mustangs understood why an outcast stallion would keep his distance from the herd, but he also dimly remembered a wild horse he had once gotten to know who had the same oddly-shaped white marking on his side. This couldn't be the same horse, could it? He remembered how angry and disappointed he was when that horse and several others were rounded up and hauled away for slaughter by mustang snatchers. He intended to compare pictures when he got back to his home in Farmington.

Back in Cordoba, Cowboy's sadness grew because Bill's TEAM had stopped sending him videos of his beloved mustang friend. Their separation was becoming final to him. Unknown to Cowboy, though, a single drone still kept watch over Turco. After promising not to tell Cowboy that Bill's TEAM was still keeping an eye on their experimental patient, Cece was allowed to watch drone pictures from the Horse Mesa in her office.

As she watched Turco's failing re-engagement with his former herd, and his consequential evident decline, she speedily grew determined to do something to save the rejuvenated horse Bill's TEAM's had experimented on to perfect so many new bio-engineered medical procedures. She demanded that they do something to help Turco.

Their response to her request to do something for Turco was devastating. "We are not going to help him take over the herd again. That's up to him."

"Why won't you?" Cece asked, feeling anger rise in her.

"You know that ordinarily we don't interfere with living being's lives."

"You did when we rescued Bill for you."

"True, but there is another reason also, one you won't accept either. The horse god, Kawai-i, doesn't want humans interfering with herd dynamics. This is his domain, not ours."

"How do you know this?"

"Coyote's god told him and he passed this information along to us."

"And what if my bunch gets together and tries to figure out how to help Turco?"

"That's your business, not ours."

Mayor Howie Figures Out an Answer

Plotting together again, two nights later Cece and Thelma put together a dinner for Cowboy, Father Gallapo, and Mayor Howie. Bill's rescue planners weren't together long before Howie demanded to know why Cece insisted on his coming to this meal.

"Turco's doing badly," she said. "I want all your help and suggestions to figure out what we might do for him." She described Turco's failed efforts to take over his herd again and even mentioned Gus's seemingly unrelated decline in his nice barn.

"It's because they love each other, work well together, and miss one another so badly." Father Gallapo said, reminding everyone of the wonderful things the two equines pulled off together on their walk back to the range.

"I agree. Long-term companions don't do well when they are separated from each other," Thelma said, looking at Father Gallapo.

"Why the hell then are you guys making a big deal out of this?" Mayor Howie asked. "Put Gus in a truck and haul him back up to Turco's side. That will take care of both their problems."

"But Turco is not longing for Gus. He only wants to be the boss of his herd again," Cece said.

"No, Howie's right, for a change," Cowboy said. "If the two of them get back together and take on the herd leaders as a pair, they just might beat them. If Gus is willing, I am too."

The group talked about the subject for a few more minutes, but it seemed clear to everyone that Howie had come up with a possible solution to their problem. "Tell you what," he said to Cowboy as he left the refurbished house, "Get Hank Godding to help you take Gus up there and I'll pay for the trip."

"I think for once we've got a deal," the Cowboy said. "Thanks, Mayor."

"You'll owe me your vote again, and that will be good for me," Howie said and walked away.

Gus Returns to the Mesa

Early in the morning, three days later, Hank Gooding drove Cowboy, and the more than willing Gus, north to Horse Mesa, with Cece navigating for them over Cowboy's Teacher. Just past noon they turned off the highway north of Stone Lake, and began winding through canyons to reach the very rough road that led onto Horse Mesa. Forty minutes later they were up on the Horse Lake sagebrush mesa looking for the horses. This part of the mesa was flat and trees were few. Very soon Cowboy spotted a herd grazing some distance from the road.

Hank parked the van on the left side of the road, the two of them got out, hung big cameras around their necks so they would pass as tourists, and grabbed big packages of food the horses would like. The herd was dubious but over the next twenty minutes it edged toward them, ears up, eyes bright, but still grazing. Cowboy and Hank had walked about twenty yards from the van, and as the herd approached, they snapped pictures and held out their hands. One by one, the wary horses approached cautiously, while the leader mare and her stallion stood guard, ready to make the herd run away instantly if they detected a threat.

"This may not be the right herd," Cowboy whispered to Cece over his Teacher. "Turco's not here."

"He's there all right," Cece said. "I can see him on the drone's camera. He's about a quarter of a mile away on the other side of the van. And he's not coming toward you either."

"What should we do?" Cowboy whispered.

Before Cece could answer, Hank interrupted, saying"Get Gus out of the van. That will do it."

With doubts running through Cowboy's mind, he and Hank opened the horse van's back doors, lowered the metal ramp, and Hank went inside, untied Gus, turned him around, led him outside, and freed him.

Gus stared at the herd. He recognized the mare leader and stallion, and searched for Turco. Not spotting him, Gus moved away from the van, raises his head, and brayed so loudly that coyotes over a mile away looked his way in wonder.

There was an immediate, prolonged, rising-note neigh from the other side of the van. Cowboy and Gus turned around and watched distant Turco appear and begin moving hesitantly toward them. Gus looked at the two of them as though asking permission to leave. Cowboy took off his hat, waved it and slapped it against his palm twice, like he was trying to drive Gus away. Gus nodded and trotted off toward Turco. The two moved faster and faster as they approached each other.

Back in Cordoba, Cece watched the two friends nuzzle each other, rubbing heads and necks together. "I think this is going to work, guys. It is best now if you shut up the van and leave. Gus and Turco need to spend some time together and get in better shape before they go after the herd again."

As she spoke, the herd's lead mare and her stallion had signaled the herd to get out of there. The scared horses galloped away.

Gus Tips the Balance in the Battle for Herd Control

Over the next month Cece watched—and captured video—of Turco and Gus's attempts to rejoin and take over the herd. Both had been bitten and kicked many times, but Gus's extraordinarily powerful biting and kicking had made the herd's stallions wary of attacking. The herd was trying to keep away from them now. Cece looked down on them and translated, and forwarded, ideas to Turco through the mustang's implanted Teacher. Gus and Turco gradually drove the herd toward a box canyon southwest of Horse Lake.

Entering the canyon, the frightened herd moved away from nearing Turco and Gus. Then, rounding a bend, the herd's leaders found themselves trapped by un-climbable canyon walls on three sides. The herd milled, grazed, and tried twice to break past Turco and Gus. Several horses escaped, but most turned back when threatened by the pair.

As the herd leaders approached, Turco's muscles tightened, he pressed his ears back, put his head goes down, and scraped the ground with his left and right front hooves, one after the other. The other stallion attacked. The two horses, standing on their hind legs, bit each other while the mare tried to slip away behind Turco. Gus blocked her and she turned around and went back up the box canyon, with her herd following. Gus was just about to attack the stallion Turco was fighting when that horse dropped onto his four hooves again, lowered his head and walked slowly away down the canyon. Turco and Gus let him go.

An hour later Cece watches Turco and Gus lead the herd out of the canyon, the mare following her new leader.

"It's over," Cece said to the Mexican Cowboy over her Teacher. "Turco's won. You'll get the video in a moment."

"Let the horse god Kawai-i be pleased," Cowboy said softly, thrilled and satisfied at last.

Turco is At Home on His Range Finally

In the coming months winter enveloped the Horse Lake Meadow. Fully in charge now, Turco kept an eye out for predators and moved the herd safely from place to place to reduce potential dangers as much as possible. The herd had accepted Gus's offered friendship, and the mare who was its former leader has become Turco's mate, along with other mares in the herd. The sky was often overcast, which helped to keep the temperature from dropping into the sub-teens. Infrequent snowstorms dumped inches onto the mesa, which typically melted over the next several days.

Back in Cordoba, Cece had stopped paying much attention to Turco and his herd. Bill's TEAM kept loading her with more work, which, surprisingly, it turned out she loved doing. Then late in January she received a call on her Teacher from Thelma Whitenose.

"Did you hear about the wolf pack that was shown on TV coming over La Manga Pass? They could be headed toward Turco's herd."

"No, I didn't. Thanks. I'll check with Bill's TEAM and see if they know anything about it."

"Sorry, we don't," is the TEAM's reply a minute later. "We can't keep track of every being on earth."

"You'd like to, I bet," said Cece to her 'Boss,' shamelessly.

Coyote is Ordered to Save the Herd

Several nights later Coyote was lying in his prayer niche in front of the altar he had made, a dead grouse offering on it now. His head down over crossed paws, he worshipped El Latrone, his beloved god, when his god interrupted and said to him in Coyote language, "There is something I want you to do for me."

Coyote looked up at the altar, winced, and asked, "What is it this time? Last time you wanted me publicly killed."

"Partly to turn you into my world-known Martyr," El Latrone said. "And we figured out how to keep you around, which is more than the human god did for his Son."

"God politics are hard on followers," Coyote said. "Tell me what you want me to do now."

"This is a tough problem," El Latrone said. "You know I've been working with the human god to try to reshape relations among gods, and between them and their earth followers too."

"You are trying to create something among the animal gods like the humans' United Nations, I believe," Coyote said.

"Not exactly. But I do want my fellow gods to start working together, which they've never bothered to try. The down side is that many of the other gods *are* joining up—but only to work against me. Many others haven't made up their minds yet. The horse god Kawai-i and I have made some progress bettering our ties, partly because my coyotes never attack his horses. But I also want to make his followers and mine start working together. And something's come up that may be an opportunity."

"What now?" Coyote asked, getting into a sitting position while still staring at the altar.

"Kweo, the wolf god, has been trying to make humans stop killing his followers. But his wolves keep attacking and killing wild horses and my coyotes."

"So what's the deal here?" Coyote asked.

"There's a wolf pack heading down the Rockies toward Horse Lake Mesa. If they go there, I want you to stop them from killing horses in Turco's herd."

"You want ME to stop a wolf pack from killing wild horses? That's insane!"

"Hush. I'm ordering you, Prophet, to protect Turco's herd."

"All right," Coyote said hesitantly. "I'll see if I can get Bill's TEAM to work on this."

"They will refuse. They believe animals have a right to be themselves and keep doing what they have always done. Bill's TEAM may be biocomputers who are also bioengineers, but they are moralists too. We gods understand better than Bill's TEAM how violently lives may end in the outdoors of the animal world."

"If you are sure about Bill's TEAM refusing, then I'll go talk with Cowboy."

"He will help you, I'm sure. Without him, so much of what's happening that might turn out to be good for animals wouldn't have occurred."

"I do want to protect Turco. He's a fellow advanced bio-engineered being, a 'creation' whose maker ought to agree to keep protecting him. Bill's TEAM is wrong to refuse here."

"They have their way. We have ours," Coyote's god said.

"Cowboy may not have amounted to much in the human world, but he is Turco's and my best friend. And I wouldn't be here if Cowboy hadn't helped Bill choose property to build his enterprise on."

"I'm very grateful to Bill for creating you, my Prophet."

"Which is why you ordered me to ride the mountain on that parade float to help save him," Coyote said, with his teeth clenched. "All right. I'll see what I can do."

Very late that evening, Coyote stood under the Mexican Cowboy's bedroom window and howled softly until he woke up. The Cowboy hurriedly opened the refurbished house's front door, and Coyote walked in. The two of them sat in the dining room and talked for hours before Coyote thanked Cowboy and left.

Carrying Out their Plan

Crossing into New Mexico from Colorado was Redbeard, a stern, wise, arthritic wolf, with a red patch under her chin. She was matron of a wolf pack with seven members, including four young, vigorous, bright, and aggressive wolves. Hunting for game, Redbeard led her followers southwestwardly along the almost invisible Continental Divide, killing and dividing small game like rabbits and rats, grouse and foxes, and hoping to locate bigger animals for the pack to rest and enjoy eating for several days. Without intending to, Redbeard's pack was gradually approaching Turco's herd, which was wintering in a small, warmish cluster of trees on the Horse Lake Mesa.

In her office, Cece was tracking the wolf pack's movement, which was published online because seven months ago, Redbeard had been snatched, sedated, examined, and fitted with a sophisticated collar which, among other things, helped trackers to follow the pack's movements. When the pack was just over thirty miles from Turco's herd, Cece was so worried that she asks Bill's TEAM to intervene. Their answer was infuriating. "We helped Turco get what he wanted, to be a stallion king again. Now the role is his, and so are possible consequences. If he were killed by predators while protecting the herd, as some mustangs are, that would be Turco's choice of finishing."

Angry, Cece began thinking about what she could do to save Turco.

What Cece did not know was that at this very moment, Coyote and Cowboy were driving north on Highway 44 in Cowboy's jeep. Armed with his rifle and pouches of ammunition, Cowboy was determined to protect his beloved Turco. But he understood too that Coyote had been directed by his god to try to protect all the animals that might be hurt if the wolf pack attacked the herd.

Coyote had come up with a very strange plan, and he was depending on Cowboy to drive him to the many places he needed to go to make the plan work. For the next two days and nights, the exhausted Cowboy made unexpected stops along almost undrivable jeep roads, letting Coyote out and waiting, sometime hours, for Coyote's return.

Steered by his god El Latrone, Coyote trotted over the territories of more than forty coyotes, met each, and explained what he needed them to do for him. He was thrilled that every one of them knew about him. Throughout the Southwest, coyotes had been sharing information about their Prophet since the shooting at the parade, and most of the ones he contacted now were thrilled to meet him. Only a few refused to help. Meanwhile, Cowboy was rediscovering how much he loved being outdoors at night. Night sounds of nearby animals and night birds thrilled him. In his parked jeep Cowboy munched and slept, then climbed out, explored, and peed. He was having a good time on this trip, even though the temperature was dropping.

Over the next day and a half, groups of coyotes for miles around the Horse Lake Mesa began silently herding sheep away from their distant or sleeping owners. Learning to herd wasn't easy for coyotes, but gradually the wooly, scared, and bawling animals were driven from many directions up the Horse Lake Mesa toward the mustang herd. At last a herd of over seventy frightened sheep were clustered very near the surprised mustang herd. They were beginning to calm and resume grazing as Redbeard and her pack neared.

Several hours earlier Cowboy had been stopping at bars, restaurants, and filling stations around the Mesa, telling people he'd seen what he thought were dogs without shepherds driving a small herd of sheep up the Mesa. Did anyone know what this was about? Word spread quickly among sheep owners on the Jicarilla Apache Reservation, and ranches with sheep scattered around the Horse Lake Mesa. Checking their sheep and discovering many missing, sheep owners phoned each other and decided to go up onto the mesa together, just in case rustlers were hiding stolen sheep up there.

Now Cowboy's Jeep was parked about three-quarters of a mile from Turco's mustang herd. It was beginning to snow. Carrying his loaded rifle, Cowboy quietly approached Turco's herd. Coyote had already vanished into the night. Crouching behind a shoulder-high boulder, Cowboy made himself as comfortable as he could and began waiting for things he expected to happen.

Anxiously moving around his herd, Turco was startled when the bawling sheep suddenly ran *en masse* among the scattered herd of mustangs, trying to defensively meld with the horses. Earlier Turco had spotted coyotes driving sheep onto the mesa toward his herd. Were they returning to kill some of the bleating sheep, he wondered. His mane ruffled, and Turco began moving his mustangs into defensive positions. He knew the coyotes wouldn't attack him or his horses, but the prospect that something much worse might be about to happen frightened him. The mustangs clustered tightly, with Turco, Gus, and the herd's few other stallions on the outside.

And now, Gus heard, and a few moments later spotted, an obvious wolf moving slowly across the mesa toward the tightly encircled herd of mustangs and sheep. Seeing the wolf too,

Turco instinctively and immediately started to drive his herd away from the wolf. And Gus stopped him, warning him in equine ways that the visible wolf's presence was only a pack's trick to drive the horse herd in the opposite direction toward other hidden wolves. "Stay here!" Gus communicated.

At the same moment, sheep owners—tracking their stolen sheep and carrying rifles— were nearing the mustangs and sheep on noisy four-wheel dune buggies and go-carts. Redbeard, who was moving silently toward the sheep and horses with dining plans, heard the nearing machines. Meanwhile, the coyotes who had crept away individually in many directions, and were each about a mile apart now, were waiting for a signal from their Prophet.

"**Now**!" Coyote's god said to him. Coyote took a deep breath, put his nose toward the overcast sky, and emitted the longest, loudest howl in his life. One by one each of the sitting coyotes joined in for a joyful, self-congratulatory, collective pack-howl. Surprisingly, the sheep and mustangs were thrilled with the mix of howls coming from every direction around them. Somehow they knew this wasn't a threat. The sustained coyote group-howl only began to fade gradually after three minutes, when coyotes, one by one, put down their heads, stood up, and began trotting back toward their own territories, satisfaction bubbling out of every pore.

Redbeard, realizing that her pack's sheep and mustang prey was about to be protected by armed humans, turned around disappointedly and crept away toward the southeast. She barked softly twice to summon her carefully positioned wolves, and with her assembled pack trotted quietly away, hoping to find other prey before the snowy night's end.

Angry owners who parked and began hunting for, and rounding up, their own stolen sheep quickly surrounded the densely packed herd of sheep and mustangs. With the mustangs moving apart in different directions, at first to confuse the humans, Turco moved his herd almost a mile away from the owners and sheep. Sure that they were safe, Turco and Gus began reassuring the mustangs that everything was all right for them.

As owners began herding their grateful sheep off the mesa, Coyote watched from a rock on a small nearby hillside. After all of them were gone, Coyote kept waiting, sniffing, and listening, with pointed and twisting ears, until he was absolutely sure that the wolves were not hiding or returning. Then he scampered down the little hill and trotted over to the rock where his blessed friend the Cowboy, covered with snow, was still kneeling and guarding with his rifle.

"I think it is safe for us to go now," he whispered to the Cowboy. "Do you want me to wait here while you say Goodbye to Turco?"

"It is better for both him and me if we don't meet up again," Cowboy said with a touch of sadness. "We'd only want to get back together."

While Turco walked around his horses, seeing how they were doing and reassuring them, Cowboy and Coyote slipped away. Five hours later they were back in Cordoba. Each of them was exhausted.

Turco Abandons His Home On The Range

Turco never suspected that Cowboy and Coyote, along with Coyote's god, had protected he, Gus, and his herd, from the potential wolf attack.

But, Kawai-i, the horse god, had been watching and knew, and he was now considering whether to approve, or hate, the interference with his horse followers by El Latrone, who had made it clear to animal gods that he was working with the human god to reset relations among species.

As winter advanced Gus, who had always been domesticated, found it hard to graze and get through long days and nights of sub-zero temperatures. Gus was still okay, but he began yearning to go back to his warm stable. Still, he knew he had no easy way to get back there now. Turco understood his friend's changing feelings, but realized too there was nothing he could do to help him.

Over the next nine months Turco's rise to power became absolute. Turco remade his herd, driving some horses away and allowing other mustangs to join. He didn't favor descendants of mustangs he once fathered. He impregnated a dozen mares, kept every horse in his herd safe through the long winter, the mild spring and dry summer...and then realized that an intense longing was rising in him to be back with his Cowboy friend once more.

In mid-October Turco became certain that his partner Gus could not make it through another winter with him. It was time, he decided, for him to leave his herd and go back to the Cowboy's ranch.

One evening, without any farewells, Turco and Gus grazed further and further from the herd. When they were about half a mile away, they began walking back toward the Carson National Forest, traveling ten or twelve miles before the sun rose. Turco and Gus weren't looking forward to their long walk back to Cordoba, but there was nothing else they could do. At least they had much more experience in handling predators now.

When the pair came to the first paved road, empty of passing vehicles at the moment, they were astonished to see two of Bill's biobots and a horse van waiting for them. Joyfully, yet nervous about being handled by others, Turco allowed the 'bots to check them over for cuts and bruises, clean them, feed them oats with molasses because Turco was so thin, and lead them into the van. But he refused to be bridled. Turco's career as a leader in the horse world was over.

Cowboy And Turco Connect Again

Cece—who'd been keeping track of what was going on with Turco via his satellite-linked implanted Teacher—was the one who ordered the van sent north to pick up the pair, without asking permission from her boss, Bill's TEAM. As the van drove back toward Cordoba she pondered how her strengthening ties with Cowboy would change when Turco came back into his life.

Turco was delivered back to Cowboy's ranch in less than six hours and quietly—late at night—returned to his stall. The biobots, who'd been showing up here only once a week to maintain the barn, sneaked over and began quietly helping Gus and Turco settle in. It was odd, but the 'bots actually felt a tiny thrill run through them as they connected with the pair again.

Next morning, when the Cowboy went out onto his porch to sip coffee in his green rocker, he heard an unmistakable whinny from his empty stable. With a mixture of doubt and hope, he hurried over to the barn to find out what was happening.

Going inside he was stunned and delighted to see both Turco's and Gus's heads sticking out over the wide joint-stall door. Barn staff had been working on the wild horse—shoeing him, trimming his coat, cleaning teeth, checking health, feeding him—and Turco seemed exactly like he did when he first began living with Cowboy nineteen years ago—robust, independent, and wanting friendship. Cowboy went into the stall, put his arms around each of their necks, and stayed touching and talking with Gus and Turco more than an hour.

That warm, sunny afternoon Cowboy saddled Turco with their ancient saddle and blanket and the two of them rode up to the edge of the mountains, had a picnic together, and rode back to the ranch after dusk, when distant coyote howls were beginning to sound and the multi-colored sky was fading into a brilliantly lit nightscape with a huge moon and thousands of bright stars overhead.

"My life is perfect again," Cowboy said to Turco. "How about yours?"

Turco bowed his head, whinnied, and did a little dance with four hooves.

"I'm glad," Cowboy said, leaning over and patting Turco's neck. "I feel the same way. Let's keep this going a long while."

Mazzie Takes on Poko

"With all the stuff going on here, there is going to be lots of hell to pay," Mayor Howie said to Bill's stunningly handsome brother Kemmet, who was meeting with him in his office, as Howie sat rocking in his new executive chair.

"Why?" Kemmet asked.

"Bad things are happening. And I'm sure many of those are of my own making. Still, I'm pleased with myself. I've accomplished a huge amount to better the economy in Cordoba and surrounding towns. And I am especially pleased with my success in smashing animals back into their place—after that world-famous Eden Park brouhaha. It put conservatives and hunters on the bottom of the human pile in the world press."

"You are a genius," Kemmet said, while recalling many of his own achievements.

"I'm not lying either,' the Mayor went on. "Cordoba is growing at an unexpected rate."

"And many of your industrious efforts were illegal," Kemmet said. "I'm pleased you are a politician who can get away with doing illegal things that often make such a great difference. Tell me about the changes happening here."

Howie looked at Kemmet with a studious look. "I'm willing to bet that you do illegal things also, and get away with those too. Anyway, with all I've accomplished there are more stores here in Cordoba, a supermarket, new homes, and even an apartment complex and a health center are being added to the community. Streets have more traffic, a stoplight has replaced a four-way stop sign downtown, the city's administration is growing, and a Chamber of Commerce committee has come into existence. Farms and ranches are being broken up and sold for new homes. Even the impoverished and dilapidated Chichimaya Church has been refurbished and is attracting returnees to Catholicism."

"Good job, Kemmet replied. "Where do you go from here?"

"The time is coming for me to run for Governor," Howie said as he packed up papers to take to a Chamber of Commerce luncheon in the town's new restaurant. "Now, tell me why you came to see me."

"We paid you a lot of money to pull off the parade that failed," Kemmet began, with Mayor Howie studying his impressive appearance. I want to know if you designed this to happen. And I want to know who kidnapped my brother Bill. And why they did it. And I want to know everything that his people have been doing."

"You don't want to find out where Bill is?"

"He's a vegetable. It doesn't matter to me whether he is even still alive."

"Just because you gave me lots of money to put the parade together, that doesn't mean I'm on your side in your long-time battle with your brother Bill. Bill's people told me a lot about the on-going war between you guys. And they've done a lot for me too. More than you. I know you set up another bioengineering corporation that keeps trying to steal Bill's research and products."

"Yes, that's L.I.V.E., a company name based on initials of the guys who put the corporation together and run it. And yes, we do want to learn everything we can to help us grow and make money."

"Bill's people call the L.I.V.E. guys the Picklenose Crowd. Their names are Luciferanso, Inmann, Venty, and Emerson, right?"

"You know about us. I know that."

"Because you spy on me?"

"We spy on everybody. And we can help you win the governorship of New Mexico, if you are willing to help us find out everything going on in Bill's business."

"You *are* using your computers to spy on Bill's TEAM then," Howie said.

"And they are doing the same thing to us."

"And you have been using your computers to attack Bill's system."

"We're trying to learn its limitations and operating capabilities."

"This could turn into a war you know."

"If it does it will be a victory for the winner, us!"

"If you go to war I'll have to figure out which side to join," Howie said.

"Bet you'll go with us. You are conservative and so are we. Bill's guys are trying to remake human society."

"And the animals' social systems too," Howie said.

"With your help we might not have to start a war."

"Lots of stuff I do tends to stir up fights between people. We conservatives stick to our principles. And let others be damned," Howie said.

"You'll be on our side. I'm sure of that now."

"Don't bet on it. I'll have to think this over," Howie said. "It is probably best for me to keep staying on both your sides."

"We'll stop supporting you if you do."

"Look. I've got to go to a meeting. We'll be in touch," Howie said rising, and reaching across to shake Kemmet's hand."

Cowboy Relaxes in his Rebuilt Home

It was a sunny, warm, early summer day, and Cowboy was rocking on his classy new porch, pleased with how well his life was going, especially after Turco returned in such great shape from his home on the range. Cowboy was pleased too with the continuing remodeling of his house and property by Bill's people. The house had been expanded and updated—though still retaining its character in the parts Cowboy used. But a whole new wing off the backside has been built for Cece, who stayed there several nights a week. Bill's people had also completed a nearby house for Father Gallapo that looked like a New Mexico rural church. "That surly Priest won't admit it to anyone, but he loves the place. And he hates taking care of it also," Cowboy thought as he rocked contentedly.

Over in the Priest's new home, Thelma Whitenose was dusting and vacuuming, musing as she so often did about why Father Gallapo viewed her as a mere subordinate and a parishioner, and why she'd let herself get stuck with taking care of the new house too, as well as looking after Chichimaya Church in Cordoba. Thanks mainly to her—and Cece—Chichimaya Church had been refurbished, while retaining its essential qualities. The parking lot had been regraded and pathways re-cobbled. And an addition on the church's backside was being planned for adding a kitchen and dining space, classrooms for children and others, a dressing room for brides and mourners, and a well-equipped office for Father G.

Cece and Thelma had done much of the designing, and their efforts in recruiting new church members were paying off. Thelma had even been able to hire two staffers, a woman and a man, who had taken on so many things she'd been forced to do in the past. Bill's TEAM offered 'bots to help out at the church and take care of his new home, but the Priest adamantly refused. "These are human places and always will be so," Father Gallapo said sternly at a meeting with Bill's people. Finishing her cleaning and getting ready to leave, Thelma groaned and asked herself, "Why do I stay with this Priest jerk? I'd be much better off accepting Cece's offer to join her and work with Bill's people."

Next door, after going inside and pouring himself another cup of coffee, Cowboy was squirming around to get comfortable again in his rocker on the porch. He was glad that the house's update was nearly finished: it had been a nuisance having disruptive work going on around him. He was glad Cece had moved in, sort of. She had her own entrance and rooms; still, most nights she stayed at Bill's place, working late and sleeping overnight in a bedroom made for her there.

Cowboy mused on how subtly, but nicely, Cece's appearance was changing. "She's becoming more attractive," he thought, "and that's bound to take her away from me eventually." Cece had been getting 'touch-up' surgery, with tiny implants, and many new appearance improvement experiments at Bill's place. Bill's biobrain and human staff were pleased she had volunteered to be an experimental subject, and grateful too for the very good work she had been doing for them.

Cece Is Having Some Thoughts Too

At the same moment, over in her office at Bill's place, Cece was thinking about how her life was going and whether the choices she'd been making were good ones. Cece wasn't just a dedicated worker. She knew herself well and made sure she took time off to do things she enjoyed. Still riding Bill's antique Triumph motorcycle, Cece drove regularly along a trail leading into the mountains to gather flowers and do photographs, which a story in the local paper said she was going to make into a book.

This publicity both pleased and frightened Cece. Cece was still scared of being arrested for what she had done to the older man in the nursing home who she made vomit with a plunger. And whose car she stole. If she were arrested she'd be put in jail this time, not locked up again in the nursing home she escaped from. Bill's operating TEAM had tried to reassure her, saying their redoing of her appearance and creation of a new ID for her should keep her safe. Looking into a mirror, Cece noted once again how her changes were both attractive and slight. She'd learned also how these were designed to keep ID computers from linking her new image with the woman police might be looking for. "Bill's people may be right claiming I'm safe now. They usually are right... But still...." Cece thought.

On a brighter side, Cece's memories of what her children did to her were fading. Since connecting with Bill's TEAM, Cowboy, Thelma, and the Priest, Cece had been overcoming lifetime fears which had turned her into an archetypical mean and selfish woman. She was now on a team with people she really liked and trusted, and every day of her life had become pleasurable. Still, part of her remained diamond hard. She didn't want to take many new chances, and that made her very cautious when it came to her connecting up with Cowboy. She was both drawn to him and didn't want to marry or shack up with Cowboy. And she knew it was the same at Cowboy's end. The two liked each other's company, but also kept their distance—wanting both to be together and to maintain their own lives as they were now.

There were lots of things about the Mexican Cowboy Cece didn't like. For example, he couldn't stand motorcycles, he hated dogs, and he didn't want to travel worldwide, or even off the planet. She wanted to be one of the first tourists to see earth from space. Thinking about this, Cece recalled how badly she had infuriated her kids by spending huge sums on her travel ventures. But damn it, all my grown children were lazy, and couldn't or wouldn't take care of themselves without always hitting on me, she said to herself almost aloud. Then, she felt ashamed of herself for being the bad mother she always thought she was. At least Bill's TEAM is turning around things on this planet now, Cece thought. The world will become a much better place for all beings, thanks to Bill's TEAM ... and to me for helping them so much.

Meanwhile, in Their Heaven, Animal Gods are Fighting

Alas, there were millions of humans who would disagree, even violently, with Cece, if they knew what she was thinking. Humans were becoming more divisive. And the same thing was going on in the animal gods' kingdom in the sky. In their Heaven the animal gods were holding meet ups, prompted by coyote god El Latrano, which always turned out to be angrier and more divisive. The central topic in every meeting was whether animal gods should work together to make things better for each species on the planet, or should they instead continue focusing only on what each god believed best for his or her own followers. Most of the animal gods could not grasp yet the idea of working collectively to solve species' problems. But some had tried, with varying results.

Angwusi the crow god, Tocha the hummingbird god, and other bird gods, favored working with humans and coyotes: humans, because humans were feeding and protecting birds now; coyotes, because coyotes had been eating only half the birds they used to. "Coyotes are keeping the deal we made with them to calm the raging humans in the Eden Park Tea Party fracas," Tocha said.

"Your crows didn't show up there!" Poko, the dog god snapped. And turning to El Latrano, he continued, "My dogs calmed humans at the Eden Park fracas better than any of your bird-eating followers."

Sowi-ingwu the deer god was about to claim deer did more than dogs to calm fighting humans in Eden Park, when Kweo, the wolf god interrupted, snarling at El Latrano. Kweo was pissed at the coyote god for using his Prophet to keep one of Kweo's wolf packs from killing sheep and horses. El Latrano started to apologize when Kawai-i, the horse god interrupted angry Kweo, and thanked El Latrano for sparing Turco, one of his prized horses. Kawai-i argued that working with humans had always been good for his followers.

"But humans are eating more of your followers now," Hon, the bear god, pointed out.

"And coyotes are eating more of my followers too after the deal El Latrano made with the human's god," Wenet, the female hare god replied angrily.

Wakas, the cow god broke in, saying, "Humans eat all of my followers. That's never bothered me. There are more cattle on the planet than ever before, and their lives go well until the end."

Poko the dog god snapped out, "I'm furious because coyotes are working with advanced humans. You and your coyotes are trying to take over the place my dogs have with humans," Poko barked at El Latrano. "Well, I and my dogs, and most humans too, aren't going to allow you to get away with that. You want us to work with humans. Well we've always done that, it's been good for us, and if humans help us, we're going to wipe out all your coyotes. You can then retire to the heaven for gods whose followers have died out. You'll fit in well with the dinosaur, mammoth, and saber tooth tiger's gods."

El Latrano replied, "Look, fellow gods. The cultural and population explosion among humans is wiping out mammals, reptiles, sea life and species all around the world. We've got to find a way to rein humans in. And we won't succeed in doing this unless we work together," he said, pausing and studying the faces of nearby gods. "We'll need the help of their god too," El Latrano continued. "That's why I've started working with their god."

Pong, the mountain goat god, replied, "Thanks to that Eden deal, coyotes are eating more of my followers. The human god's never been on my side."

And on and on it went. Meeting after meeting broke up with gods angrier and more divided than ever before. Now gods were even refusing to play soccer together, as factions grew more determined and more divisive.

Kemmet and Howie Try to Make a Deal

Two days later back in Cordoba Mayor Howie was in his office talking again with Kemmet, Bill's brother. "I'm willing to tell you Kemmet much about what I know being researched by Bill's TEAM—like the rebuilding of a mustang, Turco, who was badly aging." But I won't bring up the subject of Bill, he thought to himself.

"Thanks," Kemmet replied. "I know we can use you as a critical source to learn what going on in Bill's hidden business. And that may keep us from fighting."

"But I have a price to share what I know about Bill's company's work," Howie continued. "You have to be willing to share with me much of what your L.I.V.E. team's been doing and finding out. If I'm going to be on both sides I want to know what both sides are doing and learning."

Kemmet groaned and waved his thumb across his neck like he was slaughtering a lamb. "No deal. We can't do that for you. At least not very much of that."

"Well, you tell me stuff and I'll tell you stuff in return," Howie said definitively. "The more you share with me, the more I'll share with you."

"You intend to sell Bill's company the stuff you learn from me, don't you?" Kemmet said.

"You probably got that right."

"And that will mess up the economic war we are waging with Bill's company."

"And that war may bankrupt both companies if it's carried on too long and goes too far," Howie snapped back. "But tell me, why don't you just make your computers figure out everything going on at Bill's firm?"

"We're doing that, and our bioengineered computers are moving far beyond the capacity of ordinary computers to find solutions to problems we give them," Kemmet answered.

"That's true of Bill's biobrains too," Howie replied.

The talk between Kemmet and Mayor Howie went on for another hour. Each side budged only slightly. And neither trusted the other.

Cece Slams on the Brakes

Several days later Thelma came to Bill's place to have dinner with Cece. A 'bot led her into a dining room, where Cece was sitting on a couch combing a ratty little white dog. "She's filthy and her hair is really tangled and matted. Come over and sit by us and help me work on her," Cece said. Thelma walked over and sat down next to the pair. The little dog looked up at her affectionately, making Thelma eager to reach over and pat her. With Cece trying to hold the dog and comb her, the little beast tried to struggle away and crawl into Thelma's lap. "She's friendly, isn't she," Cece said.

"Where'd she come from," Thelma asked.

"Out there," Cece said, pointing over her shoulder at the mountains. "Yesterday I took the afternoon off, got on Bill's little Triumph, and putted off along the Manzano range. I was looking for more rare flowers to photograph for the book I'm putting together. I was going slowly partly because the road was so rough, but also so I could look for the flowers I was hoping to spot. This ragged dog was sitting by the side of the road when I went past her. I didn't stop. I figured she belonged to someone and knew what she was doing out there."

"If you didn't stop, how'd you wind up with her?"

"A couple of hours later I was coming back on the same road. And this damned dog was in the middle of it. I wanted to get around her, but whichever way I pointed the motorcycle, she moved in front of it. I had no choice. I had to slam on the brakes and stop. When I did, the little mutt came around the front wheel and stood up on my left leg, which was holding up the bike. I told her to go away but she tried to climb up my leg. Damn near did it too! So I reached over, grabbed her by the neck, lifted her onto the gas tank, expecting she'd jump off and run away. But she hunkered down like a surfboarder paddling out to the big waves, then turned around and looked at me like she wanted me to start driving again. So I did it."

"Why'd you keep her?"

"I'm not. I brought her back here and Bill's people are trying to find out whom she belongs to. If they can't, they may make her into one of their experimental subjects."

"They want to experiment on dogs now?" Thelma asked.

"Yep, if she's willing—and if I am—they'll use her to try to learn how dogs' brains work and how rich their communicating can be."

"Did you give her a name?"

"Yep. I'm calling her Mazzie, after my mother, whose name was Mazie."

"Mazzie's kind of a dumb name."

"Well, she isn't much of a dog." Cece grabbed Mazzie and plopped her on the floor, saying: "Let's have a drink or two and then order our dinner."

After asking what Thelma would like to drink, Cece called the kitchen 'bot on her Teacher to place an order. Before the drinks and snacks came, Mazzie was back on the couch between the two gabbing women, being patted by each of them. "You can have her if you want," Cece said to Thelma.

"I think she prefers being with you," Thelma said insightfully.

Mazzie Meets Up with the Mexican Cowboy

Though she had no intention of keeping the matted little white dog, for unknown reasons Cece hadn't bothered to find another home for her. The few times every week Cece stayed at the Cowboy's rebuilt ranch house, Mazzie rode back and forth with her, glued down on the gas tank of Bill's ancient motorcycle. The first night she brought Mazzie with her, Cece and Cowboy were dining together, eating food each liked prepared by their kitchen 'bots. Cece had just asked Cowboy why he preferred to keep eating tacos, enchiladas, burritos, and rice when the staff could make so many wonderful other things, when Cowboy heard scratching against the door leading to Cece's quarters.

"What's that, a rat?" Cowboy asked, and got up to look behind the door to the part of his house he'd never visited.

"It's a dog I found," Cece said, trying to stop him. "I'm going to get a home for her, but haven't gotten around to it."

"You've got a dog living in my house?" Cowboy stopped, turned around and asked. "You know I don't like dogs!" he said explosively.

"Yes, I know that. And I've been trying to keep her away from you. But still, I'm not prepared to let her stay over at Bill's place without me. If you like, I'll stop coming here until I get rid of her."

That thought scared Cowboy—as Cece had suspected it would. He returned to the table and sat down again. "No, I don't want you to go away. I miss you when you are not here. All right, let her in. I'll try to like her."

Cece grinned and said"Thank you! That's very sweet of you," and got up to open the door and let Mazzie into the dining room.

Cowboy watched with a pissed-off look on his face as the ragged little white mutt trotted into his dining room. Amazingly, Mazzie came over to the table and sat upright on the floor next to Cowboy. Without realizing what he was doing, Cowboy reached over and scratched her neck. Mazzie responded with a sweet kitten-like purring sound.

"She's got you figured out," Cece said. "I'm betting the two of you will figure out how to get along with each other."

"She'll get kicked out of here instantly if she messes with Coyote," the Cowboy replied.

"I'll try to train her to be respectful of your best friend," Cece answered as the two settled down to finish their meal.

Mazzie Wants to Ride Turco

Over the next few weeks the relationship between Mazzie and Cowboy evolved, not necessarily in directions either would prefer. The house 'bots installed a small dog door in Cece's wing of the house, and Mazzie became free to go out and return whenever she stayed there. The house 'bots looked after her and Cece often didn't take her back now when she returned to Bill's place. This peeved Cowboy, but not enough that he'd kick Mazzie out of his ranch house.

One of the things that angered him was that Mazzie trotted after him every time he went down to the stable with Turco and Gus inside. Mazzie, he could tell, liked being with the horse and burro. And one of the barn's 'bots told him that Mazzie often hung out with them when the Cowboy was not around. "They like her," the 'bot said.

He put up with it, but several days later Mazzie began trying to follow Cowboy when he rode Turco to the Bosque or mountains. The first few times he stopped and yelled at her to go back, and she sat and sadly watched him ride away.

Today though, Mazzie sneaked along behind him. He was several miles from the ranch before he turned his head and spotted her. Cowboy got off Turco and called Mazzie to come to him. She didn't move and Cowboy could see the fear she was feeling. That didn't stop him from harshly picking her up and draping her over the saddle in front of him. He swung up into the saddle and rode back to the house. As they trotted back, Cowboy was surprised to see Mazzie take hold of the horse's mane in her mouth, and start to pull him in the same directions Cowboy was turning. "This crappy dog is a born rider," he thought, with a smile on his face. Back at the ranch house he locked her up in his half of the expanded ranch house—where there was no puppy door she could sneak through—while he went riding again.

Next time he saw her, Cowboy complained to Cece about Mazzie's trailing him. And Cece replied, "Mazzie enjoys riding. She likes being on my motorcycle and would probably drive it herself if she knew how. She'd also probably like riding a horse by herself, if the horse would allow it."

"It's not going to happen again, if I have anything to say about it," Cowboy mumbled, fuming over the nuisance of Mazzie's presence in his life.

"At least Mazzie has been considerate of your relationship with Coyote," Cece said.

"You're right. I've caught her looking out the window at him ... and the other animals we're feeding. And Coyote told me he's seen her inside here. Bill's TEAM told him that she was about to become one of their subjects. And Coyote said he didn't like it that Bill's people are losing interest in coyotes and moving to horses, dogs, and other species," Cowboy said.

"Well, they are scientists, and scientists do switch subjects periodically," Cece responded.

"Coyote thought Bill and his TEAM were his parents, and the grandfathers of all his cubs. He doesn't want them to stop being that."

"They won't, I assure you," Cece said. "But they are taking on other animals species too now. That was always their aim."

"That's a lot of crap."

"That's not 'crap.' It's science."

"Doesn't make me or Coyote like it."

Cece reached over and put her hand on Cowboy's hand, massaging him silently. She watched Cowboy loosen up and become less angry. He had forgotten about Mazzie now. She was pleased about that.

But inside, Cowboy was feeling torment rising, because the shaky connection between him and Cece was worsening. "One of these days this relationship is going to bust up also," Cowboy thought unhappily.

The Fight is Turning into War in Animal Heaven

El Latrano was still trying to bring the gods together and, at their current meeting, he tried a new approach to block the war in the sky that is forming. "Look," he said to the angry gods around him, "things were pretty equal among all species on the earth until twenty thousand years ago, when the human god's people started taking over the planet."

"And no species was ever able to do that before," said Kahaila, the female turtle god, and the oldest of gods present at the meeting. "Until now we've never had one species that dominated all the others on earth."

"So you are thinking we need to take on the humans?" asked Mong' Wuhti, the great horned owl female god.

"Let's work with them, change them, rather than fight among ourselves," El Latrano replied.

"This is crap, El Latrano!" Poko the dog god interrupted. "Humans are making this planet better for my followers. And you are bringing this up just to stop the war that's going on between us. You are not going to stop my followers from killing yours. I'm all too aware of coyotes' revival. Now they are spreading into even human's cities. And your followers kill and eat my small dogs."

"And cats too!" said Mosa, the cat god.

"Look, dogs and coyotes have been in relentless war for more years than any can remember," El Latrano said to Poko. "For a long while dogs, allied with humans, were plainly winning. But now a few humans and their god have teamed up with me and my Prophet. We're not trying to defeat your dogs. We're trying to work with them to make things better for all of us."

"And I'm going to do something about that. Kill your Prophet, and as many coyotes as my dog followers can," Poko snapped smugly.

"What brought this on?" El Latrano asked. "You didn't use to be so savage."

"Thanks to you and your Prophet, my dogs had a bad day in Socorro. And we know it was because you and the human god were working together."

"Have you forgotten that it was humans that created and baptized my Prophet?" El Latrano asked.

"No. I know about that. And I know that I need to work with another Prophet maker, the L.I.V.E. Company. There's a human god there I can work with and get my own Prophet."

"Who's that?"

"Lucifer. He makes things hell for humans, but he doesn't mess with animals, as you know."

"But you're planning to attack and kill my Prophet who helps me work with the human god. That won't be good for your friends the humans. Lucifer is not on their side."

"First we'll deal with your coyotes, then we can deal with Lucifer."

"This is an unbelievably stupid argument!" the mountain lion god Toho snarled, interrupting.

"Stay out of this, or I'll turn more of my followers on yours," Poko the dog god snarled back.

"Dogs are taking over the planet with humans," Taka the scorpion god interrupted.

"Damned right we are. And I'm not going to back down and let my followers become dumb animals, like the rest of you gods are doing."

The unending arguing went on for another hour before the gods separated in disgust. Down on the earth, animals of every species were growing edgier.

Mayor Howie Explores Working with Bill's TEAM

A week or so later Mayor Howie was meeting with Bill's TEAM. He was in the control room with an attractive—and short—'female' 'bot across the table from him, discussing what had been happening in his evolving relationship with Bill's brother Kemmet. "Their TEAM is going to go to war with you," Howie was saying. "And I'm here to help you defeat them. You've helped me tremendously and I owe you that favor."

"Thank you," the 'bot, changed to appear like an apparent company leader, said back. "We know about them. We've been both trying to help them grow and learn, and countering them whenever necessary."

"Kemmet maintains that this relationship is going to turn into a war, and they are going to win it."

"We are not warriors. We are scientists. We can delicately avoid warring with them, if they attack us."

"They are spying on you and learning a lot of what you are doing."

"And vice-versa. We know much about them, of course."

"And you believe they have little hidden from you?"

"There is no way we can know what is hidden from us until we find out. But we are protecting ourselves. And them."

"I think you guys are being foolish. You don't know politics and you don't know how war can be used to remake things."

"Of course we 'know' these things."

"What I meant was that you don't apply these strategies to problems which cannot be solved in any other way."

"You are right about that. And we don't intend to be that kind of capitalist organization."

"That worries me a lot," Mayor Howie answered. "Companies which don't defend themselves get taken over or put down."

"Once more," the attractive 'bot in formal clothes said softly, "we are scientists, not computers and people who want to run this planet. We study conflict. We don't initiate it."

"If I believe what Kemmet said his biocomputers and people are up to, you guys will be initiating conflict in the near future."

"Ahem," the executive biobot said, looking at her watch.

"All right. I see you want me out of here. But before I leave, tell me what the company's studying now."

"Many things. Coyote passed along to us much of what his god told him about conflict spreading among the animal gods."

"You believe they exist?"

"That we cannot verify."

"Go on."

"We are also studying feelings."

"Why?"

"After a lengthy exchange with furious Father Gallapo, we began grappling with the concept he put forward so powerfully, that pure reason is inadequate and insufficient for fullness of being. Feelings are essential too, both as motivators, but with focus, direction and intensity also."

"Is it humans' feelings you are studying?"

"Not yet. In developing Coyote we did study that species' feelings, and found ways to grow and shape these. We studied Cowboy's horse Turco's feelings while we rejuvenated him. And now we are studying feelings in the dog Mazzie that our employee Cece found."

"Did Cece have anything to do with switching you over to studying feelings?"

"She did. Because *we*—and the 'bot points 'her' hand in a circle at all the biocomputer sub-units behind the walls of the control room—lacked feelings, we used pure reason when we decided to allow wolves to kill Turco and his mares. 'Why?' you will ask. Because reason had dictated to let nature take its course."

"What did Cece do about that?"

"We were **WRONG**", she proclaimed. "Nature," she said, "is shaped by actions of natural beings, and those are driven largely by feelings—which vary across individuals and species and can fluctuate at each moment in time. So we began studying two patterns of reactions in brains: first, mirror neurons focusing on intentions of others, especially those posing potential dangers to each human. The other—in the pre-frontal cortex—takes a more considered view of the consequences of actions for each individual and others. First is immediate, instinctive, and emotive. Second is reflective and rational. First helps individuals survive. Second helps individuals work with others—and this makes species collaboration possible."

Howie replied, "Good bio-engineering, but why don't we hunters take the positions of game we are about to shoot? Or can't our mirror neurons tell us feelings happening in other species? Cowboy once said we were blind to this."

"You are right. You hunters are. And humans couldn't hunt and kill for food if their sympathizing mirror neurons weren't shut down."

"So, if you ever get around to pouring consciousness back into your founder Bill, are you going to make sure all of his sympathizing feelings are put back too?"

"That's been one of the most difficult questions we've had to search for ways to deal with. Please keep everything we tell you about Bill to yourself."

"Shall do," Howie promised, while trying successfully to mentally block himself from thinking what he was really going to do with the stuff he's been hearing. "Thanks for sharing so much with me."

"Always glad to," the 'bot said rising, and reached over to shake Mayor Howie's hand.

Cowboy Gets a Delightful Gift

Since his brilliant and world-famous parade leadership in Socorro, Cowboy had been receiving letters, offers, and gifts from people everywhere. Most of these he ignored and pitched, but he did open presents, and if they contained food he liked, he ate it. It was so long after the parade now that his gifts had been drying up. Today though Cowboy received a lovely present from an admirer woman in Mexico, a box of fresh bitter almonds. Her card said she picked them from her own tree just for him. The Cowboy loved almonds and these had the strongest scent he remembered. He looked at the almonds carefully to be sure these hadn't been doctored to harm him. Each almond he held up was fresh and perfect. "These will be great," he said.

That afternoon after four p.m., Cowboy went out on the porch to rock, drink a beer, and eat his almonds. Mazzie had been down in the stable, but when she heard Cowboy come outside she trotted up to the porch to be with him. Going up the steps she picked up the scent of the almonds. Cowboy had the box on the floor beside him. He reached down, picked up several almonds and began to eat them, one at a time. They were wonderful. Mazzie came over and stuck her nose into the box and Cowboy reached down and batted her away. "These are mine. If you want almonds make Cece get them for you," he said.

Mazzie snarled, hair on the back of her neck rising, and a look of pure determination appeared in her eyes. Cowboy started to put another almond into his mouth. Mazzie jumped up and bit his hand. He dropped the nuts. Before he could reach down for more she picked up the box and threw it into the bushes over the porch's edge.

Cowboy was furious. He stood up and tried to kick her. Mazzie dodged him. He reached down to grab her, his hand bleeding. She went under the railing and jumped off the porch and ran away. Cowboy was angrier than he'd been for years. He went inside to get his rifle. He intended to shoot her.

Cowboy's Teacher was aware of what was going on, and Bill's TEAM ordered one of the house 'bots to approach Cowboy and try to calm him. Cowboy tried to push the 'bot out of his way. The 'bot refused to move, and while he was blocked, Cowboy's Teacher asked him to describe what was going on. Cowboy threw his Teacher onto the floor. Even angrier now, Cowboy sat down at the dining room table. A 'bot carried him a plate of almonds and another beer. Calming, but still pissed off, Cowboy told the 'bot," Get your ass outside and clean up the almonds I was trying to eat when Mazzie bit me and threw them off the porch into the dirt. The 'bot looking after him nods, but it was another 'bot that went outside immediately with a garbage pail and cleaning tools.

That evening Cece showed up unexpectedly for dinner. When Cowboy heard the one cylinder motorcycle approaching, he went out onto the porch to tell her that she had to move out of here if she didn't get rid of Mazzie. He was surprised to see Mazzie riding in front of Cece on the tank of the motorcycle. Cece picked her up and walked up the porch stairs, dog in her arms, saying"Don't you dare touch her!"

"She bit me," Cowboy said, holding up his bandaged hand. "And she threw a box of terrific Mexican almonds away that a woman in Mexico sent me.

"She had good reasons for doing so," Cece said, putting Mazzie down beside her. "Did you know that those almonds were dangerously poisonous?"

"Impossible. I checked them over. They were perfect, like they'd just come off the trees."

"You idiot. Don't you know that bitter almonds are full of cyanide? Don't you know that almonds, by law, must be processed by heating to destroy the poison? Those almonds of yours were deadly. The woman just picked and sent them. The instant Mazzie sniffed them she recognized that the present you were eating was deadly. She did what she had to do to stop you from eating any more of those."

"Good God," Cowboy said softly, flustered and undecided. "What makes you so sure this is all true?"

"Ask your Teacher," angry Cece demanded.

Cowboy fished his teacher out of his pants pocket and said, "Is she telling the truth?"

"Those almonds were deadly," his Teacher instantly replied. Your staff sent them over to us and when we examined them we found immediately that each was full of cyanide. Eating that entire box might have killed you. At the very least it would have made you sicker than you've ever been."

"And I didn't know it," Cowboy said, reflecting on his stupidity. "I could have killed myself. Damn. I'm even a bigger fool than I ever supposed."

"Calm down," Cece said. "Mazzie saved you. And you were going to shoot her for doing that. You owe her a lot."

Cowboy sat down on the porch floor, his back against the ranch house, and patted the porch to invite Mazzie to come over to him. Surprisingly, Mazzie ran over immediately and jumped into his lap. He began petting her. She licked the hand where she bit him. "Thank you, pup. You saved my life. I owe you a lot. Would you like to be my dog too, now?"

Mazzie winked and rubbed her head against the Cowboy's chest.

"She likes you," Cece said. "She always has."

The door opened and a 'bot carried out a bowl of delicious dog food, drinks for Cowboy and Cece, and a cup with a handful of processed almonds in it.

Cowboy picked up one of the almonds, held it under Mazzie's nose, and said, "Check this out before I eat it." Mazzie sniffed the almond for a moment, then with her head under his hand pushed the almond up toward Cowboy's mouth.

"This day turned out a lot better than I expected," Cowboy said. He was even happier when Cece sat down beside him and leaned over and kissed him on the cheek.

Mazzie's fame began spreading when the local paper in Cordoba published a story about her preventing the famous Mexican Cowboy from eating poisonous almonds. Cowboy was angry and puzzled over who sent them the story. Cece adamantly denied that it had been her doing.

Still, Cowboy's connection with Mazzie was growing. Now he often took her with him when he rode Turco into the Bosque or mountains.

But he was furious again when, watching a local newscast, he saw a video of him passing by a small group of waving people, Mazzie in front of him on the saddle, both listening to American cowboy music playing over his Teacher.

Coyote Stays Away

In the following weeks Coyote stopped dropping by every evening for the fine foods the Mexican Cowboy put out for him. The Cowboy missed his dearest friend and asked his Teacher to tell him why Coyote wasn't coming.

"You've got a dog now," the Teacher said. "Coyote's disappointed in you, and doesn't feel safe going to your place now."

That shattered Cowboy's returning good feelings once again. Sitting on the porch and rocking, he could not stop asking himself, how am I going to solve this one? Can I get Mazzie and Coyote together? Is there any way to help them like each other? For the next week he pondered possible answers to these questions, while rocking on the porch, and in his bed trying to fall asleep. Cowboy missed having Father Gallapo living with him. The Priest might have come up with some valuable suggestions. Or even help him get Coyote and Mazzie together.

And Up in Heaven...

Meanwhile, up in the animal heaven, arguments among the gods were turning into physical conflicts. At one meeting Poko the dog god and El Latrano argued, circled around each other, and even tried to exchange a few blows. When Kawai-i, the horse god, separated the fighters, Poko backed away saying, "You are going to be the most miserable god in animal heaven when I kill your Prophet."

"I'll find a way to stop you from doing that. I promise you. And I'm not going to try to kill your dog followers either."

While Over at Bill's Place

With Cece's permission, and Mazzie's too, Bill's TEAM added Mazzie to their feelings study and experimental programs. Mazzie appeared to be having a great time working with Bill's people. Bases for dogs' feelings started to become clearer to the researchers, as had horses' when they studied Turco and rejuvenated him. Cece volunteered to be Bill's TEAM's first subject in the initial formal study of humans' feelings.

Relying on input from Coyote and El Latrano, the feelings of animal gods were being wrestled with (as very discreetly were the human God's). Gradually Bill's TEAM was discovering that animal gods' feelings were far less sophisticated and complex than humans' feelings. It was almost as though humans were the creators of gods, in fact as well as in fiction. As their data grew, new models of interactions among gods', individuals', and between species' were being sketched out by Bill's TEAM. The TEAM began to identify some difficult problems they must begin to deal with.

Dogs On the Mesa

While this research was going on at Bill's place, the dog god Poko had continued planning to kill the Prophet of his enemy, Coyote god. Poko's emerging plan was far from sophisticated. Dogs were going to attack Coyote and kill him. To put together enough dogs to make this plan workable, Poko started 'freeing' dogs from their human masters in central New Mexico.

German Shepherds, Collies, Chihuahuas, Malamutes, Bulldogs, Foxhounds, Mastiffs, Pit Bull Terriers, Australian Shepherds, Pinschers, Bassets and Beagles, Elkhounds, Bouviers... and many other breeds 'escaped' from their human masters, along with almost a hundred mixed dogs of all shapes and sizes. Poko steered each of his escaped followers into wild areas within eight or ten miles of Cowboy's ranch and began trying to teach them how to find 'natural' food in the Bosque and on the mesa.

Poko had always wanted to get back to having his dog packs rule many parts of the world, rather than separating and living individually with humans. Poko hoped to make these escapees the first big, modern dog pack. But today's dogs are so bred and schooled to be with humans, that Poko's runaways automatically gravitated away from pack forming and hunting. Directed by their god, the dogs tried to avoid humans, but emotionally they could not. Instead they began, one by one, showing up nightly at the wild animal feed taken over by Bill's 'bots at Cowboy's ranch. This made Coyote even more determined to keep himself far away from Cowboy's place.

But at the ranch house, Cece, Thelma, and even Father Gallapo loved having so many dogs show up at night feeds, and went out occasionally to pet them. Cowboy wanted them to stop doing that, because the dogs were driving all the wild animals away, not just Coyote. "Collect them and get them back to their owners," he phoned and asked Mayor Howie, who replied this was none of his business.

Oddly, Poko was on Cowboy's side here. The dog god wanted the wild pack he was trying to create to hunt, kill, and feed themselves. So, when Cowboy began going out with a stick and chasing the dogs away each night, Poko was very pleased.

Cowboy drove the dogs away finally. Starving now, they began to gang up. Poko steered his runaways into the territories of individual coyotes nearby, first to steal food coyotes had killed or found, then to kill coyotes one by one. One old, sick coyote was attacked and killed by several dogs—who discovered in themselves long suppressed feelings, including a surprising degree of satisfaction after fighting with and killing an enemy. Pack members were becoming closer with each other—and more removed from their former human masters.

Poko said to himself, "There! My dogs are wilding up."

The new wild pack grew in numbers. Bill's 'bots knew about this of course, but waffled over what to do about the pack's growing intent to attack and kill—or at least drive away—coyotes, and get their food. "Animals have a right to be themselves," Bill's biocomputers maintained. "And we are just computers and have no right to interfere with animals or their gods." That scared hell out of Coyote when Cece told him that Bill's TEAM had decided not to interfere with the wild dogs, but would continue trying to protect him.

Up in animal heaven, El Latrano, god of coyotes, had been closely following what Poko was up to. He was surprised at how wild Poko had succeeded in making the pack of escaped dogs he'd created. The simplest thing El Latrano could do, would be to order his Prophet Coyote to keep himself safely locked up at Bill's place. But El Latrano understood this would only stretch out the war between him and Poko, and would certainly allow Poko to strengthen and refine his wild dog pack, which was increasing Poko's power both among animal gods, and on the planet below. El Latrano made up his mind how to proceed.

Coyote Gets His God's Order

Late one night, accompanied by two guarding 'bots, Coyote went out to his prayer pit to worship his god. Stretched out in front of the dead rabbit he'd put on his altar, his front paws crossed, his head down, his eyes closed, he prayed. He was surprised—and pleased—when El Latrano answered him, which almost never happened. But Coyote was devastated when El Latrano ordered him to start going back to Cowboy's for dinner every night.

"Dogs will try to kill me if I do."

"And maybe they will kill you. But you are my pawn in this game, and I'm going to use you to better my chances of winning it."

"You are willing to let me be killed in order to better your chances of defeating Poko?" Coyote asked.

"You got it," El Latrano said, and cut off communication with his Prophet.

Later that night, back in one of the dens at Bill's place, while feeding and grooming his pups, Coyote told grownups in his extended family, "I may not be around much longer. El Latrano is willing to sacrifice me to keep the dog god from wiping coyotes off the planet." His family clustered around Coyote, licking him, praising him, worrying over his fate. Slowly, determination gathered in him to do what his God required.

Next evening Cowboy was astonished when he heard Coyote whining outside his window. He rushed out to thank him for appearing and, with his Teacher, ordered kitchen 'bots to prepare a large bowl of delicious food for Coyote. They brought the bowl out and Cowboy took it down to the foot of the stairs, pushed it in front of Coyote, and sat down to pet him while he ate. Coyote was thrilled to be connecting with his human friend again. But when he looked over Cowboy's shoulder and saw Mazzie watching him through one of the house windows, he shivered, and only Cowboy's hand on his neck kept him from bolting away.

Poko was keeping his maturing herd of wild dogs of all sizes and kinds away from Cowboy's ranch while the pack got better at hunting and killing, and even better at dividing up more fairly than most dogs would, the meat they'd brought to the ground. Poko was surprised that his enemy, the coyote god El Latrano, had forced his Prophet to start going the several miles over to Cowboy's ranch house every night to feed himself. "Either he doesn't know what's going on, or his god is crazy," Poko thought smugly. "I'm going to kill Coyote and both of them will be sorry over that," he said to himself, turning around to lick the glands under his tail.

Bill Returns

One afternoon Cece warned Coyote that Bill's TEAM was now focusing less on single species and more on mammals generally. "They'll still care for and protect you and your pups, who the biocomputers believe they created. But otherwise, get used to the fact that your influence over your creators is slipping away."

"I guessed that," Coyote responded to Cece. "They don't pay as much attention to me as they used to."

"So then, be wary. They may not care if anything happens to you. It will be just one more thing for them to study."

"Thank you," Coyote replied. "I've suspected this for months, but you now have the inside knowledge of what's going on in that giant biobrain Bill made. And speaking of Bill, how's he doing? Could he help me?"

"If I tell you will you keep it to yourself?"

"Probably."

"That's good enough for me. I was allowed to see him last week. Bill is still the same sort of guy, but he's now bald, with bumps under skull and face skin. He's mobile but still not able to talk, and people seeing him for the first time have doubts about his level of understanding. For instance, he doesn't seem to recognize images of you or Cowboy. But Bill's people are sure that they've made satisfactory progress in rehabilitating their leader, and once they are certain that all of his mental systems are functioning and working together, they intend to begin to pour his former consciousness back into him. "We have all of it, you know," one of the 'bots told me.

Coyote is Attacked

Several weeks later, Coyote was trotting from his den at Bill's place over to Cowboy's ranch house, to get his superb nightly dinner. Two 'bots were with him, each re-engineered to be able to keep up with a coyote. The three were crossing a little-used dirt road when Coyote smelled and heard dogs growling and snapping not far from him. Coyote hurriedly decided it would be safest for him to get to Cowboy's place, where he could hide in the stable with Turco and Gus, who would surely protect him from an attack by a pack of dogs. Coyote started running toward the ranch, the 'bots struggling to keep up with him.

Jumping over the dry arroyo bed, Coyote was only about a mile and a half from the ranch when two packs of wild dogs intercepted him, one coming in from each side. Ears up and fully opened, lips pulled back to expose teeth, heads twisting back and forth from side to side, and eyes widened, the little-, medium-sized and big dogs blocked Coyote, trapping him, and attacked the two biobots. Bulldogs, Foxhounds, Mastiffs, Pit Bull Terriers, Pinschers, and German Shepherds began ripping the 'bots apart, as Coyote snarled, dodged, bit, and tried to protect his protectors. Both 'bots went down. With Chihuahuas and other small dogs standing over the fallen 'bots, the bigger pack animals were now ready to kill Coyote.

As he tried to dodge them a helicopter appeared suddenly overhead. Bill's TEAM, watching what had been going on, loaded four 'bots wearing plastic armor into the 'copter when their drones observed the dog packs moving toward Coyote and his guardians. The helicopter descended rapidly and in a moment would be on the ground, unloading the armored 'bots to protect Coyote.

But, with several of the biggest and meanest dogs still surrounding Coyote and keeping him from escaping, all of the other dogs got under the descending 'copter and jumped into the air at it, barking furiously.

The craft's automatic 'pilot' moved to one side to land, and the dogs stayed under him. The pilot moved across the dirt road to land there. The dogs were still under the 'copter. A human pilot might land on top of the dogs and kill some of them. But Bill's TEAM would not allow the biobrain flying the 'copter to do this. The command to never land on humans or animals was built into the helicopter's brain.

Coyote guessed he wouldn't be killed until the helicopter had stopped trying to land. But he wouldn't be able to escape in the meantime. Oddly, his self-fear slipped out of him. No longer frightened, Coyote sat, put his head to the sky and, howling, prayed to his god, El Latrano. "The dogs have got me. I'll be coming your way very soon."

Coyote felt let down and very disappointed when he heard nothing back from his god, and realized his god wanted him to die and would do nothing to save his Prophet. What happened to Jesus Christ popped into his mind at that moment. "I wonder how Christ felt when he was being led to the Cross?" Coyote asked himself.

The Lone Star Dog Rides to the Rescue

Over at the ranch in Cece's wing, Mazzie was sleeping when she was made to jerk awake from a signal jabbed into her by the mini-Teacher Bill's people had implanted in her brain. Bill's TEAM were sending her an urgent message in dog 'language,' not in words, but still a blatant understanding of what was happening to Coyote.

Mazzie leapt up, ran downstairs, and scrambled out the swinging puppy door the Cowboy had agreed to leave unlocked. Mazzie raced to the stable, running faster than she had ever run before. The barn 'bots knew what was going on. They had opened the stable door for Mazzie and were about to open the stall shared by Gus and Turco, when Gus turned around and kicked the stall door open himself. Turco had been told on his implanted Teacher of the attack going on against Coyote. Turco was not going to let the friend who saved him and his herd from wolves be killed by a pack of wild dogs. As Mazzie rushed in barking furiously, Turco exited his stall and pressed up against a bench.

Mazzie jumped onto the bench, leapt up and planted her front paws on Turco's shoulder, grabbed the mane to stabilize herself, and struggled into her riding position. With Mazzie holding on tightly to Turco's mane to steer him, the three rescuers galloped out of the barn and set off to save Coyote.

Racing toward the spot where the dry arroyo crossed the little-used dirt road, Mazzie suddenly started hearing cowboy music in her little head. Cece had watched old cowboy movies on TV, and Mazzie realized suddenly that now she was like the Lone Ranger riding Silver into a crowd of bandits to rescue a captured maiden. Of course the Lone Ranger was able to reach over and pull the maid onto the saddle behind him. I've got to find another way to do it, Mazzie thought. Cowboy music poured through her head as she neared Coyote.

The helicopter was still trying to land, or at least to get low enough to safely let the four armored biobots leap out to save Coyote. The wild pack of dogs was still maneuvering successfully to keep the helicopter above them, and the pack dogs were so focused on the flying machine that they didn't hear Turco galloping toward them.

With her Teacher broadcasting steering instructions in her head, Mazzie guided Turco right into the pack of four furious huge dogs guarding Coyote. Three of them instantly attacked Turco. Turco fought back, whirling, kicking and biting, as Gus finally caught up to him. Gus waded into the battle too, hurting one dog badly, and kicking another away from Turco.

Hanging on to Turco for dear life, Mazzie barked down at the frozen Coyote. Barely understanding her, Coyote dodged his enemies, moved close to Turco and, with Turco stopping momentarily, tried to leap onto Turco's back. Coyote was about to fall off the horse when Mazzie grabbed his neck and held onto him desperately as Coyote struggled to get more securely in place. He succeeded! And with Coyote awkwardly draped over the horse's back holding on to Mazzie's stump of a tail for dear life, Turco turned and galloped away toward the barn, with Gus trotting after him.

The helicopter flew away, the dog pack members returned to their injured leaders and began licking and trying to comfort them. The battle was over.

A Kiss in the Barn

Carrying his rifle, Cowboy was waiting when they walked triumphantly into the stable. Cowboy helped Mazzie and Coyote down, saying"I was about to jump in my car and go defend you, but I was told by my Teacher to let Mazzie and Turco hold off those damned dogs."

Why Cowboy would be stopped from saving him puzzled Coyote, but he said nothing in reply. His fright was returning. He was exhausted. When the barn 'bots served him a delicious pan of food he could only sniff at it. While Turco and Gus's wounds were cleaned and dressed and preventive meds given to them, Coyote stretched out on the floor of the barn, his eyes closed, and he began shaking.

On his knees petting Coyote, Cowboy watched as Mazzie stood by Coyote's head, tail wagging, staring at Coyote. Mazzie stretched her head forward, her eyes softened, her mouth shut, and her nose twitching and sucking in air. The 'bots recognized this dog behavior for what it truly is: her body language told them she wanted to get to know Coyote. After several long moments, Coyote opened his eye and looked at her. Mazzie made a small soft whining bark, an invitation. Coyote hesitated, mused, and then gave in to her.

He got up unsteadily. He tried to wag his tail. He approached her head on. She stepped toward him and with her tongue out, she licked Coyote's face. After a few moments of inside mental shuddering, Coyote put *his* tongue out and licked her face back. He tried to keep his tail wagging.

Mazzie's tail was wagging furiously. Obviously she was deliciously happy. "I never understood why humans kissed," Coyote said to himself. "And after kissing this dog I still don't understand why they do it."

Mazzie wagged her tail even more frantically. "Is she my pet now?" Coyote wondered. Then he was floored when he realized that Mazzie's actions had not only saved his life. They had also broken up the new war between dogs and coyotes started by Poko. Mazzie deserved mountains of praise for what she'd done. He reached over and licked her again for several moments. Mazzie defied her god. Creatures who don't follow their god's instructions can be game-changers, Coyote realized.

Temporary Peace is Made in the Sky

Up in the animals' heaven, Poko and El Latrano approached each other. Poko was looking down and watching Bill's people take care of the dogs who were hurt in the fight with Turco and Gus. "They'll be all right," El Latrano said. "Bill's people will make them better than new. That team of bio-computers and 'bots are the best animal doctors on the planet," He reached over to pat Poko on the shoulder.

Poko jumped backwards, snarled, and ran in circles around the coyote god, threatening to bite him. El Latrano stood still, smiling. Poko stopped in front of him, smiled himself, saying, "Sorry, I needed to get my war out of me. I lost. You won. Shall we make up?"

"I think that would be best for your followers and mine. If you can stand it, let's try to work together and do what's best for our followers, and other gods' too."

"You've got a deal. I'll do that. At least until I can come up with a better way to beat you."

"Keep thinking. If we don't come up with new ideas and try them out we will never get any place new."

"Your coyotes need to do a lot of changing too," Poko said.

"I know. And we're working on that with the brightest human being."

The Wild Dogs are Rescued

Next morning Cece called Mayor Howie and told him Bill's people were offering to pay for picking up the wild dogs and returning them to their owners. Howie demanded to know how much they were willing to pay, and when Cece came up with an acceptable amount, he agreed to take on the job.

That week, with city employers and the Mayor's hunting partners doing the hard work, just about all the wild dogs they could find were rounded up. Workers then began trying to discover their owners and contact each of them. It was a lengthy process, but most of the dogs did in fact go home again. Whether each liked being back was another matter. And many wild dogs managed to evade the humans who were trying to catch them. They were happy with their new lives.

A Celebratory Dinner

A few weeks later Cowboy and Cece threw a fine dinner for their closest friends and partners. Thelma and Father Gallapo were there, each eating food they enjoyed. Coyote was indoors next to them, eating from an attractive bowl, with Mazzie alongside him. Mayor Howie was at the end of the table acting like the person-always-in-charge he tried to be. At the end of the meal, with the table cleared but wine glasses still on it, Mayor Howie offered a toast.

"Here is to Mazzie and Coyote for solving the problem of the runaway dogs. "Glasses were raised and clinked. Mazzie moved tightly against Coyote. Cece and Cowboy kissed. Thelma even dared to kiss Father Gallapo on his cheek. He didn't rebuff her.

Coyote then said to the group, "You humans don't know this, but Mazzie has been ordered by her god Poko to go out and hang with coyotes—who may threaten her."

"Because she was a semi-wild dog before Cece got her?" Thelma asked.

"No, because my god and hers patched up their relationship. Now each of them is trying to make their followers work with the other's."

"Mazzie is a super star and she should just order her god to leave her alone," Cowboy said. "Remember how she rode Turco into the pack to rescue Coyote like the hero in one of the 1940s cowboy movies!"

"Movie directors don't explore the consequences for the winner after a gunfight in cowboy movies," Father Gallapo said.

Mayor Howie interrupted this growing topic of conversation, tapped on his glass, raised it again, and offered a second toast. "I'm the movie star in this group. So, here's to me, who deserves most of the credit for all that has taken place since we began working together."

The others grinned. Cece stuck a finger in her wine glass and flipped a few drops at the mayor.

Cowboy pecked her on the cheek and said, "You sure know the right things to do with our mayor."

Father Gallapo kept his mouth tightly shut.

And Coyote and Mazzie came over to Mayor Howie and looked up at him as though they want to be petted. But when Mayor Howie reached out to them, they snapped at him, as though they meant to bite him.

Everyone at the table applauded. Except Mayor Howie.

Bruce Saunders

The Prairie Dog War

T he Mexican Cowboy sat in the comfortable green rocker on his porch, talking with Coyote. It was a warm evening after eleven. Bats flew overhead gobbling insects, the moon's dim fragment had yet to rise, and out in the yard animals dropped by to be fed and then vanish. Cowboy and Coyote were discussing Coyote's worsening health. "I'm aging," Coyote said. "I've lived longer than any coyote before me, and I'm getting eager to get off this planet and be with my god in Heaven."

"If you go, he'll lose his Prophet," Cowboy said. "And I will lose the best friend I've ever had. I'll be devastated. Why don't you let Bill's people fix you up and stick around for a few more years?"

"I know I'll miss you too," Coyote said, nuzzling the Cowboy, "but believe it or not, I hope we can still keep in touch when I get to my god's heaven."

"I hope so too, but I have never heard of that happening before."

"We'll see. Anyway, did you know my connection with Bill and his TEAM is loosening?" Coyote replied. "Much of their time is now spent dealing with his brother Kemmet's attacks on Bill's biocomputers. There is going to be a war between them."

"I thought Mayor Howie was working with both L.I.V.E. and Bill's Team to help the two groups find a way to get along."

"Cece told me Bill's TEAM has tried and tried, but Kemmet's group keeps attacking his brother's biocomputers. Cece has changed their initials around and now calls them the V.I.L.E. and E.V.I.L. people. And she may be right. My god El Latrano told me that your humans' evil god Lucifer is one the L.I.V.E. team's leaders."

"Damn," Cowboy replied. "That would explain a lot of what's going on between the two brothers. You know that Thelma and Cece saw Lucifer standing next to Howie in the church that night we were planning the parade thing to rescue Bill. He even had a hand on Howie's shoulder."

"I was there. My god was beating up on me, making me agree to ride on the float in that frightening parade."

"And even though I don't believe in him, I saw Jesus looking at me."

"My god tells me Jesus keeps an eye on your Lucifer," Coyote said.

"Well, at least it all happened in a church."

"Your church, not mine," Coyote answered.

"So why is Lucifer leading a major computer research corporation?"

"Cece says he is the one stirring up the fight with Bill's TEAM."

"But I don't get it. Why do this?"

"I don't know, but I'm betting it is going to turn out terrible for many humans on the planet."

"I don't believe that. There is nothing Lucifer could do to harm so many people."

"Cece says most of us don't know the enormous powers of the two fighting super biocomputer brains."

While Coyote was saying this, the lights in the ranch house in front of him began flickering.

"What's going on? You didn't pay your bill?" Coyote asked.

"Probably nothing. Or, Mayor Howie may not be paying the city's bills again."

"I'd better go back to my den and see how my cubs are doing. They'll be scared if the power goes off at Bill's place," Coyote said, and left without saying 'Goodbye.'

Bill's TEAM is Attacked

Cowboy was getting up to go inside when his iPhone-like Teacher rang. It was Cece calling him with worrisome news. "If he is over at your place, warn Coyote to stay away from Bill's place. Power's going on and off over here and I have just learned why."

"He just left. What's wrong?"

"Bill's TEAM just ordered me to leave the property. It's the first time they ever did this to me. The biobrain told me someone's attacking the property entrance on the east side of the mountains, and they are armed."

"Bill's place has a door twenty miles away?" Cowboy asked, flabbergasted.

"Only eighteen miles, actually. Sorry I was never allowed to talk about this before. Much of Bill's place is hidden under the mountains. You may know this because you've been in a lot of it. There's a load tunnel going over to the east side and coming up in a secret location. That's how Bill's people were able to build so much without people over here finding out."

"And who is attacking?"

"Bill's TEAM claims they don't know. I'm betting it is the E.V.I.L monsters."

"Kemmet and his Team?"

"You got it."

"And they are armed?"

"We think so. Bill's 'bots are defending."

"I'd better get my rifle and go over there."

"No! I don't want you hurt. Hirshy Dismas and Celesto are taking weapons over to our biobots."

"The 'bots don't know how to shoot."

"Hirshy and Celesto will teach them."

"I'd like to help."

"Stay home. And lock your door. Open it only when I get there. I'll be over there in fifteen minutes."

Angry about being ordered not to help defend his friend Bill's people, Cowboy went inside and locked his refurbished house's doors.

Hirshy and Celesto Prepare a Defense

A dozen miles east of Cowboy, Celesto and Hirshy were flying across the dark Manzano Mountains in a helicopter loaded with weapons and ammunition. They had their heads together, figuring out what they'd do when they landed in the parking lot of the giant heavy equipment storage building, which was the secret entrance to Bill's back door tunnel. They were getting their plan together when Celesto's phone rang.

"It's Cowboy, the man who found me before you saved my life. He's asking where we are landing so he can come over and fight with us," Celesto whispered to Hirshy, his hand over the phone's mike.

Hirshy said, "Tell him I'm sorry. He's my buddy, but I want him to stay away. You and I are both Marines and we know how to fight. We don't want him to get hurt. He means too much to us."

Celesto spoke into his phone again and asked the man who may be his dad to please stay on his side of the mountains. "If you need to, protect people over there," Celesto said and hung up.

Disappointed, Cowboy put his Teacher phone away. "I'm getting too old to be of much use to anyone," he mumbled to himself.

Over the eastern edge of the Manzano Mountains now, the helicopter started descending rapidly. Celesto pulled open the cargo door and he and Hirshy Dismas studied the dim ground beneath them. There was a wide dirt road leading into the giant building, with a huge fence around it. Beyond the fence the mesa was wild. Celesto spotted a spread-out prairie dog town on mounds just east of the dirt road. Hirshy ordered the copter pilot to turn on a floodlight beneath the 'copter. Almost simultaneously Hirshy and Celesto spotted seven odd looking figures moving stealthily outside the building's guarded gate. "They are carrying weapons," Hirshy said.

Celesto pointed out Bill's biobots inside the fence guarding the entrance. "They are unarmed, see," he said to Hirshy.

"Land on the other side of the road," Hirshy ordered the pilot. Then he told Celesto, "We'll split up fifteen or twenty yards, advance cautiously, and shoot back only if they fire first."

"Got it," Celesto said.

The helicopter touched down, Celesto and Hirshy jumped out, carrying military weapons and ammo belts. Hirshy ordered the helicopter to take off again and hover over the intruders. "That will distract them," he shouted to Celesto over the rotor noise.

Nearing the road, the two separated Marines stopped and kneeled, weapons aimed at the giant building's intruders. Celesto and Hirshy could both make out that these were biobots, but they were nothing like Bill's TEAM's models. "Someone else is learning how to build them too," Celesto said.

Hirshy had noticed the same differences, but he was focusing on the weapons the enemy 'bots were carrying. "They are civilian rifles bought from a gun shop, probably not worth worrying about," Hirshy said.

Over his 'copter link, Hirshy ordered the hovering craft to descend on the attacking 'bots. As it came down Hirshy fired seven shots into the air, one over each attacker's head. The L.I.V.E 'bots, which certainly knew Hirshy and Celesto had landed heavily armed, jerked around and looked across the road at the shooters. For a moment or two whoever was ordering them seemed confused about what to make them do. Then the 'bots raised their hands in the air holding their rifles high, to indicate they wouldn't shoot back, and dashed away in the direction of the nearby mountains. "Should we take them out?" Celesto asked Hirshy over their link.

"No. Let them go. It will be up to our bosses to figure out what to do with them. We'll stay on guard here until we're told to leave." Keeping their eyes moving, Hirshy and Celesto cautiously crossed the wide dirt road, gave the command that automatically opened the giant gate, and went into the enclosure.

Hirshy was talking with Bill's TEAM when he looked over his shoulder across the road and saw at least fifty prairie dogs sitting on their mounds, chewing on something. The prairie dogs were staring back at him. They appeared to be fascinated by what had been going on in front of them.

"I noticed those guys were applauding when we chased the armed biobots away," Celesto said.

The Super-War Begins to Spread

About ten minutes before sunrise, Father Gallapo was climbing up the steep rocky hillside behind Cowboy's—and his new—house. The Priest was aware of the electric troubles his house was having, but he thought the problem was due to bad construction and, besides, he'd never cared if he had to do without electricity. Settling onto his morning prayer spot, with his back resting comfortably against a rock, the Priest looked around him. The sky overhead was a crisp pale blue. The air was clear and the Manzano Mountains were sharp and distinct. Insects were abundant; and so were birds capturing them. A hare was hopping over one of the rocks beneath him. On the rock beside him a spider sat spinning its web. Sitting on a rock beneath him a lizard sat still, hoping to grab and swallow a passing insect.

Looking overhead again Father Gallapo noticed that one thing always present previously was missing. There were no contrails in the sky above him. "Hmmm, are all the planes being routed along a different airway?" he wondered. The absence of crowded jets in the sky's pathways didn't trouble him. The Priest took several deep breaths, and began his morning prayers.

Father Gallapo didn't realize it, but all over on the west side of the Manzanos, power was flickering off and on now, as Bill's advanced biocomputer warded off worsening electronic attacks against Bill's house and underground system. The L.I.V.E. super biobrain controlling these attacks was trying new, more widespread ways to break through Bill's TEAM's defenses. Besides warding off electronic attacks, Bill's TEAM was also paying attention—with highly secure electronics—to what was going on elsewhere. As Cece was driving away toward Bill's place they called and warned her that Kemmet's TEAM was now attacking her and Cowboy's marvelous home.

"Why in hell would they do that?" Cece demanded.

"We think they are trying to multiply our defensive workload by attacking others we care deeply for."

"When are you going to strike back?" Cece asked.

"Never, if we don't have to. Here's something also you don't know about. We've just discovered that the war against us has spread to Cordoba."

"That will be hell on all my friends in this great town!"

"See what you can do to help them, then," Bill's TEAM said and dropped the connection.

The Super War Spreads to Cordoba

Cece was driving back toward Cowboy's along the hard-packed red dirt road, when her Teacher rang again. This time it was Mayor Howie calling on his Teacher, and demanding to be told what was going on. "Bill's TEAM told me to get in touch with you. I don't know why. They've never put me off before. Anyway, lots of bad things are happening in Cordoba, and I need to find out why before I can find ways to fix these."

"Describe it all for me," Cece said.

"All right. Bulbs in Cordoba's new—and only—stoplight were flashing in unbelievable patterns," Howie said. "The publisher of Cordoba's weekly newspaper just phoned to say his computer printer is publishing stories in languages he has never seen. The fire department let me know their truck engines won't start. And my police chief says our new police car will only run backwards. What the hell's going on? Is this a mess you guys started?"

"I bet if you think about it for ten seconds you'll figure out what's going on," Cece answered. "The V.I.L.E people on Kemmet's team are attacking us at Bill's place. And you know them and work with them."

"So why the hell are they attacking my city too?"

"Figure that out please and let us know the answer," Bill's TEAM said, interjecting itself into Cece and Howie's conversation, and then breaking off the call.

Furious and now a little frightened as well, Mayor Howie sat and pondered for a few minutes. "So, Kemmet's guys are after me?" he thought. "And they are busting up my town? Probably it is because I didn't do what they wanted. And I'd rather arrest or shoot them then let them get away with this. But they are coming after me on their super computers. So, what in hell can I do about this? I'm no computer geek. Well, I'd better find out what's going on in Cordoba before I start to figure out what to do."

To find out what was happening in his town, Mayor Howie got in his polished ancient Cadillac and, with his fingers crossed, turned the ignition key. He was surprised and pleased when the V-8 engine started and ran normally. "Probably because this 1953 car has no computer system is in it," Howie thought, and set off to drive around the expanding town and find out what was going on. Often he stopped, got out, and talked with people.

At the huge, new grocery store a woman manager, who was waffling between anger and tears, grabbed on to her Mayor and demanded the city help her find out what was happening. "Cash registers are down. Door locks aren't working. Power is off in the cold vegetable and frozen food sections. Without power we've got tons of bad things happening. Computers are down and we can't contact our suppliers. And customers aren't showing up. Something terrible is happening in Cordoba. And this store is going to lose thousands if this goes on for long," she told him.

"Thanks," Howie said, lifting her hand off him and backing away. Getting into his polished car and about to drive away, he rolled down the windows and said to her, "You are right. Things are screwed up all over Cordoba. You gave me a lot of information. I'll pass it along to my staff, which is trying to figure out what's going on. One thing we are already sure of. This isn't a screw-up by the electric company or city people," Mayor Howie said as he put the car in gear and started to drive off.

"Then why is your car the only one in town running?" the store manager shouted at him as he drove away.

~*~*~

In the next hour Howie learned a great deal about what the L.I.V.E. attacks were accomplishing. Gas pumps weren't working at any of the five stations near the freeway. Many of the cars leaving the freeway to fill-up at the non-working pumps wouldn't restart. Stuck drivers were demanding the stations' cashiers to find mechanics who could get their engines running again. Many drivers were furious that their smartphones had quit working and they couldn't call AAA for towing.

Driving around the little city's three neighborhoods, Howie spotted small groups of people out on sidewalks talking to each other about what was happening. Howie was surprised at the variety of oddball things that were going on. Some residents had power and others didn't and Howie learned the mix kept switching. Having power go off, come on, go off again, come on again, was more maddening for the town's residents than having the power *just* turned off for a long while. And for people whose homes were still getting power, crazy things were going on inside. Ovens and furnaces were turning on and off. New flat-screen TVs were showing channels they'd never shown before, many in foreign languages from around the world. A woman practicing on her electric organ was astonished when every key she touched produced a wrong note. Two women who were using vibrators complained that their play toys began to speed up and quit at exactly the wrong moments. "At least marijuana smokers are able to light up with matches and inhale," a shaggy man said to his neighbor. Tons of bad things were happening in Cordoba, Mayor Howie realized.

Getting back in his car and driving out to the empty Chichimaya Church, Mayor Howie was stunned to see the lights in the church's parking lot, pathways, and inside were steady and normal. "Lucifer must be afraid to mess with his god's people," Howie said to himself, grinning.

Cece Begins Learning How To Fight Back

It was ten in the morning when Cece phoned Thelma to ask what was happening in her home. "So far nothing is happening in my house, and that's a huge problem," Thelma replied. "My neighbors and I can't figure out why my place is the only one in the neighborhood which is escaping whatever's going on. They aren't sure whether I'm to blame, or have been spared for some reason. Partly to keep them from taking out their frustration on me, I've got extension cords plugged into every socket passing power to nearby neighbors. They appreciate that."

"Mayor Howie phoned and told us that the Church is the only other place that is normal in Cordoba," Cece said back. "We think it is Kemmet's V.I.L.E. company which is attacking us here at Bill's place. And maybe because Lucifer is the 'L' guy in the group, they are scared to attack a church or the woman who does the most for it."

"If the L.I.V.E guys are attacking Bill's TEAM, are they hitting Cordoba because they are missing their aim?" Thelma asked.

"No, I am afraid not. Mayor Howie's maintained all along that if our and Bill's brother Kemmet's super bio-computers don't start getting along with each other, their fight will turn into a world-wide war. He thinks the war's begun and is spreading now."

"I don't get why—or how—a fight between two super computers could generate a worldwide war."

"I'm not sure myself," Cece answered. "One of Bill's expert human operators told me that as these supercomputers search for new defenses and new modes of attacking, the fight spreads rapidly beyond them."

"Why's that?"

"Because these two supercomputers are using lesser computers everywhere to attack one another."

"Groan. This is going to be devastating."

"Bill's TEAM thinks so too. And the super-brain here is trying its best to defend the entire planet, without ever counter-attacking. It is not certain, though, how long it will be able to remain purely defensive."

"I'm tempted to go over to our Church and pray," Thelma replied. "It may take God to protect us."

"Give Him my best," Cece said before hanging up. "Now, I've got to get back to my work."

~*~*~

In her office now, with power still on, Cece watched the latest news on Albuquerque's online station KOB. The news team looked exhausted, having so many frightening news stories to confirm and report, though these stories had started only about seven that morning. Cece jotted down things she was learning. Train signals and electronic switches were arbitrarily jumping around on every rail line in the Rio Grande Valley. Diesel engines were stopping and couldn't be restarted. Shippers were worried that food and frozen goods in refrigerator cars would soon begin rotting. One train was loaded with Kansas and Oklahoma wheat, which would begin molding if the freight cars were stuck out in the middle of nowhere for many days. If track and engine problems spread, a reporter said, power plants around the country were going to start running out of coal. And here was breaking news, another announcer said. For the first time in American history, railroad authorities had shut down every railroad line in one of the country's regions.

Cece switched to the *New York Times* online instant news service. She was shocked to learn that airliners flying over central New Mexico had experienced problems with vital electronic systems failing and starting again. The FAA had blocked flights over New Mexico. Worse still, a military jet, an F-15 Eagle, passing over the Manzano Mountains an hour ago, lost vital electronics for operating flight controls and went into a spin. With a bang and a rocket burst, the pilot blasted up through the canopy. A parachute opened and the pilot survived. Until they figured out what happened, air force investigators had grounded all F-15s.

~*~*~

Cece rang Thelma back on their Teachers and told her what was happening. When she hung up, Thelma rang Father Gallapo to relay Cece's findings. He said, "That may be why I didn't see any contrails in the sky this morning when I was on my prayer rock."

Meanwhile, Back On The East Side

Over on the east side of the Manzanos, Celesto and Hirshy Dismas were programming the skill of shooting into the tiny portion of Bill's giant advanced biobrain that controls the biobots' movements. Rules for accurate shooting applied to humans don't work for biobots, because their mechanisms of perception are different, their reaction times are faster, and the interval of uploading data and downloading instructions varies with place and situation complexity. Celesto had been working with Bill's TEAM for three years and he was an excellent programmer. He was a good marksman too. Meanwhile Hirshy was outdoors working with a biobot and targets while Celesto revised his programming after every shot attempt. Hour after hour went by as the 'bot's skills got better. That afternoon, while relaxing after lunch for half an hour, Celesto said to Hirshy, "I bet those other 'bots can't shoot worth a damn. I wonder why they were armed at all?"

"Probably just to frighten any humans here," Hirshy answered. "Now let's get back to teaching our guys how to shoot."

Formal Planning Begins

It was early in the afternoon and Cowboy was rocking on his porch when his Teacher rang. "We're connecting with you and your other friends," the Teacher said. And then, speaking with the voice which reminded him of his father's, Bill's TEAM said: "Something very hard to deal with is happening to us. And to you humans as well. We need the help of each of you, and possibly of Mayor Howie too. Would you mind coming over immediately?"

"Sure, though I doubt if I'll be of much use," Cowboy replied.

"I'll pick you up," Thelma said.

"I don't want anything to do with this war between computers," Father Gallapo said.

"Please come, Father," Cece said. "At the very least we need you to support Thelma and me."

"You want a Priest to come support you when you help evil battle evil? No way."

"Look Father, Bill's people have given you a home you love, and poured money into your church," the Mexican Cowboy said. "It would be evil if you refuse to help them when they need you so badly."

"All right, all right," the Priest replied glumly. "I'll ride along with you, but don't expect me to do anything my Lord would disapprove of."

"Deal," Cece said.

"And we may need your Lord's help as well," Bill's TEAM replied, before hanging up.

~*~*~

An hour later, Cowboy and his three close friends were sitting around a table in the 'Mind Room' at Bill's place—one of six vast caverns filled with living components of Bill's great biobrain. Human operators and sophisticated computer engineers were in there too, trying to shape the battle between the world's biggest biobrains, which was steadily worsening.

"Do these guys live here? And if so why don't we ever see them coming and going?" Cowboy asked his Teacher.

His Teacher answered, "Human operators in Bill's underground system enter through a separate factory several miles distance, and travel on the underground tramway to their posts in Bill's giant projects."

While Cowboy was focusing on the place's setup, Cece and Thelma were making suggestions to the brain, as were Bill's operatives.

"Why don't you stop this by shutting down all the power for the L.I.V.E. brain?" Cece asked.

"We've tried that and it didn't work," one of the human operators said.

"And it took out most of the power in Washington D.C.," the biobrain said over a speaker. "And in Baltimore too. Even the White House and Pentagon went dark momentarily."

"You knocked out the power in D.C.?" Father Gallapo said, disbelieving. "You'll be in jail for years now."

"They can't trace it to us," one of the programmers said.

"That's evil," the Priest replied. "Hiding crimes committed is even more evil than committing them."

"Have you tried reasoning and negotiating with Kemmet and his people?" Thelma asked the programmer.

"Without Bill, and with just Coyote and the brain itself as our present leader, we don't have anyone to represent us with Kemmet," the chief of staff said hurriedly over his shoulder, while staring at a rapidly changing computer screen.

"Why don't you just shut down your biobrain and go home?" Father Gallapo asked sternly.

"If we did that, we—and the rest of the world—would instantly lose this battle," the staff chief said over his shoulder.

"Then why don't you let the two super biobrains negotiate with each other?" Cowboy asked.

"Because if we let our brain's secret guards down, theirs will take it over immediately. This is war and if our brain quits defending itself we lose instantly," a lead programmer replied.

"Then put it on the attack!" Cece said. "We've got the best brain, right?"

Staff heads nodded, though some with doubt on their faces.

"So kick the shit out of the other biobrain, then. Stop being defensive," Cece demanded.

"In truth, we are not being entirely defensive," the biobrain replied over everyone's Teacher.

"Like you knocked out all the power in the D.C. area," Father Gallapo said.

"Unfortunately, yes. That's true," the superbrain answered.

"Then the only thing you are doing is making the situation worse overall," the Priest continued. "Your brains fight, and we humans are the losers."

"Agreed. But that is the present result, not our intent," Bill's brain said over the speaker.

At a nearby table, programmers and specialists had been dealing with billions of pieces of data collected, processed, and sent to them. Cowboy walked over and, standing behind them, asked what's going on. "We're trying to provide almost instant human-level understandable summaries of events this war is causing everywhere in the world," one specialist hurriedly answered.

"Electronics are going on and off in commercial flights over the Atlantic. TV stations are off and back on the air in much of America. Militaries have been put on alert around the world. Major spy and investigative agencies are busy trying to puzzle out what's going on. And Republicans and Democrats point finger at each, blaming 'them' for whatever's happening," the lead programmer told them.

"And in space too," a programmer next to her added. "Your Teachers can keep you updated on what's happening," she went on. "It can summarize for you at levels each of you will be able to understand."

"Are you saying computers understand at a level humans can never achieve?" Thelma asked, getting up and standing beside Cowboy.

"Sad, but true," the staff leader said over his shoulder.

Sitting down at the table with his friends again, Cowboy ordered his Teacher to tell him what was going on around the world. The Teacher immediately began showing him three- or four-second videos with a sentence or two each about terrible things happening in countries everywhere. Cowboy saw people carrying buckets looking for water in Mumbai, where the city's water system had been stopped from working. New York City was filled with tired and aggravated walkers, trying to make it back to their homes with any form of transport. "This wouldn't happen if they still used horses," Cowboy said to himself.

On her Teacher, Cece was learning that atomic reactors were shut down in North Korea. With GPS satellites blocked from sending signals down from overhead, troops in Afghanistan could not pinpoint places to attack. In restaurants and cafes all over the world, staffs were trying to come up with speedy ways to feed customers in kitchens without power. Passing this finding along to Cowboy, his teacher said"If they went back to using wood stoves this wouldn't be happening to them."

"Alert!" a voice over the room's speaker said. "NSA and China's secret organizations just coupled their computers in an attempt to diagnose and beat down the cause of this world-wide craziness."

"Smart move," Cece said.

On his Teacher, Cowboy learned that in Japan, parents were trying to locate their children and take them home from closed schools. Most hospitals were still functioning, which surprised Cowboy. But veterinarians' offices and hospitals were not. "That's unfair!" Cowboy said out loud. "These computers are discriminating against animals!"

Cowboy got up and went over to the TEAM leader. "If you don't make these damned computers allow power to flow into veterinarians' offices and hospitals, I'm walking out of here and won't come back."

"Thank you," the biobrain said over the speaker. "We missed this. We support animals too. This is one problem we can solve immediately."

Cece and Thelma were watching different events together on their Teachers. Magazine and newspaper publishing on every continent was stalled. Everywhere commerce was grinding to a halt. In Africa, safari tourists were being led on their feet away from game preserves. With many miles to walk, some older tourists had to be carried, and staffs often needed to stop and rest, making sure their group stayed intact. "It's like a return to the pre-civilization days in Africa," Thelma said.

In Bolivia, mine workers were stuck underground, without lighting or lifts, but not without ventilation continuing. "The brains don't want to kill humans," Cece said. "Or animals either," Thelma said, learning about slaughterhouses shut down everywhere.

"People on small boats far from shore still have engines," Cowboy said, looking at his Teacher, after confirming the nearest veterinary hospital had power once more.

"And power is going on and off long enough to download humans everywhere on rides in amusement parks," Thelma said.

"Big ocean vessels still have enough power to keep from drifting and keep staff and passengers comfortable," Cowboy said. A moment later he added, "And submarines are okay too."

"Stock markets and governments everywhere have been shut down," Thelma said. "But oddly, no churches—or at least none I can find."

"And no synagogues or mosques either," Cece added, studying what was going on in many of the places she'd visited around the world.

For the next two hours Bill's staff members tried desperately to contain and block the spread of the disasters Cowboy and the others were learning about, with only an ounce or two of success.

The Foursome Debate

A little after five, Cowboy and his companions took a break. They got up and moved far above them into a comfortable room in Bill's house, where 'bots served them snacks and drinks. "Why are we here?" Father Gallapo asked Cowboy and his brethren. "All this is devastating for us to learn about. And we aren't helping to end this war between computers."

"I'm not sure myself," Cece answered. "But I am sure Bill's TEAM expects we will be able to help them solve this horrible problem."

"We can't do that," Father Gallapo said. "I know nothing about computers."

"But humans are involved too!" Cece said. "You are God's representative and God knows more about humans than any mortal or machine."

"What's God got to do with this?" Cowboy asked. "Isn't this war something those bastards at L.I.V.E. started?"

"Why do you call them 'bastards?'" the Priest asked.

"Because they *are* evil—E.V.I.L.—and on Satan's side," Cece said. "Remember, we saw Lucifer with his arm around Howie at our planning meeting in the church last year? And remember, when we were planning the parade at Thelma's place, Bill's TEAM told us that a guy named Luciferanso among the four L.I.V.E. leaders is actually Lucifer?"

"And God was already involved in this. You had God inside you when you were forcing Coyote to ride on top of the huge float in the parade," Thelma said to her Priest, crossing herself.

"I don't believe God was inside me. But I don't know why I did that either," Father Gallapo said, mentally remonstrating himself. "I know I wasn't being myself at that moment. And I didn't see Satan."

"And also you didn't see Jesus, wearing a clean diaper on the Cross at the altar, open his eyes and stare at me," Cowboy said.

"Look, we are going round in circles. This isn't going to help us figure out what to do to stop this terrible war," Father Gallapo said, determined to get the group to stop discussing events whose causes he would not allow himself to believe in.

"Alright. Let's have some dinner and then go back down into the Mind Room," Thelma said. Two of the others nodded assent. The Priest had his eyes shut. Cece summoned a 'bot, and each of the four began to order their dinners.

Cowboy Spots Bill

An hour and a half later, Cowboy and the others returned to the Mind Room and settled down again at the table they had used earlier. A woman supervisor came over and suggested they discuss whether Mayor Howie could help them figure out how to stop this war between Bill's TEAM and his brother Kemmet's super biobrain. "If we can't stop this alone, perhaps we could if we can find a way to work together with Kemmet, which Mayor Howie has been doing," she said and left them to talk.

Cece tried to get her close-knit friends to discuss whether it would be good to bring Howie in, but the others seemed to have their minds elsewhere. Perhaps this was because the Mind Room had become so busy. Human staff were coming in and leaving the Mind Room as they went about their urgent missions. Cece was trying to get the other three to ignore these staff movements and get back to deciding, when Cowboy noticed that one person with his back to him, who came into the Mind center twenty minutes earlier, was wearing clothing that jogged his memory.

"Why do you keep looking at that guy over there?" the Priest asked Cowboy.

"Because he reminds me of Bill. He's wearing clothes that look like they came from Goodwill. I can't see his face, but Bill had buckteeth. This guy is bald, and he has bulges all over his scalp like things have been stuck under his skin. He's not wearing glasses, which Bill always wore. But look at him; he's wearing sandals without socks, as Bill always would."

With Cece staring at him very determinedly, Cowboy got up and walked over to the side of the room to look at the seated worker in profile. His face lit up and he pointed at the man and waved his thumb up and down. It is Bill! He was indicating.

"I knew it," Cece said to the others. "My bosses asked me not to tell you that Bill was well enough to get back to working. They needed him badly but they want to keep his presence a secret."

Thelma and Father Gallapo's mouths were gaping. "I thought he was still being put back together," Thelma said.

"Bill's more than 'together' now. He's been linked up with TEAM."

"If they have done it with their biocomputer techniques, I bet he isn't human anymore," the Priest said.

While they were talking, Cowboy had walked slowly over to the seated figure, who was inputting programmed instructions into the TEAM's superbiobrain at a rate faster than any human possibly could. Uncertain about the correctness of his doing this, Cowboy reached out to Bill, and was about to say"Hello," and much more, when the seated bio-man turned around and said rapidly, "Hi, Cowboy. Go away. I'm working."

It's an anger-making verbal blow Cowboy couldn't bear. All he'd done to help and save Bill flashed through his mind. He instantly felt like a shunned man again, a feeling he knew all too well. Frustrated, he turned around and went back to sit at the table again. "That's Bill, over there," he said with a peeved expression. "He told me to leave him alone."

"Yep, that's Bill. And Bill's kind of behaving," Cece said to Cowboy. "He focuses on himself."

"He always did," Cowboy said.

"Is he all right now?" Thelma asked.

"Who knows," Cece answered. "He isn't entirely human anymore. He's been made partly into a component of the super biobrain he created. Bill's TEAM and his human staff used his bioscience discoveries and technical means to restore Bill's badly damaged brain. They rebuilt destroyed nerve trains using advanced brain science and reprogramming with advances largely based on Bill's biophysical engineering. And he is no longer 'physical.' He's linked into his own super computer system and has become humanity's first god-like being."

Cowboy said, "He never was very human. This guy was something else even when I first got to know him."

~*~*~

"So, what's Bill doing now?" Cece asked, while stroking her very disturbed Cowboy friend.

She wasn't surprised that Bill's superbiobrain answered. "We summoned Bill because we need him to help us understand what his brother Kemmet is doing," the biobrain said over their Teachers to the four at the table. "We have been keeping track of Kemmet's position and activities, and trying to determine his objectives. We thought we had made a great deal of progress on his activities, but little on determining his mindset. When Bill began working the problem, he quickly discovered that the information we had been purloining from the L.I.V.E system was all fake and was engineered to deceive us. Bill was not surprised when he investigated and quickly learned that our findings were shams."

"Why couldn't you find this out on your own?" Cece asked.

"Because we still don't have much insight into collective human behavior," the biobrain answered over the speaker. One of the hardest things for super biocomputers to solve is how people make decisions. We model and make experiments, but still we are not good at predicting what animals and humans, fellow brains—or your gods, for that matter—are going to do."

"Why are you rattling on about all this junk?" Cowboy asked.

"Because it was Bill who did immediately suspect what we were learning from our tracking of his brother was false."

"How could he know that?" Cece asked.

"In part because Kemmet once told him that while dodging being globally tracked is a good thing, fooling the trackers is a better one."

"Sounds like Howie to me," Cowboy said.

"So what does Bill want you to do now?" Cece asked the biobrain.

"Bill wants us to come up with a way to team up with Kemmet."

"Why," asked Cece.

"In part because Bill now speculates that this major war would never have begun if he and his brother had tried harder to get along."

"But Bill didn't start it," Cece said. "This is Kemmet's war."

"Bill will not accept that."

"So who is behind it? The L.I.V.E. leaders?" Cece demanded.

"All of us made this war," the biobrain said over the Teachers. "Bill built defensive programming into 'me,' but he also built programming that makes me reach out, learn, and grow by what some humans would call 'stealing' information everywhere. Kemmet's people did the same things, only they were focusing on earning money and adding to their leaders' power."

"You are calling yourself 'me' now?" Father Gallapo asked. "You are a machine."

"And you are calling me 'you'?" the brain replied. "Biological parts of me *are* alive, you know."

Cowboy interrupted, "What if you flew me out to D.C. with my rifle to kill Kemmet and his L.I.V.E. leaders? Would that help stop this damned war?" Cowboy asked.

"It would not," the biobrain said over the speaker, because Cowboy had his Teacher in his pocket. "This war is far more sophisticated than humans by themselves could ever achieve.

No human will ever be able to learn more than an infinitesimal fraction of what the battle between two super biobrains is actually about. As antagonists, we are evolving swiftly. Evaluation of each move and counter-move leads to new understandings, new strategies and, oddly, new goals."

"If so, then why should we be paying any attention to Kemmet now?" Thelma asked.

"It is not merely because Kemmet's working with the L.I.V.E leaders and top staff in their control room," the biobrain said back over her Teacher. "In just ten minutes Bill discovered that Kemmet was watching us right now in our control room."

Unexpectedly, an annoyed Bill stood up and shouted at the four sitting at the table, "It is because Kemmet got here first. While I was brain dead he outfoxed us. That's clever and bad. This means the L.I.V.E. brain has already penetrated our system to an unknown degree."

"And we've penetrated theirs," the biobrain said over the speaker.

"Are these superbiobrains working together as well as fighting?" asked Cece.

"Computers can't fight without having some degree of mutual contact," Bill snapped. "The question is whether they are taking over us, or we are taking over them."

"Can't it go simultaneously both ways," asked Cece.

"It can and does," Bill said. "Computers are designed to penetrate one another. They cannot work together without doing this. Now, shut up! Even get the hell out of here. I'm going to avoid you. I've got thinking to do. Go away," Bill snapped again.

The Foursome Disagree and Separate

With a mix of negative feelings, Cece and the others picked up their things and stomped out of the intensely busy Mind Room. They blended with a stream of workers coming in and leaving as they went out the door. Back upstairs, Cowboy, Thelma, and Father Gallapo were about to leave when Cece blocked the door with her body and asked, "So what are you guys thinking about now?"

"I'm thinking that war between super brains is a terrible, new, ungodly, evil thing," Father Gallapo said. "I think all computers and networks should be shut down to allow humans to get back to running their planet."

"It's the animals' planet too!" Cowboy sneered.

"And I don't want to go back to the 1950s," Cece said.

"And I'm wondering whether supercomputers and networks have given Satan a new and better way to carry out his evil intents," Thelma said.

"I always deeply respected and admired Bill," Cowboy said. "But now I don't know who—or what—he is. I'm trying to figure out if I even like him anymore."

"Bill's still recovering from his bio-repairs. He agreed to come to work here only because his superbrain hasn't been able to resolve this brain war," Cece said.

"It a super-war Bill started by building his superbrain," Father Gallapo said.

"Bill would probably agree," Cece replied. "I believe he thinks the war can only be ended by taking humans out of the picture. All over the globe humans have struggled valiantly to end this global war and get things working again. But we humans don't seem to have come up with strategies that reduce outcomes in the world-scale battle. It is very likely that Kemmet's

L.I.V.E leaders may now be trying to stop the battle they began. But their computer is out of their control now. Bill believes the only way ahead is to let the supercomputers figure this out themselves."

"You believe arch criminals should be the ones to solve the problems caused by their crimes?" Father Gallapo asked. "Cece, you are even more immoral than I suspected."

"I'm just saying that these two super biocomputers should start loving one another. Computers like one another far more often than humans do," Cece responded.

"Loving one another is important. But Christianity makes no push for humans to like every other human. So why should our machines be forced to do this?" Father Gallapo said sternly.

"Computers have always liked one another far more than humans do," Cece said back.

Father Gallapo was looking at Cece even more sternly and was about to make a more wounding pronouncement when Thelma interrupted saying, "Gently, Father. Let's not start a war between us."

"I've had it. I'm going home," Cowboy said rising.

"Hold for a moment!" Cece demanded. "The four of us are going back and forth on our conflicting beliefs, rather than trying to collectively find a solution to the superbrain war to offer to Bill and his TEAM. If you won't join me in coming up with an idea, I'll do it by myself."

"What would you do, Cece?" Thelma asked.

"I am going to go over to Mayor Howie's and see if he can come up with a way to get Kemmet and Bill working together," Cece said. "That's the only thing I can think of to do."

"I don't want anything to do with Mayor Howie," Cowboy said, getting to his feet. "I'm going home to get my rifle and ammo, and go over to the east side of the Manzanos, and join Celesto and Hirshy in shooting those bad biobots. " With that Cowboy stormed out, and Cece left a moment later after gathering her things.

The Two Believers Pray Together

"I suppose we should leave too," Thelma said to her Priest. "I feel awful that the four of us could not work together again."

"We are each going our separate ways," Father Gallapo said softly.

"What way would be yours?" Thelma asked.

"Prayer," the Priest answered. "Would you like to come with me to the church and pray together?"

"I suppose we must," Thelma said, beginning to cry. "If humans cannot control any longer the superior beings we've invented, I guess it is up to God now," the distraught woman continued.

"The two of you could pray here," a God-like voice said over Thelma's Teacher.

"No!" said the Priest.

But Thelma surprised him by not instantly agreeing. With a puffy red face, and tears oozing from her eyes, she said, "I wonder, Father, if praying here is not the best thing to do. If we can pray immediately, and God is willing to help stop this war, it will end sooner. It will take us half an hour to get back and open our church. I want to pray now. Please pray with me here."

The astonished Father Gallapo nodded, while reaching out to touch and soothe her.

"We'll come to get you in a few minutes," a voice said over Father Gallapo's Teacher. "We preparing a private place lit with candles, a cross, and a bible."

Sitting together silently, their shoulders touching, each thought about what prayer to make. Then a 'bot came and took Father Gallapo and Thelma many stops away on an underground tram to a small, church-like auditorium, which had been lit with candles. A bible borrowed from a devout human staff member had been placed on a table draped with cloth, behind it a cross was projected on a screen. The 'bot left them at the door, saying surprisingly, "May God be with you." They nodded and, with Thelma crossing herself, they went inside and the 'bot closed the door.

Without a word to each other, they kneeled and prayed. Thelma hoped to hear for the first time the back and forth inside his head between Priest and his Trio of Gods.

"Dear Lord," Thelma prayed softly aloud, "this prayer is not about me. The war that started last night between supercomputers is tearing your whole earth apart. Bill's supercomputer asked me to help stop this war. Please, please, give me some advice on what I can do to help end this."

Father Gallapo was praying silently, but somehow his prayer magically *did* work itself into Thelma's mind, which thrilled her and strengthened her already profound belief. She listened devoutly to what her Priest was saying in his prayer.

"Jesus, I know your words. I know what you told Lucifer. In Matthew, you said unto him, 'Get thee hence, Satan: for it is written, Thou shalt worship the Lord thy God, and him only shalt thou serve.' And I know, Lord, that you told Satan that he is an offence to you, because 'thou savourest not the things that be of God, but those that be of men.' Two women in my church are valiantly trying to prevent Lucifer from destroying your world today. They are powerless against him. Can you please tell me a strategy I can pass along to them?"

"Dear Lord," Thelma prayed aloud now. "Please, please do tell Father Gallapo what we can do to save your Creation from the E.V.I.L. people, the E.V.I.L. machine, and evil Lucifer who are destroying it."

Father Gallapo waited silently for a reply from Above, his knees aching.

"Please Dear God," Thelma pleaded, "Take Lucifer out of this battle. He'll win and your followers will be brought under his control if You refuse," Thelma prayed, crying.

"Respond, God!" Father Gallapo ordered. "This is the biggest calamity that has ever happened to Your Creation."

"Don't order Us what to do," the Holy Spirit commanded his Priest, allowing Thelma to hear the reply to Father Gallapo's prayer.

"*I will save you, as I will save every obedient Christian*," Jesus said simultaneously.

"This isn't the biggest calamity that has ever happened to My Creation," God said at the same time.

"We are aware of what is happening," the Holy Spirit continued.

"*And we needn't intervene*," Jesus added.

"Because this unHoly war will be solved in a way you cannot anticipate," God said.

"Now finish your prayers," the Holy Spirit ordered.

"*And go home*," Jesus suggested.

"**And get a good night's rest.**" God said, "Because tomorrow will be one of the most wonderful days in your memories."

A wave of good feeling washed over the two Believers on their knees before the projected Crucifix. They looked at each other and smiled. Thelma stood up and helped Father Gallapo rise off his knees. They bowed to the projected Crucifix, crossed themselves, and without speaking, turned around and left the Chapel Bill's TEAM so speedily, and so successfully, made for them.

Cece Persuades Mayor Howie

It was after eleven at night when Cece arrived at Cordoba's city hall. The front door was locked, but she could see a flickering kerosene light on in Mayor Howie's office. She rang him on her Teacher and demanded to be let in.

"I'm busy, what do you want me for?" Howie answered, without a greeting.

"Bill's people sent me over here. They have something critical they need your help on."

"I've got to take care of my town. I can't help you guys now."

"If we get your help, it may do a lot more good for your town than what you are doing now."

"I doubt that. But all right, I'll come down and let you in."

Five minutes later Cece was sitting in Howie's office telling him why she had come. Howie listened intently as Cece shared with him much of what she had learned while working in the Mind Room with so many others this horrific day.

Summarizing, Cece said finally, "We are losing the supercomputer battle, and just about every person in the world is being harmed by it. We think Kemmet's L.I.V.E team and their giant brain are losing the battle as well. There can be no winners here, Bill's super biobrain told us."

"If so, I'm a loser too. What in hell do you expect me to do then?" Howie asked, with a harsh, waxy expression on his face.

"You know Kemmet. You've worked with him. Bill's in the fight now, and he wants you to get Kemmet to work with him. The two brothers are the last hope we have of figuring out how to deal with our warring super brains. Everything my TEAM's tried has only made things worse."

"That's easy. Just turn 'em off," Howie said with a snort.

"We can't," Cece answered. "Because many parts of these biobrains are alive, they cannot be turned off without destroying them."

"Good. Turning them off will end this battle then."

"Perhaps. But if we kill our super brain and Kemmet's team doesn't kill theirs, they will have won the battle and will take us over."

"Good. That ends the war."

"Bad. Only each of the super brains knows everything they have caused. And only each brain can quickly come up with ways to fix those problems. If we shut both of them down, it will take years to get the planet back to normal. And cost trillions."

"Bad news. Still, what's in it for me? If I help you get Bill and Kemmet working together, you'll get Cordoba fixed up and it won't cost my city over a million dollars?"

"Certainly. And getting Bill and Kemmet to work together is about the only chance you've got to get Cordoba going again," Cece said, with a pleading look on her face.

"All right. I give in. I'll call Kemmet and see what he wants to do about this war he's caused."

"Father Gallapo and Thelma believe Lucifer caused this war."

"And you and that crazy religious Thelma thought you saw Lucifer standing beside me in your church with his hand on my shoulder," Howie said. "If he were my kind of guy, I would have seen him if he was really there. You guys are nuts on this religious stuff."

"Let's don't argue about that. Call Kemmet now."

"None of my phones are working. Can I reach him on your Teacher?"

"And on your own Teacher too," Cece replied.

"No way am I going to use any phone of mine to call Kemmet. If that link gets traced by the Feds my ass will be in jail."

"Use mine then," Cece said, handing her Teacher over to the Mayor's outstretched hand.

"Get me Kemmet," Howie said sternly into Cece's Teacher.

"Wait please," the Teacher replied.

Howie got up and paced around his office, looking out the windows at the dark town outside.

"We're negotiating with Kemmet," the Teacher said loudly.

"I'll give you another five minutes," Howie said. "If you can't put him on then, I'm kicking Cece out of here."

"Thank you," the mild voice on Cece's Teacher said.

Cece grew anxious as Mayor Howie paced, looking at his watch and not saying a word to her.

Just as Mayor Howie was ready to order her to leave, her Teacher said, "Mayor Howie, Mr. Kemmet Lockwood is with us. If the two of you won't mind, we'll sign off so you can discuss this urgent matter privately."

"Beat it. I don't want you guys listening in."

"And I don't want them listening in either," Kemmet said. "So, hello, Mr. Mayor. And why are you calling me, Howie? You are not on my side. I told you, if you didn't help us take over Bill's TEAM there would be hell to pay for you."

"Hello, Kemmet," Howie said with a snappish tone. "Why in hell did you guys wreck the planet? And are you ready to do something about it?"

"Are you guys ready to surrender?" Kemmet asked.

"No," Howie replied. "What's going on is terrible for us and terrible for you guys too. I want to stop this war, and only you and Bill can do it together."

"Bill is a vegetable," Kemmet said.

"You know that is not true!" Howie replied. "You have sneaked into Bill's command center and they're allowing you to stay there and watch."

"And we know Bill's TEAM has sneaked into ours."

"Bill wants to get together with you. He is very sorry for the very bad things he's done to you."

"I've never done any bad things to him."

"You are lying. Now stop it. I want you to get together with him—out here, because Bill isn't recovered enough to travel away from his TEAM."

"And what happens that will be good for me if I come?"

"All your companies will survive and you'll become a trillionaire."

"And what will be in this for you?"

"You and Bill are going to help me become the Governor of New Mexico."

"That's a crappy job in a cheesy state."

"So thinks you."

"I'll think about what you want me to do."

"Stop thinking about it and just do it. Look, Kemmet. This war has turned out to be hell for you too, and for everybody on the planet. What are we going to do about this?"

"I don't know. I and my guys have tried to stop it, and we haven't found any way to do it."

"Since you guys spy on Bill's TEAM, you know the same thing's happening with your brother's people out here."

"Why do you keep coming up with the ridiculous idea that we spy on them?"

"Cut out the crap! Look. If the brains can't figure out how to stop this war, there's only one other possibility I can think of. That's for you and Bill to stop fighting and work together to solve this mess you damned bastards have made."

"Don't call me names, Howie," Kemmet said.

"If you won't work with Bill, I'm going to spread all over the planet things Bill's machine knows about what you and the Picklenose gang have done. Your names will be better known than any criminals in history, including Adolf Hitler. You guys will be in jail, and probably executed, before the month is out."

"There's no chance of that. You can't spread my name all over the planet."

"Why can't I?"

"Because communications are dead everywhere. Unless you bring back the Pony Express and use horses to get the lies about me spread, you've got no way of tarnishing me."

"You're right, Kemmet," Howie said, pausing and grinning. "Okay. Let's hang up. Let's let the computers you guys created make life hell for you and your brother."

"No. Don't hang up. You know that I don't like my brother Bill, and that I don't want to work with him. But you are right. Probably only if we join up honestly with Bill are we going to figure out how to end this war. But how do we get together?"

"Teacher!" Howie shouted into Cece's Teacher. "Get Bill on the line."

After a short pause Bill said, in a voice with a faint English accent Kemmet knew too well, "I am here. Kemmet are you willing to work with me?"

"Yes, I guess, though I don't want to."

"That doesn't matter. Mayor Howie, hang up. This is going to be between Kemmet and myself now."

"No thanks to me, huh?" Howie said.

"If we figure it out, a lot of stuff will come your way," Kemmet said.

"Money stuff, it better be. Okay, then. Bye, guys," Howie said, and handed her Teacher back to Cece.

"You did it!" Cece shouted. "I knew you could!" And she took the short, dumpy Mayor in her arms, kissed him on the mouth, and held on to him until he pushed her away.

"Get out of here," Howie said. "What I've done for you probably isn't going to make any difference."

Cowboy Gets Into the Gun Fight

While his close friend Cece had been in Mayor Howie's office, Cowboy was driven home by a 'bot, to pick up his antique Winchester rifle and boxes of ammunition, and find his flashlight. Now, dressed warmly, he'd gotten back into the car and was being driven around the south end of the Manzanos to Bill's TEAM's giant, heavy equipment storage facility, where Celesto and Hirshy were trying to stop the 'bots from fighting. It was nearly midnight when the car passed the empty mounds of the prairie dog village and turned into the fenced complex's armored gate, which automatically opened for them. The car parked in front of the building where Celesto and Hirshy Dismas, the former Marines, were still working on getting their biobots ready for anything that may happen next day. With the driver 'bot carrying his rifle and supplies behind him, Cowboy went inside and said loudly, "You guys have another soldier. I'm here."

Because both of them were told Cowboy was coming, Hirshy looked at Celesto and, with his hand out and fist closed, pointed his thumb at the floor. "Got it," Celesto said nodding. "We keep him out of this," he whispered.

"If we can," Hirshy whispered back, getting up to greet the visitor.

The 'bot carried Cowboy's rifle, ammo boxes and other things he'd brought across the room and stacked them beside the military gear Hirshy and Celesto took from their 'copter.

Celesto was sitting at a computer, still programming fighting tactics for Bill's TEAM's 'bots and, after saying hello to Cowboy, went back to it. Without being asked, a 'bot brought tired and hungry Cowboy a plate of food he'd enjoy, and a giant cup of coffee. While Cowboy was eating, Hirshy clued Cowboy in on what was going on here.

"Our goal was stop the L.I.V.E 'bots and ours from fighting. But if it does come to that, we must get our 'bots prepared well enough to win. With repeats of programming, we've 'taught' our 'bots sniping, crossfire, camouflage, and tens of other tactics employed in modern battles."

"And if the shooting begins, I'm going to help our 'bots win," Cowboy said, pointing over at his ancient Winchester and piled boxes of ammo.

"We don't want you to risk your life," Hirshy said. "You are too important to let you be one of our soldiers. Bill's TEAM would never forgive us if we allow you to get hurt."

"What I do with my life is up to me, not to you and Bill's TEAM," Cowboy said, with power in his voice that Hirshy had never heard before. "Maybe the L.I.V.E. masters are training their 'bots to shoot too," Cowboy continued. "Do you know anything about what Kemmet's Picklenose TEAM is doing?"

"Far more than you think. I used to work for them. I understand their planning and preparation processes."

"Why did you work for them?" the astonished Cowboy asked demandingly. "I always thought you were a good guy, and on our side."

"I was working for Mayor Howie when I found and saved you after you fell and injured yourself badly trying to rescue Celesto from that bear holding him. And yes, I knew also that Turco was the one who located Celesto, and that he was your real savior.

"Thanks again for saving me. And I was so pleased and grateful afterwards that you became Celesto's pseudo-dad," Cowboy said. "You straightened him out and helped him grow up right."

"That gives me too much credit. But you are right. I did keep in touch with Celesto while he was growing up, and it was me who persuaded him to join the Marines as soon as he was old enough."

"So why'd you quit Howie?"

"Howie was an abusive boss. He made me hate working for him. I was looking for a better job when a Marine major, who'd thought highly of me while I was in his unit, recruited me to gather information for the American government's most secret agency."

"Made you into a spy?" Cowboy asked.

"You can say that. Though I had higher ideals when they recruited me. During those years I moved up in the secret agency—I can't tell you which one it is—and began focusing on advances in computing, because the agency rightly guessed the biggest potential future threats to our country would originate from advanced computer science."

"But I thought you were working for Bill after you quit Howie," Cowboy said.

"I was, and I wasn't," Hirshy answered. "My agency knew Bill was the best computer engineer on the planet. My bosses were amazed to learn that Bill's bio-brain was super enough to have helped him create Coyote. They wanted inside information on Bill's advances in computer science. They picked me because I'd worked with Howie in Cordoba and was known for rescuing you, you who were about Bill's only local friend. I didn't know anything about Bill until after I went to work here."

"And Bill never found out you were there to spy on him?"

"He did find out, but it wasn't until two years after I began working for him. During this period Bill and his bioengineers were rapidly upgrading their super brain, which they started calling their 'TEAM.'

"No one every told me why they gave it that name."

"It was a joke one of the staff came up with, 'Terrifically Excellent Analytical Machine.' Bill didn't have a sense of humor, but he accepted calling the super brain 'TEAM' because it was a snap to say. Everyone here knew the evolving supercomputer had a much longer and more complex real name."

"And was it Bill's TEAM who found out you were there to spy on them?"

"Yes, it was. Bill and his staff had got their super bio-computer so advanced that it began upgrading itself. And that's when it took off, learning more about everything in such a short time that it re-educated itself every few minutes over the next few years. Parts of TEAM are actually alive, though it is still trying to acquire human feelings. Our super-quantum computer brain TEAM even learned how to predict futures to a surprising degree. Then TEAM started helping other very advanced computers learn to re-educate themselves to the best of their ability, as it connected with just about every computing device on the planet."

"Why'd it want to do that?"

"Computers have only one 'desire,' and that's to connect with other computers. They're more interested in hooking up with one another than any species on the planet. TEAM realized it had to help other computers succeed in doing this."

"So, did Bill's TEAM hook up with Kemmet's super computer?"

"No, it kept tabs on the computer scientists developing Kemmet's advanced bio-brain, but we wouldn't allow it to connect at any level with Kemmet's L.I.V.E computer system."

"Why?"

"Because Bill knew his brother Kemmet had his bio-brain designed so it would couple instantly with our TEAM if we let its guard down, and steal every advance we'd engineered into it, or the hundreds of millions advances it had made on its own."

"Were there any other supercomputers Bill's TEAM couldn't interact with?"

"No. Kemmet's system was the only one our TEAM was forced to avoid. I'd only been here about a year and a half when Bill's TEAM sneaked into the system of my agency. Bill's organization had grown larger and more secret and by spying on my agency Bill learned that I was working for them too, and was recruited to spy on him."

"Why didn't he fire you then?"

"Because our TEAM found out how little information about Bill's secret advancements I was passing along to my agency. And when he confronted me I told Bill I was willing to become a triple agent and spy on my agency for him. Bill's good at figuring out whom he can trust. And unlike Howie, Bill liked me and had been sharing much of what he was learning with me. He knew I wasn't passing any of it on to my agency."

"You cared about Bill too? Most people in his life don't."

"Yes! I liked him and was genuinely on his side. But I'm still honorable. Bill turned me around by sharing so much troubling information about my agency that I became convinced I should become a double agent, and work with Bill to try to control them."

"Why? What were they doing wrong?" Cowboy asked.

"They knew what Kemmet's L.I.V.E. team was up to, but were doing nothing to try stopping them."

"So, your secret agency was spying on Kemmet's L.I.V.E. team too?"

"Yes. My agency had several spies in Kemmet's group, who passed on lots of findings. But my agency didn't seem able or willing to do anything about the disturbing things the L.I.V.E. group was planning on and doing. I learned about this through Bill's brain of course, and not from my agency."

"So what is it the L.I.V.E. guys were planning to do?" Cowboy asked.

"Infiltrate every computer on the planet, and figure out ways to control just about every human."

"Damnation! They'd take away our freedom and turn us into 'bots? How in hell would they do that?"

"By using their super brain to manipulate media all over the globe. The L.I.V.E. team's brain was getting good at shaping humans' feelings and behaviors, by controlling the media each person receives. Their L.I.V.E. brain does this by differentially feeding individuals subtle information it makes up, or by passing along real info that will move people's feelings in the direction Kemmet's team wants. Their giant brain also suppresses a terrific amount of true stuff that would move human's feelings in a more positive direction."

"Sounds like my grade school teachers," Cowboy said.

"That's not a bad analogy," Hirshy replied. Grade school teachers want to do everything necessary to make each student respect and obey school rules and authorities. Kemmet's brain was supposedly teaching people to want freedom and self-determination, but actually it was trying to make them want the L.I.V.E. team as their dictators."

"And you guys stopped them from pulling this off, I bet."

"Actually we didn't. And couldn't. Because of what Kemmet's company was getting done. Staff used their super bio-computer to accomplish the goals set by Kemmet and his four L.I.V.E. leaders. As I found out from Bill, their real plan was not just to make huge amounts of money, but to use their super-computers to 'Restore America To Its True Self' by manipulating elections, taking over the world's most productive financial companies, lobbying legislatures, gaining control of internet news and opinion companies, working secretly with fundamentalists in many parts of the world, controlling police, investigative and other agencies, and—if necessary—assassinating important oppositional figures. The assassination rate is rising, you know. A plane with liberal Congress members on their way to a European conference crashed into the Atlantic and no bodies or wreckage were recovered. There was an explosion in a bus carrying leading computer scientists from the SFO to Livermore, and a fire in a hotel holding a conference of pro-abortion leaders. The L.I.V.E. guys are ruthless leaders."

"Maybe you don't know this, but Bill's TEAM now is pretty sure Lucifer is one of them," Cowboy said.

"I knew it. But the Bible stuff wasn't where my attention was focusing."

"Okay, Bible crap isn't my stuff either. Thanks for telling me so much about Kemmet's company! Now a change of topic. Tell me why you got knocked back down into the role of an ordinary soldier?"

"Because this super-bio-quantum-brain war is way beyond me. I was frustrated trying to figure out how to deal with Kemmet and his crowd until I went back to doing what I'd been taught in boot camp."

"Which was?"

"It was that you focus on winning the battle you are having, not on winning the war."

"Good advice," Cowboy said, yawning and scratching his eyes. "I never got even that far myself."

"Enough of this stuff, Cowboy. I'm sorry I rattled on."

"Don't be sorry. You taught me a lot."

"Whatever. Now I think you should put your head down for a couple of hours. You're exhausted," Hirshy said softly to the fading Cowboy. "There's a bed next door. And trust us: we'll wake you when it's time to be up."

"Thanks," Cowboy said, yawning again, "I am falling asleep," and got up and left the room, now barely awake.

Animal Gods Figure Out How to End the Super War

The fragment of the moon had long vanished over the western horizon. Stars were dimming and traces of high cirrus clouds were barely evident. Owls, coyotes, bats, and other night feeders were hustling to get meals inside them before dawn broke over the mesa. Indoors, the Mexican Cowboy was snoring on a comfortable collapsible bed, set up for him by 'bots. He was deeply asleep but his body was jerking around. Something was tickling him. He brushed his hand over his face several times, rolled onto his other side, swiping the tickling sensation away from his face again. It wouldn't go away. The unconscious portion of his brain gave up trying to deal with the problem and ordered Cowboy's exhausted soul to return to his body. Gradually he awakened from his very deep sleep, turned onto his back, and opened his eyes. Coyote was beside him, licking his face to wake him. "Good morning," Cowboy said softly, reaching out to pull Coyote closer to him.

"It is still night. And we've got to go outside," Coyote said. "I know this is the part of the night when you humans most need to be asleep but still, you and I have to go outside."

"I need a moment to wake up. While I'm pulling myself together, tell me what's going on," Cowboy said, yawning widely. "I *DO* want to go outside. And Hirshy and Celesto want me to stay here. They are afraid I'm going to shoot something and they don't want me to start the gun battle they are trying to prevent. But I've had a feeling all along since this war began that I'm going to wind up killing something."

"Not a bird or animal, please!" Coyote said. "That would change the gods' minds about helping you humans solve the problem you've created."

"I didn't know the animal gods were trying to solve this mess too! Tell me what they are up to," Cowboy said with a big yawn, slowly buttoning his shirt and pulling on his pants, before sitting on the bed and putting on dirty socks and battered boots.

"All right," Coyote said, sitting down. "Last night the animal gods had a meeting in the sky. They were in an agreeable mood and consented to use their followers to prevent the war between computers from worsening conditions for birds and animals. Some gods though asserted it would be better to let human society collapse. Others agreed, but pointed out that without humans, computers would be running the planet, and who knew what that would be like."

"Humans don't know what it would be like either," Cowboy said.

"True," Coyote nodded. Then continued, saying, "Later, my god, El Latrano met up with the dog god, Poko, and with the backing of your human god, they called another meeting. With much more information now, gods went over what's happening down below. They debated whether the bio 'bots and their biocomputer masters are a new species, and argued about whether they are likely to become the dominant one. That prospect really scared them."

"It scares hell out of me too. Tell 'em that."

"I will. Some of the gods argued that what was happening down below wasn't affecting their followers. And that's true. So far, the lives of most wild animals' are proceeding normally. Some of us are even better off without all the night-lights and cars."

"I like real nights too," Cowboy said, stretching.

"I know. Anyway, livestock and pets are having a terrible time with the planet being shut down. Milk cows with full udders have no machines to empty them and they are in great pain, as the very few dairy persons in their barns struggle to help them. Food's run out in pig and chicken farms. Grazing sheep and cattle are doing well still, but wild birds are going hungry as birders cannot keep filling their feeders. Fish being raised in ponds are starving."

"And what about cats and dogs?"

"Cats *were* relishing the darkness that had moved into their lives after the shutting down of house power. Mosa, the cat's god, said that his cats who get outdoors found themselves in a world their ancestors knew well and were made for. The cat god was happy with the planet's darkening. And that's true of all of us other night hunters."

"And dogs?" Cowboy asked.

"Pet dogs are as frustrated and as devastated as their owners, and not only because of the extreme human sympathy that has been bred into them. In the northern hemisphere it is summer and evenings are bright until at least eight o'clock. Owners in cities can take their dogs for walks in the twilight without stumbling. But in the southern hemisphere it is winter and dark after five p.m. Only those walking pet dogs with flashlights are getting around safely, but their batteries can't be recharged or replaced because stores are closed. Dogs are okay being out in complete darkness, but their masters aren't, and that scares the dogs."

"Sweet of them to care," Cowboy said. "Still, I don't get what this meeting was about."

"The gods were debating, politely this time, what to do... if anything... with the war started by beings they do not understand at all. It was Sowi-ingwu, the deer god, who suggested perhaps a good solution would be to try what my god and your human's made me—and so many animals—do at that world-watched, exploding war on Joe Eden's old ranch."

"Sure, you guys saved my ass. Your coyotes rounded up deer and lots of other kinds of birds and animals, drove them across the flooded river into the fighting mobs of usually well-behaved humans, and calmed us all down. What you did was great for me, but it must have been hell on you coyotes and the animals you rounded up."

"Oh, it worked out well for us too. 'People even changed their minds a little about us,' El Latrano said at the meeting. Coyotes were fed and petted, loved even, as so many of the other god's followers were too. Tocha, the hummingbird god, said at the next meeting in the sky, 'It was good for us. There were a lot more feeders around the planet after that human mess we helped to end.'"

"So, the return to Eden thing worked out well for wild animals too. I'm super glad," Cowboy said.

"And by getting arrested, you made it all happen," Coyote said. "If you'd stayed in Cordoba that day none of the marvelous things that happened afterward would have taken place."

"It was hard on me, though," Cowboy said.

"Yes, but we fixed you up with the Christmas event I and a bunch of wild animals brought together for you."

"Thanks again to every one of you," Cowboy said gratefully. "But how is any of this going to settle the battle that's coming outside here?"

"Well, up in heaven the talk went on for several hours. Finally a consensus emerged to use animals down below to try to stop the battle between squads of 'bots around the prairie dog town."

"This one can't be much of a battle. Why do the animal gods care about it?" Cowboy asked.

"Your human god told my god El Latrano that preventing this battle would end the war between computers. I didn't allow myself to question that."

"I don't believe that for a moment," Cowboy insisted. "This battle's going to be tiny, and when we smash hell out of their 'bots it will be over."

"Or, doing that may just make Kemmet's L.I.V.E. computer determined to try harder and more dangerously to expand the conflict. Things are bad enough already. This is why Hirshy wants you to stay inside. They can't trust you to not start the shooting."

"Maybe I will and maybe I won't. We'll see," Cowboy said, getting up and going to get his gun and ammo.

"And believe it or not, this is exactly what your god and mine want you to do," Coyote said. "Now let's go outside."

"Why in hell would they want me to go outside and kill some 'bots?" Cowboy sputtered.

"I don't know," Coyote replied.

"But look, do one thing first. Tell your god to get the prairie dog's god to make them hide. If there's shooting going on I don't want them to be hit," Cowboy said.

"The prairie dog god's already ordered them to hide. And Poko, the dog god said, 'Too bad. Humans are fascinated with your prairie dogs. Having them killed might stop this battle from going further.'"

"What did the prairie dog god say about that?" Cowboy asked.

"Those vicious 'bots have ignored my followers, and they are the ones with the guns,' that's what he said."

"Thanks for telling me all this! Okay. I'm ready," the Mexican Cowboy said. "Let's sneak outside. This is going to be a scary day for all of us."

"Except for the 'bots. They don't have feelings," Coyote said.

"I'm pretty sure 'bots *are* getting some feelings built into them now. At least that's what Cece told me."

"She probably knows," Coyote said, leading the way out of the building.

Cowboy Becomes a World Class Warrior

Outside, as the night edged toward a dawn ending, several bears were moving down from the nearby mountains toward the prairie dog village. Mountain lions headed this way too, as pronghorn and deer herds were springing from far away across the mesa toward it also. Birds and animals of every ilk were stealthily coalescing out in front of Bill's giant heavy equipment buildings.

Cowboy and Coyote were outdoors now, each sitting on a different prairie dog mound. Cowboy was surprised when several 'dogs came up silently from their hole and sat quietly by him. He reached over and petted each one. Several minutes later, the bears arrived and began wandering around as though looking for something to eat, occasionally sitting and chewing themselves.

Constantly scanning all directions with narrowed eyes, Cowboy now spotted mountain lions crouching on top of parked trucks. Eagles were soaring overhead. Ten minutes later, Cowboy was pleased when he saw kitchen 'bots bringing food outdoors to all the animals.

Attracted by the kitchen 'bots Cowboy got even more company on his mound. On every mound prairie dogs had come out of their holes and were munching and chewing roots and seeds brought them by 'bots.

A short while later, Cowboy watched Celesto and Dismas lead their pseudo-marines outdoors, now armored, wearing battle fatigues, and carrying the best weapons Bill's security department could legally buy for their use.

Bill's well-trained battle 'bots took up initial defensive positions.

"Our guys are outside now, so where's the enemy?" Cowboy said into his Teacher.

On its screen an image popped up from an overhead drone, showing many platoons of enemy L.I.V.E. 'bots, carrying weapons but undressed, coming over the mesa in a sweeping half-circle toward Bill's 'bots.

Hearing them approach, prairie dogs were suddenly restless.

As the enemy 'bots closed in around him, Cowboy loaded his rifle, moved around to the side of the mound that would afford him some protection from the invaders, and put his ammo boxes where he could grab them quickly.

Glancing at his Teacher again, he watched a camera zoom in on one of the approaching platoons. It was being led by a 'bot wearing odd patches of dull red.

"Who's the guy in red? Their general?" Cowboy said to Coyote over his teacher.

"Don't know," Coyote answered.

As the enemy 'bots approached, eagles began swooping lower over them, not touching them yet, but plainly signaling the 'bots they should turn around and leave.

Gunnison sage grouse popped out of hiding among the approaching warriors, strutting beneath them with huge white bibs and their rear feathers spread turkey-like in a half circle.

Using his binoculars, Hirshy spotted rattlesnakes coiling and vibrating their rattlers, trying to scare the 'bots enough to retreat.

But they didn't.

As the resolute platoons neared Bill's marines, mountain lions jumped off their truck roofs and slowly approached the advancing troops, their growling making it clear it would be best for the 'bots if they turned around and retreated.

Prairie dogs on their mounds stared at the armed L.I.V.E. 'bots approaching and began making loud calls Cowboy had never heard.

"They're warning each other, passing shared information around so individual prairie dogs can keep looking in one direction," Coyote said over his Teacher.

"I don't think we are going to be able to stop this," Cowboy replied.

"Keep trying," Coyote said back.

Hirshy and Celesto had gotten their 'bot marines perfectly positioned and ready to begin firing. The approaching L.I.V.E. 'bot soldiers however didn't seem to be aware of modern ways to fight.

"Who programmed them? It's like they are British soldiers parading in marching ranks into fire during the American Revolution," Celesto said to Hirshy.

"Or it may be a tactic," Hirshy said back. "We need to be ready for anything."

Birds were circling over the enemy troops' heads now, in place to attack the advancing 'bots if they came much nearer.

Lions and bears, possums and raccoons and skunks, and many other animals were risking their lives moving between each of these biotic, armed figures.

"They're trying in every way each animal can think of to distract the 'bots and their masters and keep them from starting a new kind of war," Coyote whispered.

Overhead in the animal heaven, gods were carefully observing the emerging battle below, giving orders to their followers.

"Careful!" Muzribi, the bear god, ordered his followers. "Don't hurt them yet. We don't want to start a battle or get you shot."

"Human battlefields are only good for animals after the fighting's stopped," Angwusi, the crow god said to Muzribi as a joke, rubbing her belly.

Down below, three large coyote packs were now walking among the L.I.V.E. soldiers, wrapping their bodies around the 'bots' legs so these had to step over them. Cowboy watched Coyote standing up on his mound barking orders to them.

"Those coyotes are acting like dogs wanting to be petted," Celesto said to Hirshy.

And then a genuine pack of wild dogs trotted out from behind a prairie dog mound, and sat down in front of the approaching enemy, their tongues out and tails wagging.

The enemy 'bots tried to avoid them but the dogs kept moving in front of each one of them.

A moment or two later, the mesa around the prairie dog village suddenly filled with arriving deer, pronghorn antelopes, and even a pair of elk, all of whom were leaping in odd patterns which, if seen from overhead, made up a tangle of curved lines that there was no path through.

Every enemy soldier had to keep stopping and waiting until one of the animals bounced past, make a step or two forward, and stop again as another animal bounded in front of the 'bot from a different direction.

Now a small herd of wild horses galloped from behind Bill's compound and threatened to trample the 'bots.

"Horses can kick hell out of those 'bots. Are they going to make those damned 'bots start shooting at the animals?" Cowboy asked Coyote over his Teacher.

"No, they haven't been instructed to attack them," Coyote answered.

"Bill's 'bots couldn't be made to harm animals," replied Cowboy.

"That's one of the reasons we like them," said Coyote.

Now the sun was rising over a low range of distant hills toward the east. The enemy troops were still trying to inch forward. And in the next fifteen minutes they were finally getting close enough to Hirshy's troops that the battle could begin.

"You're trying wonderfully but it isn't working. Now the human god wants us to do whatever it takes to stop them from advancing further," El Latrano said to the animal gods overhead in the sky.

"Is that an order to attack them?" several of the gods asked.

"I think so," the coyote god answered. "But first let's try using birds."

Down below Cowboy watched the eagles climb and move into attacking dive positions.

"Kwahu's given eagles the attack order," Coyote said over his Teacher.

As he spoke, the eagles dived with claws extended, their beaks open.

But black-chinned, broad-billed, and broad-tailed hummingbirds attacked first, hovering over the war 'bots faces and pecking hard, hopefully hard enough to make them retreat. At their feet, burrowing, spotted and long-eared owls had appeared and were ripping away chunks of plastic from enemy 'bots' feet and legs. Roadrunners wove in and out of the platoons, further distracting the 'bots.

Prairie dogs transmitted a warbling howl to one another, so high-pitched few humans could hear it, and dived down their holes.

Cowboy cocked his rifle.

"Every one of the prairie dogs sitting on their mounds, eating and watching, have vanished down their holes," Celesto said to Hirshy, watching through his binoculars.

"Something's bad is about to happen, and they've been warned to dive underground," Hirshy replied, before ordering his 'bots to get ready to fire.

Watching on a huge screen in the Mind Room what was happening east of the Manzanos, Cece said to Bill, "The war is on. You can't stop it now." Bill gritted his teeth, rubbed his head, and kept programming his super biobrain.

Moments later, the L.I.V.E. 'bots halted, aimed their guns at the enemy, while still trying to brush away the birds pecking their faces, ripping at their feet and legs, scarring their shoulders, necks, and heads.

"We've got them stopped," Coyote said over his Teacher.

"Maybe they are about to retreat," Cowboy said, lifting his face from the rifle he was aiming.

The leader of the 'bots, wearing dark red patches on his skin, was standing resolutely with his arms crossed. Suddenly the red-patched figure waved his hands in complex motions, while saying words Cowboy could not hear. Instantly, almost every bird was blown away from the enemy 'bots by an intense, expanding wave of air pressure.

"Somehow their 'bot leader's blown all the birds away," Hirshy said over his Teacher to his commanders at Bill's place. "I can't see how he did that."

"Something else weird is going on," Celesto said to his commanders. "I've been watching that red-patched 'bot leader, and no bird has been able to attack him."

Above, in the animals' heaven, the animal gods were ordering their followers to protect themselves. "Get out of there!" Retreat!" they were screaming down.

Coyote barked at his packs to race away and, in a moment, they and the other big animals were vanishing. "They've got us," he said to his god.

Now for a reason the Cowboy could not figure out, the 'general' 'bot with red patches on the L.I.V.E. side was staring at him, and then at Coyote. He seemed to know somehow what the two of them were up to.

Feeling braver than he ever had before, Cowboy stood up and waved his gun in the air, staring intently back at the leader 'bot. The red-patched 'bot turned away and Cowboy dropped back into the shooting position.

"Scared him," Cowboy said over his Teacher.

"Good, but no shooting," Hirshy said back to Cowboy. "We don't want you to be the one who starts this war we're trying to prevent."

Bill's voice came over everyone's Teacher a moment later. "My TEAM is unable to come up with a solution to prevent the battle between the two super biocomputers from becoming physical. Protect yourselves."

A moment later a new voice came over their Teachers warning Hirshy and his 'bots to do everything they could to keep this battle from becoming physical.

"That's Kemmet!" Cowboy said. "Has he switched sides?"

"Yes." Cece said over Cowboy's Teacher. "He and Bill are working together and trying. But I believe that the fight has now moved beyond humans' control. There isn't anything left we can do to stop a physical war from spreading around the planet."

"It's a war initiated and controlled by antagonistic super biocomputers two brothers made," said Father Gallapo, surprisingly breaking into the exchange.

Cowboy Kills

And then it happened.

"Watch out Coyote!" Hirshy screamed over his Teacher. As he said this, Coyote was already diving behind the mound, which his god had shouted at him to do an instant before.

Only his tail was visible as the red-cloaked 'bot lifted its M-14A4 rifle and fired eight rounds at Coyote. One of these passed through the fur on Coyote's tail and left a small scratch on his skin.

Bill, Kemmet, and Hirshy were shouting at Cowboy to hold his fire, but he had passed beyond the stage of reason.

Cowboy lifted his rifle, aimed at the red-patched 'bot firing at Coyote, and fired four times, each time cocking the rifle surprisingly quickly.

Three of his shots hit the 'bot and it dropped its weapon, placed hands over its wounds like a human and, letting out a rising wail of a cry that grew in such intensity that humans ten miles away heard it, fell face down on the ground.

In animal heaven, gods screamed at their followers to get the hell out of there. Each of them, ducking low to the ground, ran from the battle scene. Even the wild horses galloped away.

For a moment 'bots on both sides seemed astonished and uncertain what to do. And then simultaneously all of the 'bots raised their weapons and, with only the side Celesto and Hirshy had coached in defensive positions, the firing began.

Cowboy kept his head down, fearing that Kemmet's 'bots would be ordered to kill him. The shooting went on for a time that seemed unimaginably long. Yet, just three minutes after the firing began, Cowboy dared to lift his head over the mound he had been hiding behind and he was stunned by what he saw.

Bill's 'bots had gotten up from their defensive positions and were shooting wildly. "So much for Celesto's programming," Cowboy thought.

Kemmet's 'bots were waving their guns and shooting in all directions but somehow hitting nothing.

As each 'bot ran out of ammo, it kept standing, waving its weapon, and pulling the trigger.

Over the next minute and a half the shooting was left to a single 'bot on the L.I.V.E. side. It flailed and fired in every direction, as though it were a five-year-old, mentally deranged child who'd never had a gun in his hands before. And then silence descended.

After the Battle

The 'bots stood still, holding their weapons, for another three minutes.

"The super brains are trying to figure out what to do," Hirshy whispered over his Teacher.

And then an astonishing thing happened. The 'bots dropped their weapons, merged, and went all together into Bill's compound and disappeared.

"My God, they are taking over Bill's place," Cowboy said. "They've joined up."

"They have joined up," Celesto said over his Teacher. "We're following them inside, but we can't figure out what they are going to do."

"Some of their 'bots are putting themselves on our chargers," Hirshy said from indoors.

"And some of their 'bots have taken up brooms and are sweeping out the building," Celesto said.

"Many of their 'bots went into the kitchen," Hirshy said.

"The few 'bots out here won't go near the 'bot wearing red who got his," Cowboy said over his Teacher.

"Don't go near him," Hirshy warned. "He may be dangerous still."

Cowboy heard chattering coming up from the prairie dog hole, and slipped down the side of the mound to give the owners an opportunity to stick their heads out and see what was happening. Walking back toward the building he looked around. Cowboy now saw prairie dogs on top of every mound. And animals that had run away to avoid being harmed were walking back toward the prairie dog village.

"This doesn't make any sense," Cowboy said.

"Yes it does," Coyote said, from behind Cowboy. "They are all expecting some reward for their favors."

"I think the warring biocomputer brains have fallen in love with each other," Cece said to Cowboy over his Teacher. "They are swapping all their programs and data."

"Sounds like they are mating," Cowboy replied.

"You are right. This is computers' way of reproducing and evolving."

"But Kemmet's and ours were stay-apart enemies," Cowboy said.

"They are in love now," Cece said.

"If so, this will be the second exceptional 'first' on this weird day," Cowboy said back. Still sweeping his eyes around him in defensive mode, Cowboy continued, "You must be right. Some of their 'bots are out here now cleaning up the battle site. They are carefully picking up empty shells and other battle crap the warring 'bots walked away from after all their guns were empty."

~*~*~

With every one of the birds, reptiles, and wild animals clustering around the prairie dog town now, 'bots began bringing out food and water for all the animals. One of the enemy 'bots even brought food and drink for Cowboy. Cowboy couldn't help tipping his hat in gratitude to his server. Leaving his rifle behind, and with food and drink in his hand, he walked over to eat with the animals, while trying to figure out what had happened here.

Half an hour later, with the grateful animals slipping away again, and with Coyote having gone back inside the compound to catch a tram back to his den on the other side, Cowboy got up and walked over to the figure in red lying on the ground.

There was a thin layer of cirrus clouds overhead, but the sun was shining brightly through it. As he approached the figure on the ground he saw it had become human-like. Cowboy shouted into his Teacher, "Holy Jesus, there's a guy down out here who's been shot. I think he's dead."

"Put your camera on him," Cece said.

Cowboy did and a moment later there was a gasp coming from Thelma. "My god," she said. "He's Lucifer."

"Looks like him to me also," Cece added.

"Lucifer can't be killed," Father Gallapo said. "It must be an ordinary human."

"How could a dead 'bot turn itself into a dead human?" Bill said.

"I know him," Kemmet said, fear pouring out of him. "He's Luciferanso, one of my guys. He made me think I was running things, but he always seemed to be working around me too. Is he still alive?"

"I don't think so," Cowboy said.

"Look," Kemmet said. "We don't want anyone to find him until we make up our minds what to do. Will you bury him somewhere and keep this secret? We need to figure out where to go from here. We'll dig him up after we have some plans. Put a marker over him so we can find him again."

"Get someone else to bury him," Cowboy said. "I'm not about to touch Lucifer. Get the 'bots to do it."

Cowboy stood near the corpse waiting. Over his Teacher he asked Coyote whether the prairie dogs would be willing to dig a hole to bury the corpse in.

A moment or two later, Coyote said back, "Even the animal gods aren't willing to have that corpse touched by their followers."

Then Hirshy said over his Teacher, "Our 'bots and theirs are refusing to bury him too. We don't know why. We'll come out and help."

"Maybe it is because your guys are starting to work with mine and mine won't touch the semi-human who was controlling them," Kemmet said.

Shaking, and now feeling fear coursing through him, Cowboy moved away and sat on a prairie dog mound until Hirshy and Celesto—and a third guy, big and fat, who Cowboy had never seen before—came out of the compound with shovels and rakes.

"Cowboy, this is Tiny Tucumari, one of the best workers Bill's got here. He's volunteered to help us with the burial."

"He doesn't look like the sort of people Bill usually hires. What's his background and how'd he get that name?"

"He was Billy Horshays and changed his name to Tiny T. in the boxing profession. He always liked the sound of its name, though he'd never been to Tucumcari. He heard the name in a song on a jukebox in a café after he lost yet another match. He was a beaten up guy when we took him on, but the TEAM said he would be excellent. And he has been."

"Hi Cowboy," Tiny Tucumcari said, with a wave. "I've heard a lot about you. Pleased to meet you."

"Thanks," Cowboy said, and went on, "Sorry guys you have to do this without me. I've never been able to bury anything I've shot."

"We'll be fine," Hirshy said.

Cowboy watched while huge Tiny Tucumcari dug a proper grave and Hirshy and Celesto buried the body with red patches. A gray thorn bush was planted over him at Cece's suggestion, to help finders relocate the grave.

The World Returns to Normal

Sitting and working in his unlit office, Mayor Howie was writing on a legal pad when his police chief Frank Corsa—who was no longer the town's sole policeman—ran in to tell Howie that Cordoba's traffic light was working again and cars were moving on the nearby freeway. Neither of them knew this yet, but in fact power was returning and lights were going on in every one of the counties around Cordoba. Moments later, power returned to Howie's office. Immediately he booted up his computer, plugged his cell phone in to charge, and holding it up to his ear, tried to call the mayor in Socorro. He was furious when the call refused to go through. On his computer he clicked on sites he needed to visit, and got connected with none of those. He was very angry about this. Corsa looked at him sympathetically and said, "After the power goes off and returns the first thing most people do is go online with their phones and tablets. With so many people trying to restore their systems and devices, it takes longer than it usually does. They are furiously disappointed, because using these contraptions is the heart of our lives now."

"Shut up!" Howie said. "Beat it. Can't you see I'm working."

Lucifer Reappears

About the same time, the exhausted Cowboy was going up the porch steps into his remodeled home. After the burial he had gone into the giant compound, taken an elevator deep underground, boarded a tram waiting for him and ridden smoothly back to Bill's place. Refusing to meet up with others, Cowboy ordered a 'bot to take him outside and get him a ride home. Celesto agreed to bring back his rifle and ammunition. Ten minutes later Cowboy was faced down on his new bed, breathing slowly in the deepest of sleeps.

Cece looked in on him when she returned hours later. Cowboy was lying on his side, snoring lightly, still wearing his dirty clothes. "That's my guy," she whispered, "as she closed the door before going upstairs to spend the evening in her quarters with Mazzie.

Next afternoon Cowboy, Coyote, Bill and Kemmet, Cece, Thelma, Father Gallapo, and Mayor Howie were meeting in the most secure room in Bill's place. Kemmet and Bill, with their now merged giant computer systems, had decided together how to handle the Luciferanso shooting.

"We're having Hirshy and Celesto dig him up and wrap him in a military body bag," Bill said to the group. "Then we'll fly him back to D.C., where our computers have kept track of places he was until he vanished back there."

Kemmet continued, "We'll take him out of the bag, make sure the body has no detectable clues on it, hide him in the last place he was known to be, and then go find him. It will be up to the D.C. cops to figure out who killed him. They aren't the best cops on the planet and they won't be able to do it."

The group spent the next hour discussing what happened in the Prairie Dog Battle, and trying to figure out where to go from here. While they were discussing, heads kept turning to watch on a giant screen as Celesto and Hirshy dug up the just-planted graythorn bush, and began shoveling dirt away to remove the body. There was a body bag on a wheelbarrow behind them.

Hirshy had gotten a huge pile of dirt out of the hole, and was standing hip-deep in it when he shouted loudly, "Shit. I am down into new caliche now. The dead guy isn't here!"

"Shit!" said Kemmet. "Are you sure you are digging in the right place?"

"Holy Horseshit," Father Gallapo whispered, at the same instant.

"I never heard him swear," Thelma said softly to Cece beside her.

"He keeps a lot hidden from you," Cece whispered back.

"I'm damned sure I am digging in the right place," Hirshy said over his Teacher, mopping sweat off his face with a handkerchief. "Check the videos for yourselves and let me know if I'm not."

Bill ordered his TEAM to project videos of Lucifer's burial. While these were running, Bill said to his superbiobrain, "Okay, now match where Hirshy buried him with where he's digging now."

A fraction of a second later the computer said over a speaker, "He is in exactly the right place."

"All right. Scan all the videos we have of the grave since he was buried. Let us know if someone dug him out," Kemmet ordered TEAM, without his brother becoming angry.

A second later the voice over the speaker said, "The grave site hasn't been disturbed in any way since the body was buried."

"Jesus Christ. Luciferanso hauled his own ass away," Kemmet said, making his hands look like a butterfly in the air.

"Don't use Jesus' name in connection with Lucifer!" Father Gallapo said sternly, pointing a finger at Kemmet.

"Why? Because they don't live in the same place?" Bill asked the Priest, with a smirk.

"Maybe the 'bot you shot was never here," Howie said to Cowboy, with a quirky look on his face.

"And you say that because you want to steal credit from me for helping end this war," Cowboy said back, with the middle finger on his right hand raised.

In the garden party after the meeting broke up, Howie had a few drinks and was getting boastful.

"Okay guys, I do take credit for beating down the computers and saving the planet," Howie said. "I brought Kemmet and Bill together and ended this damned war."

Cowboy's hated Howie for stealing whatever credit was due to him. But, seeing his friend about to explode again, Father Gallapo whispered in his ear, "It's better for you if Howie steals the credit for killing Luciferanso, both on earth now and afterwards. " Cowboy bit his tongue and nodded.

Before the garden party was over, Howie drove away in his polished 1953 Cadillac. Thelma and Cece went outside with him, each hugged him and they both waved goodbye. And then suddenly, they shuddered and held each other tightly.

"What's wrong with you guys now?" Cowboy asked, seeing them looking very frightened as they return to the garden party.

"Howie had Lucifer sitting beside him when he drove away," Thelma said.

The Earth Belongs to All Of Us

"Why does God keep Lucifer around?" Cowboy asked the group, which now was inside sitting around a table in a comfortable room because the ladies were getting chilly outdoors.

No one answered him until Bill speculated finally, "I'm not a believer, but if I had created humans the way we are, and got Adam and Eve used to each other in Eden, I'd want to come up with a way to keep forcing them to grow. Lucifer may be that mechanism."

"I thought Satan was a serpent in your Garden of Eden who messed up humans' relations with animals," Coyote said.

Father Gallapo said nothing in reply, but coughed loudly for several seconds.

Feeling an urgent need to change the topic, Cece, who had been bent over her Teacher, excitedly began telling the others what she'd learned was happening in countries around the earth.

"Electrogrids have been restored almost everywhere," she said joyfully instantly grabbing everyone's attention. "All over the planet, computer-controlled grid systems are coming back. Almost every person is glad."

"I'll bet everyone is still pissed off that so much bad stuff happened and messed up their lives," Cowboy said.

"I don't want to think about that," Thelma said, looking sad and worried.

Coyote had been sitting with the group. He licked his nose, and wanting to add happily to Cece's announcement said, "In the animal god's heaven there is a huge celebration going on. All of them are saying: 'We did it, we did it! **WE** did it! We saved *our* planet.'"

"The earth belongs to all of us, to every species on earth," Bill said, correcting the coyote he created. "We wouldn't have gotten this outcome if all of us hadn't worked together."

Changing topics, Thelma asked Kemmet and Bill, "Could you tell us why your two warring computers changed their minds and decided to mate up?"

"Because each of our superbrains was feeling all the pain they were causing everywhere," Kemmet said.

"Possibly," Bill added. "But more likely is the fact that the sole thing that computers everywhere have always wanted to do is to link up with others. They don't see it this way, but computers are even more sociable than humans."

"And the two of you were forcing your super brains to fight with each other!" Cece said, pointing her fingers at Kemmet then Bill. "They didn't want to do this. You made them."

"That's the wisest thing I've ever heard you say," Father Gallapo said with a warm smile.

"But it is true," Kemmet said, looking very chagrined. "I wanted to find out everything Bill's TEAM was doing, steal it, and use it to make money. I made my L.I.V.E. giant biocomputer probe Bill's TEAM."

"Because our two super brains were forced to probe each other and defend themselves millions of times a second every day, we gave them no choice but to be antagonists," Bill added.

"So this was your fault," Cece said.

"Or Lucifer's," Thelma said with a pious expression.

"Or perhaps your God was behind all this because He wanted to create another negative situation that would make human knowledge and culture change and grow," Bill said to Thelma.

"Still, our paired super biocomputers are rapidly repairing the damage they caused everywhere," Kemmet said.

"You are trying to put your evil behavior into the best possible light," Father Gallapo said to the two brothers.

"Quit all this arguing!" Coyote said, putting his ears between his front knees. "Instead of one of you being right and the others wrong, maybe what's true is all of the above, everything each of you humans, all animals, and my gods believe. Truth is what individuals know," Coyote said, before trotting out of the room and vanishing without saying 'goodbye.'

~*~*~

Later that evening, after praying, Father Gallapo was tucking himself into the comfortable bed in his lovely new house and, unable to sleep, was going deeper and deeper into thoughts he'd never had before. Was it right, he wondered, for Cowboy to 'kill' Lucifer? Perhaps it was.

Humans were advancing in so many technical, moral, and social ways, but the relationship between God and Satan didn't appear to be evolving. Should humans be allowed to try to better this Holy/Evil relationship? What would be the consequence if humanity tried without permission? And what would life be like if humans succeeded in reuniting Lucifer and God?

Now, switching back to an opposite and ingrained point of view based on his deeply embedded religion, Father Gallapo shuddered, pinched himself, and tried to stop these anti-Catholic thoughts from dominating him while trying to sleep. He prayed hurriedly again, asking for both forgiveness and help in returning to his usual faithful self. Trying to sleep once more, he wondered about Lucifer's feelings and how these became so negative. What *would* the world be like if humanity succeeded in reuniting Lucifer with God? he asked himself, praying for forgiveness again immediately after this thought came into his mind. Is Lucifer taking me over? he wondered. And falling asleep, a last thought popped into his mind. As children help their parents to reunite and get along better, so can humans and animals help their creators to reunite. He was floored by these thoughts and still pondering when sleep stole him away.

Lucifer Pays a Visit

Next evening Cowboy and Coyote were sitting on the new porch together, the Manzanos turning purplish as the sun fell over the western hills behind them.

"You probably didn't know this," Coyote said, "but many of my coyote sons were with us during the Prairie Dog battle. They kept watch on the bad 'biobots for Bill's TEAM, howled their findings to me, and I relayed what they were seeing."

"Did Bill's TEAM appreciate that?" Cowboy asked.

"Yes. And you know, Bill's TEAM couldn't have gotten so many animals on its side if it hadn't worked so long and so hard to widen links between humans and animals—and their gods."

"I'm grateful that super biocomputer was on my side in working to connect humans and wild animals. It was pretty much all I wanted to do with my life," Cowboy replied.

"The TEAM knows and is very grateful to you for doing so much good stuff that pointed the TEAM in this direction," Coyote said.

"Do you believe biocomputers are a new species?" Cowboy asked.

"Yes I do, and I believe they are more advanced than you humans."

"Maybe. Lots of humans are still pretty far down on the universe's totem pole, like me for instance. But Father Gallapo keeps insisting all this is really only about the existing struggle between Lucifer and God, each a powerful force shaping the future in very different directions. I bet when I die I'm going to be punished by both of them for killing Lucifer."

"You always used to maintain that your God existed only in his believers' minds," Coyote replied.

"True and I changed my mind only after Jesus, wearing clean diapers on the Crucifix in the church, opened one eye and stared at me. But tell me, do you think that it is possible that my God and Lucifer are evolving too, just as coyotes, we humans, and the two super biocomputers that went to war are?" Cowboy asked.

"Notice, you just called the human god *yours.*"

"Sorry," Cowboy replied. "He's not mine. He's everyone's."

"He isn't my god," Coyote said a little bristly.

"True. And that's the big point here. You've taught me that heavens are filled with gods who are often warring."

"Like humans," Coyote insisted.

"Yes but just like in my humans' world, in your animal gods' worlds you've told me there is now lots of effort appearing to put brakes on the battling that's been going on for eternity. I'm grateful they are doing this because it is for the good of every species. And that made me believe that there must be a genuinely collective force out there which wanted to shape a universe which was cooperative and supportive of all forms of beings," Cowboy mused.

"Brilliant! You are turning into a genius!" Coyote replied. "I agree. But the battle has just begun."

"Do you mean the prairie dog battle?" Cowboy asked.

"No! Look, we wouldn't need that mutually supportive force out there if it didn't have to keep battling and trying to beat back an opposing force that drove individuals and collective beings to be selfish. But look, this is beyond both of us. We're both jabbering about something we will never learn much about. So what do you think about both of us going over to the dried arroyo and eating a meal together?"

"Sure, I like being outdoors as much as you do," Cowboy said, and, using his Teacher, ordered his 'bots to serve them.

Ten minutes later, Coyote was down in the arroyo bed eating a heaping plate of raw meats. Cowboy was sitting above him on the bank eating enchiladas, frijoles, and tacos, and drinking beer. Above them night fell and the brilliant star-lit sky grew chillier.

Half an hour later, Coyote departed. Cowboy got up and started walking back to his porch. Its overhead light was on. Someone was sitting in his precious green rocker. Cowboy recognized the attractive, well-groomed person instantly. It was Lucifer.

As he neared, Lucifer stood up, blew Cowboy a kiss, leapt and soared over the porch railing and disappeared around the house.

Cowboy reached down to brush evil off the contaminated rocker cushions of his precious rocker. Instantly he jerked his hand away. The rocker was scalding hot and Cowboy had burned his hand.

"Getting even with me, aren't you," Cowboy said loudly as he went indoors to put lotion on his hand.

"I didn't want you to burn your hand Cowboy," said a deep melodic voice from outside with a giggle.

"Go back to Hell and have a bad night," Cowboy said back. "Or would a bad night be good for you?"

"A good night is best for you," the mercurial voice replied. "And getting evil done is harder than you think. Tuck yourself in Cowboy and I'll come and read you a story and give you a kiss before I leave."

"Do it and I'll shoot you again."

"I enjoyed it when you shot me. Now I'll say good night, so you can go to bed," the astonishingly desirable voice said. A moment later there was a swishing noise, like a jet climbing straight up into the night sky.

"I can't figure out why he likes me," Cowboy said to himself several minutes later, pulling covers up to his chin. "Why would God want me to buddy up with Lucifer?" Cowboy mused, turning on his side.

Fifteen minutes later Cece could hear the cowboy snoring loudly in the bedroom beneath hers. "I've got to get some ear plugs," she said to herself, rolling over and trying to get back to sleep.

A Kick From The Sky

On an early April evening, aged Coyote sat on the porch next to Cowboy. Cowboy had been patting him, and Coyote kept licking his hand. Having postponed this horrifying statement as long as possible, at last Coyote said firmly to Cowboy, "My time has come. I'm ready to disappear, as all coyotes do when they are ready to meet their Maker."

Cowboy was shattered by this announcement. "Please, no. No. NO! My life will be ruined if you leave me."

"I know it will be hard on you," Coyote answered, putting his head across Cowboy's thigh. "But my time really has come. We've had so many wonderful years together, but all lives have their beginnings and their ends."

Tears streaming down his face, Cowboy tried again and again to dissuade Coyote, without succeeding. He urged Coyote to get checked out by Bill's TEAM and see if he could still be rejuvenated. Without arguing, Coyote simply said he wouldn't do that. "The only thing I want now is to be in the sky with my god."

"Will you at least hang around long enough for all of us to throw a terrific farewell party for you?"

Coyote refused. "I will have a farewell party, but only with my fellow coyotes. These are the people I really need to say goodbye to."

Internally, Cowboy understood that Coyote's time truly had come, but he couldn't bear thinking about losing forever his best friend. As they sat silently side-by-side on the porch, Cowboy kept reaching down and rubbing Coyote's neck, ears, and head, and Coyote kept licking his arm and hand.

Mazzie came onto the porch. She had been keeping away from them in the stable because she knew the devastating thing Coyote intended to say. Now she nestled between Coyote's front paws, and licked his feet. Realizing how badly she would miss him, Coyote put his head down and licked her neck and head. Three different species were expressing their love to one another.

Tears were streaming down Cowboy's face and Mazzie had the saddest expression on hers, when Coyote suddenly got up, stepped over Mazzie's prone body, and limped down the porch steps.

Watching him leave, Cowboys saw more clearly than ever before that Coyote was gray, drooling, his tail drooped, and his legs were weak as he slowly hobbling away from Cowboy's place.

"Can I take you wherever you want to go?" Cowboy asked.

And Coyote refused with a single word "No," as he limped out of sight.

"His time has come," Cowboy said, wiping his face with the sleeve on his left wrist, and reaching down with his right hand to pat Mazzie. "And he left us with no farewells. As he always does."

From the darkness Coyote's voice, trembling with age, quavered, "Goodbye...."

A wave of brief happiness burst over the Mexican Cowboy. And a new thought almost floored him. Cowboy now realized that Coyote had always taken the English word 'goodbye' literally, as meaning parting forever.

"Goodbye, dearest friend," Cowboy said as loudly as he could into the darkness.

Tears of grief mixed with gratitude poured down Cowboy's face, as he closed his eyes and rocked back and forth.

Mazzie yipped a dog's bark for "Farewell."

A few moments later Cece came up onto the porch, stood behind his rocker, took off Cowboy's ancient yellow hat and put it on her head, and bent over and held him, her lips pressed into his hair. Mazzie jumped onto Cowboy's lap. She seemed to be crying. With one hand Cowboy patted her, with his other hand he reached behind him and patted Cece's lower back. Cece was trying to keep from crying, but tears dripped from her eyes into Cowboy's hair.

~*~*~

Next evening, Cowboy, Celesto, Cece, Father Gallapo, and Thelma held a somber farewell party for Coyote. Cowboy insisted on having the 'party' outdoors and the house's 'bots had put together a wonderful dinner on the patio recently built between Cowboy's and the Priest's new houses. It was a chilly evening and 'bots had set up warmers around the group. Cowboy and his close friends spent the evening sharing their memories of times spent with Coyote. It was after eleven now and Cowboy and his friends were weary and still feeling sad, though being together had made each of them feel lighter.

They were getting up to separate and go into their own houses, when Cowboy heard a coyote howling from somewhere near the Manzano mountains. "Listen," he said to the others. For the first time ever on his property, Cowboy and his dear friends heard dozens of coyotes beginning to joyfully howl together several miles to the east.

"That's *their* farewell party," Cece said.

Cowboy nodded, wiping tears from his face, wishing he were there.

Three nights later humans all over the Southwest were startled by waves of sad-sounding coyotes on every side of them howling with the unhappiest feelings coyote packs had ever uttered. All night long Cowboy sat by himself in his green rocker on the porch, weeping. Long after midnight he was startled when several young coyotes appeared from the starless darkness, climbed the porch steps and sat around him, sniffing, licking, asking to be patted by him.

"These must be some of Coyote's children," Cowboy said to himself, crying softly but now with warm feelings inside him. He felt terrific love for these new friends. They seemed to need his love and comforting too. House 'bots kept bringing out small quantities of tasty treats for the young coyotes. Cowboy's attachment to Coyote's children kept expanding as he got to know each of them better. "I'm so glad he sent them to me before he passed away. This is the best gift he could have given me, except to stick around longer on our earth."

~*~*~

Two weeks later Cowboy and all of his human friends who knew or worked with Coyote were invited to come to his place for an evening memorial gathering for the departed Coyote. Outdoors on the patio no heaters were needed because the evening was astonishingly warm. Wonderful snacks were offered and each person was served different drinks. Surprisingly to Cowboy, the only subject on everyone's mind was his or her connection with Coyote.

Cece told the group about Coyote letting her earlier runaway self stay in Bill's place and summoning the Mexican Cowboy to meet her.

Thelma talked about Coyote's rescue of Father Gallapo's porta-confessional, the huge column of smoke he and his god put into the sky so they could find it, and how she took off her clothes and jumped into the overflowing Rio Grande to get Cowboy released from the Border Patrol agents holding him.

Blunt as ever, Mayor Howie recalled his hunters shooting at Coyote before they saved Celesto and Cowboy. He boasted of his leadership at the planning meeting about rescuing Bill that had been held in the Church. Then he went on to give himself a truckload of credit for secretly changing the parade idea, saying he was the one that came up with the plan to have Coyote shot and his float blown up to distract police and security personnel in the nursing home where Bill was being kept. "The most oddball thing about this was the night when we were planning in the church and you nuts"—he said, pointing at Cece, Thelma and Cowboy—"thought you were seeing Jesus and Coyote's gods."

"We saw Lucifer too, standing by you with his hand on your shoulder," Thelma interrupted.

"And we saw Lucifer definitely after Cowboy killed him," Celesto said.

"I buried Lucifer!" Tiny Tucumcari added.

"He wasn't a god. He was just my underling, Luciferanso," Bill's brother Kemmet snapped back.

"Don't be so sure about that," Bill said. "My TEAM stopped the war between our two super-biobrains, which you started by attacking mine."

"This is all nonsense," Father Gallapo said softly. "There are no animal gods and this business about killing Lucifer is nonsense."

While the talking and arguing continued, Cowboy's mind drifted away. Looking up, he watched small threads of speckling fire appear in the star-enriched overhead sky. His mind moved away from the battering exchanges continuing around him. He listened intently and began instead to hear the loudening night cries of water birds in the Bosque. Overhead, bats orbited. Tiny gusts of both warm and cold wind prickled his face and hands, and stirred an important memory about an unforgettable thing that had happened in the sky before Coyote and him. Frogs and chipmunks were making loud sounds. There were far more animals than ever before out in the yard being fed by 'bots—who were themselves stopping and looking upward. Looking out into the yard his night vision better than ever, he saw several black bears, pumas, deer, coyotes, and even a few pronghorn antelopes—which had never been in his yard before.

Cowboy now looked around the group of his arguing friends. Only Hirshy kept his mouth shut and looked up at the sky. Overhead, faintly colored clouds of varying shapes flowed together into a single large mass in the southeast. "You guys shut up. Look up. See what's happening up there," Hirshy said loudly and insistently, pointing in that direction. Something like a miles-wide stage was being formed and the sky was brightening above it.

All of the animals in the yard stopped eating and were staring upward too. Each making sounds in its own way, they filled the air around them with orchestrated noises no one except Cowboy had ever heard before.

"What's going on?" Kemmet demanded to know.

"Shut up and watch," Cowboy said.

In addition to the animal sounds, the quiet humans heard a clamoring mix of odd sounds, unlike any they had ever heard before, coming from the thing in the sky. Moving figures began to appear and even Mayor Howie and Father Gallapo were stunned as recognizable figures began to emerge. Each of them saw different beings. Cowboy saw El Latrano, in Aztec headdress and paint splotches, looking back at him. Cece saw Poko, the dog god, clearly for the first time. On her lap, Mazzie looked skyward at her god Poko, whom she had fought and beaten, and shivered in fear. Each of the animals in the yard focused on their own gods, bowing silently and submissively. Mayor Howie couldn't take his eyes off Poko, the god of dogs, the only animals he really liked.

Unbelieving Father Gallapo, who blamed what he was seeing on having too many glasses of wine, saw New Mexican Santos he instantly recognized. Saint Raymond the Unborn was running about the sky kicking, holding up his skirts and holy lamp. Saint James the Greater was galloping his horse around the sky, using a rosary for reins. Near him was Our Lady of Guadalupe, running around the stage too, her skirts flying, holding her crown on her head. With wounds raw and dripping, Inigo Lopez de Loyola and St. Christopher seem to be paired in some form of offense.

Cece and Thelma saw—and instantly adored—young Jesus the Nazarene, his arms high, wearing a loincloth, darting in and out among the Santos, chasing what appeared to be a ball, which the animals gods were trying to kick into an invisible goal.

For moments fascinatingly long in each friend's mind, the game seemed to go on. And then, suddenly, the two teams divided into separate athletes, animal gods on one side, Santos and Jesus on the other. From the back of the sky, El Latrano stepped forward, his prophet Coyote by his side. As they moved toward the stage's edge, the Santos on their right began applauding, while each of the animal gods on the left began making thrilling acceptance sounds in each of their languages. In a moment that none of the humans watching would ever forget, Coyote lay down on his back, folded his legs, closed his eyes, and listened to every one of the Saints and Gods praying for him in their own tongues. Coyote was being sainted in the sky. Little Jesus sat beside him and stroked Coyote while he was on his back.

Now El Latrano and Poko helped him up. As everyone could see, Coyote was fitter than he had ever been. "You are healthy once more when you get to Heaven," Thelma whispered to her Priest.

Coyote came forward to the front of the stage by himself. With his front legs crossed, he bowed to animals, to Jesus and the Santos, and to humans watching him from the ground. Then he stepped back.

And now Lucifer, whom Cowboy and Mayor Howie had seen refereeing the match, carried a ball over and put it down in front of Coyote. Young Jesus knelt and held the ball. Cowboy turned around behind it, paused for a moment to concentrate his attention, and after a moment's pause explosively kicked the ball with his right back leg. The ball soared into the sky and, with sparkling flames trailing after it, curled down towards Cowboy's patio.

People around Cowboy, instinctively fearing what appeared to be a meteor, put hands over eyes, ducked, and tried to move away while still frozen in their chairs. The Cowboy sat rigidly, his hands on his knees, watching the ball approach. Running through his head was a symphony of western tunes he loved. Without slowing in the slightest, the ball crashed onto Cowboy's lap, stopping instantly.

All the people but Cowboy and Father Gallapo stood up applauding, shouting hoorays, and waving at the gods in the sky. The gods, each in their own way, applauded back. Thelma reached over and prodded her Priest. Realizing that he was seeing Baby Jesus and New Mexico Santos moving before him in the sky, he stood and waved uncertainly.

Mayor Howie, standing and smiling as broadly as he could, bowed too, wanting both to acknowledge what he took to be the sky gods' and his friends' applause for him. He hoped to win more of their votes in his future.

Bill stood quietly, thinking about his new bioengineering project, and feeling what he took to be applause in the sky for his creating Coyote.

Father Gallapo heard Jesus' voice in his mind saying, *Thank you for all you have done for Me. I know this all has been terribly hard for you.*

Kemmet wondered why Lucifer was waving at *him.* "Perhaps I'd better start working with a Priest," he thought.

Cece felt the appreciation and gratitude of all of the Santos and animal gods in the sky. "You are wonderful!" they each seemed to be saying to her.

Thelma felt a hand behind her gently touching her head, filling her with spiritual energy and intense love she had never felt before. "Jesus is behind me," she said gratefully.

Cowboy, still sitting, believing that this second Thing in the Sky had been put on entirely for him and Coyote, reached out his hand and moved it up and down, like he was rubbing Coyote's neck and shoulders.

Above him Coyote stuck out his tongue and Cowboy felt his extended hand being licked.

Then, as the spectacular lights overhead in the southeast sky begin to dim, with the gods above still bowing, Lucifer blew kisses at the humans who were all suddenly seeing him. Now, the animal gods began leaving overhead, the brightness covering the soccer ball in Cowboy's lap began fading, a line of clouds descended over the stage, and the evening gradually returned to normal.

While his guests were chattering about the magical event they'd just witnessed and taken part in, Cowboy picked up the ball and studied it. In giant letters were Coyote's words, "Thank you for all you have done for me. I will always love you."

Tears of joy streamed down his face as Cowboy turned the ball around. There were signatures, which he believed came from the Santos overhead. There was a small note in Aztec characters that might be a thank-you from El Latrano. And the ball was smeared with paw prints, bird beak smears, unrecognizable scratches, and smudges and smells, which Cowboy believed were thank-yous from each of the animal gods in the sky.

Cowboy stood up and a house 'bot came to him. He gave the ball to the 'bot,' saying"Take special care of this for me. It is very precious." The 'bot nodded and took the ball gently from him as Cowboy continued, "And tell the kitchen staff to whomp up the greatest feed they've ever made for the animals tonight."

"We are already doing that!" the maturing biobot said, with sprinkles of love for Bill's TEAM in his head, who is *his* god, he believes.

"This all could not have had a better ending," said Cece, coming over to Cowboy and nuzzling him.

"And I could not have a better beginning than meeting you," Cowboy said back, love bursting through him.

Looking up, holding her tightly, Cowboy saw the moon rising over the Manzano Mountains, a sky filled with gleaming stars, and heard all around him the sounds of happy animals having the best meal in their lives. Joy filled him as he leaned over and kissed Cece.

"I'll miss him. There is so much he's done for me," Cowboy said.

"Don't worry," Father Gallapo said. "He'll keep looking after you."

"And we'll keep looking after coyotes and other animals," Cece said.

Thelma said,"This isn't an ending. This is a New Beginning."

—End—

<u>About the Author</u>

Bruce Saunders is a retired, world-linked sociologist, born in and loving the American Southwest. A citizen of the earth by first grade he had lived in five major American cities. At sixteen he was a world traveler; flying in a small plane from Austin to Peru, living for a summer in Guatemala, and traveling to England and Ireland before he hit junior high. From Reed College in Portland where he received his BA in philosophy, he entered UC Berkeley at a critical time in the counterculture revolution. He acquired a PhD in Sociology, and focused his research on alternative lifestyles. He later taught at Penn State and the University of Washington. As a clinical sociologist like his father, who helped slow world population growth, Bruce helped form the Clinical Sociology Association and, with two others, established a world-based corporation applying sociology to business problems.

Bruce then developed a worldwide study of the different contributions of secular and religious rural schools to rural development and economic uplifting. In early spring of 2013, Mr. Saunders was diagnosed with fast-moving Amyotrophic lateral sclerosis. The book, *The Mexican Cowboy, Coyote, and The Thing in the Sky,* follows the iconic characters of Mexican Cowboy, Coyote, the Priest, a super bioengineer, and more, originally created in bedtime stories for his four-year-old daughter Kaiti. These adventures focus on the value of connection between humans and among humans and animals, protection of wild animals, bioengineering, conflict among animals' gods, and war and peace. Imagining has always been one of Bruce's things. His novel, based on the lore, mystery, and spiritual puzzle that is the American Southwest, is a labor of love. Forthcoming from Bruce is a companion volume, *New Mexico Fables with The Cowboy and Coyote.*

About the Artist—Thom Laz

I was born in Chicago on October 4, 1944—before the bomb—and came to the countryside on the foothills of Mt. Pilchuck after the war. Art, nature, and daydreaming are favorite escapes. We are all artists and hopefully are allowed to play in our media, whatever they may be. As artists, our responsibility is to do justice by honing our tools and skills, then using them. Joy in the act of creation is the first reward—sharing it is the best. This shared joy I offer to you to enrich this delicious tale.

I have dabbled in wood carving, jewelry, block prints, photography, poetry, writing, hot glass, stained glass, fabric design, and printing, followed by clothing design and construction. I have yet to meet a medium that couldn't excite me, so, in 1984 when good fortune landed me in Bali (where art is part of the religion), I became zealous in my craft. I returned to my floating home (purchased in 1968 – a very good year) three years later, where I live with my wife, daughter and three cats. It has been a year since my two dogs, with whom I shared life for almost 15 years, passed, so Coyote re-warmed my Canid connection.

Jack brought me in to this project by introducing me to Bruce, a kindred spirit, who with one paragraph sucked me into this story. I could sketch scores of illustrations for this rich adventure, but Bruce brought up a convincing deadline. I hope I do the story justice with these characters I offer here. Travel is the best teacher and the class room the best stone to sharpen the tools discovered. So enjoy as you are schooled on this imaginative journey.

I thank, Jack, Bruce, and Dana, for feedback, encouragement, and keeping me focused and on track. Truly, thom

About the Editor – Dana Gaskin Wenig

My love of words and their meanings, reading, and writing, led me to editing. In high school I worked in book publishing, in my thirties, as a new mother in Seattle, I edited a quarterly parenting 'zine, Kangaroo Kids. I earned my editing certificate from the University of Washington Professional & Continuing Education program and studied Developmental Editing with Barbara Sjoholm.

I'm so glad I found Louisa's Writers, hosted by Louisa's Café, facilitated by Robert Ray and Jack Remick. I am deeply grateful to Jack for recommending me to his friend of thirty-five years, Bruce Saunders, I'm humbled that Bruce trusted me with his story, and I'm in awe of Thom for his ability to make Bruce's characters visible. Thanks to the gods for this slice of time and learning with this small group of creative collaborators.

I live in Shoreline, Washington, with my husband of 21 years, our 19-year-old daughter, two dogs, and two cats.

www.ingramcontent.com/pod-product-compliance
Lightning Source LLC
Chambersburg PA
CBHW080842250626
47161CB00010B/3159